SEER
OF
SEVENWATERS

Also by Juliet Marillier

THE SEVENWATERS NOVELS
Daughter of the Forest
Son of the Shadows
Child of the Prophecy

Heir to Sevenwaters

Wolfskin
Foxmask

THE BRIDEI CHRONICLES
The Dark Mirror
Blade of Fortriu
The Well of Shades

Heart's Blood

For young adults
Wildwood Dancing
Cybele's Secret

SEER
OF
SEVENWATERS

JULIET MARILLIER

A ROC BOOK

ROC
Published by New American Library, a division of
Penguin Group (USA) Inc., 375 Hudson Street,
New York, New York 10014, USA
Penguin Group (Canada), 90 Eglinton Avenue East, Suite 700, Toronto,
Ontario M4P 2Y3, Canada (a division of Pearson Penguin Canada Inc.)
Penguin Books Ltd., 80 Strand, London WC2R 0RL, England
Penguin Ireland, 25 St. Stephen's Green, Dublin 2,
Ireland (a division of Penguin Books Ltd.)
Penguin Group (Australia), 250 Camberwell Road, Camberwell, Victoria 3124,
Australia (a division of Pearson Australia Group Pty. Ltd.)
Penguin Books India Pvt. Ltd., 11 Community Center, Panchsheel Park,
New Delhi - 110 017, India
Penguin Group (NZ), 67 Apollo Drive, Rosedale, North Shore 0632,
New Zealand (a division of Pearson New Zealand Ltd.)
Penguin Books (South Africa) (Pty.) Ltd., 24 Sturdee Avenue,
Rosebank, Johannesburg 2196, South Africa

Penguin Books Ltd., Registered Offices:
80 Strand, London WC2R 0RL, England

Published by Roc, an imprint of New American Library, a division of Penguin Group (USA)
Inc. Previously published in a Macmillan Publishers Australia Pty. Ltd. edition.

First Roc Printing, December 2010
10 9 8 7 6 5 4 3 2 1

LIBRARY OF CONGRESS CATALOGING-IN-PUBLICATION DATA:
Marillier, Juliet.
Seer of Sevenwaters/Juliet Marillier.
p.   cm.
"A Roc book."
ISBN 978-0-451-46355-5
1. Prophets—Fiction. 2. Mythology, Celtic—Fiction. I. Title.
PR9619.3.M26755S44   2010
823'.92—dc22   2010029391

Set in Palatino
Designed by Alissa Amell

Printed in the United States of America

To my granddaughter Isobel

ACKNOWLEDGMENTS

My thanks to Gaye Godfrey-Nicholls for lending me her reference books on runes and divination; to Glyn Marillier for answering my sailing queries; and to Elly Marillier for advice on medical matters, including how early medieval healers might have dealt with a serious kidney problem. The members of my writers' group provided their usual excellent advice and encouragement. My agent, Russ Galen, is a source of ongoing support.

I consulted a number of reference books before writing the runic divination scenes in this novel. Two were especially useful: *The Secret Lore of Runes and Other Ancient Alphabets* by Nigel Pennick (Rider, 1991) and *Rune Magic* by Donald Tyson (Llewellyn, 1992).

I wrote much of *Seer of Sevenwaters* while undergoing cancer treatment in 2009. During that period I received wonderful personal support from my family and friends, and also from my readers all around the world. Readers, your encouragement helped me to meet my own challenge as bravely as my characters do theirs, and I salute you.

Acknowledgments

Observant readers will notice two characters in the Sevenwaters Family Tree who do not appear in this novel. Conri and Aisha are introduced in my novella 'Twixt Firelight and Water, which appears in *Legends of Australian Fantasy*, a collection of stories by well-known fantasy writers. The anthology was published by Voyager Australia in June 2010. It was edited by Jack Dann and Jonathan Strahan.

CHARACTER LIST

Sevenwaters family

Muirrin	(*mwir*-rin)	eldest daughter of Lord Sean of Sevenwaters; healer; married to Evan
Clodagh	(*klo*-da)	third daughter of Lord Sean of Sevenwaters; married to Cathal
Sibeal	(shi-*bayl*)	fifth daughter of Lord Sean of Sevenwaters; druid in training
Johnny		their cousin, leader of the community at Inis Eala
Gareth		an Inis Eala warrior; Johnny's partner
Cormack		Johnny's younger brother
Ciarán	(*kee*-a-raun)	half brother to Lord Sean's mother; Sibeal's druid mentor
Evan		healer; married to Muirrin
Gull		Evan's father, once a celebrated warrior, now a healer
Biddy		Gull's wife, Evan's mother; Inis Eala cook

Sam   Biddy's eldest son, Inis Eala black-
                                    smith
Brenna   Sam's wife, Inis Eala fletcher
Fergal   small son of Brenna and Sam
Cathal   (*ko*-hal)   Inis Eala warrior, married to Clo-
                                    dagh; son of Mac Dara, an Other-
                                    world prince

Inis Eala warriors
Johnny   (see Sevenwaters family) leader of
                                    the community
Gareth   (see Sevenwaters family) Johnny's
                                    partner
Sigurd
Niall   (*nigh*-ull)   a musician; Alba's brother
Jouko   (*yoo*-koh)
Kalev   (*kah*-lev)
Berchan   (bar-*han*)
Oschu   (us-*shu*)
Garbh   (garv)
Rian   (*ree*-an)
Spider
Otter
Rat   married to Flidais
Badger
Wolf
Snake
Fang   Snake's dog

Inis Eala women
Biddy   (see Sevenwaters family)
Brenna   (see Sevenwaters family)
Alba   a musician; Niall's sister
Flidais   (*flid*-is)   married to Rat
Suanach   (*soo*-a-nach)

Connacht men
Brendan
Fergus
Rodan

On board *Freyja*
Felix
Paul
Knut
Svala
Donn
Thorgrim
Colm

the sevenwaters family tree

1.niamh *(m)*

⚭liam   diarmid   cormack   conor *(twins)*   finba

1.samara *(m)*   2.mari *(m)*

aisha   fernan

niamh   ⚭sean
1.fionn ui néill *(m)*   aisling *(m)*
ciaran▸

fainne   muirrin   deirdre *(twins)* cloda
darragh *(m)* evan *(m)* illann *(m)* cath

danny niamh   emer oisin

SEVENWATERS

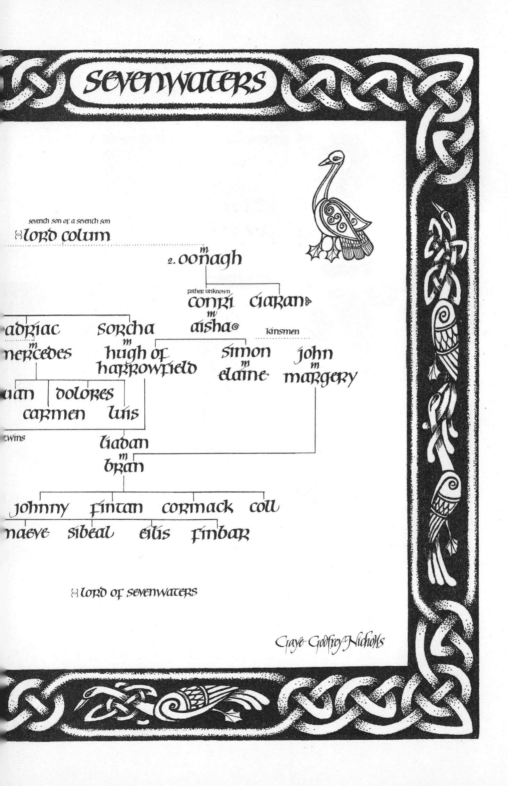

seventh son of a seventh son
⊗ LORD COLUM

2. OONAGH
m

father unknown
CONRÍ   **CIARAN ⊳**
m
AISHA ⊙   kinsmen

PADRIAC   **SORCHA**   **SIMON**   **JOHN**
m   m   m   m
MERCEDES   **HUGH OF**   **ELAINE**   **MARGERY**
            HARROWFIELD

LIAM   **DOLORES**
CARMEN   **LUIS**

twins

LIADAN
m
BRAN

JOHNNY   **FINTAN**   **CORMACK**   **COLL**
MAEVE   **SIBEAL**   **EILIS**   **FINBAR**

⊗ LORD OF SEVENWATERS

Gaye Godfrey Nicholls

PROLOGUE

Pull! *In the name of all the gods, pull!*

I haul on my oar, every muscle straining. Cold sweat shivers on my skin. Salt spray blinds me. Or do I weep? We're going to die. We're going to perish in the chill of the sea, far from home. *Pull! Pull!* We haul with our guts, with our hearts, with our last strength. We seventeen, we survivors, exhausted, sick at heart—how can we prevail against such seas? *Freyja* shudders a moment, balanced between muscle and swell, then plunges broadside toward the rocks. The waves snatch up the ship, and with a surge and a decisive smack, hurl her down on the reef.

A jagged spear of rock splits the prow. Splinters fly. The fine oak disintegrates like kindling under the axe. Fragments fall on the deck, a momentary pattern of augury, gone almost before I can read the signs: *Eolh*: protection; *Eoh*: comfort; *Nyd*: courage in the face of death. The sea surges in, erasing the runic shapes in a heartbeat. The air fills with screaming; abandoned oars fly every-where. Struck on the temple, a man falls. Another lies limp over his bench, a red stain spreading across his tunic. Others stagger along the boat, pushing, shouting. My heart thunders. I struggle to my feet. The purchase is perilous. The shuddering deck has a tilt like a church roof. The reef is opening *Freyja* as a hunter's knife opens the carcass of a deer.

"Felix! The rope, quick!"

Paul, gods, Paul with his feet still tied . . . I stagger over to where he lies half on, half off the bench, clutching a broken oar. The rope around his ankles is caught on a jagged length of split wood. A wave washes over me, drenching me to the chest and submerging him. The water recedes. Paul chokes and wheezes, sucking in air. *Freyja*'s timbers groan, grind, shatter. The ship is in her death throes. Crewmen fall, shrieking, into the maelstrom. Nowhere to climb to. Nowhere to shelter. No surface broad enough, flat enough, high enough for even one man to balance on and wait for rescue. There's land not far off; smoke rising. This storm will drown us before anyone can come.

"Here."

I crouch down, fumbling for the rope. It's underwater, the knots impossibly tight, the strands snagged fast in the broken wood. Too slow. A knife, I need a knife . . . There's a crewman dead, his corpse washing about in the narrow gap between benches. I snatch the weapon from his belt—gods, let me do this in time, let the two of us live.

I hear Paul speak behind me. "Save yourself, Felix."

As I turn back toward him a monstrous wave engulfs me. It's in my nose, my ears, my mouth. Its surging song drowns everything. Iron bands close around my chest. The sea bears me away.

CHAPTER 1

I had been just one day on Inis Eala when a ship was wrecked on the reef north of the island. I was on the cliffs, heading out with a basket over my arm to gather seaweed, when I heard the men shouting down near the settlement. As I looked out over the sea the vessel struck the rocks.

"Manannán be merciful," I murmured, horror clenching my belly tight. The waves were monstrous around that reef. It was as if a malevolent hand stirred the water, reaching up to destroy any man so foolish as to come near. The day was windy—I had kept a cautious distance from the cliff's edge, for it was a long way down—but here on the island there was no storm. A freakish turn of weather stirred the seas in one particular place out there. Did that ship bear someone who had angered the gods?

I stood frozen as the vessel smashed and twisted and broke up. Men were tossed into the water like dolls. Then, as the shouting from the settlement turned into an orderly series of commands, followed by a disciplined pattern of activity— men running to the anchorage, a flotilla of small boats being

3

launched and heading out to the rescue, women suddenly busy between infirmary and kitchen—I was able to move again, and headed back down the hill. Inis Eala was full of capable folk, but at a time like this another pair of hands could always be put to good use.

I reached the infirmary to find it full of quiet activity: women putting sheets on pallets, sweeping the stone floor, clearing space. My eldest sister, Muirrin, stood at the workbench preparing poultices while a young helper checked the supply of bandages. A pot steamed on the fire; a fragrant smell of healing herbs filled the air.

"What can I do?" I asked.

"Nothing here until they start bringing in the survivors," said Muirrin. Her black hair was scraped back under a neat head-cloth; a capacious homespun apron protected her gown. She was a picture of orderly calm.

"Where's Evan?" I asked, not seeing the tall, dark-skinned figure of her husband among the helpers.

"He went out in one of the boats. It helps to have a skilled healer there as soon as they pick the survivors up."

It had looked a substantial ship, with many oars. Norse, I guessed. Such a vessel would require a big crew. Each of the island boats had capacity for only a few passengers. The work of bringing back the survivors might take some time.

I headed for the kitchen, where my sister Clodagh was helping Biddy, cook and matriarch of the island establishment, to prepare food. A great cauldron bubbled on an iron trivet. Biddy was kneading a large lump of dough, her hands pummeling and punching with a violence that suggested her attention, like mine, was on those poor souls out there in the water. Clodagh had been chopping vegetables, but she had laid down her knife and was staring out between open shutters. The breeze caught strands of her fiery hair, tossing them around her face. One hand rested on the swell of her belly. Her child, and Cathal's, would be born within two turnings of the moon.

"Can I help?" I asked Biddy.

"You could talk to your sister," Biddy said, glancing in Clodagh's direction.

I walked over to the window. "Clodagh? Are you all right?" I followed her gaze. There was a view from here down the track to the anchorage. Across the water, the small boats were making steady progress toward the reef. The stricken ship looked almost submerged. I thought I could make out dots in the water, men swimming or floating, but the wash of the waves around those rocks made it hard to be sure.

My dreams had not shown me this. I had been weary from my long journey. Last night I had slept soundly. Now I wished I had resisted sleep and made use of my scrying bowl. But then, if I had been granted a vision of the storm, the wreck, what could I have done to prevent it? A seer was not a god, only a hapless mortal with her eyes wider open than most. Too wide, sometimes. Even as I stood here beside my sister, there was a cacophony of voices in my mind, folk shouting, screaming, praying to the gods for salvation, crying out as lost children might. It happened sometimes, my seer's gift spilling over into chaos as the thoughts and feelings of other folk rushed into my mind. It was one of the reasons my mentor, Ciarán, had sent me here to Inis Eala.

"Cathal's down there on the jetty," Clodagh said. "I know exactly what he's thinking. A freak storm, a boat wrecked so close to our shore . . . He believes it's his father stirring things up, trying to make him leave the island."

I could see the black-clad figure of Cathal, his cloak whipped by the wind, his eyes trained on the flotilla moving out across the bay. He could not go with them; everyone understood that. There was a powerful ward over Inis Eala, something ancient and good that held the whole island in its protective embrace. Here Cathal was safe from the clutches of his father, a devious prince of the Otherworld.

"What could he have done that Johnny and the others can't?" I asked, ignoring the clamor of voices in my mind.

"He could have calmed the waters, Sibeal. Maybe. But he can't even try. If he performed a feat like that beyond the confines of the island, his father would soon know about it. That man has spies everywhere. It's hard for Cathal, standing there watching men drown, knowing he could save people if it weren't for the need to protect me and the child."

"Don't blame yourself," I said, putting an arm around my sister's shoulders. "You and Cathal came here so you would be safe, and you are safe. Ask Cathal, and I'm sure he'll say that matters more to him than anything else. Besides, the storm seems to be over—the water's much calmer already. And look, they're picking someone up."

The sharp rocks jutted from the water like the toothed jaws of some ancient sea creature. Around them the waves had subsided and the ferocious gale had dwindled to a stiff breeze. Two men were leaning over the side of Johnny's boat to haul someone in. The other vessels had spread out to cover the area all around the reef.

"Thank the gods," Clodagh said quietly. She squared her shoulders and turned to walk briskly over to the cook fire. "Biddy, I'll start another batch of bread."

I wanted to help, but the voices were crowding my mind, and if I stayed here I was in danger of fainting on the floor and giving these already busy women still more work to do. I excused myself and headed out into the vegetable garden, which spread between kitchen and infirmary, protected from the prevailing winds by a dry-stone wall. I sat down with my back to the stones and bowed my head onto my knees. My body was tight with terror, the wrenching fear of men at the last extreme. I struggled to catch my breath. My vision blurred. My head was bursting. I whispered a prayer, fighting for control. "Danu hold us in your hand. Manannán be merciful."

I breathed slowly, repeating the words over and over to steady myself. The air was full of the sweet scents of thyme and calamint. The stones at my back held the sun's warmth, anchoring me in the here and now. High overhead, gulls called. Closer to hand, the island dog, Fang, appeared from a corner where she had been digging and approached me, rolling onto her back to demand attention. I reached out my hand to stroke her, glad that she was in one of her good moods, for the diminutive creature had not earned her fearsome name for nothing. I waited, my fingers keeping up a slow pattern against the dog's warm belly, and the voices screamed on. Perhaps they would not hush until all were dead.

It was some time before the cries died down sufficiently to let me move. I stretched and rose to my feet. The little dog scampered off to investigate something under a comfrey bush. Beyond the garden wall the settlement seemed near deserted, but I could hear voices from the communal dining hall that adjoined the kitchen. Nobody near the infirmary, though the door stood open. No movement near the practice yard where the main work of Inis Eala—the training of fighting men—was carried out. Everyone must be busy indoors or out on the rescue boats. But surely the small craft should be back by now. In my mind one last voice called—*Mother, help me!*—and fell silent.

Inis Eala's sheltered bay housed the long wooden jetty and an old cottage where a fisherman had once lived. I walked to the top of the steep path and looked down to see a good number of folk standing on the shore in silent clusters. Among them were Clodagh and Cathal, his arm around her shoulders, hers around his waist. I did not go down, but settled to wait on a flat rock beside the path.

Johnny's boat had turned for home. The others passed and passed again around the rocks. A few timbers floated on the swell, but the ship was gone. "Danu hold you in her hand and bring you safe to shore," I murmured. "And if it is your time to go, Morrigan guide you through the gateway. May light shine on your path; may you walk on without fear."

After a while Fang crept up beside me and settled, nose on paws, keeping her own vigil. Dogs were not allowed on Inis Eala. For this unlikely creature an exception had been made. The story went that she had been brought back from a mission by the intimidating Snake, a man whom one would expect to see accompanied by a fearsome wolfhound or barrel-chested fighting dog, not a tiny, temperamental ball of white fluff. I hoped I would

7

hear the full tale of how it had happened before my visit here was over.

"You're a lucky girl, Fang," I murmured, scratching her behind the ears. A subterranean growl rumbled through her small form, and I drew my fingers away. Fang's moods were legendary, as changeable as spring weather. "You fell on your feet, from the sound of it."

Snake was away, along with a party of fifteen men, undertaking a mission for a chieftain in the south. They had taken the largest of the Inis Eala boats, which made today's rescue effort slower than it might have been. Johnny's boat was halfway back now. Four men were rowing, my cousin among them, while Evan was in the stern, his arm around a man swathed in a big cloak. Only one. And now another of the island boats had turned for home. The crew had raised a rudimentary sail. I could not see whether this vessel carried survivors. The others maintained their pattern, searching.

I slowed my breathing, calming my wayward thoughts. I tried to set aside those anguished voices. I told myself that the rescue effort had got under way quickly, that the crew of such a ship would be fit, capable men, that many would be saved. More folk were heading down to the shore now, carrying stretchers, blankets. Johnny's boat came in to the jetty. Johnny threw a rope to Cathal, who secured the craft. The man in the cloak was helped onto the jetty. He refused a stretcher and began to climb the path with Evan on one side and Cathal on the other. The survivor was a strong-looking person of middle height, squarely built, with hair that would be fair when dry. His skin was ashen, and despite the courage that saw him attempt the path on foot, he was plainly exhausted.

They were almost at the top of the pathway when the second boat came in. The fair-haired man turned his head to look, started violently and began shouting. He seemed intent on hurling himself headlong down the path, but the combined strength of Evan and Cathal held him back.

There was a survivor on this boat, too, and it was a woman. She appeared deeply shocked, her eyes huge, her face gray-blue with cold and exhaustion. When she was helped from the boat to the jetty, her knees buckled and she collapsed onto the boards. A woman on a Norse ship. So perhaps this had not been a voyage to raid and plunder, but one of trading or searching for a place to settle. Had there been other women out there in the cold sea? Little children drowning? This woman looked as if she had gazed on hell.

Clodagh helped her up. The survivor was much taller than my sister; equal in height to most of the men down there. A blanket concealed much of her form. For a moment she looked straight up the hill toward my perch among the rocks, and a sudden sharp pain went through me, like a knife in the heart. Even as I gasped with the shock of it, the woman dropped her gaze and the pain was gone.

The fair-haired man would not go a step further until they brought the woman to the top of the path. When she reached him, he took her hands in his and kissed her on either cheek. She stood stiffly, staring through him. I thought she hardly knew where she was.

The two of them were escorted away, but I did not move. The piercing pain had unnerved me, and it was some time before my heart slowed to its usual pace. Even then, I stayed where I was. It seemed important to keep watch until the last of the little boats came home. Fang crouched by my feet, reassuring in her small warmth. I prayed. "Danu cradle you gently in her arms . . . Morrigan lead you through the gateway . . . Sleep, dear ones, sleep softly . . . " I hoped I was wrong about the children. What had that woman seen, to turn her face to stone?

When the last boat was tying up at the jetty, Johnny came to find me. The search was over. The stretchers had been used to bear seven dead men up the path to level ground. Two more limp forms lay in this final vessel.

"Sibeal," my cousin said, seating himself on the rocks beside me. "Still keeping vigil?" At his voice, Fang rolled instantly onto her back. Johnny rubbed her belly absently. His tattooed features were grim.

"Only eleven, counting the woman," I said. "It must have needed far more to man a ship that size. So many lost . . . Will the currents bring them back to this shore, Johnny? Or will they drift with the weed and the fish until there is nothing left of them?"

"The waves may wash some in here. We'll keep a watch in the likeliest places. Sibeal, we must conduct some kind of funeral rite. The two we rescued are too distressed to say much as yet, though I'm hoping the man—his name's Knut—may be ready to talk to us later today. Some of us have enough Norse to conduct a conversation, and this fellow knows a word or two of Irish."

"What about the woman?"

"Her name's Svala. Knut's wife, if I understood him right. She's deeply shocked. I haven't heard her say a word so far. It seems the gods were watching over the two of them. I'd imagine a vessel of that size needs a crew of forty or more. They were gone so quickly."

"Clodagh suspected Mac Dara's hand in it."

"Perhaps." Johnny was noncommittal.

"A Norse warrior is buried in a boat. Or a grave in the shape of a boat. I can conduct a ritual for them, something simple. Knut and Svala might add prayers of their own. When do you want to do it?"

Johnny was a leader of men. Though still young, he headed the community of Inis Eala and its school of warcraft. He was skilled at reading people. "Something's troubling you, Sibeal," he said now. "Something beyond being witness to what's unfolded here today."

"I'm all right." I would not confess to him that a very small part of me was still disturbed that Ciarán had insisted I come here to spend the summer with my sisters before I made my final pledge as a druid. That I could hold on to such a personal concern in the face of today's tragedy was selfish. "I'll be ready to help as soon as you've decided where and when to conduct the ritual. I did not expect to be performing a druid's duties here so quickly. Are they all men, the drowned ones you brought in?"

Johnny nodded. "As one would expect on such a vessel. It seems quite odd that Svala was among them. If this was a voyage of settlement there should have been more women, surely."

"They may have been first to drown."

"We'll find out in due course. I won't tax the survivors with questions yet. Come." He rose and held out his hand. "You need food, warmth and company. I'm under orders to see you're well looked after during your stay with us."

I took his arm and we walked toward the dining hall. "Whose orders?" I asked.

"Ciarán's. Didn't you wonder what was in that message he gave you to bring me?"

I grimaced. "I'd assumed it was something complicated and strategic, not an order to make sure I ate properly and got plenty of sleep."

My cousin smiled. "There was some of both in it, to tell the truth. I understand he's coming here in person to collect you at the end of summer."

A whole summer. Why had Ciarán thought it necessary to send me away for so long? I was ready to make my promise now; I had been ready for some time. True, sometimes the thoughts and feelings of others did crowd into my mind, as if I were a receptacle for anything too powerful for their own selves to encompass. But in the nemetons, as a druid, I could work on controlling that. I could learn to make it a gift, not a burden. Here on Inis Eala all I would be doing over the summer was wait. Wait until it was time to go back to Sevenwaters; wait until it was time to fulfill my vocation at last. I had known since I was six years old that the life of the spirit was my destiny. I had known since the first time the Lady of the Forest had appeared to me, a majestic, blue-cloaked figure manifesting before me unsought by a still pool under the oaks. She had recognized me as a seer; she had offered me her grave counsel. What did Ciarán think I would do here at Inis Eala? Fall in love with some strapping young warrior and allow my life to veer off its long-intended course? I would never let that happen.

"Sibeal?"

I snapped out of my reverie. "Yes, Ciarán is planning to come here and escort me home. He wants to talk to Cathal."

"Mm-hm. I'm glad you're here, at any rate. Not only because

this far-flung part of the family likes to see you, but also because the island lacks a druid or wise woman. I'm sorry I have to ask you to conduct a ritual so soon after your arrival, but folk will be pleased to see it done with the authority a druid can provide. Those poor fellows died a hard death. We must lay them to rest as well as we can."

"I'm not quite a druid yet," I said. "But I'll do my best."

There were folk in the dining hall, not laughing and talking as they usually did over their meals, but seated in subdued silence. The pots of soup and loaves of fresh-baked bread that might have fed a small army of survivors were a mute testament to the lives lost. Johnny spoke to one or two people—mostly senior members of the island community, those who had been at Inis Eala since his father's time—then came over to tell me the burial rite would take place at dusk next day, if I agreed. It would take some time to choose a suitable spot, excavate the hard island soil, then place stones in the rough shape of a boat.

"It's a while for the dead to lie waiting," I said. "I should say some prayers over them when they've been laid out."

"Thank you, Sibeal. That would be welcome. They've been taken to the net-mending shed."

"I should speak to the survivors first. I'm hoping Knut will give me the names of the dead. They should be spoken aloud, if not now, then certainly as part of tomorrow's ritual. Where are Knut and Svala? In the infirmary?"

"They'll still be there, yes. Our healers are checking what damage they've sustained. You'll find Jouko with them; he's translating for Muirrin and Evan. Sibeal, go carefully with Knut. He seems calm and composed, but these fellows were his crewmates, perhaps friends. Looking on their drowned faces will be hard for him. He speaks very little Irish. Jouko will help you."

For the duration of my stay on the island, I was in fact sleeping in the infirmary. There was scant privacy on Inis Eala, where single women slept in one communal area and single men in another, with a partitioned building for married couples. Only those with children had their own quarters. In recognition of my status as a druid and my personal need for quiet, I had been given a chamber of my own, a narrow space at one end of the building that more usually housed patients who must for one reason or another be isolated. The first time I had stepped inside this small chamber I had felt the sorrow there, and the kindness. The place was screened from the infirmary proper by a sacking curtain, and had its own door to the outside so it was possible to come in and out—for instance, to visit the privy— without walking across the main chamber. Before sleeping last night, I had marked protective runes on the walls with charcoal. It seemed they had been well chosen, for no bad dreams had visited my slumber. My druidic robe was hanging on a peg there. I would need to change before I said prayers for the fallen.

I took one step inside the infirmary door and halted, staring. I had walked into a silence so charged with unease that it made my skin prickle. Svala stood by the far wall, clad in an assortment of wet garments, a shirt, a pair of men's trousers. Her long hair hung over her shoulders and down to her knees. Her eyes were fixed on Muirrin, who stood three paces from her with a cloth in her hands. Every part of Svala was tense; my body felt her urgent need for flight. Before I could say a word Muirrin took a step toward the Norsewoman, and a sound came from Svala that made the hairs on my neck stand on end, a growling noise from deep in the throat, as if she would launch herself at my sister to rend and bite. Muirrin retreated, her face turning pale.

I cleared my throat, unsure if either had seen me come in. Svala's gaze was instantly on me, and my head began to throb. Danu aid me, what was this?

"Sibeal!" The relief in Muirrin's voice was unmistakable. "I was just . . . " She came over to draw me aside, speaking in a murmur. "I can't even get her to take off her wet things. It's as if she wants to attack me. She's cold and shocked; I need to get her warm. She won't let me near her."

"I thought Evan and Jouko were here. And Knut." The place was empty save for the two women.

"I sent them out into the garden so Svala could wash and change. I have some things of Biddy's here for her to put on. We got Knut to explain to her before the men went out. I thought maybe if she was alone with me . . . " She lowered her voice still further. "Something really terrible happened, Sibeal. Their son, Knut's and Svala's, only four years old . . . he was with them on the boat. Knut told us. She must be out of her mind with grief. She hasn't spoken a word. Sibeal, will you try to talk to her?"

Without turning toward her, I knew Svala was staring at me. I felt the power of her gaze; I felt her sorrow as I had felt the terror of those folk drowning out on the bay. A little child, the same age as my brother, Finbar. The thought of it made my heart clench tight. "I can't speak Norse," I said, knowing this was something I must attempt. A job for a druid.

"You'll surely do better than I did," Muirrin said. "At least she's looking at you as if she sees you."

I approached Svala. She was far taller than I, with the kind of figure that would draw men's eyes and make wives jealous. Her face was strong, the cheekbones high, the nose proud, the mouth well-shaped and full. Her hair was drying in the warmth from the infirmary fire; its natural shade would be sun-gold. Her eyes were the gray of a winter sea. Right now there was a disturbing blankness about those fine features. Perhaps, when the shipwreck had claimed her son, it had also washed away some vital part of her. She followed my every step as I came closer. The tumult of feelings that came from her was disturbing: grief, loss, fury, confusion. I struggled to hold it all. I breathed in a well-practiced pattern, calming myself. "Is she injured?" I asked Muirrin.

"She won't let me examine her. There are no obvious signs of physical hurt. At this point, if we can get her out of her wet clothes and into these dry ones I'll be happy."

I halted three paces from Svala, holding her gaze. Gods, my head hurt! "Svala," I said quietly, "I am a druid, a wise woman." I inclined my head to her, indicating respect and greeting, then stretched out my arms to the sides, palms up, and closed my eyes, trying to suggest *priestess* or *prayer*. "I am sorry for your loss. But now . . . you must be cold." I mimed shivering, then pretended to put on clothing. Slipping a gown over my head, smoothing the skirt down. Wrapping a shawl around my shoulders. Stepping into slippers. "Let us help you," I said.

Something stirred on her face. For a moment there was a kind of recognition in the lovely eyes. Her hands moved, graceful as fronds of weed stirred by the current, copying my gestures.

I smiled, nodded, even as my head threatened to split apart with the pain. "Yes," I said. "Dry clothes, nice and warm." I took a step closer, thinking to help her with the fastenings, and she shrank away, her hands going up before her as if to ward me off. Her fingers curled, claw-like. "I won't hurt you." It was hard to keep my voice steady. I wondered if the men were within easy call.

"Like this, see?" Muirrin spoke from behind me, and when I turned my head I saw that she was demonstrating, removing her own shawl, untying her big linen apron, laying each garment on the work bench in turn. I proceeded to do the same, hoping it would not be necessary to strip naked.

"You, too," I said, setting my shawl on a bench and pointing to Svala.

Her hands moved again, plucking at her neck, tearing at the ties of her shirt. She made a sound like a creature in pain, a deep moan of anguish or frustration.

"Danu preserve us," muttered Muirrin. "I'm wishing now I hadn't sent Knut out. It might have been better to leave him to deal with this."

Now Svala was ripping at her shirt as if suddenly she could not wait to take it off. She wrenched it over her head, revealing a pale, perfect body underneath, then tore off her trousers and threw them across the chamber with some violence. She stood before us clad only in the garment of her long hair, and fixed us with a glare of challenge.

"Good," said my sister with admirable calm. "Now dry yourself and put these on."

Svala gave her body a cursory rub with the proffered cloth,

tossed the cloth to the floor, then stood looking at me, as if waiting. Muirrin passed me Biddy's gown, and I held it out.

"Here, this is for you."

Svala shied away like a nervous horse.

"For you to wear." I started to put the gown over my own head, showing her—it would have swamped my much slighter figure. "Please," I said. Stepping forward, I put it in her hands.

We touched for the merest moment before she pulled away, seizing the garment, but for that moment I felt not only her grief, but something else. *No! Wrong! Wrong!* Her thoughts were like a monstrous, crashing wave. They were like the scourge of an icy wind. I closed my eyes, praying that I could stay on my feet and capable until this was over.

"Sibeal, are you all right?" Muirrin's astute gaze was on me. My sister, the healer.

"A slight headache. I'll be fine." I was a druid. I would be strong. I would not let this overwhelm me.

Svala donned the gown haphazardly. It was as if shock had robbed her of the ability to perform the simplest tasks. She slung the shawl over one shoulder.

Muirrin went to the back door; I heard her calling the men. I picked up the towel and moved to gather Svala's discarded garments. Before I had taken two steps she was beside me, her hand closing tight around my arm. I froze. There was no need for her to speak. That touch screamed *Help! Help me!*

Any more of this and I would be insensible on the floor. My head was pounding. My legs felt like jelly. The back door creaked open, the grip on my arm was gone, and as the three men came in I moved to the bench and sank down on it. The tide of emotion retreated. I breathed, repeating a snatch of lore in my mind. *Breath of the winds; dancing flame; peace of the earth; song of the waves.* Calm. I would be calm.

Knut went straight to his wife's side, taking her hands, murmuring in Norse. She bowed her head. She did not speak.

"She's still very upset," Muirrin said. "I haven't been able to examine her, but I don't believe she's hurt. She'll need time. Time alone with Knut, probably. Jouko, will you ask him what he thinks is best?"

I knew wheaten-haired Jouko quite well from his visits to Sevenwaters. Johnny came to our home at least once a year, since he was my father's heir, and he always brought some of his men with him. Jouko was not a Norseman, but spoke the language well. Now he translated for Knut, while Evan, tall and dark in his healer's white robe, busied himself at the worktable.

"Knut says that Svala does not speak. Not even when things are going well."

This was something of a shock.

"Does he mean she is mute?" Muirrin asked Jouko. "Is she deaf as well?"

"Not deaf, he says," Jouko translated. "She understands his speech. But yes, she is mute. Even before this sad loss she was not quite like other women."

Knut had released his wife's hands. She stood quiet by his side, her lovely face an impassive mask. The Norseman's blue eyes had been bright with feeling as he spoke, his tone heartfelt. I thought how hard it was to be a man. The child had been his, too. His son. But he could not let go as she had, could not weep and grieve and rail at the gods, for he must be strong for her. He spoke in Norse, gesturing.

"Knut says his wife will improve with time. She may find the presence of so many folk disturbing. If there is a place she can rest in quiet . . . Knut hopes Svala has not upset or offended you." Jouko's gaze went to Muirrin and then to me.

"Not at all," Muirrin said. "As for private quarters, tell Knut those are rare on Inis Eala. Maybe Biddy can arrange something. Jouko, will you explain to Knut who Sibeal is?"

"Does he know that we have the bodies of nine drowned men here?" I asked.

It seemed he did, and when Jouko explained that I was a druid, the Norseman gave me a respectful nod.

"Knut," I said directly to him, with Jouko's translation following behind, "I will be saying some prayers over the dead very soon, and conducting a burial rite tomorrow. Would you be prepared to come with me and tell me their names? I know this will be hard for you. I will not ask Svala to come." Gods, it would be an ordeal indeed, for surely every moment he looked on those drowned faces, he would see the face of his dead son.

Knut's mouth tightened as Jouko rendered my request into Norse, but he was quick enough to say he would go with me. "Wise woman," he said in heavily accented Irish. "Prayer. Good."

Not long after, Johnny came to find us. I had retreated to my chamber to put on my gray robe, while in the infirmary proper Jouko was translating for Biddy—she had come to take Svala down to the dining hall for some food, and then to the married quarters to rest. Johnny had brought another Norse speaker, Kalev. He fell in step beside me as the four of us made our way to the net-mending hut. A sharp wind had come up, bringing the smell of the sea.

The drowned had been laid out in two rows in the shelter of the shingle-roofed hut. While Johnny waited, I went quietly from one to the next with Knut beside me. The Norseman's face was waxen white.

"What is this man's name?" I asked quietly. "And this one? What can you tell me about him, Knut?"

I must remember each one, so tomorrow's ritual would be without flaw, and the departed could move through the great gateway unimpeded. This man with russet hair was Svein Njalsson; this bearded youth was Thorolf Magnusson. This man went simply by the name of Ranulf.

Knut added something to this last name, and Kalev translated: brother.

I was shocked. "This man is Knut's brother?" Gods, had there been whole families on board? The two men did share a certain squareness of the jaw, but the drowned man's features were a ghastly simulacrum of the living one's.

Kalev asked a question. Knut replied.

"No," Kalev said in his accented Irish. Kalev came from a land of lakes and forests. I had heard some of his tales on my previous visit here, and they were different from ours, full of strange water entities and tall, pale trees. "Ranulf and Thorolf were brothers."

"Then we must lay them down side by side," I said, wondering who would take the terrible news back to the mother of these dead seafarers. It might be years before she heard it. She might never know that her sons had drifted in distant waters and would lie forever among strangers. Kind strangers, certainly. I would make sure it was done with respect. But a man wants to go home, in the end.

A big, black-bearded man: Mord Asgrimsson. A very young one with a terrible wound to his head: Starkad Thorkelsson. A broad-faced, burly fellow: Sam Gundarsson.

We came to an older man, gray-bearded, who had been clad in a robe of good quality wool. The sea had treated him harshly; his skin was mottled yellow-white, his right temple bruised. Knut stood by him and shook his head.

"He doesn't know the name?" I asked my interpreter.

It seemed not. "Not a crewman," Kalev translated. "A passenger. Knut knows nothing about him."

"And what is this man's name?"

The last in line was of strapping build, youngish, brown-haired. I touched his chill hand, turning it to see that he bore what might have been a line of blisters on the swollen and discolored palm. Rowing for their lives, with nothing between them and death but the strength of their arms.

"No name," Knut said in Irish. "I not know."

I was surprised; of them all, this powerfully built young man looked most like a crewman. "Why not?" I said without thinking.

Knut did not respond.

"Kalev, ask Knut if this man was a crewman or a passenger."

"A passenger." Kalev translated Knut's response. "With the other man, yes. I know nothing about them. My job was to row, not ask questions."

I thought Johnny was going to make a comment, but he only nodded, keeping his own counsel. "Thank you, Knut," he said, coming over to put a hand on the Norseman's shoulder. "You're a brave man. You and your wife will be looked after here. When she's recovered from her ordeal we can arrange passage home for you. We need to speak about the voyage soon. With so many lost, there are messages I must send."

Knut's lips quivered as Kalev rendered this speech into Norse. A tear rolled down his cheek. He put up a hand and dashed it away.

"It's all right to weep," Johnny said quietly. "You've lost your son, so they tell me. You've lost your comrades. As for talking, it can wait until you're ready. Come, let's find you something to eat and drink. You're among friends here, Knut."

I was suddenly on the verge of weeping myself. I felt exhausted, drained of all energy. So much sorrow. So much pain. And Svala . . . I did not know what to make of her. She was a mystery, a bundle of wild emotions not fully contained in the form of a beautiful woman. As the men headed off toward the dining hall, I returned to my little chamber. I took off my robe and lay down to rest, the rags and tatters of the day's sad story making a tangled web in my mind. I closed my eyes, willing it away. *Breath of the winds; dancing flame . . .*

I woke suddenly, my mouth dry and my heart pounding. Gazing at the runic markings on the wall, at first I could make no sense of them. Something was wrong. Somewhere, something was awry.

I sat up and worked to calm my breathing. Awareness of time and place crept back to me. Had I dreamed? If so, I could recall none of it, only the panic it had left behind. I focused on the runes, seeing in them messages I had not intended when I wielded the charcoal. This was the nature and purpose of such characters— they provided a wealth of interpretations. *Eoh*. Yes, that was apt, since it could signify a staff of support in times of darkness, and this chamber had no doubt seen more than its share of those. *Gyfu*. Its wisdom was uncomfortable to face, an insight Ciarán believed I had yet to grasp: that spiritual growth must always come at a price. *You will not be ready until you understand the true worth of what you must relinquish.* There had been compassion in his eyes as he'd said this. Maybe his own understanding of this particular truth had come at a high price. But he was wrong about me. I understood what the choice meant. I loved my family. My little brother was only four years old. Of course I knew what I was giving up.

Eoh, Gyfu, Beorc, Ing. I had surrounded myself with signs of protection; I had sought to cleanse the little chamber of the sorrows of the past. All the same, something was wrong; I felt it in every part of my body. And now I was filled with the urge to act, but did not know what it was that called me.

There were no windows in the chamber, but daylight showed under the door. Perhaps I had not slept long. I donned my blue gown and tunic over the shift I was wearing, brushed and replaited my hair, put on my shoes and headed out. Perhaps I had heard something in my sleep, some commotion that had set this unrest in me. But all seemed quiet now, though there were plenty of folk about. People were always busy here. In keeping with the philosophy of the original settlement founded by Johnny's father, Bran, this was a place of hope and purpose. Working hard was one of the unspoken rules, and it applied to every man and woman on the island, from healer to druid, from warrior to teacher, from fisherman to cook.

There were two sides to this coin. Inis Eala accepted the outsider. It had room for the dispossessed, the damaged, the rootless, provided a man was prepared to break free of what held him back and offer his absolute best. On the other hand, once admitted to the small community on the island, and to Johnny's band of warriors in particular, a man got no second chances. Transgress the codes of Inis Eala, and a person would be sent away the moment a boat was free to transport him to the mainland.

I had been here once before, two years ago. I had seen what happened to men when they came to the island: how they changed, growing hard and lean, their eyes becoming brighter and more peaceful. Here trust budded and flowered. Here wary, cautious men bloomed into fine teachers, loyal friends and, in some cases, loving husbands and fathers. For women came too, with their own reasons—seeking out kinsmen, looking for new opportunities, offering particular skills. Biddy, the cook, had come to the island after her first husband, a member of Bran's original outlaw band, was killed in a terrible accident. The Painted Men had taken the widow in under the rules of comradeship. There were some complicated relationships in this community. Biddy and her second husband, Gull, were Evan's parents, which made them parents-in-law to my sister Muirrin. Through Gull, a man from a hot southern land, the Sevenwaters family had acquired an exotic, dark-skinned branch.

Whatever had disturbed my sleep, it was slow to depart. My body was tight with tension, my mind full of an urgency that had no just cause. I needed a fast walk. I judged by the light that there was still an hour or two before sunset. I would fetch a basket and complete the seaweed-gathering mission that had been interrupted earlier.

The tide was coming in. Slate-dark clouds moved overhead, chased by the westerly breeze, but I judged it would not rain before nightfall. The plant Muirrin had mentioned went by the local name of mermaid's tears. Dried, pulverized and mixed with certain other ingredients, it could be made into a tonic to strengthen the blood. There was a particular cove on the western shore of the island where I would likely find a fresh supply, she'd said. A basketful would be plenty.

I took the path I had used earlier, before the wreck. Some distance beyond the point where I had turned back last time, the way branched, and I went by the westward track. I found myself walking quickly, almost running, and forced myself to slow. Beyond the level area where the Inis Eala community was housed the island terrain was steep and treacherous, more apt for goats than men and women, and it would be foolish to take any risks while I was out alone.

At a high point I paused, making sure of my direction. There was a cave near the northwestern tip of the island, a place I intended to visit soon, for it was the source of the powerful protective net that lay over Inis Eala. The cavern had once housed a solitary member of our family who had been wise and good, but unable to mingle with other folk easily. It was a place of stillness, a home of old spirits. I would pray there; I would seek answers to the questions that troubled me. But not today, with time passing and the clouds gathering.

I found the cove, descended and filled my basket with the slippery strands of seaweed. Beyond this point the terrain rose sharply. The track branched again, one path snaking westward along a narrowing ridge, the cliffs to either side broken by tumbles of fallen stones and earth, over which erratic ways might here and there be made down to the sea. There were seals on the rocks below, and the cliffs were alive with birds. This place was refuge for many wild creatures. It felt right that it had also become a home and haven for some of the wildest of men.

I climbed back up to the path, then paused. Something still wrong. Something close at hand, holding me watchful, immobile, looking for the invisible, listening for the inaudible. The clouds massed above, heavy and dark. The sea sighed and shifted, a soft accompaniment to the high calls of the gulls. What was it that would not let me set my steps for home? My mind sought, stretched, found it . . . a thread, a breath, a flicker like a guttering flame, fading fast. There was another survivor. Somewhere out here in the dimming light, somewhere between tide and cliff face, a man lay close to death. But alive. Still alive.

Gods, what to do now? Run for help and risk losing that faint trace, run and take a chance on the light being still good enough to find him when I got back, wherever the waves had deposited him in this crooked landscape of crack and chink and crashing seas? Run and hope the rain held off until I could return with men and ropes and lanterns? Or search now, on my own? He was close by. I felt it.

No time. No choice. As I made my way out along the narrow, high neck of land, a part of me was running through all the sensible arguments—*you're too small to lift a man's weight, the tide's coming in, you didn't even bring a cloak, what if you can't reach him, what if . . . what if . . .* I took no heed. Someone was alive out here. I must find him.

The path grew narrower as it climbed, revealing dizzying drops to either side. Gulls wheeled above the rock stacks. There were white caps on the sea now. I could feel the wind's bite through the wool of my gown. The sky was growing darker.

"Where are you?" I muttered, hardly daring search my mind for the little spark of life I had sensed before, lest I find it gone forever. How could anyone have survived so long? "Breathe! Stay alive! I'm nearly there."

A gust caught me off guard and I teetered, fighting for balance. As I righted myself, heart pounding, I saw him. He lay far below me on a tiny strip of pebbles, sprawled out with his head toward the cliff face and the hungry tide lapping at his feet. Tattered dark clothing; tangled dark hair; a length of wood lying by his prone body. Perhaps it had helped buoy him until he made landfall on this unlikely shore. He looked limp, spent. So long in the water . . . He must be near death from cold and exhaustion.

I climbed down, my mind repeating the same words over and over. *Don't be dead. Don't be dead.* The cliff was a nightmare of crumbling rock, of sudden crevices and uncertain ledges. I crept and sidled, slipped and slid, tearing my palms on the clumps of rough grass as I tried to control my wayward descent. I did not think too hard about what I was doing. If my instincts had drawn me here, I must be able to save him.

I jumped the last few feet and landed with a crunch on the pebbles beside the man. A wave washed up to his knees, drenching the hem of my gown, then retreated. Manannán's curse, this tide was coming in with unnatural speed. As I crouched beside the fallen seafarer, a small gathering of gulls squawked derisive comments from the rocks nearby. I eased the man's head to the side, pushing his hair away so I could put my fingers to his neck, feeling for signs of life. Gods, he was cold! Under my fingers, a weak pulse beat. He was chalk white, save for dark bruising around the fast-closed eyes.

"Up!" I slapped his cheek hard. "Help me!"

Another wave; in no time at all, the sea would reach the foot of this cliff and be up over the rocks.

"Wake up! You must help me!" I slapped him again. No response. Gritting my teeth, I tried to lift his upper body so I could get a grip around his chest, under the arms, and drag him up. Foolish. Some women might have done it, but I was of slight build. *You are a druid, Sibeal. Use your wits. Find a solution.*

I scanned the rock face above us, searching for markers. There was the high tide point. Get the man onto the ledge just above it, and all I need do was keep him warm and wait for someone to come looking for me. As a plan it was somewhat lacking, but a definite improvement on waiting down here until we both drowned. I looked around the tiny strip of pebbles, seeking other answers, and my gaze fell on the length of wood I had noticed before. It had surely been part of the Norse ship, for carven along its elegant curve were runic signs, no doubt placed there to keep vessel and crew safe from harm. Today's storm had been too strong for any protective talisman.

Runes. Divination. Hidden meanings. From one wave to the next, I fixed my eyes on the carven symbols. "Manannán, send me wisdom," I prayed. "You've brought him this far. You must mean him to survive. Show me how to do my part."

The next wave washed in. It moved the man forward on the strand and a sound came from him, a deep groan. The water retreated. It had scattered pebbles across the carven wood, touching *Lagu, Nyd, Eh.* Three runes, and only a heartbeat of time to interpret them. Water, tides. Inner strength. A problem to be solved, a tool to be found. I was too weak to lift a man, but the sea could do it for me. "Get up!" I shouted as the man stirred, shifting on the pebbles. "Quick!"

He dragged himself up to his knees. I crouched beside him and lifted his arm over my shoulders. *Let me be strong enough to hold him against the tide. Gods give me fortitude.*

"Hold on. When the next wave comes we're going to stand up. Ready?"

A sound from him, more of a grunt than a word.

"Here it comes. One, two—"

The wave caught us, drenching me to the waist as I struggled to my feet. The man hung on. We were standing.

"Move!" I screamed, for the next one was coming fast, and it was much bigger, surely powerful enough to smash us against the rocks. "Now!"

I staggered toward the place where I had climbed down, half-dragging him with me. "Quickly!" But he could not be quick; it was taking all his strength to move one foot before the other. No chance of getting there in time. It was coming. I heard its roar behind us.

"Breathe!" I shouted. I braced my legs and threw my arms around the man's waist, holding on hard. No time to pray.

The wave hit us. I fought for purchase, clinging to my companion as the water crashed into me, chest-high, and spent itself on the rocks. All was swirling white around us, and then came the sucking undertow, and I did pray, a wordless, mindless plea. It was gone, and we were still here. He wheezed for air, the sound like a knife scraping iron. His legs were buckling. I fought to keep him on his feet.

"Well done!" I shouted. "Now up! Up, quick!"

I dragged him up, step by stumbling step onto the slippery rocks. His breathing vibrated through my body. "Up there. Next wave—up to that ledge. Higher! Up! Up!" *And let the next wave not smash my head into a boulder, or we're both gone.*

My legs ached. My shoulders felt like fire. Another step up, and another. Let me be right about how fast this uncanny tide was rising. Let this wave carry us up to the ledge. The voice of the sea thundered its challenge. Now, it was coming now.

I found a tree root between the stones and grabbed it with my left hand. My right arm was clamped around the man's waist. "Breathe!" I ordered, then took a breath deep into my chest as I had been taught. The water came, chill and hard. It was in my face, up my nose, filling my ears. My head hit something. I surfaced, my shoulder smashing against the rocks. The man was slipping from my grip, down, down and away. "No!" I shrieked in defiance of the sea, and I grabbed his hair and held on like a barnacle to its rock. "No! You're going to live!"

The wave subsided, leaving us just below the safe ledge.

"Up!" I croaked. His breathing screamed hurt. His face was ghastly white, his eyes dark hollows. I must be cruel. "Move! This way!" The next wave would get us there. It must. I got his arm around my shoulders again. He forced himself more or less upright. *Nyd*. Courage in the face of the impossible. "Good work," I said. "Keep hold of me. I won't let you go."

We struggled over a patch of sliding stones and past a projecting boulder. As the next wave roared up behind us, we reached the ledge. The surge washed us up onto it, as if weary of the game we were playing. The water receded, and we were safe.

At first all I did was breathe. With every breath my spirit filled with thanks for the blessing of air, for the gift of survival. The man breathed, too, making a sound that suggested his lungs were half full of water. He lay flat on his back beside me. Bouts of shivering coursed through his body. He was wet through, and so was I. The strength he had summoned at the last was gone now. He wouldn't be walking anywhere, even with my support. And I couldn't leave him here on his own. How long would it be before anyone thought to look for me, and how long before they found us? I had left my basket up on the path. Eventually someone would spot it and call, and I would answer. But it was cold, and growing dark, and we could not afford to wait.

You are a druid, Sibeal. Use what is here. Use what you have. What did I have? My seer's gift was strong, but it did not allow me to mind-call as some of my kinsfolk could, communicating over distance without words. Ciarán was teaching me the language of creatures and the power to manipulate the elements, but I was only a beginner, and I could think of no way my limited skills could be put to use now. If my mentor had been here on the island, he'd have sensed something wrong and come to find me. If . . . but wait. What about Cathal? Clodagh's husband was half-fey. Indeed, he was an adept in the magical arts, though he did not make use of them, having chosen to live his life as a man among men.

Might Cathal sense a message of the mind, if I tried hard enough to send it?

The man was shivering so violently that he seemed likely to fall off the ledge into the water. Gods, I hoped I was right about the tide line.

"Here," I said. "Move closer." For, though I had been foolish enough to come out here without shawl, cape or cloak, I had the warmth of my own body. On second thought, warmth was hardly the right word. I was drenched and chilled to the bone. The man was too exhausted to sit up, so I pushed and pulled him to the back of the ledge, then lay down behind him, wrapping an arm over him and pressing my body against his. It was a little improper, but necessary under the circumstances. He mumbled something. His words were in no language I could understand—they did not even sound like Norse.

"That's better," I said. "Now pray that this works. I've no wish to stay out here all night." If nobody came, we would be dead of cold before morning.

I shut my eyes and summoned the deep calm that must enter the body before one may attempt to open the eye of the mind. I set aside the perishing chill of the ledge, the dark, the restless sea. I ignored the pain in elbow, knee, hip. Water and stone had tested us hard as we performed our unlikely struggle up from the cove. Never mind that. The quiet groves of Sevenwaters were far away, but in my mind I could be there, under the great oaks, walking in dappled light. The realms of the spirit were many and wondrous. At the last point of exhaustion, one could always find a deeper strength. In time of greatest trouble, one could feel the gentle touch of peace. So I had learned. *Quiet your mind. Breathe in slowly; breathe out still more slowly. Feel the earth beneath you. You are part of the earth, she sustains and supports you. Breathe. Now let the grove open around you.*

It had never been so difficult to take the time I needed for this practice, with a man perhaps dying in my arms and my body simply refusing to be still, but shaking and trembling like a leaf in an autumn wind. Eventually I detached my mind, swam into the place where I might call and bent all my will on Cathal. I pictured him seated in the dining hall, next to Clodagh, talking about the shipwreck; I imagined him running a long-fingered hand through his black hair, then gesturing as he explained something to his wife. I called him. *Cathal! We are here.* I tried to show him the path along the narrow neck of land, the precipitous way down. I made an image of the fallen sailor. I showed myself in this place without any of the things I needed such as a lantern or a blanket.

A spattering on the rocks around us; it was starting to rain. My concentration was gone. There were tears on my face, tears of sheer exhaustion. The roaring of the waves seemed menacing, as if Mac Dara himself was stirring, stirring, reaching out to suck us down. The water was right up to the ledge. From time to time a wavelet splashed over, teasing, as if it could not quite make up its mind whether to drown us. Thus far the sea had not reached the place where we were huddled. The rain grew heavier.

"It's all right," I said, more to myself than to the man pressed close to me, who likely knew no Irish. "You'll be safe. Help is coming. This can't be for nothing. I won't believe it." If I had been a different sort of person, I might have killed for a dry cloak.

He rolled over, surprising me. His arm came around me and tightened. He said something in that foreign tongue, perhaps *Thank you*. Or maybe *Don't cry*. I pressed my cheek against the fabric of his tunic—wet through, a tear or two would make no difference—and shut my eyes. In time of trial, there is one weapon a druid always has, and that is the lore.

"How about a story?" I murmured. "I know plenty." There in the growing dark, with the hungry sea washing in and out and our bodies sharing their last warmth, I told a tale of heroes and monsters, and a tale of a boy who accidentally tasted from the cauldron of knowledge, and then I related part of our own family story, for in our past there were brothers turned into swans, and a wicked sorceress whose son was now my beloved teacher, Ciarán. Since this stranger in whose arms I lay probably did not understand a word I was saying, it hardly mattered whether any part of that story might be considered too private to tell.

"But in the end, he turned it all to the good," I said eventually. "And he taught me everything I know. Almost everything. When I go back I will make my final commitment to being a druid, and then I'll live in the nemetons all the time, and only see my family on ritual days."

"*Druide*," said the man, showing that he had not only been listening, but might even have understood a word or two. Then we both tensed, for over the washing of the waves and the screaming of the gulls, another sound came: the shrill yapping of a little dog from the path above. Fang had found us.

I sat up abruptly, elbowing my companion in the chest. "Here!" I yelled. "Down here!"

Not long after, there were lanterns, and men coming down the precipitous path—Cathal followed by Gareth and Johnny—and the blissful warmth of a dry blanket around my shoulders. I wanted to climb up by myself, but Gareth lifted me and carried me to the top as if this were the easiest path in the world. The others brought the man up between them. At the top Fang was scampering about, mightily pleased with herself, and close by stood Clodagh, warmly wrapped, with a lantern in her hand and my basket of seaweed over her other arm. Gareth set me on my feet. Clodagh put down lantern and basket and threw her arms around me.

"In the name of all the gods, Sibeal," my sister said, "has this place turned you into a fearsome warrior so soon?" She stepped back, her hands on my shoulders, and scrutinized me more closely. "You're freezing cold," she said. "And hurt, too. There's blood on your face."

"I'm fine," I said, sniffing. "Don't worry about me. He's the one who needs help—"

My knees gave way. One of the men uttered an oath. I fell into someone's arms as the world turned black.

CHAPTER 2

~Felix~

he fog lies heavy on me. It weighs me to the very bone. My eyelids struggle against it. Ebb, flow. Ebb, flow. Tides. Faces above me, coming and going.

I thought I saw a woman. Between the shadowy curtains she turned strange eyes on me. The veil came down again, and I lost her.

My eyes hurt. My head hurts. I try to turn it and my neck shrieks protest. Iron bands around my chest, tighter, tighter. Each breath a mountain to climb. If I were dead, would I feel this?

I am cold. The chill is in my bone and in my blood. Blankets piled on me. A heated stone at my feet, some kind of creature beside me in the bed. I am so cold.

*   *   *

There are three women. One comes more often, neat-featured as a marten, dark-haired, green-eyed, a line between her brows as she leans over me. The others are like her, but not quite like. The second woman has locks the color of sun on autumn leaves, and a scattering of freckles across creamy skin. The third . . . the third has eyes that startle and compel, eyes like still pools under early morning sky. They fix on me and I feel the power of them in an untouched place, deep inside. I seem to know her.

I am in the afterworld, perhaps, or on my journey there, and these are three guardians. Three goddesses? Three Fates? Which cut the thread that was my life? What do they want of me? And what . . . What . . .

Are these three sisters? There is a dark-skinned man as well, who comes to look at me, a calm-eyed man in a white robe. A physician? Sometimes he seems old, sometimes young. What place is this?

Night outside. A lamp's glow brings a landscape of moving shadows: monsters, demons, serpents. Another man sits by my bedside awhile. His face is tattooed with a raven's mask. His gaze is somber. I am at the gate of death; this is a threshold spirit, a guardian warrior. He speaks of trust, of choices and chances. He tells me I am safe here. He names the place: Inis Eala. Swan Island? I do not remember such a name. I do not remember . . .

I wake with heart hammering, my skin clammy with sweat, my mind reeling in terror, from what, I do not know. Under all these covers I am naked. Where . . . What . . . There is no question I can ask. I know nothing. Nothing. Save that, after all, perhaps I am not dead.

The neat-faced woman, the eldest sister, sits by my pallet. The dark-skinned man stands behind her, his hand on her shoulder. Young now. Her husband? He moves to slip an arm behind me, lifts me, raises a cup of water to my lips. Gods, I'm thirsty. I could drink an ocean.

"Slowly," he says. "A little at a time. That's it. Rest now."

I understand him. But the tongue he speaks is not the language of my thoughts. It is the same as the raven man used. Have I strayed far from home?

The woman fixes her emerald eyes on me. "What is your name?" she asks with careful enunciation. She gestures toward herself. "Muirrin." And to the man, "Evan." Then back toward me. "What is *your* name?" As she says this she points at me, brows raised.

I cannot answer. I have no answer. I close my eyes.

The two of them talk to each other. I catch some of it, not all. The man speaks of a ship, and someone called Knut who may know me. The woman says I do not look like a Norseman. They talk about my chest, my breathing.

"Perhaps we can get him through this," Evan says. "Let us hope Sibeal's heroic effort was not in vain."

"Sibeal would give the credit to the gods," says Muirrin. They speak further, then she goes away, her footsteps soft on the earthen floor. I let my lids fall over my eyes. Perhaps I will sleep. Is it night or day? Perhaps I will wake in terror again, not knowing what it is that sets such dread on me. Something unthinkable. Something unspeakable. It is gone from my mind, along with everything that makes sense of this day, this hour, this moment. Breath to breath. I cannot remember my dream. I cannot remember how I came to be here. I cannot remember.

~Sibeal~

Gareth insisted on carrying me all the way back to the settlement, although I could have walked perfectly well once I recovered from the faint. The man I had rescued was taken straight to the infirmary. Clodagh bustled me off to the bathhouse, where she made me soak in a tub until I was glowing pink all over, then stood over me as I put on clean clothing. She dried my hair in front of the bathhouse fire, which served the dual purpose of heating water and keeping the place warm. Biddy brought in food and drink on a tray, and the two of them refused to let me go anywhere until I had finished it all.

"I don't think you realize what a fright you gave us," Clodagh said, watching me with her arms folded. "The least you can do is be sensible now, Sibeal."

I was not even allowed to walk back to the infirmary alone—Cathal went with me, moderating his long stride to keep pace with me. My brother-in-law had his dark cloak wrapped around him. He was not saying much at all.

"Thank you," I said. "I wasn't sure if you would hear me. It was the only way I could think of to fetch someone quickly. If we'd had to wait until someone noticed I was gone, he might have died."

"So might you," Cathal said, but he did not sound as if he was judging me. "I don't suppose you thought of that."

"It did occur to me, but it seemed . . . I don't know quite how to describe it, Cathal, but something drew me out there." I thought he might understand, where others would perhaps think I had taken a foolish risk. "Part of me knew that man was still alive and needing to be found. There must be a reason for all of it."

"You worried Clodagh and Muirrin. You're their little sister and they see you as their responsibility. As for my part in this, all I can say is that your summons reached me clearly. Proving, I think, that you are druid first and little sister second." Cathal was a man who seldom smiled, but he did so now, his somber features transformed by it. "You've saved a man's life. Your sisters may scold you, but they were impressed. We all were. As for why you were called to do it, this whole episode is troubling. It was no ordinary storm."

"You think uncanny forces had a hand in it?" I was not prepared to ask him directly whether he thought his father responsible.

"Who knows?" Cathal said lightly, but the smile was gone.

We had reached the infirmary. Cathal saw me in the door, then headed off.

Unusually, Muirrin was not working, but standing by the fire, staring into the flames. Behind a makeshift screen, Evan and his father, Gull, were tending to the survivor.

"I'd like to help look after him," I said. "That would feel right."

"There's nothing you can do to help, Sibeal," Muirrin said bluntly. "Maybe you don't realize how sick he is. There's the immersion in water—that's affected his lungs. He's weakened by cold and exhaustion. And I think there's something else wrong. I must be honest. Even with the attention of skilled healers, he may not get through the next few days."

There was something deeply wrong in saving a man's life only to see him perish soon after. How could I let that happen? For a little, I listened to the low voices of Gull and Evan as they went about their work, calm and methodical. Then I said, "Muirrin, I may not be a healer, but I am a druid, or will be as soon as I get back to Sevenwaters and make my pledge. If this man is dying, what I have to offer may be what he needs most."

There was a lengthy pause. Muirrin moved to sit down on the bench by the fire, and I saw that there were tears in her eyes. My calm, competent sister, the one who always coped with everything. "I'm sorry, Sibeal," she said, scrubbing a hand across her cheek. "You scared us. We hadn't realized you weren't somewhere here in the settlement, and when Cathal suddenly jumped up and said you were out there in the dark . . . You did a very brave thing. I can't understand how you can be so calm and collected about it."

"It didn't feel dangerous at the time," I said. "As for the man, I thought I could sit by him sometimes and say a prayer or tell a story, to remind him he's among friends. I think Clodagh would take a turn, too. We won't get in your way."

"Of course," Muirrin said. "Tonight, if you like. Sibeal, we won't let him die if we can possibly prevent it. Evan and I will tend to him during the day. Gull's offered to take the night watch for as long as it's needed—there's a pallet in the corner there that we use sometimes."

"Won't Biddy object?"

Muirrin smiled. "Biddy will probably appreciate a few nights' unbroken sleep."

"Oh?" I queried, perplexed.

"Gull gets up three or four times every night to go to the privy," Muirrin said. "He can't hold his water; it's a common enough problem for older men. It's a standing joke among the fellows here, but not so amusing for him. You may as well know, since you'll probably hear him coming in and out when he's sleeping here."

"It won't bother me," I said. The privy was out the back door, beyond a particularly lush bed of medicinal herbs. "If I wake, I'll soon fall asleep again."

I sat by the fire for some time. I would not retire to bed until I had taken a closer look at the man I had wrested from the sea's grip. Eventually Evan took away the screen, and he and Gull started cleaning up the area around the pallet where the survivor lay. They'd propped him up on pillows. He was conscious, his eyes open to slits. His skin was a blanched gray-white. His hair, which I had thought black, had proven on drying to be of a deep chestnut hue. It was an interesting face, though so thin as to be almost gaunt. The brow was broad, the nose straight, the mouth generous. In health, perhaps his features would be handsome. Right now he looked wretched.

"I'll sit by him awhile now, if that suits you."

Gull had no qualms; he placed a stool by the pallet for me, smiling. I wondered what the survivor would make of this nursemaid, who looked every inch the warrior with his night-black skin, his powerful build, his hands with less than their full complement of fingers. Before the incident that had seen him maimed thus, Gull had been a fighter of exceptional skill. Afterward, when he could no longer hold a sword, he had continued to prove his worth on Inis Eala as an herbalist and healer. He had been the closest friend and confidant of Johnny's father, Bran, in the early days, and was viewed with special respect by all on the island.

"You look tired, Sibeal," Gull said now, scrutinizing me across the pallet. "Why don't I make you up an infusion, something to help you sleep? I know just the thing."

"Thank you. I feel fine." But I didn't, entirely. I had cuts and bruises everywhere, and now that I was close enough to see how ill the survivor looked, I was filled with doubts.

"Can't seem to get him warm," Gull said over his shoulder as he went to rummage for ingredients among the myriad jars and bottles on the infirmary shelves. Evan had joined Muirrin by the fire, where they were talking in low voices. "He's cold to the bone. I know how that feels."

The man was indeed cold, despite the fire in the chamber and the blankets piled on him. Bouts of trembling coursed through him. "Has he spoken to you?" I asked. "Does he understand Irish?"

"He hasn't said a word yet. Doesn't have the look of a Norseman, does he? I think Johnny's planning to bring the other fellow up before bedtime. Knut, I mean. Might reassure this one if he sees a familiar face. Now, where is that jar . . . ?"

"What are you giving my sister, Gull?" Muirrin was smiling.

"A pinch of ease-mind, hot water, a drop of honey . . . works wonders on the nerves."

I was not sure whether to be amused or insulted. One of the things folk most often commented on, when speaking of me, was my composure.

"You've had a shock." Gull had seen the look on my face. "This will keep away bad dreams."

I swallowed my pride, which had no place here. Gull was not Ciarán. But he was wise in his own way, and I could learn from him while I was on the island. I turned my attention back to the man on the pallet. "You're safe here," I said, in a voice intended for his ears only. "You're among friends. We'll look after you." Gods, his breathing must be like fire in his chest. The rasp of it was hard to listen to; each inward breath tensed his whole body. "It hurts, I know," I whispered. "But you'll get better. Manannán chose to release you. That must be for a purpose." He was watching me, conscious of my presence even if he could not understand my words. His half-open eyes were of an unusual dark blue. One long-fingered hand lay atop the bedding, and something about it caught my attention. "He has blisters, like that other man," I said in a different tone.

"They must have been rowing for their lives," said Evan.

"Wouldn't a ship's crew be rowing every day? I didn't think of it before, but their hands would be tough and calloused. This man's skin looks more like mine might after a day's hard rowing."

"What do you think it means, Sibeal?" asked Muirrin.

"Knut did say there were passengers. Perhaps this man was one of them. But surely the crew would have done the rowing, even in a storm." Those eyes still watched me, and it seemed to me there was understanding in them. "I hope you'll let us help you," I murmured, thinking of Svala.

By the time Gull had brewed his concoction, Johnny had come in with Knut and Kalev. At their feet followed Fang, looking smug. I moved away when the men approached the pallet, but not before I saw the patient close his eyes.

Knut looked down at him. His expression was grave. He spoke, and Kalev rendered it into accented Irish. "He looks very sick. Near death. Has he spoken to you?"

"Not a word," Evan said. "Can you tell us who he is, Knut?"

"Not a crewman. He was with those others. The three of them going together to the Orcades. I know nothing of their purpose. Will this man die?"

"Not if we can keep him alive." The blunt nature of Knut's question, which Kalev's translation did nothing to soften, had clearly surprised Muirrin. "My husband and I, and his father here, are all skilled healers. We'll do our best to help him."

Knut inclined his head and spoke again, but soon faltered to a halt. "I thank you for your skill and kindness," Kalev translated. "Too many have died. My son . . . "

"We're sorry for your loss, Knut." Gull spoke plainly, like the warrior he had long been. "It's a hard thing to bear. The hardest."

"The Orcades." Johnny looked thoughtful. "So that was your destination?"

Knut nodded. "The ship was to be delivered there," Kalev translated for him. "We heard, some other fellows and I, that the Orcadian Jarl would welcome new settlers, fighting men in particular. We had hopes of making a fresh start in that place. Several of my comrades had wives and children on board." There was a long silence, then Knut added something. Kalev said, "I will not go now."

There was a silence. Knut's grief and regret seeped into me, bringing me close to tears. At the same time I felt something from the man on the pallet, who appeared to be asleep but was not. He was on edge, tense as a creature in the hunter's gaze.

"You know nothing at all of this man's purpose, or that of his two fellow travelers?" Johnny asked Knut. "Where did they embark?"

"Ulfricsfjord."

I had never heard of such a place, but Johnny said, "That's the Norse name for Goosefeather Bay, north of Dublin. Knut, the trade route from the east coast of Erin to the Orcades would surely take you close to the shore of Dalriada. Inis Eala is far to the west of your natural course."

"That is so, yes. But a strange wind caught *Freyja*, driving us westward. There was no fighting it, though we rowed until our backs were breaking."

"*Freyja*," echoed Evan. "So your ship was named for the Norse goddess of spring."

"A fine vessel. A grievous loss." Knut was keeping his shoulders square and his chin up, but his tone was uneven as he spoke. Kalev translated quietly. "I hope you can save this man's life. I will come to see him every day. When he returns to himself, when he wishes to tell his tale, a familiar face may help him."

In view of the fact that Knut did not even know the other man's name, that sounded a little odd to me, but I made no comment. They had been through a nightmare together, the survivors and the fallen. If Knut was not making perfect sense, there was good reason for it.

"We'll speak more of this later," Johnny said. "Now you should go back to your wife. Thank you for helping us here." He glanced at the man on the pallet, and I thought he saw what I did: a person who was doing an excellent job of feigning sleep. "Just one thing," he added. "Do you know if this man understands Irish? Is he a Norseman?"

"Foreign," Knut said. "He knows some Norse. More, I cannot tell you. He has not spoken at all?"

"Nothing," Muirrin said.

"When he wakes, he will be confused." Knut was studying the survivor's features more closely. Perhaps he, too, had realized by now that the man was not sleeping. "Everything muddled, dreams and truth mixed, like a stew of many kinds of meat."

Muirrin gave a crooked smile. "I'll be happy if he speaks at all." She hastened to add, "I'm sorry, I meant no disrespect to your wife, Knut. I know she is mute and cannot talk to us."

"Mute, yes. And disturbed. I will go to her now. I thank you all again."

"Kalev will take you back to the sleeping quarters," Johnny said. "Rest well. Be assured this man has excellent care. If anyone can pull him through this, it's our healers."

The door closed behind Kalev and the Norseman. Johnny sat down by the sick man and addressed him quietly, in Irish, giving a brief explanation of where he was, telling him he would be safe, reassuring him that we meant him no harm. My cousin then repeated it in what sounded to my untutored ear like very passable Norse. Perhaps the presence of Kalev as interpreter had been unnecessary. This was not entirely surprising; it could be to a leader's advantage not to reveal just how much he knew of another tongue. Johnny sat on in silence for a little, while I drank my herbal draft and the others completed their packing up for the day. I noticed that the sick man had his eyes open again, and was watching Johnny with something of the same wary look he had turned on me. Just before my cousin rose, the little dog pattered across and launched herself in a wild leap for the pallet. She scrabbled up, circled a few times and settled by the invalid's side.

"She'll help keep him warm," Gull commented. "Pity we don't have a bigger dog. Evan, you and Muirrin may as well be off to bed. Sibeal and I can cope here. Johnny, with these Connacht men due any day, we'll need to talk further."

"Mm." My cousin was suddenly serious. "This has created a few more complications than I'd like, certainly. But it can wait until after the burial rite. Knut's account was somewhat sketchy. Maybe, given time, he'll be able to tell us more."

"Connacht men?" I asked.

"We've a group due to arrive for training," said Johnny. "Our unexpected visitors make that a little more difficult than it might be, but you need not concern yourself about it, Sibeal." He smiled. "We ask a great deal of you, don't we? A heroic rescue one day, a burial rite the next. It's too easy to forget how young you are."

"If my skills are needed here, I should use them," I said.

"Not what Ciarán had in mind when he sent you to Inis Eala, I'm certain, but undoubtedly fortunate for this man," Johnny said. "Now I'll bid you good night. Muirrin, Evan, will you walk back down with me?"

The infirmary hushed, save for the survivor's labored breathing. Gull lit another lamp, then came to sit on the opposite side of the pallet. The sick man lay still, his eyes once more closed. Perhaps he really was asleep now.

"You did a brave thing," Gull said quietly. "You remind me of your aunt Liadan. Not a trace of fear in you. Just the will to do what must be done."

I smiled. "I'm not sure I was brave. To tell you the truth, I was hardly even thinking at the time. It didn't feel like a choice."

"You've saved this man's life. And risked your own in the process."

"Just as you risked yours saving Bran, long ago," I said, remembering the epic story of Bran's rescue by two unlikely heroes: the slightly built Liadan and Gull with his maimed hands in blood-soaked bandages.

"Mm," Gull said. "You're right; under such circumstances a man doesn't think beyond the next step. You simply keep going until you reach the end. I had good reason for it, of course. My own life was in danger; Liadan and Johnny were at risk. And Bran was my friend. This man is a complete stranger."

I considered this. "I knew he was down there before I saw him," I said eventually. "It's part of my seer's gift, both curse and blessing. It comes out of the blue: a snatch of sensation, a thought or feeling, a half-glimpsed vision. Most often there's nothing I can do about it, because it's gone before I've had time to work out what it means. But I felt his presence; something led me to that place."

Gull thought about this for a while. "If you believe you were led to find him," he said, "does that mean he's going to survive this?"

"I hope so. Muirrin didn't sound confident of his chances. What do you think?"

"It's too early to say. I don't like that whistle in his breathing. Still, he's got some fortitude. Must have swum at least part of the way. Cú Chulainn himself couldn't survive being unconscious in the water so long. You're right about those blisters, Sibeal—his hands look painful. That may be a small problem alongside his other ailments, but it's one I can do something about. I have a salve. I'll get it out now . . . "

As soon as Gull had risen and moved away, the man opened his eyes. If he had seemed wary before, now he might have been looking into a bottomless abyss. It disconcerted me to think I might inspire such disquiet. I was not even wearing my druid's robe, only my gown and shawl with my damp hair over my shoulders.

"Gull, he's awake," I said. "Should I offer him water?"

But before Gull could answer, the heavy lids had closed again. Fang got to her feet, turned around three times on the blankets and with a sigh settled once more.

Gull tended to the sick man's blisters, his own disfigured hands gentle and sure. We kept vigil awhile, not saying much. It was good to sit quietly in the warm light of fire and lamp, letting the grim sounds and somber sights of the day settle in our minds. I had thought perhaps the whole community might be abed, but a little later Clodagh came in, with Cathal following.

"Still up, Sibeal?" It was plain that this was what my sister had expected, and the reason she had come. "Off to bed with you—go on. We'll keep Gull company awhile. Druid you may be, and hero as well, but you need your sleep."

Whether it was the draft Gull had given me or simple exhaustion catching up with me at last, I decided not to argue the point, though it seemed to me my sister, so close to her confinement time, must need rest more than I did. Cathal's presence reassured me. He would make sure Clodagh did not sit up too late. I bade them all good night and retreated to my little chamber, where a cold draft was whistling in under the door. As I slipped under the blankets, I wished there was more than one dog on the island.

Next morning, the wind turned to a scourging gale. The gray sea was churned to whitecaps and clouds blotted out the sun. Preparation of the grave site continued under the lowering sky, with men going out in teams and returning periodically to stand shivering by the kitchen fire, chilled hands wrapped around pannikins of Biddy's vegetable soup. I spent much of the day in my chamber, preparing myself for the ceremony. In the infirmary an orderly pattern of work continued, Muirrin tending to various folk who came in and out, with Clodagh's occasional help, while Gull and Evan took turns to watch over the man I had rescued. I took a shift when the others went to eat. If anything, the man looked worse. His skin was a disturbing shade of gray, and when his eyes were open there was a glazed look about them, as if he did not really see me. I held his hand and murmured prayers.

Some time later, while I sat quietly in my chamber planning the words for the ritual I would conduct at dusk, I heard Muirrin and Evan talking in the main part of the infirmary.

"Look at this. His water's as dark as oak wood."

"He's been in the sea a long time," Evan said. "That plays havoc with a man's insides. I have to say . . . " His voice fell to a murmur.

"Perhaps it's best if Sibeal doesn't know that," my sister said, at which moment I entered the infirmary proper.

"Doesn't know what?" I asked.

"You'll be upset," said Muirrin.

"I would be more upset if I thought something was being kept from me," I said. Perhaps I sounded more druid than sister, for she explained it in full as she would to a fellow healer. After long immersion in water and exposure to cold, sometimes the body lost the ability to perform certain vital tasks. The dark urine was an ominous sign. Other symptoms might follow: a failure to pass water for days, causing ill humors to build up. Or the opposite: a sudden flood, leaving the person drained and weak.

"Is there a remedy?" I asked. She'd been right; I was upset.

"Nothing we can be sure will work," Muirrin said bluntly. "Gull may know more."

After that, I stayed where I could see the sick man. Perhaps, while I watched over him and willed him to live, Morrigan would not come for him. But that was foolish; neither druid nor warrior, king nor sage had the power to cheat the gods. I was relieved when Gull came in, for his strong, quiet presence calmed me.

"Keep giving him water," he said when Muirrin explained the problem. "And vegetables. Beans, carrot, beet, turnip, whatever we have in store or in the garden. Biddy can make a soup, everything mashed up, easy to swallow."

"Just vegetables?" Muirrin sounded sceptical.

"I've seen it work before," Gull said, and my heart lifted. "It takes some time. The trick is keeping him alive until his innards start doing their job again. One of us will need to be here, making sure he's warm, seeing that he's propped up and can breathe, keeping his spirits up. You might help with that, Sibeal. Druids are full of good stories. A few of those wouldn't go amiss."

"I'll be happy to help," I told him, astonished by the way his practical speech had buoyed my spirits.

"I'd like to hear *his* story," Gull said. "This fellow's. Johnny has a party of folk out searching the coves around the island, seeing what might be washed up, and some of the things they're bringing in are a bit of a surprise."

"What things?" Muirrin asked.

"Costly things. An oak box with metal bands around it; a book with a jeweled cover; lengths of fabric, perhaps silk. Ruined now, of course. Makes me wonder if someone was bearing gifts. Maybe there was a party of emissaries on board. Sounds as if Knut doesn't know much."

"There were three men he couldn't name," I said. "This one and two of the dead."

"Ah well, the full tale will come out in time, I suppose," Gull said, stifling a yawn. "Poor fellow. Knut, I mean. As for his wife, she seems half-destroyed by grief. Biddy said nobody in the married quarters got much rest last night, with Svala's crying. Makes the prospect of sleeping up here for a while almost enticing."

By day's end the wind had died down, but the sea washed in with relentless ferocity, carving out the cliffs, scraping away the pebbly beaches, reminding us of the power that had taken so many lives in a heartbeat. The clouds hung above, massy and dark as the sun sank lower. Johnny had decided we would not wait for the late summer dusk, but would conduct the ceremony as soon as all was prepared.

Torches had been set around the chosen area, where a boat-shaped hollow had been dug out, marked with a double line of stones. We formed a solemn procession. First walked two of the tallest men on the island, one bearing a sword and shield, the other a spear. Behind them followed the fallen, each carried on a stretcher by two of Johnny's warriors. I came next in my hooded robe. I had plaited my hair and pinned it up, and in my hands I carried a shallow bowl containing herbs to be burned on the brazier we had placed by the burial site. The men and women of the island followed me. I had thought Svala might not come, but there she was, walking beside her husband, her golden hair loose, her lovely eyes quite blank.

Gull had stayed in the infirmary and one or two folk were tending to stock or infants, but almost the entire island community stood hushed around the burial site. The dead were laid in two rows, and the warriors who had led the procession placed spear, shield and sword down between the fallen. Knut had explained to us that a Norseman is laid to rest with his weapons by his side, as a recognition of his manhood—a fighting man, in particular, needed to go armed into the afterlife. As the sea had taken all these men had, the Inis Eala community had provided these shared items.

Now I stepped forward to scatter my herbs into the fire and begin my prayers. I did not perform a full druidic ritual, but tried to convey with simple words and gestures a wish that the gods, whichever of them looked kindly on us at this moment, would usher the drowned sailors safely to whatever awaited them next. The Norse, as I understood it, believed that men who died bravely in battle were elevated to the realm of the immortals, where they would feast eternally by the side of their warrior deity. Possibly the same fate was expected for a ship's crew fallen foul of wind and waves. It was a different belief from our own, but one that should nonetheless be respected.

Muirrin walked between the dead with a bowl of water and sprinkled droplets, and Brenna carried aromatic crushed leaves to strew. Johnny spoke about the bravery that took men far from their home shores in search of new opportunities, and how risks were part of being a man, and part of living a life well and fully.

When he was done, I moved between the dead, kneeling by each in turn to lay my hand on his brow, and although all I said was the name, in my spirit I called upon my own gods, the old, good gods, to ferry the departed gently on their last and most mysterious voyage.

"Thorolf Magnusson, and Ranulf his brother." Three paces. "Svein Njalsson." And the next. "Mord Asgrimsson." Dead; dead and cold. I wondered if he had a wife somewhere, keeping the hearth fire alight for his return. "Starkad Thorkelsson." So young; he had hardly begun to be a man. "Sam Gundarsson." I walked on to the gray-bearded man. "And this elder, whose name we do not know." A few steps more. "And this young man, who died before his time." Who died with blistered hands. "We honor them. The blessing of the gods be on them, and on every man, woman and child who perished when *Freyja* foundered here. For those who lie here now, and for those at rest in the deep, we speak the same prayer. May their spirits fly with the winds; may their souls be cradled in the waves; may their lives be celebrated in fine tales around the fire. May their love of family and land, of hearthstone and chieftain, of clan and kin, stay strong in their children and their children's children."

Knut's face looked hard as stone. By his side, Svala stood dry-eyed, staring straight ahead. Kalev translated for them in a murmur.

I had spoken to Knut about the next part, but it was still hard to get the words out, with the two of them right there in the circle. I cleared my throat.

"I say a special prayer for the little ones who perished. In particular, for Svein Knutsson, child of our new friends here." Tears had begun to flow down Knut's face, a stream over granite. Svala's expression showed not a flicker of change, though she must have heard me speak her son's name. "He was taken early by the gods, and is now at peace with his forebears in the place beyond death. Pray for him, and for all those lost here."

After a few moments I stepped back outside the shape of stones, and so did Muirrin and Brenna. The men who had been digging earlier took up their spades to lay the last blanket of earth over these sleepers. An eerie silence hung in the air, broken only by the whimpering of a child whose mother hushed it against her shoulder.

"Now, Sibeal?" Johnny asked quietly.

I nodded. The spades rose and fell; the earth pattered softly down, a dark rain on the shrouds of the dead. Fitful torchlight played on the circle of somber, watching faces.

It happened in a flash. One moment I was standing there, the next I was sprawled facedown on the ground, knocked off balance as Svala hurled herself forward. As I struggled to sit up she seized my shoulders, shaking me so hard my teeth rattled. A scream burst from her, high, ululating. Then Knut was dragging her off me, pulling her away, while Johnny and Cathal came to help me up.

"Are you hurt, Sibeal?"

"I'm . . . I'm fine. She took me by surprise. We must continue with the ritual, Johnny." I looked past him. There were Muirrin and Clodagh, looking somewhat paler than usual. And there was Knut, holding Svala by both arms, speaking to her in a low voice. Her chest heaved, but she was silent now. She did not meet his stern gaze; her beautiful eyes were turned on the ground.

"She was overcome by grief, I suppose," Johnny said in an undertone. "And better to release that grief than keep it locked inside. But that's no excuse for an act of violence."

It was not sorrow I had felt in the grip of her strong hands. What I had sensed was a cry for help.

"Are you sure you can continue with this, Sibeal?"

"Of course." I was still working on my breathing. "We need a final blessing, that's all. It would be right for you to say that, as leader of the community." The ritual must not end on a note of violence and discord. The gods would be deeply displeased, and the spirits of the dead would journey under a shadow.

My cousin stepped forward, a somber figure in his dark tunic, the raven markings on his cheek and brow brought to eerie life by the shifting torchlight. The sky was fading to dusk. "The gods speed you on your journey," he said quietly. "We honor your endeavors. We salute your courage. We offer our prayers for your passage to the next world. Let your memory be held in every stone of this island. Let your songs be whispered on the wind. May the tongues of bards tell your tales until the end of time."

The spades rose and fell once more. After some time, a time silent save for the thud of metal on earth and the soft descent of the soil, the hollow became a mound. Stones would be placed here to hold it firm; this boat would hold a true course to the northeast, toward these seafarers' ancestral home. In time, the vessel would bear a shivering shroud of grass.

Dusk blanketed the island. As we headed back toward the settlement and a warm fire, the rain descended in sudden sheets, drenching every man and woman among us, turning the paths to quagmires and filling each hollow with a slate-dark pool. The torches fizzled and died. Behind us the burial mound stood quiet in the fading light. The ritual was complete.

I was too tired to go to supper in the dining hall, but too unsettled to think of sleep. In the infirmary, Muirrin tended to my bruises and Clodagh brought me food and drink. Folk came and went. I heard from Evan that Knut and Svala had been offered the fisherman's hut down by the main cove, away from the rest of the community, and that Knut had accepted gladly. Svala had not appeared at supper time, Evan said, but Knut had come to the dining hall and had gone around the tables with Kalev, personally thanking every member of the community for the kindness shown to him and his wife.

Later, when Evan and Muirrin had gone to bed and I was sitting by the sick man's pallet deep in thought while Gull pottered at the workbench, Johnny came in. He nodded to Gull, then came over to me.

"How are you feeling, Sibeal? That was . . . unsettling."

"I have a bruise or two on top of the ones I got yesterday, but nothing serious."

"You did a fine job. To stay so calm, to finish the ritual . . . Ciarán would be proud of you." Johnny sat down opposite me. I felt his scrutiny. He was doing what he did so well, taking in what lay below the surface.

"Mm." I knew exactly what Ciarán would say if he were here. *What might you have done differently, Sibeal? What learning can be gleaned from this?* A druid was always learning. One sought wisdom in all that occurred, whether planned or unplanned. Right now, I was not feeling very wise. I was feeling exhausted, out of my depth and on the verge of tears. Svala needed help. She was trying to tell me so, or thus it seemed. But she had attacked me with some violence, when I was doing my best to conduct a solemn ritual in which I honored her dead son. Why would she do that? Was I wrong about that plea for help? Perhaps she was completely out of her mind, and unreachable. "I hope the gods looked kindly on us. Svala's grief has shattered her, I know that. But those men deserved better. I should have anticipated that she might act wildly and taken steps to prevent it."

"Sibeal, look at me."

I looked. It seemed an immense effort.

"You were exhausted and upset. Evan told me the man you rescued may not survive, and I can imagine your feelings on that. Yet you undertook this duty for us. After Svala's outburst you picked yourself up and we finished it. You did a good job."

I was reluctant to tell him that what had caused my collapse was more than simple weariness. The flaw that had made Ciarán send me away, the open window I seemed to have in me to the fears and sorrows of others, had never been more evident than today. To speak of it was to admit to a weakness that few knew about.

"I hope Svala can recover, given time."

"Time," echoed Johnny. "That's just what we don't have, unfortunately, with these men from Connacht due soon."

"Why does that make a difference?"

"Secrets," put in Gull from where he was chopping something at the bench. "Nobody comes to Inis Eala without prior arrangement. We're more accustomed to welcoming parties of warriors than hapless seafarers. When we have men here for training, we take precautions to ensure they learn only what we want to teach them."

"I understand that." Ever since Bran's time, they had taught not only methods of fighting, the construction of weapons and battle tactics, but many other skills a leader could put into use to maintain the advantage: mapmaking, for instance, and covert surveillance and codes. What had made Bran's outlaw band feared and envied throughout the north of Erin now made Inis Eala much sought after as a training ground for elite warriors. "What has that to do with Knut and Svala? And him?" The man on the pallet was asleep, his heavy lids closed, his face a study in white and gray.

"We know very little about them, Sibeal," Johnny said. "It seems Knut was happy to offer his services as an oarsman, and took no interest in who owned the ship or why certain folk were traveling on her. He can't even give me a name in Ulfricsfjord so I know where to send my message. My inclination would be to dispatch him and his wife, along with this fellow, over to the mainland before our visitors arrive. My people in the settlement there could arrange passage home for them. But even if this man survives, Muirrin tells me he won't be fit to travel for a long while. And Svala clearly can't go anywhere. We'll have to keep them for some time."

"I don't imagine any one of them is a spy," I said, wondering if that was what he meant, "or they would have arrived by less dramatic means."

"No, I imagine not. But while they're here, we'll have to keep an eye on them. And with this man needing so much care, our healers are going to be very busy. When we're conducting training, there are always injuries."

"I'll help, of course," I said.

"Good," Johnny said. "Sibeal, I sense you didn't give much credence to what I said before. You shouldn't let what happened at the burial weigh on your mind. I never lie to my men about their performance in the field, and I wouldn't lie to you. When I tell you that you completed your task well, you should believe me."

"Thank you, Johnny." His men reported to him as commander, and it was up to him to determine whether they had done well or not. In the absence of Ciarán, only the gods could determine my success or failure. I could not help feeling they would be watching me with some disappointment.

"You're very hard on yourself," Johnny said.

"The path is one of constant learning. Constant striving for improvement."

"Don't forget that your family is here. You may be a druid, but you should lean on us if you have need. Now I must go. Good night, Sibeal. Good night, Gull."

"Good night."

I moved over to sit on the mat before the fire, watching the patterns in the flames. Gull moved quietly around the infirmary, securing shutters, opening the door for Fang to go out, letting her back in with a muttered, "Your ladyship." Eventually he settled himself on the shelf bed in the corner. He had assured me that he slept lightly and would wake if the sick man needed him, so I should go to bed whenever I wanted to. The dog was asleep in the crook of the survivor's knees. One lamp still burned. My head was full of tumbling thoughts, and I knew I would not soon fall asleep. I listened to the sounds in the chamber: the crackling of the fire, the creak of timbers in the wind, Fang's snuffling snores, the labored wheeze of the man's breathing . . . He was awake. I knew it without going near him. Awake; alone; afraid.

I went to sit by the pallet. The man's eyes were open: windows of deepest blue. There were shadows around them, hollows in his cheeks. His skin was as pale as an underwater creature's, something that never saw the sun. His arms lay limp on the covers, the long fingers splayed. Fang had her nose pressed against his right hand. I curled my fingers around his left. Something altered in his eyes.

"I saw you were awake," I said. "My name is Sibeal. I am a druid; a wise woman." It seemed necessary to talk, even if he could not understand the words, simply to reassure him. But I could not speak of the shipwreck, the drowned, the burial, the disruption to today's ritual. He was deathly sick, and weak as a newborn lamb. I must say nothing to distress him. A story. I would tell a story.

"I don't live here on the island," I told him, "but far to the south, at Sevenwaters, where my father is chieftain. When I leave here at the end of the summer, I will not be going home to my parents and the sister and baby brother who still live there. I'll finally be making my commitment as a druid, if my mentor thinks I'm ready. I'll be living out in the Sevenwaters forest as a member of the druid community that is housed there."

Sevenwaters: its image was never far from my mind. The dappled forest paths, the seven streams in all their moods, the rocks by the lake where generations of children had sat and dreamed. The grove of young oaks. The solitary birch. Everything had a story. The keep itself, with the stone steps up to the roof where a child could sit and look out over the vast sweep of the forest. And that forest, with its capricious pathways and its hidden places, secret places housing portals to a world stranger than the strangest tale. Sevenwaters, home not only to man and woman, but to uncanny races of ancient story . . . How could mere words explain something so wondrous, so beautiful, so utterly different?

"But I'm not sad to be leaving my family," I went on, taking encouragement from the fact that my audience was watching me with apparent interest. "I've known since I was quite small that I was destined for a spiritual life. When I feel confused or distressed, when things worry me, I remind myself of the day I first learned that. I should explain that Sevenwaters, my home, is a place of many stories: tales of family, tales of mystery and magic, tales of uncanny folk. We belong to the old faith. Around us, many other families are Christian now. Increasingly that sets us apart. My father's fortifications defend not only our household and our settlements, but also the druids and . . . certain others.

"Of course, as a little girl I did not understand all this. I just knew Uncle Conor came to visit each festival day, wearing his white robe and his golden torc, and conducted the ritual. Sometimes, if we were lucky, one of us girls would be asked to help in some small way, perhaps carrying an item in a procession or joining in the singing of a prayer. I have five sisters in all, four older, one younger, as well as my baby brother. When we reached a certain age, each of us in turn had the opportunity to dance at Meán Earraigh, the spring celebration, where a young girl takes the part of the Maiden in the ritual."

I faltered, realizing this was not quite true. Maeve had not had a turn. When she was only ten years old Maeve had been burned in a terrible accident, and soon after that she had gone away to live with Aunt Liadan in Britain. My aunt's remarkable gift as a healer made her best suited to help a girl with crippled hands and a scarred face. And Clodagh had missed her turn as well, for the year that would have been hers was the year that disaster happened. The ritual had passed a grieving Sevenwaters by.

"Long before I was old enough to perform this dance myself," I said, thinking how complicated was the web of family sorrows and joys and shared experience, "I discovered the gods had a particular path in mind for me. Up until then, I don't believe the rest of my family knew how differently I saw the world. My eyes should have given it away. My sisters have green eyes, but mine, as you see, are a light blue-gray. Such eyes are shared only by those members of my family with a powerful seer's gift." I paused, an image of my little brother in my mind, with his tangle of dark hair and his clear, unswerving stare. At four years old, Finbar had the manner of a wise hermit, which was more than a little disconcerting. His eyes were like those of his namesake, the man with the swan's wing; and they were like mine. "Such a gift manifests itself in many of my kin. Some are able to speak mind to mind, without words. Some have prophetic dreams. Some are gifted in the interpretation of signs and portents. In a few of us the gift is . . . more powerful. Perilous, if not well governed.

"I knew quite early that I was not like my sisters. I never wanted to race about and play and make lots of noise. I preferred to sit quietly, watching and thinking. I had a thirst for learning; I was pestering Father's scribe to teach me reading and writing before I was three years old. I found that creatures trusted me. Observing them, I discovered I could feel, inside myself, the ways their bodies worked, their different manners of seeing and hearing, their small secrets. I did not like to be cooped up indoors too long; I needed the earth beneath my feet and the wind in my hair. But all of those things could have meant simply that I was a thoughtful, scholarly, quiet sort of child. Then, when I was five years old, I saw her."

I had learned the art of storytelling in the nemetons, and I let the silence draw out. He did understand, surely; how could such an intent expression mean anything else?

"I was alone on the rocks by the lake, close to home," I went on. "The others had gone to gather cress at the mouth of a stream.

I was looking into the water, wondering why it was I always saw something that I knew couldn't really be there—a ship on the sea, a crowd of strange, small creatures, a tower with a banner at the top—when someone spoke behind me. 'Sibeal. Turn around, child.'

"Such a voice! It was honey and sunlight, and it was stream and oak, a voice I knew was that of no human woman. I stood up and faced her. She wore a blue gown and a cloak that seemed to move of itself, wood-smoke and water and drifting cloud. Her hair was dark, her skin pale. She was taller than any woman I had ever seen, towering over my five-year-old self. How had she come here, so silently? Nobody came to Sevenwaters without my father's permission. Nobody came uninvited.

"'Sibeal. Let me look at you.' Her lustrous eyes were fixed on me in careful examination. 'Child, I am Deirdre of the Forest. I am a friend; you need not fear me.'

"'My lady,' I croaked nervously, 'welcome,' for my mother had taught me good manners. At the back of my mind were the tales I had heard of the Tuatha De Danann, the Fair Folk, some of whom were said to dwell deep in the forest of Sevenwaters. It seemed to me this lovely woman could only belong to that ancient and noble race. Indeed, I knew the name Deirdre of the Forest already, from one of our family stories.

"'Come, Sibeal,' she said, and motioned me back to the water's edge. Already, as I moved, I could see images dancing there, warriors and horses and eagles flying. 'Tell me what you see. Do not be afraid.' She knelt down beside me in her flowing gown, and I could smell summer breezes and dew on the hawthorn. I told her about the men in the water, the creatures, the strange things for which I had no names. Frightening things, sometimes. The Lady explained what it meant to see thus, and how I might start to make sense of it all. She spoke to me simply, in keeping with my age, but she did not shrink from the truth. That was the first of my lessons in being a seer. Later came learning of a different kind, Ciarán's learning, rigorous and challenging as befitted the druidic discipline, for which many years must be spent in study of the lore and other elements. Ciarán is my kinsman and mentor. I honor and respect him. But in those early years Deirdre came to me often in the forest, and her guidance formed the foundation of my quest to become a druid. I never ceased to feel wonder that she chose me, little Sibeal, to be the recipient of such wisdom."

I remembered how I had held the tremendous secret of that first visit to myself for what had seemed an absolute age at the time, but was probably only from midday to supper time, when Maeve winkled it out of me.

"In old times, folk thought of the Tuatha De Danaan as gods, or something close to gods," I told him. "The druids debate exactly what they are, and find various answers. Over the years the Fair Folk have shaped the path for the Sevenwaters family, for good or ill. Sometimes they seem a mouthpiece for the gods; more often they have their own intentions for human folk, their own plans. They are an older race than we are—wiser, subtler, longer-lived. But not so different, for they have sometimes formed bonds with men or women, and there have been children born in whom the two races are blended. Another night, I will tell you a tale of such folk." No need to explain that Cathal, who lived here at Inis Eala and was married to my sister Clodagh, was one such person, and that Ciarán was another. While we did not exactly keep such information secret—it was known on the island that Cathal's parentage was somewhat unusual—neither did we go out of our way to spread it abroad. "But for now, my story is complete, and I have kept you awake too long. Time for sleep."

I got up, reaching to tuck in the blankets. As I straightened, a fleeting smile crossed the man's wan features, and for a moment I saw him as he must be when well and happy—a fine-looking person with a sensitive mouth and thoughtful eyes. I imagined him throwing a ball for a dog, or painting a picture, or playing games with his friends. Or writing; those were not the hands of a farmer, a fisherman, a builder.

"I'll bid you good night," I said, suddenly awkward. Whatever the man was, wherever he had come from, it was for him to tell us his own tale, in his own time.

In my little chamber, huddled under my blankets as the draft seeped in under the door, I prayed that he would survive to do so. And I thought of Deirdre of the Forest, who had guided me so wisely, and whom I had not seen now for many years. *She is gone*, Ciarán had said. *Gone away over the sea, never to return*. Many of her kind had departed this shore as humankind stamped its authority on the green land of Erin. And when the wise ones are gone, oftentimes those left in their place are a lesser breed, folk for whom ambition and the lust for power overrule justice and compassion. Such a one was Mac Dara, father of Cathal. In time, this devious prince could do untold harm among the various races that shared that place, and to our kind as well. I wondered who might have the power to stop him.

CHAPTER 3

Falling men, crashing seas, gaping, long-toothed jaws. I wake. I cannot breathe. I gasp, struggling to sit up, but my body refuses to obey. Nothing works. I wheeze out a sound, the pathetic cry of a small creature in a trap. They come, one at each side of the bed, a pair of watchful spirits. They lift me, hold me, speak in gentle voices. They are dark, quiet, tall. Their names are . . . Gull. Gull and Evan. Father and son? "Breathe," Evan says. "Breathe." I try. Who would have dreamed it could be so difficult?

She was here. Stillness in person, telling me a story of trees and water and magical beings. She was here by my bed, her fingers gentle, her voice sweet and clear as a mountain stream. She was here, and now she is gone. Even the dog is gone.

After a long time, I breathe more easily. Evan washes me and changes my clothing. I piss in the pan he holds. They move away to study the contents, their faces grave. Something wrong. Evan puts on a reassuring face and comes to feed me broth. It is light outside. A cold wind whispers under the door. He asks me the same questions again. A patient man. *What is your name? Do you understand Irish?* I have no answers.

Time passes. Bright light: someone has opened the shutters. Outside the sun shines, but it is cold. I am always cold. The dog has not come back. I miss its small form next to me. Its breathing warmth, its sighs and grumbles remind me that I am alive. I think I am alive.

The rustle of a skirt over by the bench. My heart jumps. She's here! I manage to turn my head; the effort exhausts me. There is a woman, slight, dark, bending over a seated man. My heart plummets. Not Sibeal but the other one, the healer, wrapping a cloth around the fellow's arm. I close my eyes. I want to speak. I want to ask. I rehearse it in my mind. *Where is she? Where is she with her listening eyes and her truth-speaking voice?* I will not ask, lest they tell me I only imagined her.

I sleep. Waves crash, men scream, something rears huge and dark. I wake sweating, dizzy, the chamber moving around me. *I must . . . I have to . . .* Compulsion hammers in my blood and whips my heart to a breakneck gallop. *Quick, quick, almost too late . . .* The desperate images fade and are gone. By my bed sits the other sister, the one with flaming hair and skin like fresh cream. Perhaps I have been shouting. She dabs my face with a cloth, her eyes narrowed as she examines me.

"Better now?" she asks with a little smile. "Do you remember me? My name is Clodagh. You seem much troubled by your dreams. Breathe slowly."

She sits there quietly while I struggle to obey. Pain attends each inward gasp; I consider the elements of it, the tight band around my chest, the raw, burned sensation in my throat, the twinge up my neck and at my temple.

"You're fortunate to be alive," Clodagh says, touching her cool cloth to my brow. "Sibeal saved your life."

Sibeal! I don't intend to speak the name aloud, but perhaps my lips form the shape of it, because her eyes widen.

"You do understand," she murmurs. "Sibeal thought you might have some Irish. She's gone off for the day. To the seer's cave, to pray and meditate. She will be back by supper time."

A dark-haired man enters, and Clodagh gets up to greet him. "Cathal!"

I watch them as they talk. When Cathal looks at Clodagh, his eyes soften. She turns the same tender gaze on him. She is heavy with child. Husband and wife, I think. There is a strangeness about Cathal, a touch of the night forest, the mist over the lake, the forbidden well. He puts me in mind of Sibeal's striking tale. Now he is telling his wife that she looks tired and should be resting, not tending to me.

"Muirrin's coming back soon," she says calmly. "I'm fine, Cathal. You know how hard I find it to be idle."

Cathal glowers. He looks formidable. "What about the child?"

"Women dig gardens and weave blankets and gather crops all the time, and the children they carry are none the worse for it," Clodagh tells him, formidable in her turn. "I will do perfectly well here until Muirrin gets back. Don't you have some work of your own to do, with these visitors due any day?"

"Dear one," Cathal says, putting his arms around her, "I'm sorry. I can't help worrying." He touches the place where her gown covers the shape of the child. "I'd keep guard over the two of you day and night if I could."

She returns the embrace, and I avert my gaze. The moment is tender, beautiful. It is not for my eyes.

"Go on, Cathal," Clodagh says to her husband. "Johnny needs you."

With some reluctance, he goes. Clodagh approaches with a bowl of the brew they've been spooning into my mouth as if I were an infant. She feeds me a few mouthfuls, a wretched process for both of us. I swallow obediently and am soon exhausted. She helps me lie back. "Sleep now," she says. She mimes it, head pillowed on hands. "I'll be here if you need anything. Rest well."

Her manner is that of a person used to giving orders and accustomed to being obeyed. I close my eyes and lie still as she bustles around the chamber performing various tasks. I play games with fate. *If I can hold my breath to a slow count of thirty, Sibeal will come. If she tells another story tonight, I will start to remember . . .*

~Sibeal~

The seer's cave was at the northern point of Inis Eala. I reached the place through a narrow aperture in the rocky headland, from which a dark tunnel wound further and further in. Eventually I rounded a corner and stepped out into a hidden cavern. The walls curved up and in; it felt like standing inside a flower. In the center of the floor lay a still pool. Light entered through an opening at the roof's apex and the cloudless sky turned the water beneath to a sweet blue. I stood for some time, looking, sensing. Here was profound quiet, deepest serenity. I could feel a presence, something wise, old and somehow sad.

I set down the bag I had carried, spread out my cloak on the flat stones by the pool and sat there, cross-legged. I would meditate. I would pray. Perhaps I would scry. I was certain my kinsman Finbar, the one after whom my little brother had been named, must have used the water of this pool as a dark mirror, a tool for the seer's eye. He had dwelt here alone for many years, sheltered on Inis Eala by the kindness of Bran and Liadan. It was commonly believed that the forces of good that kept the island safe were centered in this cavern. Long before the coming of Bran and his band of outlaws, Inis

Eala had been spoken of as a sacred place, a place of old gods. But it seemed to me, as to all my family, that Finbar's tenancy had strengthened the spiritual power of the cave and indeed of the island itself.

His story was a sad one. As young men, he and his brothers had been turned into swans by a vindictive stepmother. After three years they had been saved by their sister, but Finbar had been left with a wing in place of one arm. He was condemned to live between worlds.

I owed Finbar a great debt. He had died saving Ciarán's life. Without that sacrifice, my mentor would not have lived to return to the druid community. In time I thought others, too, would understand just what Finbar's selfless act had achieved. I had seen something in Ciarán's future that was so momentous, so terrifying, that I was hardly prepared to think about it, let alone tell him what I suspected might lie in store for him. The seer's gift let in both light and shadow; not for nothing were we trained to caution and reserve. I wondered, sometimes, how much Ciarán had gleaned of his own destiny, and whether he ever suspected that I, his young protégé, might have insights beyond his knowledge.

I would spend the day alone in this cavern that had been Finbar's home for so long. Fang had settled to wait at the tunnel entry, everything about her pose suggesting duty, not inclination. It was only when I was in the cave that I remembered something Uncle Conor had told me: that in his man-bird form, Finbar had been terrified of dogs. Just as well Fang would not come in, for it seemed to me that lonely man's presence lingered here, long after his death. I could sense his sorrow, his quiet, his deep thoughts. I could feel the courage that had drawn him out of his sanctuary, perhaps knowing that he would never return.

"I'm sorry," I murmured to Finbar's shade. "Sorry that your life was not happier; sorry that I came close to disrespecting the memories in this place. I welcome your presence. I honor your courage. I hope your wisdom will guide me to right choices." But the only answer was the restless whispering of the sea.

*   *   *

It was not until I had spent some hours in meditation that I felt ready to seek wisdom in the calm pool. I drank from the water skin I had brought, considering what insights I most keenly sought today. Cathal, with the blood of the Tuatha De Danann running in his veins, could command a particular vision to the scrying vessel when he needed it—he would either see what he sought or nothing at all. A person such as myself, with two human parents, was unlikely to possess such ability, but what I could do was still considerable. I had been a seer since my childhood, born with an unusual talent. I could not wish I had no such skill, for it was god-given. I only wished I were better able to control it, and better able to withstand the difficulties it created.

As with rune rods, the usual practice with scrying was to request an answer to a particular question, or clarification of a puzzle or quandary. What the seer then saw in the scrying vessel might be an answer to that question or to any other. It might seem to have no relevance at all to what one wanted to know. The vision might be of past, present or future, or might deal with the difficult *may be* or the heart-wrenching *might have been*. I had seen things that made me sick; I had seen things that made me weep. I had seen things that made me desperately afraid. Much of what I had seen, I had not spoken of to anyone.

I took time to sink into a trance. The long meditation had not quite wiped the last two days' upheaval from my mind. As the sun moved across the sky and the light from the opening in the cave roof shifted and changed, I asked the first of my questions.

I feel Svala's pain. I feel her cry for help. How can she be reached?

For a long time the water of the pool showed only a series of ripples, a subtle, deep pattern. Then all at once waves were crashing over my head, crushing the breath from my body; hands were clamped around my arms like iron bands, something was dragging me over gritty sand, and I was screaming, screaming . . . no, that was not my voice but the shouting of men, *Don't leave us! What are you doing? For pity's sake, don't leave us!* The hands heaved me up, threw me down. My head struck something, and all went dark in the still pool. I breathed, and breathed again, and the nightmare vision was gone.

I took time to recover, using long-practiced techniques to calm myself. Gods, that had been so real! I would not try to interpret it now. I drank from my water skin. I listened to the cries of gulls beyond the opening in the cave roof, and the endless wash of the sea. I thought of the man brought to me by those chill waves. When my heart had ceased to hammer, when my breathing was slow and even, I asked my second question. Not, *Will he survive?* I did not want an answer to that; I needed hope.

Thanks to Manannán's mercy, I saved a man from the sea. What is it he needs most?

I waited, keeping my mind open and empty. I breathed. The pool lay still before me, not a ripple on its glassy surface, now darkening under the sky of late afternoon.

Start with a name. The words reached my mind as clearly as if they had been spoken aloud. Where my own reflection had been in the water, I now saw a man's. He was a disheveled person with hair of every color from black to white, and a long, thin face, and eyes just like mine. He wore an ancient garment, tattered and torn, and in place of his left arm he had a swan's wing. *A man needs a name.*

Finbar. By all the gods. My instincts had been right; some part of him still lingered in this place where he had been almost content. Could I ask more, or would he vanish the moment I spoke?

He must already have a name. I formed the words in my mind, but held myself silent. *But he's too weak to tell us what it is.*

You must choose a name for him. It is the first step.

I nodded, my gaze held by the compelling eyes, my skin prickling at the utter strangeness of this. I did not know if I could ask any more; but oh, I had so much to say to him, so much I wanted to tell him . . . I must risk one thing, even if it meant I lost the image. *There is a tiny boy at Sevenwaters now. Named after you. My brother. I think he will be a seer. You are loved still; held in highest esteem.*

A fleeting smile. The strange eyes were bright.

Act swiftly, Sibeal. He needs your help. The water stirred. A shadow passed across the cavern, turning my skin to gooseflesh, and the image faded to nothing.

I stayed in the cavern, pondering Finbar's words, until the light told me it was time to return to the settlement. Fang would surely have gone home long ago. I put on my cloak and gathered my belongings. "Farewell," I whispered. "Thank you." But there was no answer. Still, Finbar was here. I felt his presence in the deep quiet of the stone, and in the dark stillness of the water, and in the gentle patch of sky. What had he meant? Choosing a name for a man who doubtless had a perfectly good one of his own seemed an odd thing to do, and hardly urgent. I stepped out of the cave and into the narrow, dark passageway. I could not forget that first vision, the crashing waves, the cruel hands, the screaming. Past or future? Fact or possibility?

Fang was still waiting at the tunnel entry, hunkered down on the narrow path, shivering.

"You poor thing." I bent to stroke her, and she snapped at my fingers. "I'm sorry you had to wait in the cold," I murmured, straightening, "but not sorry enough to let you bite me. Come on."

Once she realized we were heading for shelter and supper, the little dog scampered ahead, good temper restored. I walked briskly, and as I went I considered what name might suit a man hovering between life and death. I could think of no good reason to give him a name other than his own. A name could be a symbol, of course—it could denote some inner quality. On Inis Eala, names were especially important. That had started with Johnny's father, Bran. Aunt Liadan had given him that name. Up until then he had gone only by his title of Chief. She had named him for the raven, since his body was decorated with an elaborate pattern based on that bird's plumage. The band of outlaw mercenaries he had gathered around him all bore animal names: Gull, Spider, Snake and so on. These men were now the senior warriors of Inis Eala, with a special status in the community. I could not think what animal my man would be named for, even if that was appropriate in his case. He was too sick to show his true colors. What lingered of his real self was all in his eyes, eyes that were wary of questions, but thirsty for tales. Perhaps a name would give him strength until he was well enough to talk to us. That meant I should choose a name denoting courage.

"What do you think, Fang?" I asked as we paused to rest on the way, I sitting on a rock beside the cliff path, the dog standing with ears pricked, watching a group of island sheep that grazed with confidence on the precipitous slope below us. "How about Conall? You'd like that one; it means 'strong as a hound.' Or maybe Ardal?"

There was a small cove below us. From my vantage point I had a clear view of the wavelets washing in, the pale stones of the beach. There were larger rocks at the cliff's foot, and in their shelter crouched a lone figure. She was barefoot, her gown dark to the knees with water. Shawl and cloak had been abandoned on the stones nearby. The sun was low in the sky; it touched her golden hair and illuminated her pale skin. Her hands were busy with something, and I saw a difference in her, as if here in this isolated place, alone with the sea and the sky, she had relaxed her guard.

"We're going down there," I murmured to Fang.

As I rose, the dog ran ahead down the steep path toward the cove. I followed more slowly, for the long day spent alone had turned my mood from storm to calm. Sunlight brushed the ocean with a patina of silver; beside me the grasses bent before the breeze, and the sheep conversed on the cliffs in gentle bleats, the ewes grazing below their young on the treacherous slope. No one could be despondent on such a day.

Svala was absorbed in whatever she was doing. The dog and I were on the pebbly beach before she realized she was no longer alone. Crouched in place, she lifted her head and looked toward me, her body suddenly still.

"I mean no harm," I said, stopping where I was. Instinct made me crouch as well, so I would not be looking down at her. There was a distance of twelve paces between us; I would go no closer unless she showed signs of trust. Fang had halted by my side. A growl rumbled through her small body. "Hush, Fang," I murmured, but the dog did not obey. "Svala, may I talk to you?" Oh, for a few words of Norse! A simple greeting would go a long way. What was that laid out in the stones before her? Fish bones? I had heard of entrails used in augury, bones, too. Those looked too small and too disordered for such a purpose. Svala's pose had shifted. Now she resembled a creature on guard over something precious, a nest, a treasure.

When I had talked to the man in the infirmary, I had done so in the belief that he understood at least part of what I was saying. It was different with Svala. Either she had no Irish at all, or she was shutting out what she did not want to hear. I gestured toward her—*you*—then put my hands over my eyes as if weeping—*sad*. Then I cupped my hands together and placed them over my heart. *I feel your sorrow.*

She was so still; she was like a lovely thing carved in pale stone. But her eyes were not blank now. They were wide and clear, gray as the ocean under cloud, and they were turned on me with some understanding.

I gestured again. *You—me*—then arms stretched toward her and curled into an embrace—*friends?*

Above us on the cliff top, a ewe bleated a warning call to her lamb. Fang was off up the pathway, a blur of white. I waited, watching the woman, looking again at the material over which she crouched so protectively. Bones, yes. A welter of them, the ribs of one sizeable catch and of several smaller ones, an assortment of other bones, gleaming white in the sunlight. Picked clean of flesh. It was not the debris of a human meal, for nobody on the island would leave scraps on the shore like this, and besides, there was no sign of a fire. Perhaps gulls had pecked away the shreds of meat. Why had Svala gathered the remnants together?

You—those—augury? This last was hard to illustrate. I placed a hand to my brow, as if to show thought, then repeated a gesture I had used once before with her, stretching out my arms to the sides, palms upwards. She showed no sign of comprehension.

"Never mind," I said, rising to my feet. "Just know that I am a friend, and I would like to help you—"

Svala had got up, too. She stretched out a hand toward me, with something on the palm. With the other hand she beckoned me closer. My heart lurched with surprise. Up on the cliff top, Fang was barking. I hoped she was not chasing sheep.

"What is that?" I asked, taking slow steps toward Svala.

No reply. As I came nearer, I saw that the small item she was holding out, offering me, was a morsel of fish. Raw fish. *Be careful, Sibeal. This may be your only chance with her.*

Svala made a sound, not words, but a murmur of encouragement whose meaning I could guess. *Take, share. This is for you.*

"Thank you," I said, and accepted the fish. "Did you catch this yourself?" I tried to mime the meaning. There was no sign of fishing line or net, nothing at all but the barefoot woman and her pile of clean bones.

Svala murmured again; it was almost like a song, a sad one full of liquid sounds. She performed her own mime for my benefit, and proved better at it than I, for I understood straightaway. *Eat. Good.* As I tried to absorb the strangeness of her request— eat a gobbet of raw fish?—I saw that her fingers were greasy, and that around her full-lipped mouth was a smear of oil. Those bones were not tools of augury. They were the remains of her meal.

Strange indeed. What kind of place did this woman come from, that she ate like a wild creature? There was no choice; she had made a gesture of trust, and if I wanted her to accept my help, I could not rebuff that gesture.

"Thank you, Svala," I said. I took a deep breath and put the fish in my mouth, trying not to wince as I chewed. I hoped very much that what I was eating was freshly caught, and not something she had found washed up on the shore. It was slippery, stringy, a challenge to the teeth. It tasted of salt water and wildness. I swallowed it down. A pity I could not have slipped it surreptitiously to Fang, who would have considered it a treat. I bowed my head courteously in an attempt to convey gratitude. "You are generous to share. The last mouthful!" I indicated the bones, grateful that she had not presented me with a whole fish.

Svala nodded. Then, abruptly, her hands came out again, this time to close around my upper arms. Gods, she was strong!

"You're hurting me," I said, not letting my voice rise.

In response, she turned me around so she was holding me from behind and began to walk me down toward the sea. I grappled with the possibility that she was quite mad, and that she was about to drown me. Out here, at the foot of the cliff, nobody would hear my screams. Fang, perhaps; but what could she do? By the time she fetched help I would be drifting out there, as limp and lifeless as those poor men we had buried. *Breathe slowly, Sibeal. She shared her food with you. That was a sign of friendship.*

Now we were in the shallows. Svala released her hold and came to stand beside me with one hand on my shoulder. I stood still, though the sea was washing over my shoes and drenching the hem of my gown. An exercise in trust. She stretched her free arm out toward the horizon as if trying to catch hold of something out there, something longed for, something precious. Too far. Too far to reach. The look on her face made my heart falter; the tumult of feelings that coursed through me almost stopped my breath. Loss, bereavement, fury, despair, yearning ... I closed my eyes, near-overwhelmed. Images came then: huge seas crashing; rocks looming, their forms those of monsters crouched to spring; dark kelp swirling in a thick mat. And sounds: men shouting, and over their desperate voices the calling of something else, a deep bellow of pain that gripped at my vitals. My heart juddered in my breast. I trembled with horror.

A call from the cliff top: no eldritch thing, but the voice of a man. My eyes sprang open, and I half turned. Knut was coming down the path, striding faster than was quite safe on the steep slope. Svala did not turn, but I felt her body freeze. The animation drained from her features.

"Are you all right?" I murmured, but she made no response. As her husband strode down the shore toward us, we waded back to dry land.

Knut's fair skin was flushed with embarrassment. Avoiding my eye, he came up to Svala, fished out a handkerchief and proceeded to wipe her mouth as if she were an infant that was still learning to feed itself. He spoke to her gently. I guessed he was telling her he'd been worried and was glad he had found her. His glance took in the pile of fish bones, his wife's wet clothing, the garments she had abandoned on the rocks, her bare feet. It was plain that he wished I had not seen this.

"Troubled you . . . regret, sorry," he said to me in stumbling Irish. "My wife . . . disturbed." His hand was firm around her arm. Svala stood quietly by him, head bowed, shoulders drooping.

"No trouble." It seemed he was mortified, ashamed of his wife. The red flush went all the way down his neck. And there, graven on a smooth stone and strung on a fraying strip of darkened hide, was something on which I could comment without any danger of making the situation still more awkward. I put my hand to my own neck and said, "I see you are wearing a rune. *Eolh.* Sometimes called the claw." It was a powerful symbol of protection. If I had been a crewman on a oceangoing ship, I might have chosen the same sign.

Knut's tight jaw relaxed somewhat. "*Eolh,*" he echoed, tucking the charm back under his tunic. "Keep safe. From sea, storm."

"Knut . . . " How could I say this without offending him? "Your wife—she offered me food. She did not upset me in any way. I believe she was trying to talk to me, to tell me something."

I tried not to speak across her, even though she could not understand my words. Her husband had treated her as if she were either a child or a half-wit. She was certainly no child; and after seeing her eyes unguarded, I was beginning to wonder if we had all underestimated her ability to think for herself.

"No speak Irish good," Knut said, then spoke to Svala in Norse, pointing to the clothing she had left on the rocks. He released his hold on her, and she moved over to collect her shawl and cloak, obedient as a chastened dog. It unnerved me to watch them, for so much about this felt wrong—her silent subservience, his obvious embarrassment. They were husband and wife, yet today there was nothing between them of the tender respect that I saw every day between my sisters and their husbands, or between Biddy and Gull, or indeed between my mother and father. Were Norse customs so different?

"I must go now," I muttered, waving vaguely toward the top of the path, where Fang could be seen investigating something under a stone. "I wish you well," I said, looking over at Svala. But she was wrapping the shawl around her shoulders, her back to me, and did not turn.

"You, not talk." Knut put his fingers to his lips, pointed to me, indicated his wife with a sweep of the hand. "Not say." He gestured in the general direction of the settlement. "Not say . . . Johnny . . . wife, here."

"I won't tell anyone," I said. I did not fully understand Knut's motive, but it did seem best that this episode did not become the subject of gossip within the community. "No talk. No tell."

Knut managed a smile and a nod.

"Farewell, then. Farewell, Svala."

I climbed up the path more briskly than was quite comfortable. At the top I whistled to Fang, then headed off toward the settlement without a backward glance.

"And so," I told my family, "I chose a name for him."

We were in the dining hall, where the Inis Eala community sat to supper at four long tables, in no particular order. Folk liked to mingle here. However, it was common for kin to sit together, and so here we were at the table nearest the cooking fire. Johnny sat with Gareth, who was his lover as well as his best friend and comrade in arms—this unusual arrangement was simply part of everyday life on Inis Eala, where folk were somewhat more tolerant than on the mainland. Clodagh and Cathal were here, along with Muirrin, Gull, Biddy's son Sam and his wife, Brenna. Evan was in the infirmary where, I was told, our patient was still alive but no better. Biddy was occupied with supervising her assistants, who were coming to and fro with cauldrons of soup and platters of bread. She herself would eat later, when she had ensured everyone else was adequately fed.

I had given an abridged account of my day. A trip to the cave; quiet meditation; some insights gained, which I did not describe. A suggestion that I name the nameless survivor, at least until he started to talk to us. I made no mention of Finbar. I said nothing of my odd meeting with Knut and Svala. I had made a promise and would keep it. The two of them had come to supper well after me, and were sitting on the far side of the chamber next to Kalev.

Svala had changed her gown and brushed her hair. I could not see if she had shoes on. Her eyes were downcast. She pushed the food around on her platter, but I did not see a morsel pass her lips. Knut was talking to the people seated around them, presumably exercising his few words of Irish. He had recovered from his embarrassment and was smiling; there was a ripple of laughter at his table. The only sign of unease was in his restless fingers, twisting and turning the amulet he wore around his neck.

"A name would certainly be useful," Muirrin said, "at least until we know what his real one is. He seems reluctant to give it; he must understand our simple requests for him to tell us, even if he knows no more than a word or two of Irish. What have you chosen, Sibeal?"

"Ardal," I said. "A man with so many challenges ahead of him needs a brave name."

There was a little silence around me as my family considered this, while at the other tables the clank of spoons on platters, the chink of goblets and the convivial talk went on. In fact, the place was not as noisy as usual; on the night of my arrival it had been hard to make oneself heard. Tonight was different. We were consuming the food that had been prepared to feed shipwreck survivors. It would be some days, I thought, before the community returned to its nightly round of after-supper songs and tales.

"Ardal," mused Gareth. "Means exceptional courage, doesn't it? A man couldn't complain about a name like that. He might have some trouble living up to it."

"It's a good choice," Johnny said. "Better a name to aspire to than one that means little. We would all hope to be strong in adversity."

The talk turned to practical matters, as the men discussed the impending arrival of their visitors and how arrangements for training and for security would be handled. Even invited guests on the island, it seemed, were more or less constantly watched.

"It's done with some subtlety, Sibeal," Gareth said, seeing my expression. "They won't know there's a guard over them."

"Not unless someone steps beyond the boundaries of acceptable behavior," added Johnny. "On the day our guests arrive, we set out the rules for them. And we generally give a display, an introduction to the kind of work we do here. It's as much entertainment as education. We open up the training area to everyone for that."

"Even druids are expected to come along and scream encouragement, Sibeal," said Clodagh with a grin. It was good to see her smile. I had noticed how pale and tired she looked. Cathal was hardly better. There were dark smudges under his eyes.

"Sibeal's hardly the screaming kind," observed Sam. He was the island blacksmith and took after Biddy in looks, being big, solid and fair. His brother Clem had wed a mainland girl and now lived and worked in the settlement on the other side, looking after the transport of goods and men across the water.

"Ah, well," I said, "I have seen your combat bouts at Sevenwaters, so I have an idea of what's expected. But if you want an enthusiastic shouter, it's a shame I didn't bring my little sister with me." Eilis, now twelve years old, had long been intensely interested in all matters of warcraft, and indeed had persuaded one or two of Johnny's men to teach her various techniques when they were in our household on their yearly visits. Eilis did not so much scream as offer an expert commentary, complete with helpful suggestions.

Supper drew to a close; the dining hall began to empty. Biddy came to sit down beside Gull and have her own meal while her assistants moved around the tables, collecting the platters for washing. Johnny would stay here awhile, for it was customary for members of the community to bring their questions and disputes to him after the meal so everything could be sorted out fairly. One of his rules, a good one for a place like this where, in effect, there was no escaping the rest of the inhabitants, was that the sun should not set on anyone's anger. Johnny would listen calmly, arbitrate, offer advice, sometimes give orders. There were one or two men standing by the open area where, on a happier night, musicians would gather to entertain the crowd. It was plain that they were waiting to be heard.

"I'll bid you all good night," I said, rising to my feet. The sooner I went to the infirmary, the sooner Evan could come down and have his supper. Perhaps I would get a little time alone with the sick man, so I could tell him his new name without an audience. "Biddy, is there anything you'd like taken over to the infirmary?"

"Ah, yes, Sibeal, thank you." Biddy got up and fetched a small covered pot. "Not what I'd be wanting for my own supper, I must say; not even a bone boiled up in the brew to give it a bit of flavor. This is all the poor fellow can take, Gull tells me. You can warm it up on the infirmary fire."

"Don't try to feed it to him yourself, Sibeal," cautioned Muirrin. "Wait for Gull. The man's still having serious problems with his breathing, and that makes it hard for him to swallow without choking."

The look in my sister's eyes stayed with me as I walked to the infirmary, my path lit by torches that were set around the settlement on poles. I had seen in her expression that she thought the man—Ardal, I must start calling him that—would not survive. Remembering those sad, shrouded corpses laid to rest so far from home, I felt a sudden determination to prove her wrong.

As the invalid was asleep, Evan agreed to go for his own supper. I set the pot by the fire and settled myself on the bench nearby. In my mind, I rehearsed a lengthy passage of lore suited to the midsummer celebration. As I was the only druid on Inis Eala, it seemed likely I would be conducting the rite here. I would at least offer my services.

"Sibeal."

A harsh whisper from the pallet. Not asleep then; not any longer. The deep blue eyes were on me, and the expression on the gaunt features so shocked me that for some moments I could neither move nor speak. Not fear; not confusion; nothing that I would have expected. He looked . . . transformed. As if, deathly sick as he was, my presence filled him with joy. No man had ever looked at me in that way before, and I found it deeply unsettling.

"Sibeal." He spoke my name again, pronouncing it oddly. The one word cost him dear; he gasped for air.

"Don't try to talk." I moved at last, wondering if I had imagined what I saw, for that look was gone now, replaced by the fierce expression of someone whose whole mind is concentrated on breathing. "Here, I will move these pillows, make you more comfortable . . . " I did so, slipping an arm behind his shoulders to lift him, wedging the pillows into place. I had hoped for time alone with him. Now I was all too aware that I was no healer, and that if he took a turn for the worse I would not be much help at all. A jug and cup stood on a shelf not far away. I should offer him water, at least.

I held the cup for him. He sipped, swallowed. Some went down; more spilled onto the bedding. A wheezing, painful breath. My own chest ached.

"More?" I asked.

He made a little sound, not speech, and took one more sip. The effort had worn him out. He sank back on the pillows.

"That's good," I said, though his weakness horrified me. "Breathe slowly if you can . . . in, two, three; out, two, three . . . " I demonstrated, placing a hand on my ribs.

He managed a nod. No more words. I sat down on the stool by his pallet, reaching out to touch his hand. "You're cold," I said. "We need Fang. Little dog. Name, Fang." I imitated her yap and pointed to the spot where she had lain in the curve of his knees to warm him. A faint smile appeared on his face. This, he had certainly understood. "Coming soon, with Gull, I expect."

He was silent. He seemed to be waiting.

"You remembered my name," I said, indicating myself. "Sibeal." I pointed to him. "Can you tell me your name?"

No smile now. His long hands were restless, plucking at the woolen cloth of the blanket.

"Do you remember?" I asked on an impulse. "Do you remember the little cove, and how I came down and found you? The waves carrying us higher, the wood with the runic markings, the stories I told to hold back the darkness?"

No response. It seemed to me his gaze was turned inward now, though his eyes still rested on me. Too weary to think; too weary to listen. But I should try to explain about the name.

"I spent today in prayer and meditation." I wished I knew whether it was necessary to keep illustrating with gestures; it did feel a little foolish. "I went to a cave, a place of the gods, where wisdom can be sought."

Footsteps outside and Fang's familiar yap—Gull was here. "I was told that I must give you a name," I said. "I've chosen the name Ardal, if you agree to that. It means 'unusual courage.' We'll use it only until you can tell us your own name, of course." I went through the ritual of pointing once more. "My name, Sibeal. Your name, Ardal. For now."

The door creaked open as I was speaking, and Gull came in with the dog at his heels. "Did you tell him what it means, Sibeal?" he asked.

That surprised me. "I did. Do you think he understands?"

"That's what you believe, isn't it? Knut said he was on the ship as a passenger, not crew. The fellow may be more scholar than warrior. Could be a scribe, maybe a cleric of some kind. I think I've seen some understanding on his face when you talk. Could be all manner of reasons why he's not speaking to us, sheer exhaustion being the most likely. I'll warm up the soup, shall I? Let's get him fed before we worry about anything else."

"I'll do it." I moved to the fire, wanting a little time to think. I could not forget the look Ardal had turned on me when he woke, as if the sight of me was a gift. It seemed quite wrong; and yet it had touched me, filling my heart with warmth. A strange day indeed: Finbar's shade in the water, Svala with her fish and now this.

"This island is an odd place, Gull," I said, stirring the little pot.

"Inis Eala changes folk." He was hanging his cloak on a peg, his back to me. "Brings out the truth in them for better or worse. For some it's quick. For some it takes far longer." He removed his outdoor boots and set them at the foot of his own pallet. "You all right, Sibeal?"

"Me?"

"Don't sound so surprised. You've only been here a couple of days, and look at everything that's happened. Wasn't this supposed to be a time of rest for you, this summer on the island?"

"Well, yes." My sisters had been talking, evidently. "But if there's work for me to do, I should do it. Anything from conducting a burial rite to helping look after a sick man."

"And rescuing folk from the sea." There was kindness in Gull's deep voice. "How old are you, sixteen?"

"I'm the same age Aunt Liadan was when she rescued Bran," I pointed out. "I'm the same age Clodagh was when she went into the Otherworld to save Cathal. And I'm the same age my mother was when she married my father. I'm not a child who needs protecting." *But I am a seer who feels too much, and Ciarán thinks that makes me a liability.* "Besides," I added for my own benefit as much as anything, "I've spent a large part of the last four years in the nemetons." I lifted the pot off the fire. "I've been trained to keep vigils, to go without food, to manage on very little sleep. I'm stronger than I look."

"You're young for that kind of life," he said, his tone noncommittal.

"Too young, you think?"

"That's not for me to say. I heard part of what you told him last night. You sound sure of yourself."

"I've known for a long time that my feet would tread this path," I said.

"Mm-hm. You're lucky, then. For most of us it takes half a lifetime before we really know. You've only got to look at the fellows who end up here. Wasted their young years, most of them, taking one wrong turning after another. Some, fate's treated harshly; some have only themselves to blame. But it's never too late for a fellow to change, not even if he's five-and-thirty with a weight of trouble on his shoulders. Or five-and-forty, for that matter. Now, we'd best feed this young man his supper, such as it is." He poured a measure of the broth from pot to bowl, his dark eyes thoughtful. "It must be good to have that bright, straight path before you," he said. "Walking forward under the gaze of the gods, and everything clean and certain."

"Mm." The path was not always so bright and straight, not when Ciarán had decided that after all those years of study and discipline I still was not ready.

Between us, Gull and I got half the bowl of soup into Ardal before it became plain he was too tired to go on. Gull took the bowl and set it down on the floor. Fang made short work of the leftovers.

I fetched a damp cloth and wiped Ardal's face. In my mind, sharply, I saw Knut doing the same for Svala. It was sad that he felt shamed by her behavior. Of course it must be hard for him, here among strangers, trying to watch over her. I wondered if she had ever been able to speak. Had she once sat and plied distaff and needle with other women, exchanging tales of husbands and children, the domestic chatter of an ordinary settlement? Perhaps she should be offered that sort of companionship here. I might suggest it to Clodagh.

Fang had finished her unexpected meal, and now made a mighty leap onto the pallet. She circled three times, as was her habit, then settled by Ardal's side with a contented sigh. His long fingers moved to rest on the small warmth of her curled-up body. There was a softening of his features as he watched her; a stirring of something in his eyes. The skin of his hand was scarcely darker than the dog's white hair.

"A long day," Gull observed.

"For all of us," I said.

"No storytelling tonight?"

While I was giving this some thought, I saw Gull stifle a huge yawn.

"I'll sit up with Ardal awhile," I said. "Why don't you get some sleep? I'll wake you if I need you."

"Sure?"

"Yes, I'm sure."

"One or two things Ardal and I need to get done first. You'd best turn your back awhile."

I took a candle and went to my chamber while Gull tended to Ardal's personal needs. I set the candle down on the storage chest, where its flame guttered in the chill draft from under the door, illuminating the charcoal runes I had marked on the walls. Something nudged at my mind. It had been a rune-marked timber from the Norse ship that had borne Ardal to safe shore, that and

Manannán's mercy. Perhaps this was not a night for storytelling, but for a divination.

Moving the candle, I opened the chest and lifted out the bag that held my rune rods. There were twenty-four of them, crafted by my hands and consecrated with my blood. Folded around them in the bag was my ritual cloth of plain linen. Feeling the weight of them, the comforting solidity, I thought they might have some answers for me.

"Sibeal? We're done here."

Back in the infirmary, Gull was poring over the pan before taking it out to the privy. Ardal lay quiet, eyes open, hand curved around the little dog. His face was ash-pale.

"Any improvement?" I asked Gull in a murmur.

"Looks much the same. He needs to keep drinking water. The more the better. Washes the poisons out." Another yawn. "I'll just go and empty this, and then I'll be off to bed. If you're sure."

"We'll be fine."

While he completed his errand, I took out the ritual cloth and spread it flat in front of the fire. I sat cross-legged before it, watching the shadows on the pale linen as the flames danced on the hearth. Gull came back in, barred the door, wished me good night and settled on his shelf bed. Ardal lay still; perhaps he too would sleep soon. I breathed in a slow rhythm. Inwardly, I repeated a short prayer. My mind gradually opened to a state in which it could receive the wisdom of the divination.

Time passed; perhaps a great deal of time, perhaps not so long. At length I reached into the bag again and wrapped my hands around the bundle of birch rods. I bunched them together over the cloth, feeling their power, the knowledge within. I closed my eyes and, in silence, asked my question. *How best can I help this man whom I have named?*

I let the rods go. The knocking music of their fall took me for a moment into the heart of Sevenwaters forest. I imagined I had been sitting all day by a still pool, deep in trance. I smelled the fresh scent of pine needles; a high chorus of birdsong sounded above me. The floor on which I sat became the earth of a Sevenwaters clearing; the hearth fire was a blaze kindled on flat stones in the grove where Ciarán loved to meditate.

Eyes fast shut, I reached out and took up one rod, a second, a third, letting instinct guide my choice. For a moment I held the three against my heart. I opened my eyes.

Os, Ger, Nyd. They settled in my mind, beginning to combine and shadow and influence one another. Some ideas came quickly. *Nyd* could be interpreted as the last extreme of courage, the kind of courage a man might show when death looked him in the face, perhaps in the form of a wild sea. I had seen the crossed lines of *Nyd* down on that cold shore, when pebbles had washed over certain runes carved on the ship's timber. Immense, almost insane fortitude; deep inner strength.

Nyd with *Os.* Prophecy and revelation. Calm and wisdom. Perhaps the courage was deep inside, a conviction born of faith; perhaps it was my own courage and faith that were being called upon. I had asked how I could help.

But then there was *Ger*, which turned things on their heads. *Ger* could mean reversals, but it could also signify the fulfillment of visions and the completion of quests. Full circle. Perhaps a mission lay ahead. Ardal's? Would he live long enough to attempt such a thing? Maybe the mission was mine.

"Sibeal."

I started so violently that I dropped the three rods into my lap. Ardal had turned his head to look at me. He was gesturing for me to come closer.

I gathered up the rods, the chosen three in my right hand, the others in my skirt, and rose to my feet. I felt shaky and sick. A meditative trance cannot be broken so abruptly without cost to the seer. I had not realized he was watching.

I approached the bed. "You startled me," I said.

"Sibeal." He spoke my name carefully; I could hear his effort to get it right. He added another word that I did not understand, then indicated the rods. *Show me.*

There was no special need for secrecy. The Norse lived in many parts of our land. Their signs appeared on door frames, on ships' timbers, on weaponry, on protective talismans like the one Knut wore around his neck. Their interpretation might be an arcane art, but the signs were not in themselves forbidden. I fanned the rods out across the pallet beside Ardal, then helped him to sit up.

"Rune rods," I said, keeping my voice to a murmur. "Used in divination. The signs that came to my hand indicated a mission ahead. Perhaps for you, perhaps for me, perhaps for the two of us together. Whatever it is, it will require great courage."

Ardal was studying the rods closely. Now he began to move them around. I sat in silence, waiting. Gull lay still under his blankets, already asleep. Eventually Ardal took up one rod, another, a third. He held them on his open palm, showing me.

"*Is. Ger. Lagu,*" I indicated each in turn as a prickle of strangeness ran over my flesh. This was no random choice. *Ger*: reversal or completion, as in my own divination. *Lagu*: a sign of the moon, full of mystery. And whether it was my own preparation for the ritual, or whether it was my openness to the pain of others, I thought I knew why he had chosen these three.

"You can't trust," I said, looking into his eyes. "Not me, not the others, not anyone. You feel as if you're walking on shifting ground." I saw it in his face. "Nothing certain, nothing sure, nothing to hold on to." He bowed his head. "But you have *Lagu* with *Ger*. That means you can achieve a goal. It's close to the result of my divination—it concerns a quest or mission, a matter coming full circle. Yes?"

He put down two rods but retained one. *Is*: literally, ice, which turns fluid to frozen solid, closing in, shutting down . . . The locking of life in stillness. As I hesitated, knowing I was on the brink of a discovery, Ardal held the *Is* rod against his heart.

"This refers to you, yourself?" I whispered. "Shut in? Shut out?"

He showed me the rune again, then lifted a hand to touch his brow. He moved his fingers to and fro before his eyes as if to indicate dizziness.

"Shut in; confused; unable to think clearly," I said, letting my thoughts wander through the possibilities. "Beset by nightmares, dreams, visions . . . "

He waited for me to work it out.

"I know you want to tell me something," I said. "I might keep on guessing and guessing, and still not understand what it is. It seems to me that you can understand some Irish at least. Can't you talk to me? It's safe here; we are all friends. But you won't even tell us your name."

Ardal made a sound of frustration. His left hand formed a fist on the blankets. In the shadows, Gull stirred.

"Hush," I said, "never mind. I'm upsetting you." I reached to gather the rune rods. Perhaps I should wake Gull. There was a wildness in Ardal's eyes, a shivering in his thin frame. In his right hand he clutched the rod carven with *Is*.

For a moment I considered that he might be out of his wits. Perhaps he had not understood anything at all, and my belief that he knew enough Irish to follow my stories and my conversation was born out of my desire that it should be so. Perhaps I had persuaded myself that I had reached him, simply because I could not bear to be a failure. I sighed and reached out for the last rod.

Ardal gave it to me. As he did so, he lifted his other hand and sketched out the same gestures as before, touching his brow, waving his fingers before his eyes. Oh, the look in those eyes! *Think, Sibeal. He wants you to understand. He wants it as desperately as you want him to speak.*

The rune: *Is*. The hand to the head: *my mind, my thoughts*. The fingers moving in ripples. Chaos? Dreams?

He pointed to me. "Sibeal." He spoke my name in his rasping whisper. He pointed to himself, and then to the rune rod in my hand.

"*Is* represents you, shut off from the rest of us. I understand that part."

"Sibeal," he said again, pointing to me. Then pointed to himself and repeated the rippling gesture, as if to indicate a swirling confusion in his mind.

I realized, with a sudden chilling clarity, that this was the same exchange Muirrin, Gull and I had tried already—*my name, your name*. "Oh, gods," I said, cold to the bone. "You can't remember anything. You can't even remember your name."

CHAPTER 4

~Felix~

Day and night blur into one. Folk come and go, doors open and close. In the time between, my ears cannot escape a ghastly music: the crackling, wheezing, creaking variations of my breath. Sleep comes in snatches. My time is measured by the steady ritual of my keepers. Gull's kind, ugly hands lifting me, turning me, keeping me clean. What lies in his past, that he bears such scars, yet gazes on the world with perfect serenity? Evan, calm and tall, tending to me with practiced care. His eyes assess me. I see him thinking: *He will live another day.* Capable, hardworking Muirrin. They all depend on her.

And Sibeal. Her gaze like a clear well, her words drops of rain on my parched ground. I have hardly seen her. Since the night when she showed me the runes, a fog has come down over me. They fought to keep me alive, I think. Time passed; days, perhaps many days. Once or twice I heard her: *Evan, can I help? I could sit with him.* And the answer: *He's so weak, he would not know you were there.* If I had had the strength, I would have wept at that.

*   *   *

Without a past, I was adrift. Without a name, I was nothing. She gave me a name like a bright flame of courage. She believes in me. That is the ladder I will climb, to escape this pit of shadows.

I find it hard to speak. The words will not come out, though they are in my mind. I try. I manage *Yes, No, That hurts*. Something weighs on me, something heavy. I have carried a darkness out of this wreck. Sibeal, where are you?

I am one step further from the abyss. Gull and Evan examine my water, muttering together. I hear Gull say, *holding his own*. They must believe I can survive this, or Evan would not keep feeding me this endless broth. He has explained that it will make me better; it will help my body work the way it should. Where is the remedy for my mind?

He washes me, dries me, tucks me up as if I were a baby. I am so weak. *Sleep, Ardal*, he says. The dog jumps up and settles beside me. A good companion; a simple friend. Fang. I do not care for that name. They say she bites. I have not seen it.

Drifting, close to sleep, I think of my own little dog. That first day, I ran home from the farm with him in my arms, most precious, most thrilling of gifts. *I will call him Noz.* My father laughed. *Night? That's a grand name for such a scrap!* But the name was perfect. Black as coal. Black as a raven. Black as dark of the moon. When Noz hid under the covers, all I could see were his bright eyes.

Visitors: three men in warrior garb. One is a man who came before. A rune around his neck on a rough strip of hide: *Eolh*.

"He's too weak to see anyone," Muirrin tells them. "We nearly lost him, three times over."

"We'll keep it brief," says a fellow with wheaten fair hair. "Knut just wants to see how he's doing, wish him well."

"Then let Knut talk to him alone, and not for long. Explain that to Knut, Jouko." Muirrin is severe.

Jouko translates for Knut. Another tongue; not my own, though I understand it well. Jouko and the third man wait by the door, talking quietly together, while Knut comes over to my pallet and sits down, his pose that of a comrade come to make kind enquiries. "I hope you are feeling better, my friend," he says. His tone is amiable, but his smile chills me.

I want to close my eyes, to will him away, but his gaze holds me. A friend? I think not. There is death in this man's eyes.

Knut's voice drops to a murmur. "They say you've lost your memory. They say you can hardly put two words together. Maybe that's true and maybe not. But understand this. Speak one word about what happened, one single word, and *sshhk*—" He draws a finger across his throat in unmistakable illustration. He has his back to the others. "Just so we're clear."

I cannot remain silent in the face of this. "How dare you threaten me?" I say, using the same tongue. But what I intend as a defiant challenge comes out as a feeble whisper. The others go on talking; my protest has carried no further than Knut's ears.

He laughs at me. He makes it the chuckle of a man seeking to lift a wounded comrade's spirits. "Fool," he murmurs. "You'll hold your tongue if you set any value on your wretched life." He rises to his feet. "I'm glad to see you looking so much brighter, comrade." His tone is hearty now. "They're looking after you well."

Jouko translates this for Muirrin's benefit.

"He tires easily," she says. "The effects of long immersion in seawater, the cold, the shock of the whole thing—it's taken a heavy toll. You'd best leave us now."

I let my lids fall over my eyes. The door opens, shuts. Muirrin is busy with something over at her worktable. I lie still. It is a long time before my heart slows. I read a message in that man's cold eyes. *How unfortunate that you did not die.*

I sleep and dream. A cart comes down the track by the farm. I'm picking berries. The basket is woven with a pattern of sunflowers. I'm not tall enough to reach the best fruit. As I stand on tiptoes, stretching up, I hear the carter's shout and a strange, squealing noise cut off sharply. I run, but Noz is already dead. Dead in the road. *Stupid dog,* says the man. *Went right under the wheels. You all right, lad?* I wake with my face all tears, my fingers reaching to touch the little dog that breathes gently by my side. The little dog that is not black, but pure white.

~Sibeal~

Ardal took a turn for the worse, and the Inis Eala healers became very busy indeed, brewing drafts, applying poultices, trying to draw the poisons out with leeches. Walking into the infirmary, I heard the desperate rasp of his breathing and smelled the miasma of sickness and defeat. My own role included everything from sweeping the floor and washing bandages to holding Ardal's hand by candlelight and willing him to take one more breath. I fell into bed so exhausted that I hardly knew whether I was awake or asleep. I dreamed of great waves, perilous rocks, men screaming in despair. In the mornings I woke with thumping heart and clammy skin, and murmured a prayer of thanks that the nightmare was not real. My first act on rising from my bed was to go through and check that Ardal was still breathing.

He no longer looked at me with recognition. When he could summon sufficient strength to open his eyes, he seemed to be gazing on fathomless dark. He did not speak, either in Norse or Irish. Muirrin looked shattered, Evan somber. Even Gull had stopped saying our patient might survive, though he remained calm and composed, attending to anything and everything with gentle hands and kindly words.

I did not go to the seer's cave. I did not go anywhere much; the four walls of the infirmary were the boundaries of my world. I had saved Ardal's life. The runes had shown a mission for him, a call to action I was coming to believe must be obeyed by the two of us. He couldn't die.

It was hard to pray, hard to conduct a conversation, hard even to think straight. My stomach was knotted tight; my head was muzzy with unshed tears. Everything was awry. I had tended to the sick before, but that had been nothing like this. I felt, oddly, as if part of me were in that man lying on the pallet, fighting Morrigan's will. If he died, part of me would die with him.

Eventually a day came when Muirrin ordered me out. "Go on, Sibeal. You must have a rest from this, even if it's only for a morning. Go and see Clodagh. Or chat to Biddy, and let her feed you."

"I can't. What if he dies while I'm not here?"

Muirrin put her arm around me. "You can't keep him alive by sheer force of will," she said. "We're doing the very best we can, Sibeal. You know that. But you won't help Ardal, or us, if you get so exhausted you become sick as well. Go on, now. Get some fresh air, at least."

Biddy was in the kitchen, gutting fish. She sat me down and put a bowl of porridge in front of me.

"Eat," she ordered. "You look like a little ghost. Every mouthful, Sibeal. And drink this mead. I want to see some color in your cheeks."

I ate, though the food tasted like ashes. I watched her awhile, realizing that while absorbed in Ardal's struggle I had lost sight of others on the island who might have needed me.

"How is Svala?" I asked. "Is she better now that she and Knut are lodged on their own?" It was days since I had left the infirmary; so many days I had lost count.

"I haven't seen much of her, Sibeal." Biddy had her fair hair tied back in a scarf; her red-knuckled hands were wielding the knife with precision. "She comes to supper with Knut, but she doesn't seem over-fond of my cooking. I've hardly seen her eat a morsel, and she's a big woman. I took food down to the hut a couple of times. She didn't invite me in. The place was a mess, from what I could see, bedding all over the floor, clothing thrown into corners. Either she's not much of a housewife, or she's still too overcome by her grief to bother with such things. As for the food, she took the dish from my hands, backed inside and shut the door in my face. I feel quite sorry for Knut. He's a good man, always willing to set his hand to a task if there's a need. And he's got his own grief to deal with."

"Svala seems ill at ease among us. As if she's not used to having people around her. I wonder where they lived before."

"Grief does strange things to a person," Biddy said. "You maybe haven't lived long enough to see it. When I lost my first husband I lost sight of hope for a bit. If it hadn't been for the boys, Sam and Clem, I would have found it hard to go on. But when you've got little ones wanting their supper or climbing on your knee to give you a hug, you do go on, no matter how badly it hurts. I felt alone. That was the worst part of it. And then the fellows came, Snake and Gull, all the way to Britain, and fetched me and the boys back here. I had no intention of marrying again; the hurt was too raw. If anyone had told me I'd wed that wild-looking black man with feathers in his hair and less than his full complement of fingers, I'd have thought it was a bad joke." She smiled, the knife stilling in her hand. "Every day I ask the gods to bless Bran for his goodness in sending them for me," she said softly. "I'm the luckiest woman in the world, Sibeal, to have found two such men in one lifetime. My Evan was the kindest husband anyone could want. Gull is . . . well, he's like no other. He and I, we've each been through our share of sorrow and loss. And we've had rare happiness together." Abruptly, she turned a searching look on me. "You'll miss that, with the future you've chosen for yourself. You'll never know the joy and terror of loving someone the way I love Gull, or the way your sisters love their men."

"But I hear the voices of the gods," I said. "And the great silences. The joy of the spirit must surely surpass the joy of the flesh."

Biddy smiled. "It's not just the flesh, though that is certainly a good part of it. If it was up to me, which it never would be, I'd say a person should wed first and have a couple of little ones, and then decide whether the life of the spirit is better and finer than an ordinary sort of existence."

"But then, if you decided it was, you'd have to leave your family to become a druid. That would be doing things the wrong way around."

"I'd have thought a person could do both," Biddy said. "I'd have thought being a wife and mother, or a husband and father, might make a person wiser and more thoughtful. And that might make them better at being a druid or a priest or whatever it was. But nobody's asking me."

I could have explained about the years and years it took to memorize the great body of lore a druid needed. I could have described the fasting, the solitude, the various tests of endurance. The need for silence; the long periods of prayer. But I was too tired and dispirited to summon the words.

"I hope I haven't upset you," Biddy said. "An honest opinion, that's what it was. What happens if you make the decision, and take these vows or whatever they are, and then change your mind about it?"

"I won't change my mind. And you haven't upset me, Biddy. I like people to be honest."

"About Svala," she said. "Maybe she's best left to herself. They may not stay long, anyway, her and Knut. Johnny will be wanting them off the island as soon as she's fit to travel. I suppose they'll go back where they came from. Poor things; a voyage to find a new home, such hopes, and ending the way it did."

"Mm."

It was sad indeed. For each of those who were drowned, there was a story like that of Knut and Svala, a tale of opportunities lost, of paths cut abruptly short, of folk left behind. Ardal's must not end that way. It must not.

"Sibeal?" Biddy was watching me closely. "Why don't you go out for a walk? It's a lovely day. Gull told me you were working too hard, and I see it's so. Finish that food first, and then go out and enjoy the sunshine. You won't make things better by wearing yourself out, lass."

"I should be there. With Ardal. It feels right."

"Ardal wouldn't want you getting sick on his behalf, not if he's got any common sense at all."

She was right, of course. Besides, if I went straight back to the infirmary, Muirrin would only shoo me out again.

I had not explored the eastern end of Inis Eala, so I headed that way, skirting the women's quarters. Down by the scattering of small huts that housed folk with children, a young woman I knew as Alba was playing with a mob of small boys and girls. Their game involved chasing, catching and making a range of animal noises. I lifted a hand in greeting. Alba, flushed and laughing, waved wildly back.

A group of men was working on an almost-complete cottage, two thatching the roof, others laying stones for a pathway. Tall, lanky Spider was supervising them, and I stopped to greet him.

"What do you think, Sibeal?" he asked, casting his eye over the humble but pleasing dwelling.

"You've done a fine job. Is this Clodagh's and Cathal's new house?"

"That's right, and it's a pleasure to build it for them. Should be finished well before that baby arrives; our extra worker has made all the difference." Spider jerked his head in the direction of the men heaving slabs of stone into place, and I saw that one of them was Knut, stripped to the waist and dripping with sweat. He straightened as he saw me, and gave me a nod.

"That fellow does the work of two." Spider grinned at the Norseman. "Don't know how we managed without him."

"You walking," Knut called, addressing me in Irish. "All alone. Not safe."

I was taken aback, and could not think what to say to him.

"Man go with you. Better."

Spider's grin widened. He made no attempt to speak for me.

"I'm used to walking on my own," I said. What did Knut think I was, a pampered princess with no common sense at all? If this was his attitude, no wonder his wife's tendency to wander barefoot on the shore troubled him. "I am a druid; I go under the protection of the gods."

It was not possible to tell if Knut had understood me. He stood there studying me, arms folded. I had no idea what he was thinking.

"I'll bid you good morning, Spider," I said. "Muirrin sent me out for fresh air and exercise, so I'd better make sure I get them."

As I was turning away, Knut spoke again. "The man. Very sick. Die soon, yes?" Before I could reply he added, "Sad."

Knut did not sound especially sad, but then, his Irish was limited—perhaps he did not realize how blunt his speech sounded.

"Ardal is still alive." My tone was sharper than was quite courteous. Out here, with the sunshine on my face and the wind in my hair, I had begun to feel that perhaps everything would be all right; that Ardal would win his fight, and achieve his mission, and . . . I had not thought beyond that point. Knut's words had conjured images of Ardal racked with coughing, Ardal shaking as he vomited into a basin, Ardal lying insensible on the bed while I tried to see if his chest was still rising and falling. "He won't die if I have anything to do with it."

I turned my back and walked away, striding fast. I did not slow until I was sure I had gone beyond sight of the men. My heart was pounding. I breathed deeply and tried to calm myself. This was ridiculous. A druid was serene and composed, striving for wisdom every moment of every day. A single ill-considered remark should not have the power to upset me so much.

The tracks at this eastern end of Inis Eala were little more than goat paths, narrow and uneven. At some distance ahead there loomed a great rocky outcrop surrounded by grazing sheep. In fact, the rock formation did somewhat resemble an enormous ram. I imagined him as a guardian spirit, watching over these ewes as they ate their breakfast, and the thought made me smile.

By the time I reached the rocks I was tired. I would sit here a moment, drink some water from the skin I had brought, then go back to the settlement. I had already been away from the infirmary too long.

Gazing over toward the sea as I drank, I saw something unusual in this stark landscape: a pair of small trees side by side not far from the cliff's edge. They were of no kind I recognized, and that in itself was surprising, for a druid knows trees. These bore needles of a dark gray-green, and their branches were gnarled and knotted like the fingers of an old man. When I walked over to examine them more closely, I saw a path leading down the cliff to the shore below. And there on the sand, a still figure in his dark cloak, was my brother-in-law Cathal.

He was alone. He had not seen me. I imagined, if he had come to this out-of-the-way place so early in the day, he did not want company. But I stayed where I was, watching him, unable to make myself move away.

Cathal was facing the sea, his arms outstretched, palms toward the water. The expression on his face was one of deepest concentration; he looked to be in another world. Every part of his stance told me he was casting a spell. I watched in wonder. Cathal never used his skills in magic on Inis Eala. He had come here to be a man among men. He had come here to forget he was Mac Dara's son. And yet, here before me, his father's legacy was on full display.

The sea stilled. Where only moments earlier the cove had been alive with the wash of waves rolling in and breaking into shivering lace, now the water lay quiet under the morning sky, tranquil as a lake, safe enough for a tiny child to play in. Not the least ripple stirred. I held my breath. I had never seen anything like this. Surely not even Ciarán could perform such a feat.

Cathal's arms came down to his sides, and he brought his hands up before him, moving them in a sequence too complex for me to follow. The sea stirred; waves arose once more, coming in to crash each in its turn onto the pale sand. A gull came down and landed beside Cathal, followed by another. Now they were coming in their dozens, alighting on the sand all around him, two on his shoulders, one perched on his dark head, until they formed a gathering of twice fifty or more. For a moment I wondered why it seemed so odd, and then I realized the birds were completely silent: no calling, no squawking, no sound at all. Cathal lifted his arms, and the flock arose as one, winging away to the east.

I should leave. Either that or I should let Cathal know he had an audience. I opened my mouth to call, but before I could say a word he turned and looked straight up at me. A moment later he was headed up the path.

"I'm sorry," I said as he came up to me. "I was out walking and happened to see you. I didn't think—"

"That I practiced these arts anymore? I have not done so for some time, Sibeal. It always seemed best not to do anything that might attract my father's attention. The ward over the island should keep us from his notice, but one can never be completely sure of it. All changes in time. It is perilous to forget that." Cathal hesitated, giving me a penetrating look. "May I speak further, Sibeal? You have plenty to trouble you just now, I know, but . . . "

"Of course. I understand this is in confidence. Such matters are not for spreading abroad."

Cathal nodded. "Shall we walk back?" And as we headed off side by side, "I have begun to practice, yes. Since the wreck . . . I hope I never face such a choice again, Sibeal. I know I could have helped those folk, saved lives, and yet I did not act for fear of endangering my own dear ones. No wonder . . . no wonder my dreams have been troubling. What I have seen . . . It seems important to be sure I can still exercise certain special skills. Indeed, I must work to sharpen them." He was looking particularly grave.

"You spoke of dreams, Cathal. What kind of dreams?"

"The same dream has visited me every night since the ship foundered on our reef. It is intense, mysterious, less like a dream than a vision. There is a storm in it, and voices screaming. It's dark. Full of violence and disruption. I wake with a sense of urgency, but I cannot understand why."

My own nights had been visited by images of storm and disquiet, something akin to the scrying visions of those first days. My charcoal runes had not been effective long. "I wonder what it was that came to Inis Eala the day *Freyja* foundered," I mused. "Two men and a woman, certainly. And something more."

"Even before the wreck, I had begun practicing my craft again. Clodagh knows; nobody else. Our child will be born soon. I will need every weapon I have to keep him safe."

"Him?"

"I pray that it will be a girl, for then Mac Dara's interest will not be so strong. But I sense that we will have a son. I would do anything, anything at all to ensure my father does not come near our child. If I must counter his magic with magic of my own, I will do it." A shiver went through his tall frame. "But I hope it will not come to that."

"Have you visited the scrying pool, Cathal?" I asked with some hesitation. "That could provide you with some clarity." With his particular gifts, scrying could indeed provide a window on the future. Whether he would want to look through that window was another matter. I knew that if I had been able to see plain truth in the water, as Cathal could, I might well turn away from scrying altogether.

"I am too much of a coward for that," he said. "Besides, the questions I would want to ask fall outside accepted practice—they are too close to my own interests. For now I will simply wait, and hone my skills, and hope. If the dreams persist I will seek your advice again."

Cathal walked back with me; if the house builders saw us, perhaps Knut thought that more appropriate than a young woman going out on her own. His odd remark had made me wonder again about Svala and that odd scene at the cove. She had seemed almost a different person when her husband was not close at hand. I must seek her out some time; try again to reach her. But not until Ardal recovered.

"The yellow flag's up," Cathal said as we crested a rise.

"Yellow flag? What flag?"

"In the settlement on the mainland. Over there, look."

In the distance, to the south, I could make out the bright pennant flying above a rooftop on the far shore. Among the small fishing vessels moored at the mainland jetty a larger boat stood out, one that had not been there yesterday.

"It means the Connacht men have arrived," Cathal said. "Someone will go over and fetch them later. We don't allow visitors to come straight to Inis Eala. Clem checks that everything's in order before he hoists the signal. The combat display will be tomorrow."

"I should think I'll miss it. I'll be needed in the infirmary."

A silence. When I glanced at him, Cathal gave an odd little smile. "Attached to this fellow Ardal, aren't you?"

"Attached. What does that mean?"

"You're fond of him."

"I did pull him out of the sea, more or less."

"Johnny pulled Knut out of the sea. There's no special fondness there, though Knut has certainly become well-liked."

"It's not quite the same, Cathal. What exactly are you trying to tell me?"

He sighed. "Nothing, Sibeal. I'm hoping you may be able to spare a little time for Clodagh, that's all. She had great hopes of your visit, but she's seen little of you. She misses her family, Deirdre in particular. And, from what I hear, Ardal is getting expert attention from our three healers. Clodagh might appreciate your company for the combat display in particular. She gets anxious when I'm involved in such things, especially now, while she's carrying the child."

"I'm sorry. I've been selfish. Of course I'll be there."

"Selfish? No, Sibeal, quite the opposite. Think of this as a personal favor I'm asking. I love my wife. I want her to be happy. That is why I . . ."

That is why I practice magic, even when in the longer term it may endanger those I love best.

"I know, Cathal," I said.

*   *   *

I spent the rest of the day in the infirmary. Ardal seemed to be holding his own, and at one point even whispered in Irish, "Thank you, Sibeal." This brought tears flooding to my eyes, and I saw Muirrin looking at me oddly. When Gull finally ordered me off to bed, I retreated to my chamber and a restless sleep in which the same dreams returned: mountainous seas, impossible cliffs, screams, blood, darkness.

In the morning, after a noisy breakfast in the dining hall—the Connacht men swelled the number of warriors, filling the place, and everyone seemed to be talking at once—all I wanted to do was spend the day by Ardal's side. Perhaps he would say more today. Perhaps he would start to talk to me properly. But I had made a promise, so I sought out Clodagh in the cramped space she and Cathal shared in the married quarters. My sister was rummaging through a storage chest.

"Ah, there it is!" Clodagh said, fishing out a skein of wool and adding it to her basket. "This green is for Spider's cloak. I'm making each of the men who has helped build our house a new garment fashioned in his choice of pattern and colors."

I knew without asking that she would have done everything herself: spinning, dyeing, weaving, sewing. A gift of her own hands, as the house was of theirs. Along with her clever fingers, Clodagh had always had a generous heart.

"Spider told me you'd been up to see the house," she said as we headed out toward the work room. "Aren't they doing a wonderful job? I love the way people work here. Even the most mundane tasks are carried out with such care. You could almost call it joy."

It was true. I only had to watch Biddy cooking or Sam polishing a sword or Gull cutting herbs in the garden to know it. "It's odd," I said. "I mean, this place is a training ground for warriors. It prepares men to deliver hurt and death. And yet people do their work as a druid does, in an awareness of wonder. With a knowledge that the breath of the gods flows through their bodies and quickens their blood."

"Johnny doesn't keep this place going in order to whip up conflict, Sibeal," Clodagh said. "He provides training so that, when they have to fight, people know how to do it properly. There are men here who haven't much to offer the world except their combat skills. Men who, if they did not have a home and a role on the island, would have nowhere to go and nothing to live for."

I considered the small number of islanders who remained from the original outlaw band. Gull, Spider, Rat, the absent Snake. A handful of others. "It won't always be that way," I said.

"No, Sibeal. And Johnny won't always be here to lead them. When Father dies, he'll be chieftain of Sevenwaters, and will have to give this up. I believe the community will keep going. Someone else will become leader. You say it's odd that the people here live their lives in the knowledge of goodness, with the purpose of the island being warcraft. But Erin was founded on war. Men will always fight; it's in their nature. They may as well be properly prepared for it."

My mind had wandered down a different track. "Would Cathal become leader here when Johnny moves on?" I asked.

A long pause. Clodagh rubbed at an invisible speck on her sleeve, not looking at me. "You know me, Sibeal," she said eventually, her tone constrained. "I'm an ordinary woman with no visionary abilities at all. But I feel in my bones that we'll be gone from here before that time. My instincts tell me Cathal will be caught up in momentous events whether he wants it or not. I hope I'm wrong. I would be perfectly happy to stay on Inis Eala." After a moment she added, "I do miss the family. I wish I could see Eilis and Finbar and our parents sometimes. And I'd love to visit Deirdre. I can't believe my own twin has two children and I've never even seen them. But I've made my choice, and I wouldn't change that."

As we walked across the yard, the men were heading over to their practice area, a circular enclosure surrounded by a double stone wall higher than a tall man. Clodagh led me with confidence against the flow of warriors—they stepped courteously aside to let us pass—and into the long thatched building, where two little girls were busily carding wool while women plied distaff and spindle or worked at looms. A basket by one woman's side contained a sleeping baby. A fire crackled on a hearth, warming the room so fingers would not be too stiff for delicate crafts. Morning sun streamed in through the open shutters, bathing the orderly scene in light.

Clodagh admired one woman's weaving and another's embroidery, then fetched her distaff and spindle and a basket of carded wool, and started spinning a fine, even thread. I found some plain mending to do—our mother had made sure we were all competent in such skills—and settled beside her. The women had plenty to talk about. I found myself answering a flood of questions about what it was like for a girl to be a druid and why I would choose such a life. I answered as well as I could, and in turn heard much about the various paths that had brought these women to the unusual community of Inis Eala.

Alba, whose brother Niall was one of Johnny's men, had run away from home rather than be wed in payment of a family debt. The debt had been quietly settled; Johnny had a talent for making things happen without undue fuss. Alba had not brought any particular skills with her, other than the ability to play the fiddle and sing, but she had found her place here. "I mend nets and look after children," she said with a grin. "And I suppose I might make someone a good wife, when I decide whom I like best. Aren't you sad to miss all that, Sibeal?"

"If she was," Clodagh said crisply, "I don't suppose she would have done all those years of preparation to be a druid."

"It's a fair question," I said. "No, I don't think I will miss what I've never had. A druid has a close bond with the gods; closer, I believe, than the bond between a wife and her husband, or between a mother and her child."

Now it was Clodagh who looked at me askance.

"You don't agree?" I said.

"I can't possibly say, Sibeal, never having had a spiritual vocation. And nor can you, never having had a sweetheart or been a mother. It's hard for me to believe anything is stronger than the bond between parent and child. A mother would do anything to keep her baby safe. Anything."

I could not argue with her. Although her own child was not yet born, Clodagh had proven her theory already, when she journeyed to the Otherworld to wrest our baby brother from Mac Dara's clutches, and at the same time returned a child of that uncanny realm to his own mother.

"Maybe some of us are not cut out for motherhood," I said. "I know the path I've chosen is the one I must take. I've always known."

"You're lucky, then," said a rosy-cheeked girl named Suanach. "Lucky you were so sure, and lucky you had a choice. Some of us didn't; at least, not until we came here to the island. Look at Flidais."

The slender, delicate Flidais had told her story already, and a dark one it was: she had fled an abusive family, and had arrived in the settlement across the water with no more than the clothing on her back. Time had healed her wounds, both those of the body and those of the mind. Now she was wed to the much older Rat, and their daughter was one of the two children busy with the wool.

"Of course," one of the other women said, "anyone's path can take a twist and a turn. Even yours, Sibeal. What if you decided to use your talents, not as a druid, but as a scribe or musician? A wandering storyteller?"

I had finished my seam. "It doesn't feel like my own decision," I told her. "If the gods call me to follow a certain path, that is the way I must go. Even if my personal inclination draws me elsewhere."

Suddenly everyone's attention was on me.

"Not that it does," I added hastily, feeling an unwelcome blush rise to my cheeks. "I did not come here with the idea of snaring a likely husband. Although I suppose there would be plenty offering in a place like this."

"Speaking of storytellers and musicians," said Alba, perhaps seeing my embarrassment, "Johnny has said we can have entertainment after supper tonight, in honor of our visitors' arrival. No dancing; it's too soon for that. Still, it should be fun. Sibeal, will you give us a tale? I expect you have a rare talent for it, being a druid. Niall and I will provide the music, with one or two others."

"Of course," I said, but my heart sank. The way things were going, I would be spending very little of today in the infirmary. *I'm sorry*, I said in my mind, hoping, foolishly, that somehow he would hear it.

Later in the morning, Brenna came to the door to summon us. The men were ready for an audience. As one, the women downed tools and headed for the combat area.

We entered through an archway set in the double wall. The heavy iron gates that usually barred this access had been swung open to let us in. Between the two walls were various chambers in which weaponry was stored and other specialized activities were carried out, including, I presumed, tuition in the more covert parts of the training offered on the island.

Inside the enclosure a broad area of hard-packed earth was circled by a double row of benches. The place could accommodate anything from a bout of wrestling between two men to a mock battle of twenty against twenty. The warriors of the island maintained their skills even when there were no visitors to be trained. Requests for their services came in frequently—such an expert fighting force could handle a broad range of assignments. Johnny chose their missions carefully; I knew he accepted perhaps one in ten such requests. As a future chieftain of Sevenwaters, he could not afford to make new enemies.

The benches soon filled up.

"Everyone'll be here," said Brenna, who was seated on my right. "Or nearly everyone. It'll be loud when things get going, Sibeal."

It already seemed loud to me, the level of excitement building as more and more folk came in, the women and children being joined by quite a few of the men.

"Only a handful of the men will be fighting," said Clodagh, who was on my left. "This is carefully planned, to show the visitors what we can do and what they will be striving for while they're with us. Of course, most of our men will be helping with the training, once it gets going. I expect Muirrin and Evan will have a few bruises and sprains to deal with; it always happens. How's your man doing?"

"All right," I said. "He's not my man, Clodagh. Just a person who cheated death, with a little help from me."

"Mm-hm. You have been spending rather a lot of time in the infirmary."

"Look," I said, changing the subject, "there's Svala with Knut and Kalev. I didn't expect to see her here, with so many people around."

"She looks as if she'd rather be somewhere else," observed Brenna.

"She certainly keeps herself to herself," Clodagh said. "I invited her to join us in the work room any morning. Or at least, I asked Kalev to ask Knut to tell her she'd be welcome. Norsewomen are usually skilled embroiderers, so I've heard. But Knut said she prefers to be on her own. She seems so sad."

Svala did not look sad now, simply detached. While Knut moved about greeting one man after another, exchanging smiles and friendly words, she remained standing at the back, not watching her husband or anything in particular. Her hair had been tamed into an untidy plait, over which she wore a linen head cloth. It did little to diminish her beauty, and I saw eyes turning toward her, those of the Connacht men in particular. His greetings over, Knut came back to stand beside her. Kalev said something and the two men laughed.

A sudden hush. A pair of combatants moved onto the fighting area, knives at their belts: fair-haired Jouko and the more solidly built Niall, brother of Alba. The combatants faced Johnny, who was seated with Gareth among the throng, and inclined their heads in a gesture of acknowledgment. A moment later they were circling each other in fighting stance, and the crowd erupted in screams of encouragement and shouts of advice: "Go for his knees, Jouko! Niall, watch your back!" If I had thought the gathering loud before, it was nothing to this.

The bout was intense and serious. Jouko was more agile than Niall; he fought like a dancer. Niall seemed stronger. I thought he might prevail, provided he could pin the northerner down at some point. I thought of animals—Jouko a stag, Niall a boar—as they whirled and struck and dodged from one side of the fighting area to the other and back again. Then, to a gasp from the onlookers, Jouko tripped his opponent with a move that was powerful, economical and entirely unexpected. Niall's knife went flying as he fell. Seizing his advantage, Jouko was kneeling astride the other man in an instant, his own knife against Niall's throat.

"Cease!" called Johnny. "Well done." Jouko slipped the knife back into his belt, rose to his feet and held out a hand to help Niall up. They acknowledged the crowd's enthusiastic approval with brief nods, then left the field of battle.

Johnny now stood up in his place; heads turned toward him. "Welcome, all." My cousin did not raise his voice, but the crowd hushed; some men have a natural authority, and Johnny had more than most. "A particular greeting to our contingent from Connacht; you've made a long journey to be here. That bout was just a taste of what's to come. Today we have on show some of our skills, some of our weapons, some of the men who'll be working with you during your stay. Your chieftain has explained to me what he needs you to learn, and from tomorrow you'll be divided into groups and allocated one of our men as tutor. You're here because you're the best of the best. Our job is to make you even better. Work hard, observe our rules, and you'll return to Connacht sharpened to precision.

"The rules are simple on Inis Eala. Your tutors will explain them again later, but here's the gist of it. If you break the codes of behavior we observe here, you'll not only be sent home straightaway, but so will the rest of your group. We don't ask any more of you than we ask of our own men and women. The first rule is respect. That goes for all of us, all the time: put it into practice in word and deed, every moment of every day. The second rule is that nobody leaves the island without my permission. Our boats go across to the mainland every few days, and there may be reason for one or two of you to go with them on occasion. Don't even think of expeditions of your own.

"The third rule is honesty. If you make an error, face up to it, come out with it. The last rule is this: we don't let the sun set on our anger. Likely there'll be disputes as we go along. We're none of us beyond annoyance, jealousy, the feelings that arise when we're working hard and getting tired and bruised, and something happens to cause offense. Settle your grievances quickly, and if you can't, bring them to me after supper on the same day and I'll help you sort things out. If you feel a need to use your fists to resolve a problem, do it properly, out in the open with a third man as arbiter, and once the bout's done, let that be an end of it." Johnny looked around as if to include each of the Connacht men in his speech. "You'll have questions. We'll make time for them when today's bouts are over. We're going to show you some new swords fashioned by our expert smith here. Stand up, Sam, so everyone can see you."

Sam rose to his full, imposing height, his buttercup hair bright in the sunlight. He gave a genial grin.

"The new weapons are lighter, easier to handle, in every way an improvement on the heavy swords most of us have been using," Johnny went on. "We'll be training you in their use—skill with the traditional broadsword won't make you an expert with these—and we'll ask for your comments, too. If your chieftain wants to make use of such weapons in future he'll need to have a smith trained in their manufacture. We can provide that training."

We watched Spider and Otter testing Sam's new blades. They looked ill-matched, one tall and thin, the other sturdy and barrel-chested. But neither easily gained the advantage. The bout had them moving light-footed across the open space, their agility and strength belying the fact that each had seen more than forty summers.

"These swords allow the men to move about much more easily," explained Brenna. "Sam learned how to make them from a Frankish smith who stayed here a couple of winters. And he's added some improvements of his own. See how quickly the men recover from a swing? You couldn't do that with the old swords unless you had arms like Cú Chulainn's."

"And these have a sharper point," said Clodagh. "More like a spear point. They can inflict a wound by stabbing, not just hacking. You can't do that with the old ones; they're simply too heavy for it."

"Mm-hm," I murmured. Living at Inis Eala provided a woman with an unusual breadth of knowledge.

Otter got under Spider's guard and could have slashed him across the thighs, but made the blow a smack with the flat of the blade, demonstrating remarkable control. Some time later, Spider turned unexpectedly and delivered, not a knockout hit, but a delicate tap to Otter's leather-capped head. Johnny called out to them to stop, and they did. Spider draped a long arm around his friend's shoulders; Otter brought his blade up in a salute to Johnny and to the cheering onlookers.

Next up was Rat, who defeated the much younger Oran after a lengthy bout. Flidais, a wisp of a woman, screamed fit to scare the gulls from the sky, and once the battle was over her husband stepped over the benches to gather her up in his arms and give her a hearty kiss.

Gareth took on a big man whose name I did not catch and eventually won, though to my untutored eye the contest looked very even. Then a pair of others battled it out with heavy broadswords, which restricted the combatants—well-muscled men, the two of them—to ponderous swings and lurching movements. It was dramatically clear how the new blades changed the manner of fighting.

"A broadsword like those can cleave a man's skull in two," explained Clodagh calmly. "Or hew off his arm or leg. But what makes them lethal also hampers the user. Once you start the swing, the whole weight of your body goes into it."

"I see."

"And that means," put in Brenna, "that if your weapon comes down in the wrong place, your opponent can kill you while you're still trying to retrieve it."

Quite soon Johnny called a halt. The combatants were glistening with sweat and breathing hard as they came forward to acknowledge the crowd's applause. When the cheering died down, Johnny stood to speak again.

"While our visitors are here, we'll have an open session like this once every seven days. Next time, you Connacht men are welcome to participate. It'll be on the basis of challenges. If you want to take part, let Rat know a few days beforehand. Choose an opponent, one of yours or one of ours. If that man accepts, the bout goes ahead. Rat, stand up."

Rat obliged.

"Rat's been fighting since I was a babe in swaddling," Johnny said. "He's in charge of the challenge days. Connacht men, we'll expect to see each of you participate at least once before your departure." Judging by the buzz of talk among the men, I thought Rat was likely to have more takers than there would be time for. "I'll answer everyone's questions after this final bout. Ready, men?"

Now it seemed Cathal was to fight, and his opponent was Kalev. As they stepped out onto the open ground, what looked like the entire complement of Inis Eala warriors came in ones and twos to settle on the benches around the practice area, until every seat was full and folk were standing all around the outside of the circle.

"Big audience," I whispered to my sister.

"The men like to watch Cathal fight," Clodagh murmured. She sounded calm, but she had gripped my hand hard enough to bruise me.

Both combatants wore the same kind of clothing as the other fighters had: padded wool garments with a leather breast-piece over the tunic, protective straps buckled around forearms and shins, and a cap-like leather helm. Each bore one of the lightweight swords.

Now that his bout was over, Niall had come to sit between Brenna and Alba. "Count of fifty," I heard him say to the man behind him.

"I'll give you seventy."

"Done. Don't like your chances."

"Five-and-forty," someone else was saying.

"Wagers?" I asked, wondering how you could lay a wager without naming the man you expected to win.

"That's right," Niall said, touching a clenched fist with that of the man behind him, which seemed to denote an agreement. "You don't wager on anyone beating Cathal. Not unless he's fighting Johnny. We put our stake on how long his opponent can last. Mind you, Johnny may have asked them to keep it going today, since this is in the nature of a demonstration. I might lose my two coppers. Doesn't matter; I'll win them back soon enough."

"I see." I watched as the two men adopted the fighting pose, swords at the ready, eyes intent on each other, ready to read a move when it was no more than a gleam in the opponent's eye. "And if Cathal fights Johnny, who gets your wager?"

Niall grinned. "We don't wager on those bouts. Johnny always seems to have a little something in reserve. Must be his father's magic. They say Bran was a superb fighter. Fearless."

I did not look at Clodagh. If Cathal had chosen to use *his* father's magic, he could have defeated any human opponent, even the superbly gifted Johnny.

Kalev and Cathal were of similar build, tall and spare; they appeared well-matched. It was apparent within moments why this bout had been kept until last: it was a cut above anything we had seen. I was surprised at Kalev's adept touch, his lightning-quick feet, for when I had seen him before he always looked a little awkward, as if he had hardly grown into his height. But of course he would not have been selected for this particular bout unless he had been able to make his opponent work hard, at least for the count of fifty or seventy or whatever it was to be.

"Kalev's good," I hissed into Clodagh's ear as the crowd yelled and stamped its feet in encouragement.

"One of our best." She was still holding my hand uncomfortably tight.

The two men were pressed together, their weapons locked, their eyes hard. The swords scraped, the sound harsh as the scream of a crow, and the position broke. The combatants circled each other. Kalev was breathing hard. Several men around me were counting on their fingers.

Kalev stepped to the left, feinted to the right, came up behind Cathal, ready to strike. But Cathal was not there; his move had been so swift I had hardly seen it. My eyes met Clodagh's.

"He's just very quick," my sister said. "No tricks; at least, not the kind you're thinking of."

She was right. It became plain, as Kalev tried one technique after another and Cathal was always a little too fast for him, that my brother-in-law was simply the better fighter.

The Connacht men were on the edge of their seats, silent amid the raucous throng. Johnny was not shouting. He was not even watching the fight, it seemed to me, but observing the behavior of the visitors, as if he had started assessing their quality before they had even begun their training.

"Eight-and-forty, nine-and-forty," Niall was muttering. "A pox on it."

Kalev was still on his feet. His contribution had been far more than mere self-defence. Several good blows had met their targets, but Cathal's speed—almost, but not quite, uncanny—gave him the advantage. Kalev's features were intent, his eyes narrowed. If he knew defeat was inevitable, that wasn't stopping him from putting all he had into the fight.

"Eight-and-fifty, nine-and-fifty . . . "

Suddenly Kalev was in retreat, backing across the open ground before the swift and deadly action of Cathal's sword arm. He staggered, went down on one knee, braced himself as best he could to hold back the onslaught. With his weapon's hilt gripped in both hands, Cathal performed a twisting maneuver, and Kalev's sword fell to the ground.

"Cease." Johnny's tone was level; if he had any opinion on the skill just demonstrated by his men, he gave no indication of it. Kalev got up, retrieved his weapon, came to stand by Cathal. The crowd roared its appreciation, and the two men acknowledged it with the customary slight dip of the head. Kalev looked tired. Cathal was impassive. "Well done, all who participated today," Johnny said. "That's the end of our display. Food and drink for everyone in the dining hall shortly. Connacht men, gather around. We'll give you some further details and introduce you to your tutors. And I'll answer any questions."

The women and children, and many of the men, headed for the exit.

"Wait, Sibeal, we'll go out when the worst of the crowd is through the gate," Clodagh said. "I'm getting so big now, I tend to be in people's way."

"Closer to seventy," Niall muttered to himself, after checking his fingers several times over. "Ah, well, it's only a couple of coppers." He headed down to join the group of men gathering around Johnny.

My sister and I were heading out at the back of the throng when I heard raised voices behind me, an intense exchange in Norse. Then came Knut's voice, speaking in heavily accented Irish.

"I fight. New sword, seven days. I fight that one."

We turned, Clodagh and I. Knut had moved against the flow of the crowd, and now stood in the group next to Johnny. Jouko had hold of the Norseman's arm and was addressing him in a fierce undertone, probably saying something like, *be quiet, you fool, this is not how it's done.* He might as well not have been there. Knut's attention was all on Johnny. His gaze was fierce, his shoulders were set square and his booted feet were apart; it was a warrior's pose. He had certainly grabbed the attention of the group. The Connacht men eyed him with curiosity; the Inis Eala men with bemused astonishment.

It was hard to surprise Johnny, but for a moment I saw him lost for words.

"Jouko," said Rat, "explain to Knut that the bouts are only for the men in training, our summer visitors. Besides, nobody's going to be proficient with the new sword in seven days. Even supposing a man could be, he wouldn't last to the count of ten against Cathal."

So it was Cathal that the Norseman had challenged. Knut must be stupid. Hadn't he seen that last bout?

Knut's response to Jouko was emphatic.

"Knut is keen to test his skills against Cathal's." There was a note of apology in Jouko's translation. "He asks this as a special favor of you, Johnny. He does not expect to be part of the training, only to have the use of one of Sam's blades for practice until the next challenges. He is a fighting man, and wishes to show you what he can do. I'm sorry. I did explain, as well as I could."

"I fight," Knut said in Irish. "Show heart. Strong. Fight best man here."

Cathal unfolded his long frame from his seat and stood to face the Norseman. "Then you don't want me," he said. "Johnny is my superior with the sword, whether it's the old broadsword or the new weapon. And I don't suppose you have the gall to challenge *him*."

There was a little silence, broken only by Jouko's murmured translation.

"Me, you. Good fight." Knut's gaze met Cathal's, blue eyes fiercely intent, black ones, if anything, mildly amused. Among the men there was a stirring, a whispering, as everyone waited for Johnny's response.

"Your request will be given consideration, Knut." Johnny's tone was calm as always. "As Rat explained, the bouts are intended as part of our visitors' training, and to keep our men's skills sharp. If you and your wife are still here on the island in seven days, and if Rat judges it wise to allow you the use of one of Sam's blades in the meantime, you may get a chance to prove yourself."

If this was intended as a not-too-subtle suggestion that Knut had bitten off more than any man could chew, it was lost on the Norseman. "I fight. You give me sword, I show."

"There's no doubting your courage," Johnny said, giving him a look that was impossible to read. "Any other questions?"

"Come on, Sibeal." Clodagh grabbed my sleeve and headed toward the gate. No sign of Svala; she had already left. Perhaps Knut's behavior was as embarrassing to her as hers was to him.

At breakfast Cathal had asked me to make sure Clodagh rested in the afternoon. After a bite to eat, she and I went to the married quarters, where I sat by her bedside and told stories until she fell asleep, blanket tucked over her expanding form. With her flame-colored curls spread across the pillow and her features smoothed by the sleep that had quickly overtaken her, she looked young and vulnerable. Not for the first time, I felt like an older sister, not a younger.

I tiptoed out and made my way to the infirmary. I visited the privy, brushed my hair and washed my face. Then I went to stand beside the sleeping Ardal, half of me wanting him to wake up so he would know I was there, the other half knowing this peaceful slumber was what he most needed.

Muirrin was hanging bunches of seaweed up to dry. "This kind's called newt's tail," she explained. "It's effective in an infusion for easing cramps. Tastes not unlike cress." When I did not reply, she looked over at me and added, "He's doing better, Sibeal. He's been resting a lot more comfortably, and Evan says his water's not so dark."

I looked down at the sleeping man. "Has he said anything today? Talked to you at all?"

"Don't expect too much, Sibeal. Breathing is enough of a mountain for him to climb. In fact, he asked for you, in quite presentable Irish. I told him you'd be here later."

A small, warm glow had awoken within me. "Thank you," I said.

A silence followed. When I looked across, my sister's hands had stilled at their work and she was studying me intently. "Does his fate matter so much to you?" Muirrin asked quietly.

I nodded, pleating a corner of Ardal's blanket in my fingers. Fang was nowhere to be seen. She'd be needed later. The nights were cold; I did not envy Gull the three trips he made each night out to the privy and back. I had become almost reassured by the pattern of them, the creaking of the back door as he went out, the creaking as he came back in. I was used to falling asleep quickly once I knew Gull was inside again. But I was always glad of the warmth of my blankets and the shelter of my little chamber.

"Why, Sibeal?"

I believe our fates are tied up together. I could not say that to the ever-practical Muirrin. "I believe I can help him," I said. "Later, I mean, when he's stronger."

"Well, it does look as if you may get your opportunity. I think we'll be able to pull him through this. Your man's a fighter. Sibeal, you're not crying, are you?"

"Of course not. Muirrin, I'm going to my room awhile now. I've agreed to tell a story after supper, and I must decide on one."

I managed to hold back the tears just long enough to get past the curtain that screened my chamber. I sank down on the pallet, put my head in my hands and allowed myself to weep.

CHAPTER 5

And so," I said later, to the hushed audience in the dining hall, "Osgar drew his sword and gave battle, and he slew the Gray Man; and at the sight of her brother lying in his blood, Ailne fell stone dead from grief. And as for the Fianna, they feasted long into the night on the fine food and drink they found in that place, and slept late into the morning. But when they awoke, all was gone: the dun, the rich tapestries, the fine accoutrements, even the grim cell in which their captor had immured them. There was only the grass and the trees and the sun rising in the sky, telling them it was time to move on. You'd have thought nothing at all had happened to them, save for the sheepskin Conan wore on his back, as if it were part of his own body. In all the years of his life, that skin stayed with him, and when his wife cut his hair for him, she had to shear his wool as well. As she was a practical woman like my sister here," I gave a nod in Clodagh's direction, "she kept it until she had enough, then spun and wove it into all manner of useful items. And that is the end of my tale."

Uproarious applause told me I had chosen it well—it was a

story they would all know already, concerning the great warrior Finn and his band, and how they fell foul of Ailne and her fey brother. Such tales made good entertainment without sparking debate or touching the heart too deeply; it was suitable for tonight. Knut was shouting approval with the rest of them. Svala was absent. Perhaps she was all alone down in the fisherman's cottage, huddled over a small fire, or sitting by a single, guttering candle. No, that was wrong. I imagined her on the shore, staring out into the west in the dark; or walking, her bare feet steady and sure across the pebbles of the beach. Or sitting on the rocks under the rising moon, waiting for the seals to swim by. Her heart aching, aching for a loss that could never be made good . . .

Someone thrust a cup of mead into my hand. I almost dropped it into my lap, so startled was I—for a moment, the wave of sorrow had borne me to another place.

"All right, Sibeal?" Gareth came to take the cup from me and set it on the table close by.

"I'm fine, but—"

"You will stay for the music, Sibeal?" It was Alba, her hair tied back in a ribbon, her fiddle and bow in her hands. She glanced sideways as she waited for my reply, and one of the Connacht men, a handsome, red-haired fellow, smiled as if he had been waiting for her to notice him. Alba grinned, showing her dimples. Behind her, Niall was plucking notes on his harp, frowning, tightening a peg or two.

I had been about to plead exhaustion and make my escape. "Of course," I said. "I've been looking forward to it."

Alba and her brother were expert musicians. They were joined by a deft-fingered fellow on the whistle and two very fine drummers. I could see that people were itching to dance, but holding back out of respect for Knut and the recent losses. It seemed to me that Knut would have been up and dancing himself, with or without his wife—he was tapping his foot—if anyone had suggested it. On another occasion I would have enjoyed the music. Tonight, I could only wait until I might leave without offending anyone.

"May I introduce myself and my friend here?" A courteous voice: the warrior standing in front of me was one of the visitors, not Alba's redhead but a shorter man with a genial smile and a head of dark curls. "I'm Brendan, son of Marcán, and he's Fergus. Both of us from the district of Long Hill, originally. That was a fine tale."

"Thank you. I am Sibeal, daughter of Lord Sean of Sevenwaters, as you know. Johnny's cousin. A druid, or on the way to becoming one."

"May we sit here, Sibeal?"

I nodded; I could hardly say no. Then I had one of them on either side of me, and the music playing on, and all I could think about was Ardal lying awake in the infirmary, like a little boy waiting for his mother to come and tuck him in. Though, of course, it was nothing like the same.

". . . and my father's land stretches from the west coast across to Hidden Lake," one of the men was saying.

"Mm," I murmured, considering whether I might amuse Ardal with a story, should he still be awake when I finally got there.

". . . hoping to end it, once and for all. Fursa Uí Conchobhair has long had his eye on Curnán's holdings; if we don't put a stop to it now, it'll soon go much further than cattle raids . . . "

"Mm."

Clodagh was looking tired again, despite her afternoon sleep. She sat at the far table with Cathal, her head resting on his shoulder. The music continued, but folk with children were beginning to extricate them from the crowd and shepherd them off to bed. Johnny was deep in conversation with the leader of the Connacht men, perhaps mapping out the next day's activities. They were moving objects about on the table as if to indicate a battle plan: *this spoon is the bridge over the stream, and this bowl the lake . . .*

I realized that one of the men had just asked me a question, and I had no idea what it was. Which of them was Brendan and which Fergus? As I floundered for something to say, the tall figure of Kalev loomed before me.

"That was a fine story, Sibeal. If you wish, I will escort you back to the infirmary—I need to speak to Evan. When you are ready."

A savior in unlikely form. "Thank you," I said, rising to my feet. "I'll bid you good night," I said to the two Connacht men, smiling at each of them and allowing Kalev to take my arm. "Thank you," I murmured again as we moved away between the tables. "I did need rescuing."

Kalev flushed. "They expect much of you. More than is reasonable."

"I'm happy to contribute a tale or two. It's part of a druid's job."

He said nothing until we were out of doors and walking across to the infirmary. The wind was rising; the torches made long flaming banners, lighting the way.

"You tell tales, you tend to the sick, you speak prayers for the dead, you bestow your smile on the man who fights and on the man who passes you the basket of bread," Kalev said, surprising me. "You are young."

I thought about this awhile. "I started down this path when I was much younger," I told him. "It's a calling. It doesn't seem unreasonable. Only when—" I stopped myself. After all, I did not know this man very well.

"When your thoughts take you elsewhere, and men expect you to show fascination at their own small tales?"

Kalev had come uncomfortably close to the mark. "It was discourteous of me," I said. "I let my mind wander."

"Here, let me open the door for you." We were at the infirmary. Through the cracks between the shutters, lamplight shone, and smoke rose from the chimney.

"Thank you, Kalev," I said before we went in. "You're very thoughtful. And perceptive."

No reply to that save a familiar reddening of the cheeks, visible even in the half-light.

Inside, Evan was packing up, ready to hand over to Gull. And Ardal was awake. His eyes were on me from the moment I stepped through the door; I felt his gaze as I might have felt the warmth of a fire. Now I was the one with burning cheeks.

"How is he?" I asked, glancing at Evan.

"I'm pleased," said my brother-in-law. "The signs are better to-day. We'll move him when Father arrives. Kalev, perhaps you'd stay and help us. We must get some clean blankets on the bed."

"Of course," Kalev said. "Evan, I've something to put to you before Gull arrives."

"Mm?"

As they talked, I went to sit by Ardal's pallet. "I'm here," I murmured as the other two men continued their conversation over by the workbench. I took his hand. He was still deathly pale, the skin stretched tight over the strong bones of his face. It made his eyes look huge, their brightness almost uncanny. "You look better," I said. "That makes me happy."

His thumb moved against my palm; I felt his touch somewhere deep inside me, disturbing, intimate. Wrong. And yet I could not bear to take my hand away.

"I missed you," he whispered.

My cheeks grew hot, embarrassing me. It was his unfamiliarity with Irish that made him speak thus, no doubt, giving the words an intimacy he had not intended. I could not think what to say.

". . . fellow could do with some support," Kalev was saying to Evan. "Maybe the challenge was foolish, but he has made it now, and we are all of the opinion that Johnny will let him go through with it, if only to illustrate the dangers of acting on impulse. Knut is well liked. If Sam won't let him have a sword, the men will lend him one, and some of us are prepared to give him some practice in between our other duties. But seven days . . . that is not much time. He needs some expert instruction, and our best are all occupied with the Connacht men."

"What about you?" Evan asked.

"You know I cannot teach as Gull can. Besides, I am required to work with the visitors. But I will not ask your father to help if to do so will cause offense or bring back sorrowful memories."

There was a pause. "You should ask him," Evan said. "Provided you can be there to demonstrate on occasion, I believe Father will be delighted to do the teaching part. He never admits to it, but he misses fighting more than anyone imagines. Are you so keen to see Cathal defeated?"

Kalev chuckled. "That is unlikely, Evan. Some of the men think Knut misguided. Most saw the courage behind his bold challenge. He will not defeat Cathal; nobody expects that. But Knut is a warrior like us, and far from home. It seems right that we help him to acquit himself as well as he can."

"What does Cathal say?" I could not help asking.

"Once I have Gull's answer," said Kalev, "I will find out."

Soon after, Gull arrived, bearing the inevitable pot of broth. While I heated it, the men lifted Ardal from the bed, wrapped a blanket around his shoulders and installed him in a chair by the fire. As if she had merely waited until this disruption should be over, Fang yapped outside the door, and when I let her in she ran straight to Ardal and leapt onto his knee. I saw him wince as she landed, but when I would have lifted her down, Ardal put out a hand to stop me. "*Nann*," he murmured, or something like it. *No*.

The men were talking about Knut and the challenge. "I suppose I could give him a bit of advice," Gull said. His voice was as calm as if he'd been asked to help with planting a row of carrots, but his shoulders had straightened as Kalev had put the request to him. I wondered if people forgot that he had once been a warrior of superb skills and dauntless courage. Did they still tell the tale of how he had rescued Bran from incarceration? "I like Knut's spirit. I like a man who can summon good humor even after such a disaster has befallen him. Though challenging Cathal was perhaps taking things too far. On the other hand, I do wonder if what you're suggesting is quite fair."

"You can't believe this will give Knut the advantage," Evan said as he whisked the blankets from the bed and threw them into a corner.

"Hardly," said his father, who had fetched a container of aromatic dried leaves. Scents of lavender, peppermint and chamomile arose as he sprinkled them over the straw-filled mattress. "He's got seven days practice with the new swords, we're not offering him the training the other men are getting, and his ordeal in the shipwreck must have weakened him, not to speak of the fact that he hasn't so much as touched a weapon since he got here. If he'd challenged one of the Connacht men I might be tempted to lay a wager, odds on the Norseman. But Cathal? It'd take a miracle. Between us, we might prepare him to the point where he won't embarrass himself utterly. I mention fairness because . . . well, I don't suppose this is what Johnny would expect us to do."

Kalev smiled. "I think it is exactly what he would expect us to do. Now that you have agreed, Gull, I will tell both Johnny and Cathal what we plan."

"You'd have no hope of keeping it secret anyway," Gull said with a grimace. He stood with arms folded as Evan and Kalev remade the bed with clean blankets taken from a storage chest. I thought I saw Clodagh's touch in the neatly folded supply. "We'll have to snatch time when we can. Johnny will only sanction this if it doesn't interfere with anyone's regular work."

"I'll help in here," I offered. "I can't do the heavy work, but I can give Ardal his meals and keep an eye on him while you're busy during the day, Gull."

"Thank you, Sibeal." Gull smiled at me. "Your visit to Inis Eala is hardly the rest Johnny tells me it was intended to be."

"I never asked for a rest," I said. "I'm very happy to help."

"Better get Ardal back to bed," Evan said when the pallet was freshly made up. "Then we'll leave you to it, Father. My belly's rumbling."

Gull glanced across to Ardal, seated with the fire's glow warming his hollow features and the little dog curled peacefully on his knee. "Leave him for now," he said. "Sibeal and I will manage."

"I don't think—"

"Go on, Evan. The man's barely been out of his bed since he got here. You and Kalev take those blankets down to Biddy. Ardal's only got to stagger a few steps across the chamber. We'll cope."

Evan's gaze passed over us: a man with damaged hands, a slight girl of sixteen. "Good night, then," he said.

"Good night, Sibeal, Gull," said Kalev, and the two of them went out.

"Well, then," said Gull. "You'd best eat something, Ardal. Sibeal can help you. And then we might have a tale. Firelight's best for tales. Kalev was saying you entertained them down there with the story of Finn and the Grey Man, Sibeal."

"That's right."

"That probably makes it my turn now. Have a think about what you'd like to hear."

I filled a bowl with broth and, after a moment's hesitation, passed the spoon to Ardal. "I'll hold the bowl," I said. "See if you can feed yourself."

As each mouthful made its way from vessel to lips, the spoon shaking with some violence in Ardal's hand, I stood still and quiet by him. I saw how much it hurt him to swallow; I knew how desperately he was working not to fail this simple challenge.

"You're doing well, Ardal," I said when he was nearly finished. "Feeding yourself may seem a little thing, something a child could do. But it's not; it's another step toward being yourself again. It takes not only bravery, but strength and hope. Perhaps you'll start to remember soon."

"I've never seen it before," said Gull, coming to sit on the opposite bench. "A man losing his memory entirely, I mean. I've seen them get confused for a while after a blow to the head, but that doesn't last so long. On the other hand, what's happened to him—Ardal—is not so different from how it's been for a good few of us here, over the years. We move on, things change, and certain parts of our own story get shut away inside us. For a lot of us, the past has a line drawn across it. *Before* is something we don't look at often."

The soup was finished. "Good work, Ardal," I murmured, taking the spoon from his fingers. Fang snapped at me.

"Deiz, *nann!*" Ardal said, and the dog subsided, growling. Gull and I both stared at him.

"Given Fang a new name?" Gull asked quietly. "Deiz, is it?"

Ardal looked at us. "A better name than Fang, I think," he said. "It means day." He smiled.

Whether or not Snake would be pleased to find his dog renamed when he returned home was neither here nor there. Ardal had just taken a huge stride forward. Gull and I exchanged grins of delight.

"Seems your Irish is much better than we thought," Gull observed without emphasis. "I wonder, now . . . I don't suppose you remember a lad called Corentin, Sibeal, who was with us here a few years back. Ardal puts me in mind of him. There's something of the same look about him, and something in the accent, too. Corentin hailed from Armorica, close to Gaulish territories."

Ardal had dropped his gaze; the long lashes shielded his eyes. If these names meant something to him, he was not saying, not yet. We must tread delicately.

"Gull, you mentioned men here not wanting to think about *before*," I said, changing the subject. "Before what? Before coming to Inis Eala?"

"For some." Gull looked down at his hands, strong, damaged, telling a tale of their own. "For others it's earlier. Death; loss; war. A deed that's best forgotten. For me the line got drawn when I met the Chief. When I recall the time before, I don't think of what happened so much. I remember how it felt to be on the brink of giving up and to be bodily hauled back. He taught me hope. Funny thing was, he didn't learn it for himself until your aunt Liadan brought him out of his own dark place. That was a remarkable time, Sibeal. Still gives me chills to think of it."

"How did she do it?" Thanks to Ciarán, I knew more of this story than most of my sisters did. Bran and Gull had both been imprisoned and tortured, and Liadan, flouting convention as she so often did, had rushed to their aid. Bran had been very ill afterward, locked inside himself. My parents did not speak of those events. Unlike other parts of our family history, which formed part of our after-supper repertory of tales, this story had a blanket of silence over it.

"How did she bring him back?" echoed Gull. "She had all of us tell the Chief stories. We spoke to him of how he'd found each of us when we were at our lowest and given us another chance, another life, a better one than the wretched thing of *before*."

"Why don't you tell that story tonight?" I suggested. "How you and Aunt Liadan saved Bran from his enemy, I mean. I know Ciarán helped you."

Perhaps my voice had changed when I spoke this name, for Gull smiled.

"Think a lot of that fellow, don't you?"

"I owe him more than I can say. He's not just my kinsman, he's my mentor. My teacher. And far more."

"Must be a lot more, if he's convinced a young woman of your age to commit herself to a spiritual life. Are there other females among these druids of yours?"

"Three."

"Young? Old? What kind of woman chooses that path?"

"They're all quite a bit older than me," I said. There would, in fact, be a gap of some thirty years between me and the youngest of them, but I did not tell him that. "It's not so much a matter of choosing, as of being chosen."

"Mm-hm. These women druids, they take a part in teaching you, do they?"

"They are not scholars like Ciarán or my uncle Conor. Ciarán teaches all the young druids. Conor has particular branches of study that he shares with me." After a little I added, "Last time I told Ardal a story, it was about my choice of a spiritual life. He won't want to hear all this again."

"I wish to hear," Ardal said.

"That doesn't surprise me," Gull said. "Your vocation has been a frequent topic of conversation among the young men of Inis Eala since your arrival, Sibeal. Shortage of marriageable women here, you'll have noticed. When Liadan visits, she's generally treated as something close to a goddess. Evan and Cathal are considered remarkably fortunate to have wed two of her nieces. When a third niece appears, young, comely and not spoken for, it's natural for the men to debate whether she should be following her mentor into a life of self-denial and prayer, or taking the kind of path your aunt did. Of course, Liadan wasn't simply choosing to wed and have children when she stayed with Bran. When she took on the

Chief, she took on all of us, a ragtag mob of the dispossessed, all desperate for a share of the magic she carried within her. It wasn't just Bran who loved her; it was every last flawed and disreputable one of us." He put his chin on his hand, remembering. "Sibeal, when the lads here talk about your choices, they wonder why you wouldn't want a chance to live a full life and make some fellow happy."

"You shock me, Gull. I can't believe the men have been talking about this."

"It's all perfectly respectful. I don't suppose any of the fellows thinks he'd have the least chance of diverting you from your vocation. When you're in your gray robe with your hair plaited up tight, you look severe enough to scare the boldest away. But they can dream. Lot of dreams here on the island."

I had nothing to say to this. I sat without speaking for a while, watching the steady movement of Ardal's hand against Fang's white hair. A druid was always learning; the journey was lifelong. My feelings on Gull's speech were decidedly mixed. It seemed to me I had just learned several things, some of them quite unexpected.

"What do you think is the best kind of story, Sibeal?" Gull's deep voice was like a soft cloak, comforting and warm. "The true kind, or a tale of marvels and magic?"

"A wonder tale can be truer than true," I said. I had learned, during my time in the nemetons, that the deepest kind of truth can be found in the strangest and wildest of stories. One may not meet a fire-breathing dragon on the way to the well. One may not encounter an army of toothed snakes in the woodshed. That does not make the wisdom in those tales any less real.

"I am no scholar," said Gull, flashing a smile. "And I am no druid, as you well know. But I grew up listening to some of the oddest tales of all, tales from a hot southern land where serpents lurk under stones and the sky rains red dust. It was a land rich in spirits and omens. If we are housed here long enough, the three of us, I will tell you stories of that realm. Tonight I will give you the tale you asked for, Sibeal. Only . . . " He hesitated. "I'm not certain how much you already know. There were dark matters in that time, the early time of Bran's friendship with Liadan. I don't think your father wished certain details to be spread abroad."

I stirred the fire with the iron poker. The embers shifted and settled. "Because of Ciarán, I know most of the story," I said. "Others here on Inis Eala must know it, too, since many of the island men were there when you rescued Bran. At least, that's what I have heard from one source or another."

"As to that," Gull said, "there are many rescues in the family story. You added another, Sibeal, when you plucked Ardal from the grip of the ocean. It was, in fact, our second encounter with this mentor of yours, that time when Bran escaped from a certain place of incarceration." Gull glanced at me, then at Ardal, his eyes glinting in the firelight. "Ardal, you haven't seen much of this place where you've ended up, brought in half drowned as you were. You'll have gathered from the talk around you that men come to this island to learn specific kinds of fighting. Sibeal's cousin Johnny runs a school of combat, highly specialized, highly organized, based on principles of discipline and control. And excellence. It's a place like no other. That's why so many want to come here, indeed far more than can be admitted.

"But it wasn't always thus, and the folk who live here weren't always employed as tutors in warcraft. Many of us were outcasts, existing beyond the margins of ordinary society, without homes or families to go to, without a direction to follow save that of survival. And the Chief, the man who founded this place and who brought us all together into a community with a spirit and a purpose, was just another miscreant fleeing the authorities." Gull thought about this a little, his dark gaze moving from Ardal to me as he folded his mangled hands on his knee. "That's not quite accurate. A miscreant, yes, in some folk's eyes at least. An outlaw, yes. A mercenary—that, too. But the Chief was never *just* anything. He was always more. Born to lead. Born to inspire. Born to make a difference. Some folk have that quality, no matter how great the disadvantages that are put in their way. He was one of those.

"Well, he picked up the rest of us one by one, got us out of our own hellholes, gave us hope, showed us how to be men again. We became known as the Painted Men: the Chief's skin markings were part of his identity, and the rest of us got our own in turn, each choosing an animal to pattern himself on. My black skin hardly shows such marks. I got my name from the feathers I used to wear in my hair, back in the old days. I liked the idea of the seagull, there was a freedom in it that appealed to me. I came a long way to reach this island; I left a lot behind."

Gull did not look sad. Perhaps those things, those people were too far gone now, in miles and in years, to bring tears to his eyes anymore. I knew, from Muirrin, that he had lost his entire family in a bloody massacre before he first met Bran. It had taken an immense effort on his Chief's part to drag him out of despair. Over and over, Bran had done this kind of thing to assemble his original band of followers. And, of course, once they learned how to hope again, they learned how to help one another. It was a remarkable story.

Ardal was watching Gull closely, his eyes intent.

"Back then," Gull went on, "we were a motley band of warriors. We had skills. We knew how to work together. But as men we still had much to learn. There were a lot of broken pieces of us to be mended. And he—the Chief—was more broken than many, for all his outer strength. He'd been hurt as a child, and he'd hidden that deep.

"There came a time when he and I were betrayed to an old enemy and taken prisoner. This fellow thought he could play on our particular weaknesses to get what he wanted." Gull shot me a glance; I think he was not quite sure whether I knew that the enemy in question had been my mother's own brother, Eamonn. "He knew the Chief had a terror of confined places, and that he feared the dark more than anything. So he shut him up in a hole under the floor with barely room to breathe and none to move. I was luckier: thrown in a dungeon and strung up by the wrists. Trouble was, each time the Chief was taken out of his little cubbyhole and subjected to questioning, and each time he refused to

124

talk, I lost one finger." He held up his maimed hands. "We had a code, the Painted Men. We never gave in to that kind of pressure. I knew the Chief wouldn't talk to save me. This fellow wasn't going to keep his word anyway. He wanted the Chief dead; once he'd had his bit of fun, he'd dispatch him without a second thought. Our captor had a double grudge. The Chief had bested him in battle. And he'd taken his woman, or at least the woman this fellow believed was his intended. Matter of pride. We were never going to be released alive."

Although I knew the story from Ciarán, it was still shocking to hear it told. The passage of so many years did not make it any less cruel. If the precise details of what Eamonn had done to Gull and Bran had never been known to my mother, she had surely been aware of her brother's love for Liadan and his jealous hatred of the man who had taken her from him.

"Well, there I am," Gull said, "in this fellow's fortress, strung up with my arms fair breaking out of their sockets and my hands somewhat the worse for wear after a little butchery, wondering how we're going to get out of this one, when in walks Liadan accompanied by a guard with a torch. She's come all the way from her own home on a hunch, a sudden concern for Bran's safety. What agreement she's reached with our captor I have no idea, but suddenly she's giving orders and someone's cutting me down—gods, that was the worst pain you can imagine, the feeling coming back to my arms—and then we're off to find the Chief. Somehow this young woman, about the same age as Sibeal here and of very similar appearance, has bargained to get the two of us out of that place. Just to make the tale all the more astonishing, I should tell you that she has a little baby with her, in a sling on her back."

"That baby was Johnny," I said. Ardal looked at me in surprise. "Yes, the same Johnny who now leads the community here, and who's come to speak to you once or twice. He is the eldest of Bran's sons."

"Bran being the Chief," Gull explained, "though Bran was not his real name, but one Liadan gave him, since she wouldn't use the other. Well, we found him, and a sorry state he was in, unconscious and cramped from being stuffed into a hole not big enough to house a scrap of a dog like Fang there, let alone a fully grown man. Liadan couldn't carry him. I was hardly better placed, my arms aching, my hands in bloody rags. But I was all the help she had.

"It so happened that the fortress in question was located in the middle of a swamp, a place where one wrong step meant sinking into mud over your head. There was a causeway, but we weren't offered the use of that. Instead we had to make our way from one clump of foliage to the next, a stride, a leap, an act of blind faith. Liadan had the child on her back; I had the Chief across my shoulders. Our captor was a man who enjoyed games. To be fair, he said, he planned to let us progress a certain distance before his archers began using us for target practice."

Ardal murmured something that sounded like an Armorican oath.

"It was late in the day," Gull went on, his eyes going distant as if still, so many years later, he saw the scene with terrible clarity. "The light was fading. Liadan was a slight girl, not tall; it was hard for her to jump from one safe purchase to the next. I was nearly spent. If ever there was a time to abandon hope, that was it. But he'd always given us hope, each one of us in our own darkest moment; he'd always told us that it was worth going on, that we could find a solution, that we simply needed to be the best we could. And there was this girl, with her little child, who'd shown the courage of a seasoned warrior. I'd no choice but to match that. Still, things were looking grim.

"Just when we'd reached a point where there seemed no way on, help came. First there was a light, moving across the surface of the bog toward us. As it came closer, I saw that it had the form of a bird, a raven. That was an eldritch thing; gives me goose bumps just thinking of it. As it passed, beneath it the foliage of the water plants began to weave itself together and to flatten out, making a kind of pathway. We didn't stop to think too hard. The raven reached us, turned, and headed away again. We followed. Liadan sang a lullaby. The baby quieted. We walked on that mat of woven fronds, not questioning how it was all holding together or whether it could bear our weight safely. I glanced back once or twice as we went, thinking that if we could use this path, so could our pursuers. But the path was vanishing even as we crossed it; nobody would be following us this way.

"I hardly had the strength to feel relief, only the will to put one foot in front of the other, to keep the Chief balanced across my shoulders, to set aside the pain in my hands. So we crossed over the swamp, and there he was, waiting on the other side: your Ciarán, Sibeal, though he was not a druid back in those days, more of a sorcerer, I think. The flame-shaped bird turned into an ordinary raven and settled itself on his shoulder, and he greeted us. And out of the dusk, one by one, stepped forward our own men, ready to take us to safety. I'll tell you something, those ragtag warriors with their beaten-up faces were the most beautiful sight in the world.

"That, of course, was only a small part of the story. The Chief was sunk in darkness; Liadan brought him light. She healed him, body and spirit. But we all played our part, Ardal. As he lay locked in his nightmare, we all found something of hope in our past, something he had given us, and we spoke to him of that. We reminded him that he was not an outcast, a wretch, a piece of rubbish thrown on the scrap heap, but a man of worth and goodness, a man whose courage shone from him, a man who always thought of others before himself." Gull's white teeth flashed in a sudden smile. "All this is his doing: this island; this school; this place of community and purpose. Though, of course, he's left it in his son's hands. The Chief and Liadan, they've moved on. Sometimes, when Bran visits Inis Eala, I get the feeling he'd rather still be here. Still, a man does what he's called to do. And that's the end of my story. Liadan saved Bran from captivity and death. Sibeal rescued you from the sea. But for her, you'd have perished that night. They're exceptional folk in the Sevenwaters family. Johnny carries on his father's traditions here, which means you can trust him, and you can trust me. If there's something in the past that you don't want to remember, something difficult, just know that if ever there was a place where a man can make a fresh start, Inis Eala is that place. As long as you tell the truth, nobody will judge you."

"I remember nothing," Ardal whispered. "Nothing at all."

CHAPTER 6

~Felix~

I t is night. Gull's sleep is a warrior's; he would wake in an instant. From Sibeal's chamber, silence. I picture her deep in slumber, the clear eyes closed, the sweet mouth in repose. Her dark hair rippling down across the covers that blanket her slight form. A druid, committed to a lifelong journey of the spirit. I have encountered druids before, I think. But none like her.

It is night and I am awake. Somewhere beyond these walls there is a man who would kill me for my memories. It was no idle threat; his eyes were like hard frost. What is it he fears so?

I have nothing to tell, nothing of any account. My mind is a shell, empty save for a rattle of old images. Noz, my dog. A row of olive trees. A cart on a dusty road. And now, as I lie here in the dark with eyes wide open, a bog, a mist, a stirring of the uncanny.

Gull sleeps quiet in his corner, untroubled by what his tale has awoken. I see barren hills. It is desolate, empty country where folk scratch a sparse living and forlorn spirits wander. A haze wraps the slopes, rendering them uncertain, treacherous. Below, down below, lies Yeun Ellez, where strange lights come and go. The dark ooze is patched with eruptions of ominous bubbles. Rank pools defy the probing of the longest stick. There are places where an object, thrown in, vanishes as if seized by an invisible hand. Flickering; fading; changing. A gateway to another world . . .

Who told me this? Is it a tale recounted around the fire, a thing of magic and wonder from time past? I remember the voice, a seasoned voice, expert in the telling of stories. I see the eyes, a vivid blue, the skin like old parchment. A hand in mine, knotted fingers warm with love. Is this a true memory? Have I conjured this from my real life, the life I have forgotten? Lying here on this pallet in the darkness, I see the Ankou striding out of the swamp, rags dripping bog water, eyes ghastly with mad intent, hands tipped with scythe-like nails black as pitch. His flesh is pale; his stride is long. My heart sounds a drum beat. My feet are rooted to the ground. Slowly, I begin to sink. I am on a steady, inexorable descent to the place beneath. Terror snatches away my breath. I stretch my mouth in a silent scream.

If you will go there, Felix, at least go armed with knowledge. The wise old voice speaks in my mind and I am back in the chamber again, in the dark, and the Ankou is gone. My heart is knocking at the walls of my chest; chill sweat coats my skin. I have made some sound, surely. But Gull does not stir, and in the little chamber beyond the curtain all is silence.

Felix. I think that is my name. I will not tell them. In this place of secret threats, knowledge is dangerous. The brave name Sibeal has given me will serve. I shiver, remembering that man's gesture, the knife across the throat. Is that how he would do it? Or would it be a sudden cord around the neck, or poison drops in the jug? Perhaps I harmed someone dear to him. Or stole his treasure.

Maybe I betrayed his trust. No. Use your wits, Felix. He fears my knowledge. I have seen something. I have witnessed something he wants forgotten, something he does not wish these good people to know about. The hair prickles on my neck; my heart is chill. Remember, Felix. Why can't you remember?

I do not think I will sleep tonight. Oh, Sibeal, I wish you would come through that doorway, come and sit here by me. I wish you were close with your sweet clear voice and your eyes full of faraway things. Help me to remember, Sibeal. Help me. All I know is that I have a task, a mission, and time is running all too swiftly. I must remember before it is too late. Vanquish demons . . . Confront the Ankou . . . Be a hero, as Gull and his Liadan were in their own tale . . . hah! What manner of hero is this, who for so long could not bring himself to speak aloud? Deiz, little dog, you show more courage than I, with your bold forays up and down my pallet and your warning growls. Yet here you are, no bigger than a squirrel.

The night seems long. There is a deep quiet, broken by the occasional cry of a sea bird passing overhead, and the sleepy bleating of sheep. Gull gets up and goes out. He comes back; stands by my bedside yawning.

"Awake, Ardal? I'll get you some water." The candle set carefully down on the stool by my bed; the cup lifted between his palms. Twin flames shining in the dark eyes. "Here," he says. I prop myself on an elbow and take the cup in my own hands, surprising him. Tomorrow, I will show Sibeal that I can do this. "Good," Gull murmurs. "Lie back now." And, as he returns to his own bed, "The gods guard your sleep."

My arm hurts. My shoulder hurts. My throat aches. What a hero! That small effort has worn me out.

*   *   *

That man said that if I spoke he would kill me. What of those who tend to me? When I remember, when I tell my tale, perhaps I will imperil not just my wretched self, but all those who hear me. Perhaps my very presence endangers them. Who knows what manner of man I am?

While I wait for the dawn, I imagine an augury for Sibeal. In my mind I hold the rune rods bunched in my hand, loosely, while I ask the question. *What lies ahead for Sibeal? What paths will she be offered?* I let my imaginary rods fall as they will, making a pattern on the linen of the ritual cloth. Three lie across the others: these are the runes of augury. *Daeg; Beorc; Gyfu.*

What would you say, Sibeal, if you could see this? There is love in it, and sacrifice, and completion. There is a bright light in time of darkness. There is, in the end, an understanding that comes from deep in the spirit. Those men Gull spoke of, those who hope, foolishly, selfishly, that you might not be entirely committed to your future path—for you are young in years, if not in wisdom— hope in vain. If ever there was a druid's augury, this is it. From a man like me, this path must lead you far, far away.

~Sibeal~

"Sibeal, may I speak with you?"

I jumped, startled; I had not heard Cathal coming. "Of course. You're abroad early." I was seated on the rocks overlooking the little cove where I had encountered Svala, the day Knut asked me to keep her secrets to myself.

"You, too."

"I usually go walking before breakfast." It was a journey to greet earth and wind, sun and cloud and hovering gulls. It helped me step forth from the wild landscape of dreams.

Cathal seated himself beside me, gazing out to the rocky islets off the coast. He looked grim. Today the sea matched his mood; it was a sullen gray under scudding clouds. For a while, neither of us spoke. When the silence had almost become awkward, Cathal said, "Sibeal, we spoke before about scrying."

"Mm-hm."

"The dreams continue. They persist, night by night the same."

"What is it you want to know, and cannot bring yourself to ask?"

"About the child: if it will be born safely, if it will thrive and be well. About Clodagh." His jaw was set tight. Someone who did not know him might have thought the look in his eyes was anger. Perhaps, in part, it was; anger that he was driven to this. "I need to know, Sibeal. I thought perhaps you . . . ?"

I had seen nothing concerning Clodagh and her baby; I had not sought guidance on the matter and I had no intention of doing so. Now, with a suddenness that was becoming familiar since my arrival on Inis Eala, an image came to me: a tiny child, a boy, lying naked on a shawl of many colors. He was so small. Even my little brother, Finbar, born many days before his time, had from the first been more robust than that. Or did I misremember? Watching over the babe was a tall, black-cloaked man. They were out of doors, in the shade of old oaks. I could not quite see the man's face, but it was surely Cathal. I hoped it was Cathal. The vision faded.

"Your fear is shared by every man who is about to become a father for the first time, Cathal." With an effort, I kept my voice calm. I put from my mind the knowledge that Cathal and his father were so alike that even Clodagh had mistaken Mac Dara for his son the first time she saw him. "Clodagh is young and healthy. And there's expert help here on the island; Muirrin will look after her. Unless you've suddenly decided you must go back to Sevenwaters, surely there's nothing to worry about." But there was; it was written all over him. And this was not a man to let his fears overwhelm him; this was a warrior, strong and skillful, a man others looked up to.

"My dreams are full of storm, violence, death." Cathal knotted his fingers together. "I'm losing sleep over them, and so is Clodagh. You said before that you believed the shipwreck had left more than two men and a woman on this shore. Sibeal, something is wrong here, deeply wrong. I have heard more than one person speak of ill omens, of shadows and portents. I am not the only man on Inis Eala troubled by his dreams. My father has a long reach. Even here, in this protected place, I carry talismans to keep his influence at bay."

Cathal had given Clodagh his green glass ring, handed down over many generations of his mother's family. That ring had helped keep Cathal safe as a child. Its protective magic had won him and Clodagh their release from the Otherworld, when Mac Dara would have trapped his son there. Maybe it was safe for them on Inis Eala, but I had noticed Clodagh still wore the ring, and Cathal carried a cargo of charms sewn into the lining of his long cloak.

"My dreams have been the same," I told him. "Dark, violent, frightening. But—shadows and portents? What exactly have people been saying?"

"Thus far it's no more than a general unease among the men. It may die a natural death. I have heard some talk."

"What talk, Cathal? And what has this to do with Clodagh and your child?"

He was sitting with elbows on knees, his hands still interlaced. He did not look at me. "Perhaps nothing," he said quietly. "But with every unusual event, with every surprise, I fear my father's influence. The sudden squall that wrecked the ship out there . . . It was no ordinary storm. I saw an uncanny hand in it, and I suspect others did as well. And . . . "

"Go on, Cathal," I said after a while. "I may not be able to give you the answers you want, but I will listen without judging, and I'll betray no confidences."

"What you saw the other morning was only a small example of what I can do. I could have helped them. Those wretched souls. I could have been on one of the boats. I could have . . . " He looked utterly wretched.

"That was a fierce storm, Cathal." *An unnaturally fierce storm.* "Even you could not have held back those waves, or stopped that gale from blowing *Freyja* onto the rocks." In my heart, I wondered. He was Mac Dara's son, after all.

"I should have tried," Cathal said. "Instead I put my own needs first: the need to escape my father's notice, the need to keep my family safe. Meanwhile the wives and children of other men perished before my eyes. No wonder I am visited by nightmares."

"If you go beyond the boundaries of Inis Eala, if you reveal yourself and if your father finds you," I said carefully, feeling somewhat out of my depth, "Clodagh could be left on her own with the child."

"And so I did not act. I am a coward, Sibeal. If I could know what lies in her future, if I could be assured they will be safe, the two of them . . . "

"Have you sought answers in the scrying bowl? Have you used other tools of divination?"

The waves washed into the cove below us, a whispering song in the quiet of early morning. "You know I have not," he said.

"Then don't ask me to do it. She's my sister."

Cathal did not reply.

"Besides," I said, "my visions are often fragmentary, cryptic, full of symbols. They are open to many interpretations. There are no neat windows into the future. It would alarm me if there were—that would surely mean that we have no power to influence what is to come."

My companion gave a mirthless smile. "If one could see a possible future, one might then take steps to ensure it did not come about."

"We're not gods," I said. "There's good reason why a divination is never carried out on one's own behalf. If you obtained answers, you could find yourself paralyzed by them."

"I understand." After a moment he added, "Sometimes I wonder how someone so young can be so wise."

I grimaced. "I don't always feel wise. But that is the druid path: it lasts a lifetime, and one never stops learning."

*   *   *

With the arrival of the Connacht men came changes to the daily pattern on Inis Eala. Training began early in the morning and lasted until supper time. Both island men and visitors were either shut away in the practice area where we could not see them, or spread out across the island rehearsing various maneuvers. I saw them heading out with coils of rope, and heard that they were practicing cliff scaling. I wondered if the Connacht warriors were preparing for a particular assault back home, perhaps an attack by stealth on an island fortress deemed unassailable. Nobody was talking about that. Biddy and her assistants prepared enormous meals, which were devoured in near silence. Folk went early to bed.

The men snatched time for themselves when they could. I rarely saw anyone use it to rest, despite the exhaustion that shadowed even the faces of the Inis Eala men. Instead, they matched up in pairs and practiced for the challenges. It became common to stumble upon a fight when going to hang up washing or draw water from the well. Every spare corner seemed to house one of these intense contests, fought with swords, knives, staves, bare fists.

These bouts were conducted under the eye of anyone who happened to pass by. Out at the back of the infirmary, beyond the drystone wall that sheltered the herb garden, a similar but less public activity was taking place: Gull and Kalev were training Knut. Going out to stake up plants or spread straw, I would see Kalev and Knut locked in combat, using the new swords, while Gull circled, eyes narrowed, observing and instructing. And once or twice I saw Gull and Knut working in Kalev's absence, the Norseman practicing with his weapon, the teacher correcting his student's grip or the position of his upper body without the need for any common language but that of combat. I could see from the look on Gull's face—his eyes bright and intent, his jaw firm—that the warrior he had been lay not far beneath the healer he had become. He was enjoying himself. As for Knut, the hard work of preparation seemed to suit him. When he spoke to me in passing his manner was quietly courteous. He had the look of a man who has begun to find content.

By the third day Rat had ceased agreeing to challenges; the program was full. None of the Connacht men had put his hand up to fight with the new swords. Still, the visitors were eager to show their mettle. Plenty had requested bouts against their own or the islanders, and a couple of the Inis Eala men had challenged the most promising of the visitors. It would be an entertaining day.

My conversation with Cathal had troubled me. I said nothing of it to Clodagh, but made sure I spent time with her each day, whether it was keeping her company in the mornings as she spun or wove or helped with the hundred and one tasks required to keep the community going, or sitting by her in the afternoons while she lay on her bed resting. Left to herself, Clodagh would have kept on working. I had heard her say that a daytime sleep was a ridiculous indulgence. Her increasing weariness frustrated her. Like our mother, Clodagh was wont to fill her time with activity so that there would not be too much opportunity to dwell on troubling possibilities. I told her stories as she fell asleep. I chose them carefully, and my sister saw right through me.

"You are determined to have me believe in happy endings, Sibeal."

"Don't you believe in them?"

A shadow passed across her face. "Perhaps I've had my share of good fortune already."

"Nonsense," I told her. "You're one of the strongest people I know. You're chock-full of courage and goodness. You'll make your own happy endings."

"I hope so. But I do feel tired, Sibeal. Tired and weak. I hate that. And I'm worried about Cathal. His dreams are terrible. Last night he woke up shouting, and he refused to tell me what the nightmare was."

"A dream is not reality," I said. "As for being tired, you don't need me to point out that women who are soon to give birth do feel weary. You could ask Muirrin for a tonic."

Clodagh grimaced. "The last one she gave me tasted like rotting seaweed."

"No doubt a very efficacious cure can be brewed from rotting seaweed," I said, smiling. "One might get better by sheer force of will, simply to avoid a second dose. Now shut your eyes and I'll tell you the story about the clurichaun wars."

"I know that one already."

"Ah, but I've made up my own version, especially designed for an audience of warriors, and I want to try it out before I tell it in the dining hall."

I was telling a lot of stories. There were the ones that sent Clodagh to sleep, and the ones that entertained the scattering of folk who stayed in the hall after supper, and there were Ardal's stories, the tales I kept for later in the evening, to be shared in the quiet of the infirmary.

Ardal was showing a fierce determination to get well again. He reached a new milestone each day—feeding himself, getting up from the pallet unassisted, walking to the fire with his hand on Evan's shoulder. They were of a similar height, and when I saw them standing side by side I was shocked. Ardal was so painfully thin, his arms skeletal, his borrowed robe hanging loose from his frame. Beside the well-built Evan he seemed a wraith.

Those who tended Ardal during the day found it hard to believe he had a good command of Irish, though Gull and I assured them it was so. To them the patient spoke only those few words that were essential to help them in their work. At night, when the others were gone, he stepped past other milestones, though I sensed a wariness in him even when only Gull and I were present. The two of us took turns to tell stories, choosing by instinct. Some tales were for comfort or reassurance. With others we hoped to give Ardal something to hold on to, a rope with which he might begin to haul in the complex net of the past. Sometimes we simply talked, and each night Ardal contributed a little more. If his memory was still lost in the fog somewhere, there was no doubting his will to recover it. As for his Irish, though it was strongly accented, it proved to be so fluent, I began to think he must have lived here for some years. Gull and I discussed this in private, for we both wondered why our charge had chosen to conceal his knowledge of our tongue for so long. Gull said that in another man he would have suspected an ulterior motive—an attempt to glean information under false pretenses. I thought the shock of being shipwrecked, coupled with the loss of memory, would be enough to make anyone act oddly. I could not imagine what I would do if such a calamity befell me. With everything gone, even the knowledge of one's own identity, what could a person cling to? There would be nobody to trust.

"Armorica," mused Gull one night, picking up the idea he had mentioned about Ardal's possible origins, "now that sounds like a place with some good tales. Corentin had a few. Full of people turning into creatures, or creatures turning into people. One in particular I remember, where a whole city was sunk beneath the sea by a woman's disobedience. It ended by telling that if you sailed in a particular bay under certain conditions of wind and tide, you could still hear the sound of bells ringing from under the water. I don't know if that's true or just part of the tale. It would be more than a little disturbing."

"Douarnenez," said Ardal. "The bay of Douarnenez."

We were by the fire, the three of us, Ardal propped in the chair, Gull on the bench and I cross-legged on a mat before the hearth. Fang was in her usual spot, curled on Ardal's knee.

"You know this tale?" Gull's tone was calm; several times now we had trembled on the brink of a discovery, a moment of revelation as Ardal seemed to recognize something, only to see him retreat almost instantly into silence.

"Perhaps I have dreamed this. The bay . . . the bells . . . the waves washing over . . . "

I watched the flames licking the turves of peat. I listened to the night sounds of the infirmary, the faint hissing and crackling of the fire, the creaking of timbers in the wind, the dog's steady breathing. I thought of home hearths and times shared. The past had shaped me: the family, the keep, the forest, the tales and songs, the joys and sorrows and challenges. The loss of my twin brothers within a day of their birth, when I was hardly old enough to understand what death meant; years later, when my mother had almost believed it too late, the wondrous arrival of baby Finbar. Cousin Fainne's brief, turbulent stay in our household. The fire that had scarred my sister Maeve, and her painful journey to recovery, one of the few times I had seen Muirrin cry. Ciarán's decision that he would teach me. Clodagh's quest to save Cathal from his father. My own father, so steady and wise, the strong center of household and community. Eilis's irrepressible love of life. Everything was part of me, every little thing. I could not think of any safe question to ask.

"Breizh," Ardal said. "That is the true name. Armorica is a name given by the Romans."

"Your Irish is fluent, Ardal," Gull said. "It's not a particularly easy language to learn. You'll discover, once Evan lets you out of the infirmary, that we're a community of folk from everywhere. In the early days, Bran's men spoke an interesting blended tongue, mostly Irish, but with words borrowed from here and there, a contribution from everyone. We used to be on the move then, keeping one step ahead of trouble, taking on one mission after another, running from one bolt-hole to the next. That's changed now. We're settled here, and everyone speaks Irish, since we provide a service for Irish kings and chieftains who need their men trained up. You can see from the hue of my skin that I'm not from these parts, and nor is my wife, who lived in Britain before we brought her here. We're like pebbles on a riverbed, all shapes, sizes and colors thrown together. Among us we get by in a dozen different tongues. Corentin's the only fellow we've had from—what was it, Brez?"

"Breizh." The response was little more than a whisper.

"Breizh." Gull tried the odd word, attempting Ardal's rolled "r" and soft ending. "Corentin spoke good Irish, too. Perhaps the men of Breizh have a scholarly streak. He learned his at the court of an Irish king, before he came to us. We were sorry to see Corentin go."

"Why did he leave?" I asked. Once a man was accepted into the Inis Eala community, it was extremely unusual for him to depart by his own choice.

"He went home. A message came to tell him that his father had died, and his mother was having difficulty holding on to the family land. Some kind of territorial struggle. Pity we couldn't send a band of fighters to help him, but I expect he put what he'd learned here to good use."

"An Irish king," Ardal said, turning his deep blue eyes on Gull. "What was the king's name?"

"Ah, that I can't tell you," said Gull. "Johnny might remember, or Sigurd, when he gets back. Sigurd was Corentin's friend."

"Ardal," I ventured, "I did wonder if some of the items washed up on the shore here, after the shipwreck, were gifts from one person of high standing to another. They did not seem to be trade goods. Knut didn't know who they belonged to or what their purpose was. Do you think, if you looked at them . . . ?"

A shiver ran through Ardal. His right hand curled around the dog, as if he sought comfort in her sleeping warmth. "I cannot yet walk more than the few paces from bed to fireside."

"They could be brought here. There are lengths of silk, once lovely, I imagine, but ruined by the sea. A box containing silver adornments, earrings, armlets; the remains of a book in jeweled covers, the ink all washed away, so there is no telling if it was a Christian psalter or a collection of ancient tales."

"Paul," whispered Ardal all of a sudden, staring into the fire. "Where is Paul?"

Silence, broken only by the sound of the night wind beyond the four walls. My heart stood still.

"I don't know, lad," said Gull quietly.

"He was a good swimmer," Ardal said. "Only a year my elder, but far stronger in all ways. We would go, sometimes, to Yeun Ellez, to the place where they said the Ankou dwelt in the swamp, rising when he chose. We feared him, and yet we were drawn to that forbidden place, enthralled by the terror of it. *I dare you, Fe—*" A sudden halt, as Ardal tripped on a word he did not want to speak. The eyes went down again. "*I dare you*, he would say. *I dare you to go right down to the edge, all by yourself, and stand there to the count of twenty.* How could I not meet that challenge? I did what he bid me, my knees knocking in terror, the dark water spreading out before me. Any moment the Ankou would rise, I knew it, he would come out of the water and seize me, and he would take me down below, never to return. I imagined drowning, how it would feel, the water coming over my head, into my nose and mouth, the pain in my chest like fire, the cold knowledge of death . . . I counted, one, two, three, all the way to twenty, and the Ankou stayed under the water. Then I turned and bolted. But Paul was gone."

A charged silence.

"Your brother?" Gull's voice was soft.

"My brother. My big, strong brother, who challenged me and teased me and looked after me. I shouted, *Paul! Paul, where are you?* But the only answer was the silence of the trees, and the darkness of Yeun Ellez. While I was counting, while I was waiting, the Ankou had taken him. I ran home alone, weeping. It was my fault. I had not kept him in sight, I had not thought, I had let him be stolen away and drowned . . . " His face was sheet-white. He was right there, living it. "And when I got home," Ardal said, "there was Paul sitting on the step waiting for me, grinning from ear to ear as I ran up with my nose streaming, my chest heaving, my face all over tears. He had always been a fast runner. I was so angry I hit him. Then he took me off to wash my face, so that nobody would know I had been crying."

"Oh, gods," I said after a moment. "So he played a trick on you. Children do cruel things sometimes."

"Ardal," said Gull, "what is this Ankou?"

"He is the helper of Death. In the swamp, yes, but more often on the road, in a cart full of stones. Coming for a man, a woman, a frail child. Coming to take you away. At night, in bed with the covers over our heads, we would listen for the rumble of the wheels, the shifting of the stones." Ardal lifted his head and looked straight at me. "And he comes in the sea. A great wave. Smashing, crashing, over our heads. Sibeal, where is Paul?"

How much did he remember? Childhood and adulthood, past and present seemed mixed in his mind. I imagined him listening now to the creaking and rattling of roof and walls in the wind, and hearing the voice of the Ankou calling him. *It is your time.* If I spoke a wrong word here, if I trod too heavily, I might send him into a place darker than this Yeun Ellez.

"Ardal," I said quietly, "your brother—Paul—was he with you on the ship?"

"My brother," Ardal said, his voice unsteady. "He was strong. Always a strong swimmer. But not . . . nobody could . . . I tried to untie it, I tried, but it was too tight, and the wave came . . . " He put his hands over his face.

"Oh, for a jug of Biddy's best mead," muttered Gull. "Pity is, a man in Ardal's condition isn't allowed strong drink." He glanced at me, perhaps thinking the same thought: that man who had lain among the drowned, a tall young man with hair of the same brown as Ardal's, could have been his brother. The man before us seemed too frail to hear it, too distressed to answer the question that might make it fact. *The Ankou came for your brother. He came from the sea.*

"We need not speak of this now, Ardal," I said, moving to crouch by him and laying my hand on his knee. Fang stirred, growling in her sleep. "It's good that you are starting to remember, but there's no rush." Knut had said those two drowned men, the nameless passengers, were traveling with Ardal. I shrank from the need to tell him what I knew; yet as a druid I must summon the fortitude to do it. I remembered Knut suggesting Ardal's memories would be confused when they returned, the truth wrapped up in the garments of nightmare.

"As we've told you," I said gently, "there were only three survivors from the shipwreck: Knut, Svala and you." There was no kind way to say this.

Ardal lifted his head; took away the screen of his hands. "In the water . . . how long was I in the water?"

"A long time. The ship struck in the morning. Knut and Svala were picked up not long afterward. I found you late in the afternoon, close to dusk. But they say you couldn't have been in the sea all that time, not even if you were holding onto floating timbers. No man could have survived so long. Johnny thinks you may have been on that beach for some time before I found you."

For a moment, Ardal's thin features looked ferocious. "He was strong. He could have swum to shore. They killed him. They drowned him. The knots . . . "

"So your brother was on the ship?" Gull asked. "The two of you were traveling together?"

A long silence.

"When I go home," Ardal said, "perhaps he will be waiting again, on the step, and he will laugh at me. *Tricked you, F—*" That catch again, before he could say the word he did not want us to hear. His name? "He will get up, a tall man now, and put his arm around my shoulders. *Dry those tears, brother. The Ankou doesn't take me so easily.*"

I had to tell him. I had to say it. "Ardal, we brought some men here for burial; nine of them in all. There was—" My voice cracked. "According to Knut, two of those drowned men were traveling companions of yours. He did not know their names. One was young, a tall, well-built man with brown hair and pale skin. He looked quite like you, Ardal. If it was your brother, I'm deeply sorry that you have lost him. There was an older man, too. Knut said you were going somewhere as a group."

"Older . . . I do not know . . . " The strong planes of Ardal's face were bathed in tears. "I do not know what came before. Only the wave, and Paul . . . If my fingers had been quicker, if I had untied it . . . So strong, he would have swum to shore . . . I could have saved him."

"Untied what?" asked Gull after a moment.

"The—the—" Ardal faltered. "No, I cannot speak of this. No more, no more of it."

"I'm sorry," I said inadequately. "Your brother was laid to rest with prayers and respect. I'm sorry it had to be done before you were well enough to know, and to be there. When you can walk outside, I'll take you to see the place." I wondered why Ardal blamed himself for his brother's death. I had seen the ship crash onto the reef. I had seen how quickly the sea devoured it. Doubtless there had been other strong swimmers among the crew, but they had drowned nonetheless. "I understand how sad you must be, and I won't talk about this any more, not tonight. But I would remind you of the runes and what they said for you, Ardal. A mission. Courage in the face of adversity. As the memories return, as they stir in your mind, fix on that. You were saved for a purpose."

Gull had got up and was quietly preparing for the night, checking the door and the shutters, quenching the lamp so we were left in candlelight and firelight, tidying Ardal's bedding.

"You truly believe that, Sibeal?" Ardal's voice was a murmur. He dashed a hand across his cheeks. "If there is a mission, a quest, why not Paul? Why me?"

"Here, take my hand. There is no saying why one man dies before another. The gods make their choices, and we are powerless to gainsay them. All we can do is live our lives the best we can. With love and courage and goodness. I can see you loved your brother very much. He would want you to go on in hope; to fulfil your mission, whatever that may be."

"What if I do not remember? What if the past is lost forever? There are so many pathways, mazes, traps. I could wander until I am old, and never find a way out."

I could feel the fine trembling in his hand. "It is not lost," I said firmly. "Already it is coming back to you. You will remember. You will fulfill your mission. We believe in you, Gull and I. Believe in yourself; make it so."

None of us slept a great deal that night. Each time Gull got up to visit the privy, with Fang pattering after him, I woke. Twice I heard the two men talking and went through to see if all was well. Ardal had been disturbed by dark dreams whose details he would not share. My own dreams had been of an endless search along twisting pathways, for what I did not know. I had heard Ciarán's voice saying, *The true mission lies within you, Sibeal. If you have not learned that, you have learned nothing.* After that, I was glad to sit awhile before the fire, my cloak around my shoulders. Gull heated up the rest of the soup and the three of us shared it.

"Had some odd dreams myself," said Gull. "Past acts of violence. Sorrows best left sleeping. It feels as if we're stirring up monsters."

* * *

The day dawned fine and sunny. The wind had died down and the sea around Inis Eala sparkled under a cloudless sky. I made my way to the dining hall, yawning, to find Clodagh in excellent spirits.

"I thought we might gather mushrooms this morning, Sibeal."

"Mm."

"It's an ideal morning for it. I can show you a part of the island where you've never been before. You'll like it; there's a little grove of apples, circled by hawthorn."

"Really?" The rocky shores and whipping winds of Inis Eala did not seem conducive to the growth of anything beyond the grasses that nourished the hardy island sheep. I had seen twisted thorn trees, their roots lodged deep in rocky clefts; I had seen a few lone junipers leaning before the gale, like bent old men. Apples, I had not seen.

"Bring a basket and I'll show you."

By the time we had gathered baskets and cloaks, most of the men were heading off to another day's hard work in the practice yard. On the way out of the infirmary I met Kalev coming in. Knut was behind him; both men bore swords.

"You're starting early," I observed. Gull would be as tired as I was. Just as well he was not required to give practical demonstrations.

"I am sorry to disturb you." Kalev was as courteous as ever. "The Connacht men learn certain tricks with the sword today, and my services will be required soon. Now is the only time to work with Knut."

"Of course. Knut, I didn't see Svala at breakfast."

Kalev translated this, but Knut answered me direct, in Irish.

"Wife sad. Not want food." He took in the shawl tied around my shoulders and the basket over my arm. "You go walk?"

"With my sister. I'll bid you both good day." Was I wrong in thinking his question somewhat inappropriate? Since he had begun training with Gull, Knut had been unfailingly polite to me, but I was finding that each time I met him I liked him a little less. That made no sense; there was no foundation for it save a casual remark or two and an oddity in the way he dealt with his wife. And Svala was odd enough in herself to make that almost inevitable.

Clodagh was waiting for me, her basket over her arm.

"Are you sure you're up to a long walk?" I asked.

"I was the one who suggested it, remember? If I had to lie down and rest all the time I'd go crazy. Even Cathal can hardly disapprove of a gentle stroll to pick mushrooms."

We made our way along the westward path, leaving the settlement behind us. Years had passed since my last visit here, and I realized the island was bigger than I had remembered. We skirted the place of the boat burial and headed across an area of gentle dips and rises carpeted by scrubby grass. For some time we walked in companionable silence. Sheep exchanged quiet bleats as they grazed; a flock of geese honked warnings at us from the shores of a reed-fringed pond.

"There's a spring over this next hill," Clodagh said. "The fresh water brings all kinds of birds. I knew you'd like this walk. You miss the forest, don't you?"

"Inis Eala is very different. A challenge."

Clodagh smiled. "Spoken like a druid, Sibeal. You treat every experience as an exercise in learning. You never seem to lose your temper or feel doubt or have a bad day as the rest of us do; you think everything through like a wise old person. But then, even as a child you were unusually self-possessed."

I considered this remark. "You say that as if it's a bad thing."

"I don't mean it like that. I always admired you for it."

"But?" I had heard the reservation in her tone.

"I don't know. I just . . . well, I suppose I wonder if it's entirely good for you to keep such control over your feelings. Feelings can be uncomfortable, but they're part of being alive: joy and sorrow, excitement, fear, hurt. Imagine a story in which every character was in perfect control of himself all the time. It would be somewhat lacking, in my opinion."

I grimaced. "I'm beginning to suspect a conspiracy. Everywhere I turn, someone's challenging my vocation, either by out-lining the delights of marriage and motherhood, or by suggesting there's something amiss because I don't scream and shout when I'm upset."

"I didn't mean—"

"Clodagh, believe me, I have plenty of doubts. About myself, about my future, about my suitability to follow the druid path. I have no doubt at all that the gods have called me, and that means I must do my best. As for self-control, I've been trained to main-tain it, outwardly at least. Not showing emotion doesn't mean you don't feel it." After a little I added, "Your story would be one in which every character was a druid, I suppose. In fact, people have been known to lose their tempers in the nemetons. You'd be surprised how heated the debate can get over the correct way to conduct a ritual."

We walked up a slight rise and paused. Below us lay a secluded hollow, a sudden surprise of many greens amidst the dun and gray of the island. A ring of hawthorns sheltered the grove of ap-ple trees, which put me in mind of graceful women in verdant gowns, perhaps preparing to dance. Short gowns; the sheep had nibbled as high as they could stretch. It was a lovely place, full of calm and sweetness.

"These trees give remarkably good fruit," Clodagh said. "Crisp and juicy. You'll be gone before this season's crop ripens. The mushrooms are over on that side."

An impressive crop of broad, cream caps rose above the grass. I made Clodagh sit and rest while I picked, filling both baskets quickly.

"How is Ardal doing?" she asked as she watched me work.

"Better. Remembering one or two things. It seems his brother was on the ship, too. He is quite confused. I had to explain that if his brother was on board, he must have drowned. Ardal seemed to believe that was somehow his fault."

"Oh, so he's remembered the wreck? What did he say?"

I sat back on my heels, seeing Ardal's shadowed eyes and tear-stained face. "I don't think he remembers much. Just a wave coming over and swallowing them up. He said he couldn't untie something, but he wouldn't explain what. His mind jumps around, one moment in childhood, the next dealing with something recent. And he mixes old tales with real life." Or perhaps it was that the old tales helped make sense of real life. "We did learn that he comes from Armorica, only he called it Breizh. A long way."

"They'll go home quite soon, I suppose," Clodagh said. "The three of them."

"Not for a while yet. Ardal can't walk more than a few steps."

"Speaking of walking, we may as well head back. Biddy should be delighted with that harvest."

I helped Clodagh to her feet. "What's she planning to do with them?"

"Put some in a fish stew and string up the rest to dry," Clodagh said, reaching for her basket. "Nothing's wasted here. No, no, Sibeal, I can carry it. I'm not completely helpless."

"I'd never dare suggest such a thing," I said, laughing. "But I wouldn't want to risk Cathal's displeasure by tiring you out. Shall we walk back the other way, round by the cliffs?"

It was as we walked above the third cove that we saw her. She was on the beach below us, standing with hands on hips and legs apart, looking down at something. Along the shore, at around the tide line, stretched a winding shape of piled-up pebbles and coarse sand, decorated here and there with patches of weed or large shells. Its creator regarded it with concentration, her hair in wet strands over her shoulders and down her back. Under its meager concealment, Svala was stark naked.

"What is she doing?" whispered Clodagh as we stood staring, paralyzed with shock. Summer it might be, but this was hardly a warm day. And there were men all over the island.

"It's a snake," I murmured, taking a better look at Svala's creation. "Look, she's given it shell eyes, and—no, perhaps not a snake. It's too fat, and it has legs. A dragon? She must be freezing.

And anyone could come past and see her. We'll have to go down and talk to her. Or maybe just I will go; that path looks rather steep."

"I'll manage. We can leave the baskets here."

Partway down the path, I halted suddenly.

"Watch out!" Clodagh was behind me. "I nearly walked into you."

"I saw something." My eye had caught a slight movement, up on the cliffs at the other side of the bay, where bushes screened the path. A sheep? Whatever it had been, it was gone now. "I thought . . . For a moment, I thought it was a man. Someone hiding, watching her. But surely nobody would do that."

"Not if they heard Johnny's speech to the new arrivals. It must have been a sheep."

We headed on down to the shore. Svala had heard us. She turned to watch us approach, making no attempt at all to cover herself up. Her clothing lay strewn on the ground, sand and pebbles scattered across it as if she had gone about her work of digging and building with single-minded concentration. As her gaze went from me to Clodagh and back to me, I wondered if she might flee like a wild creature, leaving her garments behind.

"Don't go too close," I whispered to my sister. "Good morning, Svala," I said, halting a few paces from the Norsewoman. "What have you made?" I gestured toward the sand creature. Now that we were close, I realized how big it was; she must have been here since sunrise.

Svala regarded me for a few moments, then reached out her hand, beckoning me closer. She did not speak, but walked the full length of the creature, gesturing busily all the way, and as I followed her I thought I understood: *See how bright his eyes are, how shining his skin. See his strong legs, his fearsome tail! And the teeth!* Like a little child wanting its mother's praise for something fashioned with painstaking care. The teeth were of pointed shells, and gave her dragon an expression somewhere between ferocious and comical.

"Fine, very fine," I said, nodding and smiling. "But you—cold."

I mimed shivering, wrapping my arms around myself. In fact, Svala showed no sign that she was either cold or embarrassed by being discovered naked. She stood beside me, a proud figure of a woman, breasts high and full, waist narrow, hips generous, the hair on her body of the same gold as her long tresses. Her skin was uniformly pale and unblemished, and there was not a goose bump on her. She did have a certain amount of coarse sand stuck to her here and there, and I wondered if she had been swimming before she began her labor of love.

Behind us, Clodagh had gathered up Svala's gown and was attempting to shake off the sand. The shawl that had lain beside it looked drenched. There was nothing else for Svala to put on.

"You should get dressed." I illustrated. "Cold. And men could see you." I gestured to the top of the cliffs. "That path, men walk. See you, no clothes. Not good."

In response, Svala knelt down by the creature's head, looking into the blank shell eyes. She crooned a little tuneless song.

"Svala," Clodagh said, coming up, "I will lend you my cloak. Here." She untied it and held it out.

"Best come back now," I said. "Come with us. Or at least put your clothes on, so the men don't see you like this."

She must have understood; our gestures were quite clear. Still, she made no move. The little song went on, rising and falling; it was perhaps a lullaby, perhaps a lament.

"Your creature will be washed away when the tide comes in," I said. "That is sad. So much work." Her song held the sorrow of a child when the sea swallows its creation. It was a goodbye.

Svala rose to her feet, her eyes closed now as her song came to an end. She reached out, blind, and put her hand around my arm. My ears heard the child's grief, and my eyes saw the magnificent woman, like a goddess from ancient story. But my heart felt, deep within, a terrible loss, a thing too wrenching ever to be expressed in words. My body was filled with her anguish. Dimly, I heard Clodagh cry out, and then I was on my knees on the sand, my hands to my head.

It was Svala who helped me to my feet. I felt the strength in her arms, the power in her hands. And when I opened my eyes and looked into hers, I knew that what I had felt for a little, she felt every moment of every day. She wore her sorrow as she wore her own skin.

I did not tell her that I understood. I knew nobody could, save perhaps someone who had experienced what she had. I tried to show her with my eyes, and with my hand on her shoulder, that I had felt something of her grief, and that I was a friend. After that, she let Clodagh help her on with the wet gown and slung the warm cloak casually around her shoulders. But she would not come home with us. Instead, she seated herself cross-legged by the sand creature's head, laid her hand on its neck and stared out to sea.

From the cliff top we looked back down. Svala sat motionless, as if keeping vigil. Perhaps she was waiting for the tide to come in.

"Are you all right, Sibeal?" Clodagh asked. "For a moment down there I thought you were going to faint. You're still very pale."

"I'm fine now." The wave of feeling had ebbed quickly, leaving my heart numb. To hold so much within her . . . no wonder Svala seemed sometimes to exist in a different world from the rest of us.

"We should tell someone about this," Clodagh said as we walked on. "She's like a small child, with no sense of danger. Let alone propriety."

"Mm." If she wandered about without her clothes, Svala had the capacity to cause mayhem, especially with the Connacht men on the island. I tried to imagine telling Knut what we had seen and knew I could not do it, either directly or—still more embarrassing—through Jouko or Kalev. Faced with such a task, I was far more unwed young girl than wise druid. I was not even sure I could bring myself to broach the subject with Gull.

"You can leave this to me, Sibeal," Clodagh said. "I'll speak to Cathal, he can pass it on to Johnny, and if Johnny thinks Knut should know, he'll tell him. This adds to the urgent need to get them off the island."

"I have seen her behaving rather oddly before, but not like this.

Last time . . . Knut came, and he dealt with it. But he seemed embarrassed by her, almost ashamed of her. It makes me wonder if even he understands."

"Understands what?"

"I know Svala's behavior is strange. But I don't believe she's out of her wits, Clodagh. When we were down there, just for a moment I felt the force of her grief, and it was overwhelming. I know she lost her son; I know how terrible that must be. But I wonder if something else lies in her past, something more than the shipwreck and her son's death. I sense there's a story that needs to be told, and that until it comes out, we won't be able to help her."

"If there were, why wouldn't Knut have told it? It's not as if Svala can tell us in words."

It was a reasonable question. "Maybe it's something only she knows about. Or Knut could know more than he's chosen to tell."

"If you're right," Clodagh mused, "it could be tied up with Ardal. Perhaps when he regains his memory it will all come out, whatever it is."

"Maybe."

"You know what the men are saying, don't you?" Clodagh gave me her basket to hold as we negotiated a stile. "That he has brought ill luck to the island. That wherever he goes, he casts a shadow."

"Ardal?" This shocked me. Cathal had not suggested the talk of portents and omens was associated with anyone in particular. "Why would they think that?"

"I don't know, Sibeal. Don't sound so upset; it's probably just idle talk. Maybe it was the odd way he was found, or the fact that he reached shore alive at all after such a long time in the water. The shipwreck unsettled everyone. Folk are edgy. It's not just Cathal who wishes he had done more, it's all of them. They don't like to see men lost when there's a chance to save them. If so many perished so quickly, they're saying, why did that one man survive, especially after so long in the water? Then there was the freak storm that caused the wreck; there are plenty of theories about that."

"You mean people are saying it was Ardal's presence on board that made the sea carry *Freyja* onto the rocks? What do they think he is, an evil spirit?"

"They just think he brings bad luck, Sibeal. Don't look so worried. They'll realize soon enough that there's no foundation for such superstitions."

~Felix~

She is troubled. Nothing outward; her voice is controlled, her features are grave and composed. But something disturbs her; I see it in her eyes.

Gull is abed early after a long day of work. Tomorrow, Knut's fight takes place. It has troubled me to see that man cross this chamber every day; that man with cold eyes. As he passes, he turns his gaze on me. Sometimes he greets me—*Comrade, how are you?*—but he need not speak for me to know his enmity. And still I cannot remember. They say he was a crewman. They say his wife was on board with him. And his son. Drowned. I remember nothing, nothing at all save Paul, and the knots, and the wave coming over. When the sea came, it took everything.

Today I have worked again on regaining my strength. I can walk from bed to fireside and back with my hand on a man's shoulder, or a woman's, for balance. Seven steps each way. Gull made Sibeal demonstrate that she had the strength to support me before he agreed to retire for the night. I cannot yet go abroad. Those seven steps rob me of breath. I am like a child's doll, a manikin stuffed with wool. Weak. Too weak to defend myself, save with words.

Now, at last, I can speak to Sibeal alone.

"What is in your thoughts, Sibeal?"

She glances up at me, surprised. Her favorite place is on the mat before the hearth. I do not think it is the warmth she seeks, but visions in the flames. "I was considering whether to cast the runes again."

"What is the question you need answered?"

The flames flicker in her eyes. "It doesn't matter," she says.

"That cannot be true. Cast the runes for a trivial question? You are a druid. You would not do that."

She makes no answer for a while. Her words, when they come, are hesitant. "Some things may be better not shared."

"Sibeal, look at me." She looks, taken aback by my tone. "Do you believe me unworthy of the truth?"

She wraps her arms around herself as if, even there before the hearth, she is touched by a deep cold. "I can't tell you this, Ardal. It is someone else's secret." After a moment she adds, "I haven't lied to you, just held something back."

"You said your question did not matter. I do not think that can be true."

"In fact," Sibeal says, and I see I have upset her, "if I cast the runes again tonight I would hardly know which question to choose. Several matters are exercising my mind, all equally troubling."

"Are all these matters better not shared?"

She looks up at me. I feel a jolt to the heart; it is the same each time I look into her eyes. There is no one else in the world with such eyes. She does not answer my question.

"Ah, well," I say, "I can understand. I am no more than a piece of flotsam, washed up at random on your shore. I come clad only in the garments of today, with no mantle of history about me. I am a stranger even to myself. What right have I to demand truth from you? My every word might be a lie."

Sibeal smiles. "If I were given three guesses as to what you were before you came here, my first guess would be a student of philosophy."

I am in the library at St. Laorans. *By all the saints, Felix, you astonish me with such an argument*, says Brother Bernez. *Better not speak thus before others, for if your theories on the nature of deity should reach the ears of Duke Remont, you would bring down trouble not only on this old teacher, but on yourself and on all your family.* Light falls through a colored window to gleam on his tonsured head, crowning him with jewels of cobalt and crimson. His eyes are kind. *I'm serious, Felix*, the old philosopher says. *The days when one could put forth such ideas openly are gone. Under Remont's rule, one does not challenge the teachings of the established faith. Your father could lose his position at court.*

I ask him, *How can it be wrong to search for truth?*

"What is it, Ardal?" Sibeal's voice brings me back. She has risen to her knees, her face white. "What do you see?"

"I . . . " It was there for a moment, so clear: the sun, the stone walls of the monastery, my wise friend . . . *Your father could lose his position at court* . . . But he did not. He did not, because I went away in time. I went, and Paul came with me.

You can't go on your own. Who's going to keep you out of trouble if I'm not there?

I don't even know where I'm going, Paul. I might never come back.

We're brothers, remember? You don't get rid of me so easily.

"Are you all right?" Sibeal's eyes are troubled. She puts her hand on my knee as she did once before, and its warmth is good.

"I . . . " It was so vivid, so real. A true memory, surely. Why can't I remember what came after? "A philosopher," I croak. "What would be your second guess?"

She knows I need time. "A priest in training," she says.

"And your third?"

Her smile quiets my thumping heart. It puts courage in my veins. "A poet," says Sibeal.

I breathe. My chest hurts; since the sea, all is not as it should be there. "Sibeal, you know that I remembered a little, before. About my brother. Memories from a long time ago."

She waits.

I glance over my shoulder toward Gull.

"Fast asleep," Sibeal says in a murmur.

"The past is coming back, but in small pieces. My true name. Some of the circumstances that led me and my brother to leave our home. But . . . I think it may be better if I do not give you the account of it. What I remember . . . it is of no consequence."

"Why not? Your name, your origins, the voyage—if you don't tell us those things, how can Johnny help you get home?"

It is a bitter understanding. If Paul is dead, if that memory is true, then someone must bear the news to our mother and father. Someone must take the tale to Breizh. A long way back. Further than this wayward son's feet will ever bear him.

"I cannot go home, Sibeal. I bring danger. I bring shadows. I bring ill luck. Better if the Ankou had taken me, that day in Yeun Ellez. Better, perhaps, that I had never been born. Then my brother would be alive."

"That is not true." Sibeal's eyes are wide in a face turned inexplicably pale. A white owl. She fixes me with a particular gaze. I think she sees right inside me. "You cannot know what would have happened if you had not been there. You cannot invent a past that never was. There is only *this* life, and the way forward."

I make no reply, and after some time she adds, "Ardal, we will cast the runes again. Not to seek wisdom on any of the dilemmas I spoke of earlier, but to make sense of this for you. I believe a mission lies before you. Of its nature I know nothing at all. But perhaps you need to execute that mission for your brother's sake. In doing so, you might make some sense of his death."

"Or prove to him that, now he is gone, I can be brave without him."

"You'll have me weeping, Ardal."

"You? I do not think so."

"Do you believe me incapable of tears?" she asks, turning her gaze away.

"I think you hold them inside," I say, "fearful to let them go, because you believe that is a sign of weakness." If I am right, and I think I am, she must consider me a poor example of a man. When they told me Paul was drowned, I wept a lake of tears.

"Ardal?"

"Yes, Sibeal?"

"You won't be going on without Paul. He is dead, yes. Most likely laid in his grave to the sound of my prayers. But he will walk with you step by step for the rest of your life. You will feel his presence in the air you breathe. In the cry of a gull you will hear his laughter; in the wash of the sea you'll hear him whispering to you, late at night, telling you a story after the candles are quenched. You will remember his goodness and courage every time you see a man help a comrade. You'll see his strong features, his humor, his kindness, when one day you have a son of your own."

If Sibeal cannot shed tears, I surely can. She fishes in the pouch at her waist for a square of linen, reaches up, puts it in my hand.

"He was a stranger to you. But it's as if you know him."

"I know you, Ardal. I hear the love in your voice when you speak of him. Your words tell me the kind of man he was."

We cast the runes together, on a ritual cloth before the fire. I want to sit on the mat opposite Sibeal, but she is afraid she will not be able to get me to my feet and back to bed afterward, so I remain in my chair, shame making my cheeks hot. Tomorrow I will work harder. I will walk further. I will make myself strong again.

Sibeal closes her eyes—such long lashes—and breathes deeply, her back straight, her hands relaxed in her lap. I cannot manage this manner of breathing, not now. My chest hurts when I try; my breath rasps, disturbing Sibeal's concentration as she sinks deeper into the receptive state of mind required for a divination. I close my eyes instead, summoning up an image of birches in the wind, of standing stones in a circle, of a shimmering lake under a pale dawn sky. I stroke the dog. I attempt to banish from my mind all distracting thoughts. I wait.

When Sibeal is ready she picks up the bag. The rods shift inside, as if knocking gently on the door of understanding, and I open my eyes. She looses the string. Instead of casting the rods onto the cloth, she lifts the bag within my reach. Our hands touch for a moment as, together, we let the rods fall out onto the linen square. Together we examine the pattern before us.

I have wondered if we will be shown the same runes Sibeal plucked from the bundle that first night: *Os, Ger* and *Nyd*. But although three rods lie on top of the others, all are different. Before us now lie *Ken, Gyfu, Sigel*. A voice sounds in my mind, the voice of Magnus who taught me: *The runes will not speak to you if you rush*

them. Let the meanings settle in your thoughts, let them blend and com-
bine for you, or you'll make no sense of them at all. Wisdom doesn't come
like a spring tide. It's more like the slow unfolding of an oak, from acorn
to sapling. Before that oak becomes a tall tree, you will be old. Magnus, a friend, a teacher . . . I see him, big, broad, yellow-bearded. A
Norseman. A kinsman. My mother's brother. I see him beside me
at a table, and before us a set of rune rods much like Sibeal's, but
fashioned from a darker wood, perhaps oak.

"You speak first, Ardal."

I start with some violence. The memory leaves me; here is the
fire, the dog, the darkened infirmary. Here is Sibeal, who has spoken with quiet calm, and does not deserve such a response.

"I'm sorry, I—" I cannot go on.

"Ardal," Sibeal says, "I know you understand the lore of runes.
You can interpret what you see here without reference to the past.
There's no need to touch on those matters you're so reluctant to
talk about. When I cast the runes I asked a question about your
pathway forward." After a moment she adds, "I would prefer you
to give your interpretation before I give mine. I want to be sure I
am not influencing you."

"Very well," I say, wondering what a druid will think of my
reading. Is she testing me? I am not unskilled, but by Sibeal's stan-
dards I must seem a raw novice. "*Ken* is light in the darkness;
vision; the illumination of things hidden. *Gyfu*, a gift. The gift of
talent in the service of the gods, or through service to others. *Sigel*,
sunlight, vision, achievement."

Sibeal sits quietly, not rushing me. She looks down at the
scattered rods, her dark lashes screening her eyes. The firelight
touches her skin to glowing rose.

I find the courage to go on. I must risk offending her. "You are
the gift and the light, Sibeal. In the darkness of unknowing that
has come upon me, you are the flaming torch that leads me forward. My eyes are blinded by the mist of forgetting; you are the
clear vision that keeps my feet on the path. You choose to help me
because you are a servant of the gods, and you see this as a mission laid on you, a duty required by your spiritual vocation."

Abruptly, her eyes are on me, clear and searching. "Duty? You think I'm helping you out of *duty*?" She remembers Gull and lowers her voice. "You have a strange idea of what a druid is, Ardal. First you accuse me of being unable to feel as others do, and now this."

"I tell the truth, as I see it. Maybe my truth offends you. Would you prefer a lie?"

"Of course not." It is the first time I have heard her sound sharp. "I should not have asked you for your interpretation. No wonder your answer was somewhat . . . "

Instead of holding my tongue as I should, I blunder in deeper. "Why are you helping me, Sibeal?"

She folds her hands in her lap, frowning. "You have disturbed the divination," she says in a small, cool voice.

"There," I say, "you change the subject, you detach yourself again, as if to look in your heart is too dangerous. Is this reserve something they teach you, your Ciarán and his fellows? Always to hold back, always to keep control, never to show the world your true self, a living, breathing woman? Is this what your gods require of you?"

She stares at me. After a moment she says, "The preparation to become a druid is very long, Ardal. I have spent a good deal of the last four years in the nemetons at Sevenwaters, much of it alone in prayer, or memorizing the lore, or finding out how much I still have to learn. If I allow my own feelings to crowd my mind, there will be no room left for the voices of the gods. If I expend my strength on my own everyday concerns, I cannot walk my spiritual path as I should." She pauses then, reflecting on what she has said. "I didn't express that well," she adds. "Ardal, I must be detached. That's one of the reasons I'm here, at Inis Eala. Because I have such difficulty, sometimes, in separating myself from what other people feel. It is something I must learn to do before I make my final promise."

"I am not talking about what other people feel, Sibeal. I am talking about what *you* feel."

"What I feel doesn't matter." It is a simple statement, and it saddens me beyond measure.

"Then you waste what you have to give," I say quietly. "To be less than honest with yourself makes your pledge to the gods only half a gift." I picture Brother Bernez, with his merry eyes and his droll wisdom; his family was vast, and he loved to talk of them. He spoke, too, of the anguish with which he made the choice, long ago, to dedicate himself to God. "Four years, you say. So you have been undergoing this training since you were . . . ?"

"Twelve. It is quite usual." Her whole face is closed up; her tone is as chilly as I have ever heard it.

"And since you were twelve, you have been self-contained, serene, thoughtful, dedicated to the will of the gods. A dutiful servant."

She says nothing. I remember the tale she told, that first night. I suspect she has not wept, laughed or stamped her foot in anger since she was a child of five or six. I gaze on her face, though by now I need not look at her features to see her; I carry her image deep within me. There is hurt in her eyes, though she will not release it in tears. Why have I challenged her thus? What am I expecting, a declaration of love? Wretched Felix. You never could learn to keep your mouth shut.

"I will give you my interpretation of the runes," Sibeal says, turning her gaze down toward the ritual cloth. Her manner is that of a teacher correcting a wayward student. "The way forward is no longer obscure as it was before. The light of the gods shines down on our pathway. The mission can be completed. But it's not straightforward. The possibility of victory is balanced by the presence of death in these runes. That may relate to your brother and to the others who perished in the sea. But *Sigel* also tells us we can summon the strength to hold back the forces that conspire against us. We can resist the chaotic influences that attended my first divination, the night you used *Is* to tell me you had lost your memory. *Ken* is not simply light as in a torch or lamp; it also signifies the light of knowledge. *Ken* and *Is* are opposites, Ardal. Against the frozen immobility of *Is*, *Ken* is transformation."

When I do not reply, she continues, "A runic divination works on many levels, from the most esoteric to the simplest and most direct. My interpretation is a druid's; it differs from yours, but does not invalidate it." A deep, gulping breath. "Ardal—"

"I'm sorry if I hurt you, Sibeal."

"I don't do what I do out of duty, but out of love."

I am not fool enough to interpret this in the way I would like to. I wait for her to go on.

"We are all joined in spirit, Ardal. Every man, woman and child; every creature, every blade of grass, every apple on the tree. Every wave that breaks on the shore. How can I not help?" Her tone changes, softens. "It was a stranger I found on the shore. But now you're my friend. As for your interpretation of the runes, I did guess you might be a poet, and what you said makes me think I was correct."

A smile creeps onto my face. "I am sorry I disturbed the divination. I seem to have a talent for that."

"If we discuss it calmly, I may avoid a headache. The interpretation seems clear."

"But are there not many interpretations, including conflicting ones? Could not one say, for instance, that the most significant element in this divination is the link or joining? *Gyfu* can be interpreted as the union of two disparate elements. *Ken*, the torch, does not only bring light. The torch sees wood destroyed, but heat and light created. Perhaps this divination deals with change. With transmutation, not simply on the physical level but on the spiritual one as well."

"That's all very well, Ardal." Sibeal is starting to relax now. She is far more comfortable with a philosophical debate than with a discussion of her own feelings. "But to perform this divination fully, you should relate your general interpretation to the question I asked when we cast the rods. Or, more aptly, to one of your own, one you do not share with me. It was incorrect for us to attempt ritual practice together. We should not do so again."

"Why is it incorrect?"

She flushes slightly. "You are untrained. And . . . No, I can't explain. It feels wrong. My instincts tell me it is unwise."

"I am not untrained," I say quietly. "I may not have your level of skill, but I have received good guidance in this, as in other learning. There was a . . . there was a Norseman in my own family, a scholar who taught me runic lore."

"So you've remembered more," Sibeal says. "Tell me."

"Of the wreck, the voyage, of recent times I remember nothing. What is in my mind is a clatter of old bones, a shred or two of a distant past." I hesitate. This is not quite true; and I have just challenged Sibeal to be more truthful. "I left home because my presence endangered others," I tell her. "Paul came to watch over me, and he died. I bring misfortune, Sibeal. I bring ill luck. I will not draw you into that circle of shadow."

Sibeal reaches out her hands and gathers the rods in. The clattering sound wakes Deiz, who jumps down from my knee. Sibeal begins to pack the rods away. "I never want to hear you say that again, about bringing ill luck." Her voice is stern. "I will not believe that to be true of any man."

"That is what Paul said." I see him beside me on the deck of a ship, a trading boat, the crew not Norsemen but Gauls. *That's rubbish, Felix. It's just circumstances, that's all. You do have a tendency to speak out when another man might find it prudent to hold his tongue, that's true enough. But that doesn't mean you carry some kind of cloak of doom with you.*

"Then Paul was a wise man as well as a kind one."

"And I killed him."

I hear her draw a breath. "The sea killed him," she says.

"I was too slow, too clumsy. I could not untie it . . . " I shut my mouth on the words. His voice, his face, the rope around his ankles, the knots . . . the wave . . .

Calmly, Sibeal continues to replace the rods in their bag. "It happened so quickly," she says in a murmur. "I was watching from the cliffs out there. My first full day on Inis Eala. It must have been chaos on the ship. I suppose people were trapped as everything broke up. And the waves were . . . of an unusual size."

Save yourself, Felix. It washes over me again. I close my eyes, lost in the darkness.

*   *   *

Later, when Sibeal is abed, I lie awake and watch the shifting shadows thrown by the banked-up fire. The last lamp is quenched, the last candle extinguished. I breathe. How long will it take for my body to be whole again, how many days, how many turnings of the tide before I am strong enough for this task, this unknown task the runes lay on me?

Deiz presses close against my side, sighing in her sleep. She trusts me. It is a small blessing; a dog forgives much. I wish I could pray. I wish I could believe in a benign deity, a good father who holds us safe and heals our wounds. I wish I could believe my brother has gone to a better place. But I lost my faith in that god long ago. I lost my trust when I saw men claim power for themselves in his name. There are other gods; other paths. In time, perhaps my feet will carry me onto a true way. Perhaps I will wander until I die. Perhaps I will die tomorrow, or the next day, or the next, on the end of Knut's sword, all for a truth that I cannot remember.

CHAPTER 7

~Sibeal~

O n the day of the challenges I rose early as usual and went out walking, accompanied by Fang. Muirrin, who had patched up hundreds of injured combatants during her years on the island, would stay in the infirmary with Ardal while the bouts were on, ready to tend to anyone who needed her. Her presence there had a twofold purpose; Evan judged Ardal still too unwell to be left on his own.

A great deal of interest had been sparked by Knut's challenge to Cathal, and even more interest once it became known that Gull was training the challenger. This meant both Gull and Evan, along with almost the entire male population of Inis Eala, would be watching the two battle it out this morning. It meant a good audience for the earlier bouts, in which the Connacht men would demonstrate their skill. I wondered whether I might skip those and be present only for Cathal's fight. Probably not; Clodagh would be keyed up already, needing me for support.

Fang had been behaving oddly all morning. She would scamper along for a while, then stop dead in her tracks, her whole body tense, her ears pricked. Once or twice this sudden alert was accompanied by a sound, not the customary low growl but a faint whimper. When I bent down to check if she had a thorn in her paw she snapped at me. I walked on, and in a while she was running along beside me as if there were nothing at all out of the ordinary.

"What is your story, little dog?" I asked her. "Another of those that can't be told?"

She ignored me, but three more times before we came back to the settlement she did it again: the sudden halt, the still, alert pose, as if she had caught a scent she could not ignore. Once the low buildings of the settlement were in sight, Fang seemed to forget whatever it was, racing ahead of me toward the kitchen where Biddy could be relied upon to provide a bowl of tasty leftovers.

Despite the early hour, the dining hall was near full. Men made wagers, discussed strategies and techniques, debated the likely results of each bout. Women offered opinions and exchanged jests as to the relative prowess of their husbands, brothers or sweethearts. Knut was with Kalev at the far table, deep in conversation. If he had had second thoughts about his rash challenge, he showed no sign of unease. I did not see Svala.

There was a small island of quiet where my family sat. Cathal appeared to have finished his breakfast; Clodagh had barely touched hers. He looked as if his mind was elsewhere. She was pale. Gareth and Johnny conversed in murmurs, their attention only on each other. Sam and Brenna were eating their porridge in the purposeful manner of folk who have a full day's work ahead of them.

I seated myself beside Gull and Evan. Biddy ladled porridge. A steaming bowlful appeared before me, and I realized I had no appetite at all. In my mind, a man was falling, falling from a great height . . . A wave arose, washing him from the rocks, seizing him in its grip, turning him upside down and around about . . . Jaws snatched him, tossing him high; blood filled the air in great drenching sprays . . .

"What's wrong, Sibeal?" Evan's murmur broke the vision, and

I was at the table once more, my brother-in-law's steadying hand on my arm.

Breathe. Breathe deeply. "Nothing," I said as my heart slowed. *Falling, falling down . . . faster and faster still . . .* "I'm a little tired, that's all."

"Best eat your breakfast," Gull advised, starting on his own. "No wonder you're tired. Up late talking, hmm?"

I felt an unwelcome blush warm my cheeks. How much of last night's conversation had he heard? I was certain he'd been asleep when I checked. "Quite late, yes." I took up my spoon.

"Up late talking?" Cathal was back from wherever his thoughts had led him. "Not to Gull, I gather. I hear your fellow's recovering his memory."

"Some." I made myself swallow a spoonful of porridge. "It's patchy."

"So what is he?" Cathal asked. "A fighter, a priest, a craftsman, a scholar?"

"Not a fighter. And I think not a priest, though I did wonder about that. He seems to like debate."

Clodagh gazed at me across the table. "No wonder you were up late talking, Sibeal. He sounds just your type."

I grimaced at her in sisterly fashion.

"I hear he speaks very good Irish when he's alone with you and Gull," commented Johnny, who had been diverted from his conversation with Gareth. "One might suppose he has been in these parts awhile. Possibly his brother, too."

"Where is this brother now?" asked Gareth.

"Drowned," I said. "I think Ardal's brother was one of those we laid to rest after the wreck. There was one among the dead who resembled him. Ardal remembered a wave coming and his brother being washed away. And something about knots, trying to unfasten knots . . . " My voice faded as I realized my companions at the table were looking at something behind me. I turned my head to see Kalev standing there, waiting for me to finish. Beside him was Knut.

"I do not mean to interrupt, Sibeal," Kalev said. "When you are finished, we wish to speak to Gull about this morning's activities."

But Knut's light blue eyes were fixed on me. "The man remembers?" His look was like a sudden blade, making my heart thump in fright. Before I could say a word, he added, "He is better. Is good, yes?"

"Better than he was, certainly," I said with hard-won steadiness. It was clear that nobody else had noticed anything unusual. Had I imagined that moment? "But still very sick."

"You say brother?"

He understood more Irish than I realized. "It seems likely his brother was on the ship with him, yes. One of those we buried. One of the men whose names you did not know."

Kalev translated this for Knut, then rendered the Norseman's reply: "How much does the stranger remember? Has he told his tale?"

"He hasn't said much. Most of what he remembers is from long ago, when he and Paul—his brother—were little boys. I suppose it will come back to him in bits and pieces over time. He's still quite weak. Gull and I don't want to push him too hard."

Knut spoke again.

"Knut says that if the story comes out, perhaps Ardal will tell it to you, Sibeal." A familiar blush colored Kalev's cheeks as he spoke. "He has heard the two of you are very close."

A pox on Knut! How dare he make such a suggestive remark in front of my family? I opened my mouth to answer, then shut it again. The best response was a dignified silence.

Gull rose to his feet. "We'll have our little talk outside, boys." He looked across at Cathal. "Should be a good bout."

"May the best man win," said Cathal lightly.

There was time to fill before the fighting started. Biddy, sensitive to Clodagh's distracted mood, sent the two of us off to the root cellar to fetch vegetables. When that was done she set us to chopping while she plucked and gutted chickens. My knife moved steadily:

red-gold circles of carrot like little suns, creamy slices of turnip, pungent, translucent slivers of onion. On Biddy's side of the table a drift of feathers filled the air, a strange summer snow.

"Are you coming out to watch the fighting, Biddy?" Clodagh asked.

"I'll venture over to see how the Norseman stands up against Cathal. If that man of mine works a miracle, I don't want to have to tell him I missed it."

The knife stilled in my hand. *A man falling, falling . . . blood on the stones. A scream cut off sharply. His head . . . oh gods, his head, where it had struck . . .* I sat down abruptly, my hands to my brow, mumbling something about feeling faint.

Clodagh brought me a cup of mead, a heady brew for so early in the morning. I gulped a mouthful down. My sister had seated herself beside me, her hand on my shoulder.

"What did you see, Sibeal?" Last time we had watched Cathal fight, she had been edgy. The closer it came to the time of her delivery, I thought, the more difficult it would be for Clodagh to see her husband in any danger.

"Nothing to worry about," I said. "A snatch of Sight, that's all." Who was that falling man and why had I seen him?

Biddy had the chickens hanging up on strings as she worked on them. A bucket stood underneath to catch the entrails. I could not look at this without seeing the image again: a man's head smashed on stone, the contents splattered, a feast for squawking gulls. "Excuse me," I murmured and made a hasty exit into the kitchen garden, where I spewed up my meager breakfast in a corner. I felt suddenly cold and shaky. *I bring shadows. I bring ill luck.* I had told Ardal not to say such things, not even to think them. But I felt the chill. I felt the shadow. Whether he was right, and he had indeed brought a darkness with him to the island, or whether another force was at play among us, I felt its grip and was afraid.

I waited until I was reasonably composed before going back in.

"Better?" Clodagh scrutinized me.

"I'm fine. It was nothing."

"Maybe you'd go and pick me a nice bunch of parsley, Sibeal," said Biddy, wiping her brow with the back of her hand.

Clodagh made to get up and come with me, but I waved her back down. "I'll do it," I said. "You stay here and chat with Biddy."

"All right, Sibeal." The fact that she agreed without argument showed me how tired she was. But Clodagh had not changed so much. As I headed out, knife in hand, I heard her say, "I'll pluck that other chicken for you, shall I?"

The day was growing warmer. I took my time wandering up the path of the walled garden, from the part near the kitchen door, with its straw-covered vegetable beds and orderly lines of stakes, to the area closer to the infirmary, where both culinary and medicinal herbs grew in profusion. Stone benches were set at this end, among the plants. It would be a good place for Ardal to sit out in the sun when he was stronger.

The herbs were looking especially well kept, thanks in part to the time I had spent trimming, staking and generally tending to everything. It was a form of meditation, one I especially enjoyed. With both hands in the earth and the scent of growth all around me, I felt the working of a powerful spirit, an essence that had no name, but was part of me, and at the same time part of these bushes of lavender and wormwood, and part of the sheep grazing on the cliff tops and the apple trees in the little grove and the pebbles in the coves of Inis Eala. Even now, crouching to take a few green leaves from one plant, a sprig or two from another, I whispered acknowledgment and blessing, and felt my heart grow calmer. *For this bounty, I thank you. For this gift, I am grateful.*

It did not take long to gather enough for Biddy's purposes. There would be time to slip into the infirmary and bid Ardal good morning before I went back. I hesitated, remembering last night. He had unsettled me. Perhaps I had done the same to him. Still, we were unlikely to have any awkward moments with Muirrin there.

Outside the back entrance to the infirmary, I halted. Voices came from behind the closed door, and their tone was disturbing.

Silence followed, and I found that still more disturbing. I pushed open the door.

Ardal was lying in bed. Close beside him stood Knut, looking down at him. There was nothing at all untoward about the scene, yet a wash of emotions flooded through me as I approached: unease, resentment, a furious courage. And sheer terror. There was no telling which man held which feelings within him. Knut's expression was all courtesy; Ardal's face I could not see.

"Better," Knut said, glancing in my direction, then indicating the other man. "Good. I go now."

I found myself momentarily unable to speak. The tumult crowded out everything else.

"You watch?" Knut asked me. "Good fight, you watch?"

Ardal spat out some words of Norse. I had never heard such a tone from him. Knut stared at him a moment, then threw his head back and laughed. The front door opened, and there was Muirrin with a cloth-covered bowl in her hands. "Knut," she said, surprised. "Why are you here?"

"See him," Knut said, jerking his chin toward the bed. "I go now. Fight soon." He directed a smile of sorts in my general direction, and was gone.

I found words. "I thought Evan said Ardal was too sick to be left on his own." I could still feel the tension of that encounter, without any idea of what the two men had said to each other.

Muirrin put her bowl on the worktable. "I was only gone a moment, Sibeal. I have a man coming in shortly with a painfully swollen ankle. I couldn't make up this poultice without a trip to the storeroom. And Ardal's fine, as you see."

There was no way to convey what I had felt on first entering the chamber. It was one thing to have the gift of Sight, to be open to the voices of the gods, to be attuned to visions, omens and portents. It was another to be a vessel into which poured, apparently at random, a volatile blend of other people's love and hate, cowardice and courage, envy, greed and desire. One thing I had learned. Knut and Ardal together spelled peril.

"Sibeal." Ardal's whisper drew me to his bedside, where I sank down on the stool. "Don't concern yourself about me. There's no need." But there was. I'd have had to be blind not to notice how pale he was. He took my hand, holding it tightly.

"If you're going to be here, Sibeal," my sister said, "you can find me some bandages. I anticipate a few more cuts and bruises this morning. The Connacht men may be shaping up well, but they don't have our men's experience."

"I can't stay," I said. "I wish I could. I've promised to be with Clodagh for the morning. Isn't there someone else to help you?"

"Later, yes. This morning every woman on the island will be at the bouts. Never mind, I can cope." She moved across to tend to the fire.

"Sibeal, be careful," Ardal whispered.

"What do you mean?" I was whispering, too, leaning close. "Careful of what?" It wouldn't be me out there with a sword in my hand this morning.

"Don't go out walking on your own." His eyes were full of trouble. "Please."

This again? What on earth had Knut said to him? "Ardal, I go walking on my own every single day. Not only do I possess sound common sense, but I go under the protection of the gods."

"Please, Sibeal. Please do as I ask."

"I thought you said you were needed elsewhere." Muirrin came back over, wiping her hands on a cloth.

Ardal released my hand, and I rose to my feet. "I'll be fine," I told him. "I know how to look after myself." In the back of my mind was the vision, a man plunging off the cliff path and down to oblivion. "I'll come back as soon as the bouts are over."

"Are you all right, Sibeal?" Muirrin had realized all was not well with me, and now came across to put her hand against my brow and examine my face with narrowed eyes. "Don't tell me you've been having nightmares, too."

"You mean you have? What kind of nightmares?"

Muirrin grimaced. "Healers' nightmares. You can probably imagine. I don't usually dream much. Evan and I tend to be so tired we sleep like logs, and if we dream, we don't remember it.

These last few nights have been difficult. You'd better go, Sibeal. You're right, the best place for you today is with Clodagh."

With a great effort of will and some well-learned techniques, I managed to show Clodagh a smiling face. When it was time for the bouts I took my seat next to her, with Alba on my other side. Until this was all over, I would concentrate on nothing but the excellent combat skills on display. I would not think of that vision of violent death. I would not think of ill luck. I would forget the venom that had filled the air when I walked into the infirmary earlier, hinting at a story neither Knut nor Ardal had yet told us.

The Connacht men had shown good judgment in their challenges. Most pairs of combatants were well matched, and Johnny's call of "Cease!" came more commonly with two men still on their feet and fighting, rather than with one sprawled on the ground or forcibly relieved of his weapon. While each bout was carried out with fierce intensity, the whole thing was conducted in an atmosphere of goodwill, the crowd shouting encouragement even-handedly—that was, at the tops of their voices, whether it was a Connacht man or one of their own—and offering congratulations at the end in the same manner. The place was packed, with a press of folk standing at the back behind the seats.

There were ten bouts in all, each of them a display of rare skill and, in some cases, something approaching grace. I noted again Jouko's lightness on his feet and Niall's ability to stand as strong as an ox against blows that would have felled another fighter. I admired the speed and balance of the Connacht man who had spoken to me the night I had told a story after supper—what was his name? Brendan?—and learned that Kalev was as talented in unarmed combat as he was with the sword. Both Brendan and Kalev made a point of meeting my eye before and after their bouts, as if keen that I should take notice. *If my life had taken a different path, and I'd wanted a sweetheart,* I told them silently, *I wouldn't be choosing a warrior, no matter how impressive his fighting skills.* For

173

it came to me that to love a man whose livelihood placed him at constant risk might take quite a toll on a woman's heart.

"Only one more to go before Cathal meets Knut," Clodagh said, glancing across the crowd. Gull's group was shifting to make room for Biddy, who had just come in. More folk were squeezing into the narrow space behind the benches. It seemed to me every man, woman and child on the island might be gathered here today. With one notable exception.

"I can't see Svala," said Flidais, who was sitting beyond Alba. "I know she keeps herself to herself, but surely she'll come and watch her husband fight; it's not exactly a run-of-the-mill challenge."

Alba craned her neck. "Perhaps Knut hasn't told her. Or maybe she thinks he's been foolish. She wouldn't be alone in that opinion."

Clodagh and I exchanged a glance.

"Perhaps she doesn't like fighting," I said.

"A Norsewoman?" Alba's brows went up. "She'd have been watching this kind of thing since she was an infant."

Down in the combat area, an Inis Eala man was preparing for the next bout, checking his knife, tightening his belt, glancing at a young woman in the crowd, who responded with a cheerful wave. His face was decorated with a pattern resembling a badger's mask. No sign of an opponent. After a little, Rat stood up and bellowed: "Rodan of Carna! Out there testing your charm on the ladies, are you?" A roar of appreciative laughter greeted this, though Rat's demeanor was less than amiable; he looked mightily displeased. To be late showed a lack of self-discipline, a quality as essential to a warrior as it was to a druid. "Get your sorry self out here before I count to twenty or your match is forfeit!"

The crowd hushed. People looked around, expecting a sheepish Rodan to come running from whatever corner he was in. We waited. If Rat was indeed counting to twenty, he was doing it under his breath, and quite slowly.

"That fellow Rodan's in trouble," observed Alba. "Had to happen eventually. Suanach was saying he worked quite hard to talk himself into her bed, didn't want to take no for an answer. Tried the same thing with Flidais, until she told him she was Rat's wife. If anyone gets them all sent packing it'll be him—I put my two coppers on it."

"Fifteen! Sixteen!" yelled Rat. "Don't test my patience any further, man!"

A man falling, falling away down . . . a rag doll tumbling through the air, russet hair streaming, limbs thrashing . . .

"Alba," I said, as chill fingers wrapped themselves around my heart, "is Rodan a red-haired man?"

"That's right, Sibeal. He's the fellow I thought I liked. Huh! All that man wants is to get under a girl's skirt, and he's not too fussy about which girl it is."

I was on my feet, my skin clammy with dread. "Clodagh, I'm sorry, I have to go," I muttered, and elbowed my way through the crowd to the gateway as, behind me, Rat called Rodan's name one last time. "Sorry, excuse me, feeling sick—"

I was out. What now? In my head the vision repeated itself, a man teetering on the cliff top, the fall, the long, long fall, the landing—oh gods, russet hair splashed with violent crimson—the screaming celebration of gulls. *Run, Sibeal! Run, run, you can reach him in time!* For why would I be shown this, if I had not the power to prevent it?

I ran, letting instinct guide me as it had when I found Ardal washed up in the cove. My feet followed their own path; I was not aware of choosing left or right, up or down. I ran until my chest was tight with pain and my knees were giving way under me. Out from the settlement, along the cliff path toward the point that housed Finbar's cave, past one small bay, another, a third . . . Nearly there . . . Part of me, the part that still had room for logic, said I should have brought someone with me, one of the men, or at least should have told Clodagh where I was going and why. Should have told Johnny. Should have fetched a rope. *Don't go out walking on your own . . .*

Before I found the place, I heard the gulls and knew I had come too late. Ahead I could see the way around the northwest point, where the cave entry was concealed between rocks. On my left the hillside rose in a slope fit only for mountain goats. To my right, two strides from the path, earth gave way to sea in a dizzying drop. The place below was alive with squawks and screams. I halted, gasping for breath, my eyes and nose streaming. The cliff edge was jagged, slit by many narrow ravines; tufts of sharp-leaved grass grew here and there.

One step closer. Two steps. I peered over, my heart sounding a drumbeat of terror. I could see nothing but the darkness of the sea and the pale lacework of waves at the edge of the rocks. I backed up, lay down on my belly and wriggled forward until my head was over the edge. *A woman falling, falling . . . dark hair streaming upwards, mouth open in a silent shriek . . . Stop it, Sibeal. Do what must be done here.* I looked down and there was the substance of my vision, complete in every detail. Rodan had landed in the shape of the rune *Nyd*: defiance in the face of certain death. I inched back from the drop, got to my knees and retched up what little fluid was left in my stomach.

No time to give in to weakness. I must take stock of the place so others could locate it quickly. Johnny would want to retrieve the body. That would need to be arranged in haste, or the sea would rob that man of his chance to be laid to rest with due ritual. I could see no way down, but perhaps the men would find one.

I moved along the path, looking for anything out of place, and wondering what might have drawn a Connacht man all the way out here on the very day he was due to step up and demonstrate his skills. "What were you?" I mused. "Were you a Christian? Were you of the old faith? Perhaps you were a godless man." I supposed I would be the one speaking prayers over Rodan before he was laid to rest. All I knew about him was that he had found it hard to take no for an answer.

I could see where he had gone over. In one place the earth beside the path had been disturbed, and toward the edge his feet had scored deep marks. I saw him losing his balance, flailing with his arms, desperate to keep safe purchase. *His feet slipping. His eyes wide. His mouth stretched in a last great cry. Nooooo . . .*

"Gods be merciful to this man," I murmured. "Manannán, I ask you not to take his remains, but to allow him burial here, under the gaze of his friends." The news Johnny must send back to Connacht might be softened just a little if he could tell Rodan's chieftain that we had buried him with dignity. "But if your waves must carry him away, I pray that they rock him gently, as if he were a child new-minted, sleeping in his cradle. Morrigan, Dark Lady, know that Rodan was a warrior, and far from home. Lead him safely through the final doorway. On his new journey, may he find peace."

I had a square of linen in my pouch. This I placed on the path opposite the spot where Rodan had fallen. I weighted it with a stone. I took a deep, steadying breath, then headed back toward the settlement. I ran; not as fast as before, but as fast as I could manage. Before I had gone very far, I saw two tall men coming the other way: Gareth and Kalev, heading toward me at a purposeful jog.

"By all the gods, Sibeal," Gareth observed as we met, "you run as fast as a deer. What is it, what's happened?"

I sat down suddenly on the rocks. "You'll find him just along there," I said, wondering if the way everything was spinning around me meant I was about to faint, and feeling immensely grateful that I had not done so on the cliff's edge. "Rodan. He's dead. At the foot of the cliff. I marked the place." I put my head in my hands. "As for running fast, I was not fast enough."

Kalev went ahead to look, while Gareth waited with me, crouched down with his arm around my shoulders. Then Kalev ran back to the settlement with the news, and Gareth and I followed more slowly. He explained that Rodan's body could be fetched up by men on ropes; they'd need to move quickly before the tide came in much further, but there should be time.

It was only after we had reached the settlement and Gareth had passed me into Clodagh's care that I remembered Knut's bout with Cathal.

"What happened?" I asked my sister, who was steering me toward the kitchen. "How did Knut acquit himself?"

"Amazingly well," Clodagh said. "He lost, of course. In the end. But everyone was impressed. He's a fighter of outstanding skill. The men gave Cathal a rousing cheer when he finally managed to divest Knut of his sword. But not as loud as the cheer Knut got. Everyone's suggesting Johnny should offer him a place here if he wants it."

People were going in and out of the dining hall, and I suspected there would be a press inside. "Clodagh, I would rather be somewhere quiet, on my own," I said. "Can we go to the infirmary?"

"Later," Clodagh said. "They're busy in there. One of the Connacht men has a deep cut—a knife slipped—and his two friends seem determined not to leave his side until they're sure Muirrin has given him the care he needs. Another man is having his ankle tended to." She eyed me narrowly. "I'll find you a quiet corner."

"But—"

"No arguments, Sibeal. To be frank, you look terrible. Your face is a greenish color, and you're shaking—look." She took my hand and held it up before me. I could not keep it steady. "See? You can't argue with that."

Installed in a cozy nook close to the fire with Clodagh's shawl around my shoulders and a cup of warm spiced ale between my hands, I sat quietly as people came and went. It was the usual practice to provide a hearty meal after a morning of bouts, but Rodan's death had disturbed the pattern. There were plenty of folk in the hall, and most of them were eating, but the talk was in lowered voices and many of the familiar faces were absent. I saw Knut among a group of island warriors. They were talking quietly, sipping their ale, gesturing in a way that suggested perhaps they were discussing the morning's combat. The Knut I saw now seemed unlike the man who had stood over Ardal this morning. Then, I had felt fury and terror spilling from the two of them. Now, exchanging easy banter with his comrades, Knut looked perfectly at home. He looked as if he belonged.

"Rat's keeping the rest of the Connacht men over in the practice area for now," Clodagh explained. "Johnny's talking to them. And Gareth's organizing the party to go and retrieve the body. This will be challenging for Johnny. It's not the kind of news he'd want brought home from a stay on the island."

At some point, Johnny would summon me to tell what I had

seen; to relate the vision that had drawn me out to that cliff top, and the reality I had found. I could not retire to my chamber until that duty was done. I must eat and drink. I must collect my wits. It was hard to do that amid the comings and goings, the noise of voices and clattering pans, the smell of spices and wood smoke. Why had I been shown the falling man? Why had that vision come to me when it was too late? Or had it? My mind had been on my own concerns, and on Ardal in particular. I had been distracted. The warning had been clear enough. The terrible truth was that if I had told someone the first time I saw the vision, I might have saved Rodan's life.

Ardal. I wanted Ardal. I wanted to talk to him, just the two of us alone. I wanted to release the churning mass of guilt and confusion that was building inside me. Ardal would listen without judging me. I could tell him anything. He would hold my hand and make me feel better again. But that made no sense at all. It was upside down and back to front, and I did not want to consider what it meant. I clutched my cup more tightly, wondering when my hands would stop shaking. A druid. Almost a druid. Falling apart like an overwrought child.

I was not accustomed to feeling this way, almost as if I were drowning. *Summon a simple technique, Sibeal, something you know so well you can do it without thinking.* A pattern of breathing, slow and steady. That was the key to calm. It was the first thing every novice learned in the nemetons.

It wouldn't come. My heart raced, my head whirled, my body was possessed by bouts of shivering. I was on the verge of tears. It would not do. Soon I must face Johnny. *Eat. Drink. Be calm*, I ordered myself. I nibbled the newly baked roll Biddy brought me. I sipped my ale. When I had achieved some measure of control over my wayward thoughts, I asked myself why a fit young man, with friends and skill and, I supposed, a good future ahead of him, would wander off, lose his balance and fall to his death.

After a while someone came to fetch me, and there was an awkward interview in which Clodagh and I sat at a table with Johnny and the leader of the Connacht men, with one or two others in attendance, and I gave my account of what had happened. I felt as if I were somewhere else, watching myself as I spoke calmly and precisely, not forgetting any detail. It was obvious how Rodan had died. I had no idea why. Perhaps his friends could cast some light on that.

I agreed to conduct a burial rite next day. Rodan had not been a man of faith, but his father followed the old ways, and the Connacht chieftain wanted to be able to tell the family their son had been laid to rest with appropriate prayers. I expressed my sympathy for the loss, and the three Connacht warriors who were present thanked me. It had been necessary to explain to them that I was a seer, and that a flash of Sight had led me to the fallen man. I did not say that I had seen the vision before, several times, and had mentioned it to nobody. When we were done, Johnny walked to the door with me, and before I went out, he said in an undertone, "We'll speak further of this, Sibeal."

"Mm," I murmured. I saw on his face that he knew I was holding something back, and I wondered if he, too, had not spoken with complete frankness in the presence of those other men.

"But not now," Johnny said. "You look quite ill. Best go and lie down for a while." His gray eyes were searching. "You can't save everyone."

~Felix~

Night falls once more. At last it is quiet.

A man died today, in a fall from a cliff top. The infirmary was full of folk; I heard this news as they spoke together. One of the visitors. An accident. I saw the glances they gave me, the men who came in and out with their wounds to be dressed and their friends in attendance. I read the message in their cold eyes, their grim-set mouths. They looked, then turned their backs on me. *That's him. That's the ill luck man.* Even the warriors who are only visiting this island give me those looks. I am not welcome here.

Perhaps I never was. What am I to this community but a burden and a trouble? I should go. As soon as I can, I will go and take my ill luck with me. Never mind the mission. Never mind the shadow that hovers just beyond the grasp of my mind, the darkness that nudges at me, seeking to be understood. I might linger here all summer and not remember. I might linger here forever, a blight on this place and its good people.

Gull comes to tend to me, gentle as always. He helps me wash and dry myself. He holds the pan for me, then squints at my water, nodding sagely.

"Gull," I tell him, "I will go soon."

"Mm-hm." He sets the pan by the door, ready to be emptied. "And where would you be going?"

"Away. Away from the island."

"That was always the intention, of course," says Gull, coming to stand by the pallet, on whose edge I sit awkwardly, my shoulders slumped, my legs dangling. "That you'd all go home when you were well, yourself, Knut and Svala. But you're not well yet, Ardal. It'll be some time before you're fit to travel. You must know that."

I do know. If I were well, I would have hurt Knut when he came this morning. I would have done him harm. I still see his eyes, cold with fear, hot with violent anger. He chose the moment when Muirrin went out; he must have been keeping watch. In an instant, there he was in the infirmary, right beside my bed. I had not even time to sit up.

"You remembered," he said. "You told."

"I remember nothing."

"You're lying. The girl, Sibeal. You told her about your brother."

I felt my whole body tighten. Sibeal. To hear her name from his lips filled me with horror.

"The two of you are close, aren't you?" Knut said, and he made a crude gesture with his hands. "That's what they're all saying. Girl can't stay away from you, druid as she claims to be. Did you know she likes wandering along those cliff paths all by herself? Slight little thing—a puff of wind could blow her away."

181

"How dare you!" I struggled to rise. He put his big hand on my shoulder and pushed me back down. "How dare you threaten her?"

"Ah. I see that I've touched a raw spot. Seems I was right, you do set a higher value on her life than on your own. I could kill you now, of course—you're as weak as a newborn babe. But that would attract too much attention."

"If you lay a finger on her, I'll—"

"You'll what? Stamp your foot? Cry? Spare me. It's within your power to protect the girl. Just keep your wretched mouth shut."

I wanted to put my hands around his neck and squeeze the life out of him. But my only strength was in my words, and my words made him laugh.

"Gull, I must leave this place," I say now. "I bring danger. I bring ill luck."

He busies himself collecting towel and cloth and bucket, hanging a garment from a peg, throwing another in a corner, finding me a clean shirt. "I've always been of the belief that a person's luck comes of itself," he says after a while. "You can't bring ill luck unless you have ill intent. But I'm not an expert on such matters. You should ask Sibeal; she's the druid."

"Where is she, Gull?" All day she has been gone. All day, my fear for her has grown, a cold heaviness in my gut.

"She went straight to her little chamber to rest. Difficult day for her."

Alarm darts through my veins. "Difficult, what do you mean?"

"She found that man's body," Gull says. "It upset her."

I am silent. This part of the story, I did not hear.

"I expect she'll tell you about it herself when she's ready. Or maybe not; she's had to give her account of it several times over, so Johnny can be quite sure what happened."

"There is some doubt?"

Gull is suddenly busy again, folding something; he's said too much already, perhaps.

"Gull?"

"Mm?"

"If Sibeal wakes, if she comes to sit by the fire tonight, I wish to speak to her alone."

"Oh, yes? You know, I suppose, that there are two reasons why I'm spending my nights in here and not in my own bed with my wife to keep me warm. One is to watch over you. The other's to provide respectability for Sibeal, since it's not quite right for her to be sleeping here with you in the next chamber. My presence makes it almost acceptable. Sibeal's family would not approve of my leaving the two of you on your own after dark."

"Just for a little," I say. "I wish only to talk to her, Gull, nothing more. I have none of those feelings toward her, the kind you imply . . . "

He looks at me, and I look at him. "Bollocks," he says.

"I do not think I know this word." I need not know it to understand his meaning.

"Rubbish. Maybe you and she like ideas and arguments. Maybe you share a bent for scholarship. But I'm a man, Ardal, same as you. There's much more than that between you."

I manage a smile. He has surprised me. Am I so transparent? "You speak like a father to a wayward son," I tell him. "Very well, I amend what I said before. My feelings for Sibeal are many and complex. Foremost among them, always, will be respect. I respect her as a druid, as a scholar and as a woman. Look me in the eye as I say this, Gull, and tell me I am a liar."

Gull grins. Now I have surprised him. "Then we'll leave the decision up to Sibeal," he says. "She may still be too tired to want anything more than a bowl of food and a good night's sleep."

"Gull?"

"Mm?"

"Thank you. I am sorry your wife must sleep alone."

"Ah, well," he says, "I expect we'll make up for it later. How about trying a walk over to the fire? If you're so keen to be off the island and away, we'd best keep working on those legs."

*   *   *

Gull is yawning by the time Sibeal emerges from her little chamber at the end of the infirmary. Her face is pale; there are smudges of exhaustion around her lovely eyes. She hugs her shawl close about her. If I could be that shawl, I would shield her with the warmth of my arms and the courage of my heart. I would keep her from all harm. Gods, how this weakness fetters me!

"You stayed up," Sibeal says, coming over to the fire where the two of us are sitting. She looks shaky on her feet, as if she might faint. "I'm sorry, I'm out of tune with time today. You should both be abed." She turns those eyes on me in a look of such care and concern that it stops my words.

"No trouble," Gull says easily. "I've been telling Ardal about today's fighting, which I suspect doesn't interest him in the least." He gets up. "Sit here, Sibeal."

"They were saying Knut acquitted himself remarkably well," says Sibeal. "You must be pleased."

He grins widely. "I enjoyed those seven days' work, I can't deny it. Bran would have been amused if he could have seen it. He always said the peaceable healer was only a thin skin covering the man I once was. Not sure I agree, to tell the truth. I love the skill a man can put into play in a good fight, the speed and strength of it, the strategy beforehand and the instinct that comes in the heat of combat. But I've had my fill of bloodshed. Patching folk up suits me better than killing them these days. Must be getting old."

"Not old, just wise," Sibeal says.

"Did you rest well, Sibeal?" I ask, though I can see the answer is no.

She shivers. "I would say my dreams were unwelcome, but I expect there is some wisdom to be gleaned from them. They were dark and confused; it will take me time to work out their meaning. Did they bring Rodan's body back, Gull?"

Gull nods, somber now. "Johnny wanted me to ask you if you're sure about performing the rite tomorrow."

"Of course."

"For now," says Gull, "I'm under instructions to make sure you eat and drink. Biddy has something set aside for you."

"I'm really not hungry."

"The strictest of instructions, from your sisters. You need not walk down to the kitchen. I can fetch your supper for you." Gull glances at me. "Ardal wants to talk to you on your own. If you're agreeable to that, I'll take time for a drink and a chat with Biddy before I come back. If you're not agreeable, I'll put my head out the door and whistle someone up."

"Thank you, Gull. We'll be fine by ourselves." She's looking into the flames, her eyes suspiciously bright. Holding back tears? What was in those dreams?

We are silent awhile when Gull is gone. The fire flickers; the shadows move; the night wind rattles the shutters.

"What did you want to talk about?" she asks, her voice small and tight.

I expected her to seek explanations. Why did I warn her not to go out alone? Why would I take it upon myself to say such a thing? I have no good answer ready; I cannot tell her what Knut said. She would go straight to Johnny, and Johnny would confront Knut, and in one form or another, disaster would follow. Knut will stop at nothing to keep me from talking. Whatever lies behind this veil of forgetting, it must be powerful indeed. The only way I can keep Sibeal safe is by leaving Inis Eala. I am not strong enough yet, but Gull will help me. He trained Knut to expertise with the sword in seven days, after all. Surely he can train me to walk, to run, to be my own master again. Then I will go. I had planned to tell her I have decided this. Instead I say, "You talk, Sibeal. I will listen."

So she tells me: the vision she had of a falling man, seen over and over before it came true, and how she did not act until it was too late. She describes the dead man down on the rocks, his head broken open. She doubts that she should perform the burial rite, although she has already agreed, for she thinks perhaps she is not fitted for the calling of a druid after all. Inadequate. Confused. These are only some of the things she calls herself. I sit silent, listening.

"How can I do it?" Sibeal asks, not expecting an answer from me. "How can I go out there and speak prayers over the body of a man who, but for my lack of insight, might still be alive today? All I needed to do was talk to someone, describe the man in the vision, work out who he was and warn him. But my mind was on other things, and I didn't tell anyone. What would Ciarán think of me?" I see something remarkable: tears spilling from her eyes and flooding her pale cheeks. She seems unaware of them. "Ardal, I know the Sight does not always show the truth. It doesn't predict the future or reflect the past—it shows us images we can put together to make answers. You understand that, don't you? Oh, gods, now it sounds as if I'm making excuses . . . I can't get past the belief that this is my fault. That I was warned so I could stop it from happening and that I was too slow to act. What would Rodan's family think if they knew he would be laid to rest by the person who let him die? Why can't I get this right, Ardal, why?" She turns her brimming eyes on me, then buries her face in her hands.

I am up, on my feet. I take four steps and sit down on the bench beside her. My heart is pounding, a drum for dancing. My arms go around her shoulders. She turns toward me and presses her face against my chest. I hold her; she weeps. I remember all the things I said to her last night, and I am ashamed of myself.

We sit for some time thus. I am hoping Muirrin does not decide to come back with Gull to check on Sibeal's welfare. Our pose could be that of a brother comforting a sister; it is quite chaste. My thoughts, however, are not those of a brother. Gull has seen this already. I raise a hand to stroke Sibeal's hair, fine, rippling hair, as dark as a crow's wing. She is like a girl from an old tale, a forbidden princess, an enchantress in a mysterious wood. She is the rarest creature I have encountered in all my life. Even in the lost part, the part I cannot remember, there can surely have been nobody like her.

"Hush," I murmur. "There, now." And after a while I hum a tune, as if I were lulling a child.

"Ardal," she says, her voice muffled against my shirt. A clean shirt; I thank Gull for that.

"Mm?"

"What is that song?"

"A lullaby. *I will call a hundred larks from the meadow, to sing my little one to sleep. I will call a hundred owls from the dark forest, to watch over my little one's cradle. I will summon a hundred stars from the heavens, to light my little one's dreams.*" My mother's voice comes to me, singing in the Norse tongue, and I see her blue eyes with their tilted corners, her flaxen braid coiled like a golden crown around her head, her linen apron with its rows of red embroidery, houses and horses and trees. I learned both tongues from the cradle, *Brezhoneg* and Norse. No wonder I have a facility for translation. I would like my mother to meet Sibeal, but I know this will never happen.

"What a lovely song. Gods, I didn't know I had so many tears in me." She sits up; withdraws her arms from around my waist. I release her. It feels like giving up my heart. But perhaps that is already lost.

Sibeal is delving for a handkerchief. She finds one tucked into her belt, wipes her eyes, struggles to compose herself. Even with red eyes and streaming nose, she is beautiful. Suddenly she sits straight, staring at me. "Ardal! You walked by yourself!"

So I did. Only now do I realize it. "Four steps," I say, feeling my mouth twist. "A true feat of strength."

"You did something you couldn't do before. Four steps today, perhaps eight tomorrow. Evan did say it might be midsummer before you are well enough to travel. I'm truly proud of you, Ardal."

And now I can no more tell her I must leave the island than I can summon the hundred stars I sang of. I should go away. I must go. I am the ill luck man, bringer of doom and destruction. I am the one who should have drowned with the ship; I am the one who should have fallen from the cliff. But I live, and every moment I am here I put her life at risk. *Say it, Felix.* I cannot. For tonight, let me pretend that I can stay here. Let me pretend that I can hold her in my arms again; let me dream of a future with the two of us in it, together. Let me believe in miracles.

CHAPTER 8

Rodan was buried among the island's own departed, who lay in an area sheltered by a dry-stone wall, on a rise with a fine view westward over the sea. A message had been sent to his chieftain in Connacht, carried by a man from the mainland settlement. As for Rodan's comrades, they would stay and see out the full period of their training. All of them said that was what he would have expected.

Too much death. Too much unease. Each morning I got up, intending to walk to the seer's cave and spend the day in meditation and prayer. Each morning I found a reason not to go: Clodagh had a sore back; Muirrin was busy with injured men and needed help; the garden had to be weeded; I should be keeping an eye on Ardal, who had developed a sudden fierce will to be strong again and was inclined to exhaust himself working too hard at it. He could walk out into the garden now, and sit in the sun watching as I dug and pruned and harvested. Whether he had remembered any more of his past, I had no idea. He had gone very quiet, even with me.

In this manner days passed, days in which I became more and more aware of the mutterings in the community about ill luck and who might have brought it to Inis Eala. Now every accidental fall, every dispute, every small reversal seemed to reinforce the belief that an evil had come among them. Johnny told me that the foolish talk would pass, and that I should not let it concern me. My sisters dismissed it. Cathal's mouth grew tighter, his face paler as he heard it. His eyes were haunted. I knew he was thinking about his father.

To reach the seer's cave I must go past the place where Rodan had fallen. I could not put off the expedition forever. On a clear, bright morning I set out with my provisions and my warm cloak, and Fang in attendance. I would go to that place on the cliff top and offer prayers for Rodan's spirit. Then I would walk on to spend the day in Finbar's sanctuary. I would seek a wisdom higher than that of humankind.

Fang's behavior had grown still odder. She would run a short distance, then halt as if turned to stone, her muzzle pointed out to sea. When she was in this pose, the dog was impervious to all else. There was no point in calling her. Even passing sheep were ignored. Then, abruptly, Fang would come back to herself and run after me as if nothing had happened. "What is it, little dog?" I asked her as we followed the track toward the cliffs. "What do you see?" But the only reply was the rush of the waves below us, and the high calling of the birds.

Fang's erratic pace made the walk slower than it might have been. I was sufficiently concerned for her welfare not to go so far ahead that the dog might lose sight of me. Then again, perhaps I was a coward. Perhaps my feet were dragging because I did not want to reach that place where Rodan had gone over. I gritted my teeth and walked on.

I rounded a corner with the dog at my heels and my heart faltered. A naked figure stood poised, arms stretched out as if for flight, bare feet on the very edge of the cliff. Her hair streamed in the wind; her eyes were fixed on the horizon, away to the north. Svala, like a lovely carven figurehead. If I made a sound, if I startled her, she would fall. She was standing in exactly the spot where Rodan had gone over.

Fang had no such scruples. She pushed past me, trotted ahead along the path and stopped to sniff at the heap of clothing Svala had abandoned on the ground.

"Svala," I said in a murmur. "Step back from the edge." Even as I spoke, my mind showed me an image of her falling.

She turned, gloriously confident of her balance, and walked over to the path. She stooped to pick up her gown. My heart was pounding, my palms clammy. I forced myself to breathe.

"You frightened me," I said. "I thought . . . " No, I would not tell her what I had thought, for it was obviously wrong. She'd had no intention of jumping. I saw that in her proud stance and in her calm eyes. "Never mind," I said, knowing she could not understand.

Svala donned gown and shawl. She did not seem to have shoes with her. Once dressed, she moved to one side to let me pass on my way to the cave. It was not until I had gone some distance along the track that I realized she was following me, steady and silent, a few paces behind.

Logic said, *She's big, she's strong, she's unpredictable, and the path is narrow.* Instinct said, *Walk on,* so I did, even though it became apparent when I turned to look that Fang was not coming with us. We reached the opening that led to Finbar's cave. I slipped through, making my way along the narrow, dim tunnel, and Svala came after me, quiet as a shadow. I should have been frightened, perhaps. But it felt right that she was here with me. It felt like a turning point.

Wild creature that she so often seemed, Svala understood from the first why I was in the cave. A moment after I settled cross-legged by the still pool, she was there by my side, back straight, hands loose in her lap, eyes on the water. She stayed beside me as I went through my slow patterns of breathing; as I spoke prayers, repeated passages of lore and waited for the wisdom of the gods. Not a sound did she utter. Not a move did she make.

My preparation was long. I waited until the sun struck down through the opening above the water, filling the shadowy cavern with gold. The pool became a vessel of light. Now. Now was the time.

I gazed upon the surface and in my mind I said: *I was led to save Ardal's life so he could fulfill a mission. The runes seemed to confirm it. Both of us believed it was urgent that he remember and act. But he will not tell what he has remembered. It seems to me that this silence makes the whispers louder, the talk of an ill luck man. That sets a shadow on everyone. How will the truth be known?*

Nothing. Nothing at all but the light on the water and the steady sound of Svala's breathing. All this time she had kept watch beside me. I waited, and it seemed to me the cave grew quieter, and the water clearer, as if it had nothing at all to show. The gods were silent. Even Finbar would not help me. It was all too easy to supply my own answer. *You are distracted. Your mind strays all too easily. As a seer, you are becoming unreliable.*

Svala's hand closed around my arm. After so long in trance, I jumped at her touch like a startled hare. My heart raced. I glanced across, and she met my eyes, putting a finger to her lips. *Shhh.* Still holding on to me, she turned her gaze back on the pool, and after a moment I did the same.

Something was stirring on the water's surface now. A vision was taking form. Waves crashing onto rocks; a ship tossed about by monstrous seas. Even as I saw it in the water, I felt the decking shudder under my feet, the whip of salt spray, the bruising thump of folk thrown this way and that. A gale. A storm. A tempest, sweeping the vessel before it like a scrap of debris. A powerful dread gripped me; it fettered me more tightly than Svala's strong hand. *This will destroy us. No man can survive such a storm . . .*

And then, land. Rearing up with a dark inevitability, land. A craggy island, a lonely mountain rising from the sea, wearing a white skirt of breakers. The ship barreled forward, propelled by the surge. In my mind, men were screaming, cursing, calling to their gods to save them. The vessel plowed on, and now I could see a narrow opening between two rocky headlands, and beyond it a bay, and a strip of level, pebbly shore. *To oars!* someone shouted.

There was a juddering, a shivering, and the ship's course

changed. Not straight for the rocks now, but toward that gap, heading for safe water. *Pull! Pull!* The vessel entered the narrow passage, the rocks so close I could see the shellfish clinging to the dark surfaces. Monstrous cliffs loomed to either side; the boat was in shadow. *Pull!* And then we were in the bay, the rowers gasping with effort, the ship slowing as they rested their arms. Safe. Oh gods, safe at last.

Like a bolt of lightning from a clear sky it comes, rearing out of the water right by the prow, taller than an oak tree, taller than a castle tower. Its eyes are bright with malice, its claws sharp as scythes, its mouth . . . Oh, its mouth lined with long white teeth, and its slavering, blue-green tongue . . . Its neck snakes from side to side. Looking, choosing: *Which will I take first?* Men scream. They scramble for crossbows, spears, knives. *Pull!* yells someone with more presence of mind than the others, and the crew takes up oars, turning the ship in an attempt to evade the beast. The creature's monstrous head whips down to deck level; its foul breath sets us choking and gasping. It toys with us awhile, moving one way, the other way, so the ship cannot pass. It slaps the water with its tail, making great waves. *Pull! Pull!* One man, at least, keeps his terror in check. Closer to the shore now, closer still and . . . A scream like ripping cloth as the creature reaches out a forefoot and, with a stabbing movement, plunges its claw through a crewman's chest, impaling him. It tosses him high, opens its jaws, catches him as he falls and, in a convulsive gulp, swallows him whole.

Breathe, Sibeal. The vision faded to shreds and fragments; the boat on an erratic course toward the shore, wild-eyed men rowing with the strength of sheer terror; the water-beast opening its long-toothed mouth to show a welter of bloody flesh and splintered bone, then reaching out for another hapless crewman. Before I could see him taken the vision was gone, and there was nothing but the calm water of the seer's pool, golden under the midday sun. *Breathe. Use what you have learned.*

My gut twisted in revulsion, my skin crawled, my heart shrank from the horror of it. I breathed. I prayed. I worked on not being sick. When I could move, I turned to Svala, who had taken her hand from my arm and was waiting, silent, beside me. The look on her face shocked me. Svala was smiling. Her eyes were full of light, as if what she had seen had uplifted her and made her joyous. Perhaps her vision had been quite different from mine. Perhaps the gods had granted her a glimpse of happier times, before she came to Inis Eala, before she suffered the loss that broke her heart.

I reached for my water skin, took out the stopper and drank deeply. I offered it to Svala, but she pushed it away. Making a cup of her hands, she took water from the seer's pool, lifting it to her mouth to drink. I was shocked; it seemed an act of sacrilege.

Svala was trying to tell me something, gesturing. The pool; herself—fingers tapping her breastbone with some force—then a sweeping movement toward the cave entry. The pool again, herself, then me, then a mime that was unmistakably of rowing. *I want to go. I must go there. You take me.*

"You can't mean that," I breathed. "You can't." Go to that place of monsters and impossible waves? Svala and me, rowing beside each other? I must have misunderstood. But then, if she had seen a different vision, perhaps she was asking to go somewhere else, somewhere she could not describe to me. *I want to go home. Back to the place I come from.*

"You will go home, Svala," I said, ignoring the talk I had heard in the dining hall, about Knut perhaps being invited to stay for a trial period on Inis Eala, where his superb combat skills would be an asset. "You and Knut. Johnny can arrange for you to go as soon as he's satisfied that you're well enough." I wondered about that. One could not describe the strapping Svala as unwell, but she was not as other women were, and I could understand Johnny's reluctance to send her over to the mainland settlement or beyond. I could not see her living her life in any ordinary village or indeed any ordinary household. Knut did his best to protect her, but he could hardly do so all the time, and she had the capacity to wreak havoc. "A ship, yes. A voyage to . . . the place you set out from. Ulfricsfjord. Not with me. With Knut. Your husband." That, I could not mime, but I hoped she would recognize the names.

Svala rose to her considerable height, towering over me where I knelt by the water. Her fists were clenched. She looked at me, then spat, precisely, on the cavern floor beside her feet. A sound issued from her, an explosion of fury and frustration.

I felt somewhat as a child might on finding itself alone in a field with a horned bull. Her anger frightened me. We were far from the settlement and I no longer had Fang with me. But then, I had not discouraged her from coming with me. It was possible we both wanted the same thing: truth. I must try harder to understand.

"A serpent," I said, kneeling up and indicating the shape with my hands, next to the pool. "Mouth, bites, like this. Claws, like this." I forced myself into a bizarre reenactment of the hideous scene—gods, I had seen this; in my first vision of Rodan's fall I had seen a man taken by a sea monster—and saw instant recognition in Svala's eyes. Disarmed in an instant, she squatted down next to me, watching in apparent fascination.

Boat. How could I show a boat? Ah—the half-empty water skin. I pushed the stopper in firmly, then floated the skin along the pond, showing with my hands the rowers, the shore to which they were heading. As the cumbersome vessel passed Svala, she reached out to add her own part to the story, using her arm, her hand, her fingers to play the part of the monster. *Snap! I take this man for my first bite. Snatch! I take this one now. And now this, and this . . .* There was no longer any doubt that we had seen the same vision.

I brought the vessel back to the side of the pond, beached it and left it, rising to my feet. "This place?" I asked her, motioning toward the little scene. "You, I, go *this* place?"

She leapt up and seized my arms with both hands, nodding, smiling with an energy that was almost frenzied. *At last! At last someone understands!*

"But *why*? Why, Svala? And where is it?" I swept my hand in a circle, then pointed north, south, east, west.

Her arm rose with complete confidence. *Due north.* Due north? What lay there? The Orcades, destination of their original voyage, were to the northeast. I knew of no land at all to the north.

"I wish you could explain why," I said, more to myself than to my companion. "That might be the key to everything. If only you could tell me your story, Svala."

She put her arms around me, shocking me profoundly, for it was the last thing I had expected from her. I returned the gesture, saddened that I had not fully understood, and perhaps never would; concerned that what she seemed to want was a crazy thing, a thing that made no sense at all, even if I had been able to make it happen.

Svala murmured something, not words, more of a singing sound, like a snatch of mournful chant. She was so much taller than I that in this embrace my cheek was against her heart, and in the moment of her singing I felt its message beating straight into me, the rhythm that of a great marching drum. *Home! Home!*

Dear gods. Home? That island with not a scrap of anything growing on it, that rock beset by howling winds and mountainous seas? No one could survive in such a place. I tried to imagine Knut and Svala eking out a living in some isolated hut, scraping shellfish off the rocks and bolting their door at night while the monster swam about the bay. Impossible. I could not believe it. They could not have come from such a place. Besides, it was our reef the boat had been wrecked on, not that of a wild, far-off isle. It made no sense at all.

"I'll try to help," I murmured, not knowing where to start. A place like that was surely home to nothing but sea creatures, and even those probably had the common sense to keep away lest they become the monster's next meal. Perhaps the vision was entirely symbolic.

We walked back toward the settlement. Fang was still nowhere to be seen, but halfway along the track we met Knut coming the other way. His face was pale, his jaw tight, his eyes furious. He strode up to us and took hold of Svala's arm. She stood quiet in his grasp, eyes down.

"Where you go?" He hurled the question at me. "I look—wife—everywhere." A sweep of the arm.

"We've been walking." Every part of me was on edge.

"Sorry," Knut said, far too late for me to believe he meant it. He attempted a smile and achieved a grimace. "Worried. Wife . . . "

Lost for the right word, he tapped the side of his head. "Not safe wander here. I look all over."

"Knut," I said with some hesitation, "where did you live before you came here? Where is your home, yours and Svala's?"

He narrowed his eyes. "No speak Irish good," he said.

"Never mind." I wondered if he lost his rudimentary Irish when asked a question he did not want to answer. "I'll go on ahead, then. Thank you for coming with me, Svala."

I went past them, and as I walked away I heard him speaking to her in a furious undertone. I wondered very much about the increasing talk that Knut might settle on the island. No doubt he would fit in well. He was, to all accounts, a warrior of great skill, and people seemed to like him. Since I would be leaving Inis Eala at the end of summer, the fact that I felt an instinctive distrust of the man was irrelevant. I did not think Svala could ever be happy here.

Perhaps I should share today's vision with Johnny. Or with someone else—Gull, Clodagh, Cathal? Should I talk to Knut properly, with Jouko or Kalev present to translate? Perhaps I should wait until I had a clearer idea of what those images had meant, the images that made no sense at all, for among the many faces on the stricken vessel there had been three I knew: Ardal, white as linen, his jaw set grimly; the young man I thought was his brother, Paul, pushing someone out of the way, seizing an oar, shouting orders. And Knut, rowing with the rest of them. Not a vision of the future or of a possible future. I had seen Paul's drowned body here on the island; I had performed his burial rite. In the vision he had been alive, strong. He had been the one who took control, wresting order from chaos. The images had been of time past, imagined or real. If it was real, then when he had given Johnny his sketchy account of the voyage, Knut had only told half the story.

~Felix~

I walk. From this side to that, from that side to this. I pause for breath, willing strength to my limbs. Then again, from this side to that side. Muirrin eyes me as she tends to a man's knee, but makes no comment.

Sibeal has gone to the seer's cave, the place she spoke of, where she can find peace and set her thoughts in order. I think she is angry with me. She would have me tell what I have remembered, piece by piece. She cannot understand why I hold my silence. There is something hidden in my mind, something perilous. I think it has the power to wreak havoc here.

The ill luck man. Too many have suffered because of me. To and fro I walk, to and fro, and with each pace I think of them: my father, who almost lost the Duke's favor because I could not stop my tongue; my mother, who had two fine sons and now has none; my brother, who was the friend of my heart and the companion of my journey, and who is dead. I cannot stay here. Who is to say the shipwreck was not my fault, caused by some act of negligence that I have forgotten? Who is to say what disasters I may have caused in that lost time? I must leave this place without delay.

Gull comes, and we go outside to sit on the bench in the garden.

"No more walking for now," he says, settling beside me. "Attempting too much too soon is asking for failure. Practice breathing. It is part of the cure. You nearly died, Ardal. Your body must learn to work again, and it cannot learn if you wear it out."

"This is too slow," I grumble, knowing my wise friend deserves better for the time and care he gives me. I am not angry with Gull, only with my weak body.

"If you want to find yourself back in bed for another turning of the moon, then by all means ignore my advice. You asked me to help you, Ardal. If I were training a man to fight again after a battle injury, I'd pace him just the way I'm pacing you."

I straighten my back. I attempt a few long breaths of the kind I've been shown, filling my chest slowly, stopping just before the worst of the pain will hit me. Afterward, I say, "I'm sorry."

"That's fine, provided you keep listening to good advice when it's given. We'll sit here a bit longer, and then we'll try some work on your arms."

*　　*　　*

He makes me bend and stretch, and it tires me. I do as I'm told. Gull declares himself satisfied by my efforts. When he tells me it is time to go inside and lie down awhile, for my body needs frequent rest, I bite back the words that spring to my lips: *There's no time for rest!* Truth to tell, my limbs ache, my chest hurts, I want the comfort of my bed more than anything. Almost anything.

As I sit by Gull, wondering if I can summon the strength to climb the two steps to the back door, that door opens and Johnny and Cathal come out, the latter carrying a sizeable box bound with leather straps.

"What's this?" Gull asks.

"We'd like a word with Ardal." Johnny turns to me. "These are some of the items washed up after the wreck. We want you to look at them, see if they help jog your memory." He glances at Gull. "Is now a good time? You could leave us awhile, if you like. Go and see Biddy."

Gull grins. "You think I'm neglecting my wife? I doubt she'll want me under her feet when she's busy in the kitchen."

Johnny returns the smile; he is not a particularly handsome man, but there is a gravity and balance in his features that compels the eye. The swirling raven tattoo only adds further distinction. "Go on," he says. "We can manage here without you."

Cathal isn't saying anything. He has placed the box on the seat beside me, and now unfastens the straps. When Gull is gone, he lifts the lid.

"I'm happy to hear you are improving, Ardal," says Johnny. "I know from Gull that your own efforts have played a part in your recovery." He hesitates, then goes on. "You understand, I'm sure, how important it is for me to know about the vessel, the crew, the cargo, the purpose of the voyage, so I can inform the appropriate people about these losses. I dispatched a message to Ulfricsfjord some time ago, based on what Knut told me. But his knowledge is limited, and I can't be sure my message went to the right quarter."

"Sibeal says you're holding back information." Cathal is far more blunt. I hear the hostility in his voice. "You must tell Johnny everything you can remember. Why you were on the ship, who else was with you, whose resources made the voyage possible. What brought you to Erin in the first place."

"Ardal," Johnny says, "if you've recalled anything at all that may be relevant to what has occurred, you must tell me. Inis Eala is under my leadership. I am responsible for the welfare of its people and the safety of its community. While visitors are here, I ask of them the same standard of behavior I expect from every man and woman on this island. That includes telling the full truth."

Seated on the bench with the two of them standing in front of me, I feel somewhat at a disadvantage. I do not know how to answer Johnny. "I remember nothing of the wreck, or of the voyage," I tell him, "except that my brother was there, and then a wave came over and washed me away."

"The voyage was to the Orcades, Knut told me. A promise of settlement for the crew, some of whom had wives with them. Some other purpose for yourself, your brother, and an older man who traveled with you."

"I remember nothing of that." I meet his eyes, and hope he can see that on this matter I am indeed telling the truth.

"We want you to look at the items in the box, Ardal," Johnny says. "It seems to me they may relate to your mission in some way. I have a few theories, but I want your ideas before I put them to you."

I sense what he leaves unsaid. *Otherwise you may latch on to whatever is most convenient, so you need not tell us the truth.* "Very well," I say. What was it Sibeal said they had found? Silks? The covers of a book?

Cathal takes the things out one by one and lays them on the bench. The length of fabric is a shadow of what it was; the sea has turned its original rich violet to a faint red-blue, and salt crusts the delicate folds. The silver arm-rings and torc are tarnished, the pages of the great book are blank of calligraphy. The sea has drowned all its wisdom. It was once a book of tales, scribed in half-uncial, with tiny illustrations of creatures and flowers. A lovely thing. There are smaller items, trinkets for the Jarl's wife and daughter: a flock of tiny bronze birds, a little coffer bound with silver and decorated with bright enamels, an elaborate finger-ring. I was there the day Eoghan chose that cloth. He said it would look fine on the Jarl's daughter, she being of Norse blood and fair as a spring morning. I know the man who made the little bronze birds. I remember my brother's delight when the prince showed us the book. Paul cannot read. Could not read. He smiled at the tiny foxes and owls and badgers, the fierce-eyed crow and the white pony.

In my mind, Knut draws his finger across his neck. *Shhhhk!* Even as the memories of that time flood back—ah, Matha, wise councillor, it seems you, too, were lost to the sea—I say to Johnny, "I am most grateful for the kindness and care you have shown me. But I cannot tell you anything about these items." I will not lie to him, and that is not a lie.

"Let me put another question," Johnny says levelly. "Sibeal believes you are a man of some education. Imagine these goods before they were damaged by the sea. For what purpose might such items be on a ship traveling from Ulfricsfjord to the Orcades, do you think? You can answer that question without the need to be specific."

"I am no trader."

Cathal reaches out, takes me by the arms and hauls me to my feet. He does not let go once I'm up. "Answer the question," he says. In the quiet of that tone there is a menace that chills my heart.

"Costly items," I say. For a moment I consider telling them what I have just remembered: my time at Muredach's court, my acquaintance with his son Eoghan, prince of Munster, the mission to the Jarl. Can there be anything there that would cause Knut to make his threats? I do not know. I cannot know. I remember nothing after I first stepped onto *Freyja*, save the storm, and Paul, and the wave. It is too great a risk. I hold Sibeal's life in my hands. "I imagine they might have been a gift," I say. "All seem of very fine quality. Such a gift might be made by a king or prince, an influential chieftain. The book suggests a monastic involvement, perhaps."

"Let him go, Cathal," Johnny says, not raising his voice, and Cathal complies. My arms hurt where he held me. Why is he so hostile? "Have you any idea which king, prince or influential chieftain might choose to send such gifts to the Orcades, Ardal? Are you quite sure you have not seen them before?"

"I am sure of very little." Gods, those others—there were five others with us, Artan and Donn, Fiac and Demman, young Colm on his first sea voyage, all of us set out from Muredach's court— were they on the ship when it foundered? All gone, all drowned? My knees stop supporting me and I slump back onto the bench, willing the two men to go away and leave me with my tangled thoughts.

Perhaps I have turned white, for Johnny says, "No more for now. Pack the things up, Cathal. I want another word with Muirrin, then I'll walk back over with you." He goes into the infirmary.

Cathal packs. It does not take long. Nobody comes. When he is done he moves to lean against the wall beside me. It is a casual pose, almost lounging. His eyes tell me quite a different story. This is a man I do not want as an enemy.

"I have something to say to you." Cathal is keeping his tone level. "I'll say it quickly. I have family here on the island. I have a wife I love more than life itself, and a child yet unborn. If someone has sent you here, someone with ill intent toward me, know that I have the capacity to destroy you and that I will do so without hesitation. Sibeal's fondness for you will make not a scrap of difference. Now tell me the truth, Ardal. On whose orders have you come here? What fell master set you in our midst to wreak your havoc on our dreams?"

I am too surprised to respond. Cathal believes I was sent here to do him harm, to injure his loved ones? Why would he think that? I open my mouth to tell him his suspicions are nonsense, then close it again. While any part of my past remains forgotten, I cannot know why I am on this island or for what purpose. Yes, I traveled north on a mission for the king of Munster. We bore betrothal gifts from his son to the daughter of the Orcadian Jarl, lovely things she never received. It was a peaceable mission, and my role in it merely that of interpreter. But until I can remember what went awry, what left us broken and sinking on the rocks off Inis Eala, I cannot assure Cathal that I am blameless. I cannot tell him anything. And I want to tell, not because he is formidable and I fear him, though that is true, but because I hear the sincerity in his voice, and the pain.

The silence has drawn out. He is waiting, night-black eyes fixed on me. "I do not remember everything, Cathal," I tell him. "If your enemy seeks you out, I think it unlikely he would use me as his agent."

"Unlikely." His tone is flat. "That answer is inadequate, Ardal. I don't trust a man who holds back information when he need not. You've remembered something. I see it in your eyes. It was there the moment I lifted those things out of the box. I can think of only one reason why you won't talk, and I don't like that reason. *Why were you on the ship? Who sent you, and for what purpose?*"

I say nothing. I will Johnny to come back. A moment later, I hear his voice from within the infirmary, bidding Muirrin a courteous farewell. I breathe again.

"If anything happens to Clodagh," Cathal says in a furious undertone, "or to the child, I'll make you talk, Ardal. I can do it, believe me. Another warning. You'd best step back from your friendship with Sibeal. She's young, she saved your life under extraordinary circumstances, and she feels a bond of sorts, no doubt. It can't be good for her to get involved with a man who won't tell the truth. Whatever it is you're doing, don't embroil my wife's young sister in it."

I swallow my rage. In a way, his attack is justified. "As soon as I am strong enough I will leave this place," I said. "I wish you and your family nothing but good, Cathal. But don't you see, I can't—" My voice cracks; I am not yet as strong as I need to be. "Until I remember all of it, there is no certainty," I say more quietly. "Not for you; not for me; not for anyone here. That's the curse of the ill luck man."

His eyes have narrowed. "What do you mean?" he asks, his tone quite different.

I do not answer, for across the garden someone else is approaching: Knut, tight-jawed, striding fast. As he comes up to us, Johnny emerges from the infirmary.

Knut's ice-blue gaze sweeps over us, pausing on the box, which is now closed and strapped. "Look for wife," he explains. "You see her?"

"No," says Cathal.

"Svala's not here," adds Johnny.

Knut looks at me. "None of us has seen her," I say in Norse. There is an unspoken question on his face. He's been shown this box before; he knows what it holds. He's seen me with Cathal. His eyes ask: *What have you told, ill luck man?* He turns on his heel and leaves.

I see the jetty at Ulfricsfjord, men loading supplies, the crew readying the vessel to sail. One of them has Knut's face. Paul is keeping guard over the box that holds the gifts and the chest with its cargo of silver pieces. Colm is excited, his gaze going everywhere, his enthusiasm spreading to the rest of them, even the weathered Norse crewmen. The others tease him, saying he'll be sure to meet a buxom Norse girl and achieve another first along the way. A girl. A woman. But not on the ship, because there are no women on *Freyja*. A crew of Norse sailors, a party of Irish courtiers, and with them a pair of brothers, *Breizhiz* both.

I'm on the verge of saying it to Johnny and Cathal. *This woman, Svala—she was not on the ship when it left Ulfricsfjord.* What the significance of that is, I have no idea, but the need to tell is strong in me. My memory of Knut's eyes stops my tongue. There is peril in that last, lost memory. In this moment I understand what Cathal is feeling, the turmoil that has led him to threaten me. Misery washes through me. I look up at Johnny, and he looks back at me. A strong, clever, just man; a true leader. A man who would listen, I think, if I told the truth. But what good is an incomplete truth, one in which the missing piece might place them all in peril, the wife and child for whom Cathal so fears, generous Gull, and Sibeal, most precious of all?

"I want to leave the island," I tell Johnny. "The moment I can fend for myself, you must send me away."

~Sibeal~

I would tell Ardal about Svala's vision first. He might interpret it as something cryptic, needing scholarly consideration. After all, the scene had been like something from an ancient story, with its lonely isle, its massive seas, its fearsome monster and desperate men. But perhaps Ardal would tell me it was true. Perhaps he would remember.

I walked briskly back to the settlement. As I passed the dining hall, the door opened and Clodagh stuck her head out. "Sibeal! Come in here!"

Inside, I was somewhat surprised to see Muirrin seated in the kitchen corner with a cup of mead before her on the table and her cheeks flushed a becoming shade of pink. Biddy sat beside her, and Brenna opposite. "What's this?" I asked, seating myself beside Brenna and accepting the mead I was offered. Muirrin was hardly seen outside the infirmary during the day, and for a moment I had been concerned that some misfortune had occurred, another disaster for which the community could blame the ill luck man. But there were smiles all around.

"Tell her, Muirrin," said Clodagh.

"Tell me what?"

My eldest sister looked at me across the table. I saw the joy that lit her eyes, and guessed the news before she spoke. "Sibeal, I'm expecting a child. At last! I thought it would never happen, and now . . . " She had tears in her eyes.

"Oh, Muirrin, that's wonderful. Congratulations." I went around the table to embrace her, thinking how far my mind had drifted, these last years, from the concerns of hearth and home. I had never considered it unusual that after more than six years of marriage Muirrin and Evan had no children. It had not occurred to me that they might have wanted them, perhaps badly, and have faced the possibility of never being parents. I had simply thought of them as healers, dedicated to their profession.

"I've suspected it for a while," Muirrin said, "but I didn't tell anyone except Evan, because . . . well, we've been disappointed before, thinking I was with child and then . . . But I'm sure now. I even have a little belly—look."

Muirrin was a small, slender woman, like all of us sisters. Under the practical homespun of her gown, her stomach was indeed very slightly rounded. Even I knew this meant her pregnancy was a fair way on, three turnings of the moon or four. Looking at Clodagh, whose form currently resembled that of a very ripe fruit, I felt a deep shiver of unease. The dreams, the visions, the murmurings among the islanders . . . *Gods, keep my sisters safe*, I prayed. *Let their children be born whole and healthy.*

"We're all taking the afternoon off work, even Muirrin," Clodagh said. "We're going to find a nice corner in the sun and sit there doing absolutely nothing. You, too, Sibeal."

A protest was on my lips, but I held it back. I had never seen that look on Muirrin's face before, save perhaps when she told us Evan had asked her to be his wife. Her happiness was a gift of great worth, and I would do nothing at all to spoil it. "Biddy, you'll be a grandmother again!" I said. Clem and Annie had three children, Sam and Brenna one.

Biddy's amiable features were pink with pleasure. "And that man of mine will be a grandfather," she said. "Not that he doesn't think of my lads as his own, of course. But this is different."

Evan was the only one of Biddy's three sons who had been fathered by Gull. Sam and Clem were the offspring of her first husband. It was easy to imagine Gull as grandfather to a tiny child. I saw him singing songs; telling tales; holding a small hand in his big, maimed one and leading his grandson down to the shore to watch the boats come in. Yes, it was a boy I saw: a curly-headed mite with almond skin and mischievous dark eyes. A sturdy, healthy child. I remembered my vision of Clodagh's infant, tiny and frail, naked in the forest, and suppressed a shiver. "Has Gull heard the news?" I asked.

"Muirrin told him earlier," Biddy said. "He needs time to come to terms with such tidings, welcome as they are. Brings back the past, you see. He doesn't talk about it, but a long time ago, years before he and I were wed, he lost his whole family, mother and father, sisters and brothers, wife and children, all slain by raiders. He'd have done away with himself, but for the Chief's intervention. Gull's content here. He loves the family he has now. But that sort of thing never goes away. The shadow lingers. He'll look at his new grandchild and see the babes he lost." I saw a trace of that shadow on her own face, and wondered how many times she had gentled Gull through his nightmares.

The apple grove would have been a good place to sit and talk, but Clodagh could not manage such a long walk today. The baby had shifted and was pressing down awkwardly, her back was aching, and between her discomfort and Cathal's dreams, she was short of sleep.

"Not the kitchen garden," said Brenna firmly. "If Muirrin's in sight of the infirmary she'll be wanting to go back up there and start brewing something. Nowhere near the work room, or Clodagh won't be able to keep her hands off the loom. I don't know what it is with you Sevenwaters girls, but you seem to like being constantly busy."

"It's our mother's influence," Clodagh said. "She never was comfortable with idleness. Why don't we go to that sheltered area out the back of the married quarters?"

"Take some of those oatcakes with you," said Biddy, who evidently did not plan to come with us. "And a bit of cheese. Sibeal, I'll give you a basket."

It was no surprise to me that Clodagh went to her chamber and fetched her embroidery, so she would have something to do while we talked. She was working a border on a tiny tunic, fronds of seaweed and curious goggle-eyed fish. "You won't have to sew a stitch for your baby," she told Muirrin with a smile, settling on one of the two wooden benches placed in this sunny corner. The wall of the married quarters screened us from one side, and a lone blackthorn from the other. "Everything I've made for mine can be handed on."

"Just as well," Muirrin said wryly. "I may be able to stitch a wound, but I doubt if I'd be up to such delicate work as that. My infant will be proud to wear your handiwork, Clodagh."

"I've already passed Fergal's smallest garments on to Annie's youngest," Brenna put in. "He's grown apace. Takes after his father."

"Where is Fergal this afternoon?" I asked idly.

"With a clutch of other children, under Alba's care. By the time she settles down and has a child of her own, she'll be expert." Brenna's tone changed. "It shocks me to think Alba liked that fellow, Rodan, gods rest his spirit. I saw through him the moment he tried to worm his way into Suanach's favor. According to her, Rodan assumed she'd be ready to open her legs as soon as he asked her." She glanced at me. "I hope I don't offend you, Sibeal. We women can be rather frank in our discussion when there are no men around to hear us."

"Rodan must have thought himself irresistible." Clodagh stabbed her needle into the linen with more force than was strictly necessary. "No sooner did he get a refusal from Suanach than he was trying again with Flidais. We should not speak ill of the dead, of course. But I'll be happy when these Connacht men are gone. It hasn't been a good time. There's unrest everywhere."

The seed of an idea had started to grow in my mind, and I did not like it much at all. Svala naked on the shore, playing with sand as if she were a child. Something half-seen in the bushes on the cliff top. I had dismissed my thoughts of a watcher. Svala earlier today, on the cliff's edge. My heart tightened. I must be wrong. Surely I must be wrong. "Brenna," I asked, "do you think it was true, what the Connacht men seemed to be saying about Rodan at the time of the burial, that he didn't care much whether a woman was married or single? That if he was attracted to her he'd approach her anyway?"

Three pairs of startled eyes turned in my direction; nobody had expected such a question from me.

"I heard a few remarks along those lines," Brenna said. "Flidais was of the opinion that it was her husband's identity that put Rodan off, rather than the fact of her being wed in the first place. Nobody in his right mind would want to get on the wrong side of Rat. Why would you ask such a thing, Sibeal?"

"I had a strange encounter with Svala today and I was just thinking . . . I was wondering if Rodan might ever have tried to . . . "

Brenna looked at Clodagh who said, "Anyone who made advances to Svala would have Knut to contend with. Everyone's seen how Knut can fight. And everyone knows he's very proud of his handsome wife, unusual woman that she is. According to Cathal, Knut talks about her in a way that makes some of the men quite jealous. He almost brags about her."

"She's the kind of woman men lust after," Brenna said. "What fellow's going to care if she's a few stalks short of the full haystack, when she's built like the goddess of love?"

"Sibeal," said Muirrin, "you can't be suggesting Knut had something to do with Rodan's death."

"Not exactly, but—"

"Even if Rodan did take advantage of Svala," said Clodagh, "and I don't suppose we'll ever know if that's so, Knut couldn't be responsible for his death. Rodan went missing during the morning's combat session. Knut was present the entire time."

But Svala wasn't. My mind showed me that magnificent figure on the cliff's edge, spreading her arms to the wind, hair like a wild banner, eyes bright with . . . vindication? It was all too easy to reshape that scene into one where Rodan, drawn to the place by desire for a woman who was, without a doubt, the best prize on the island, met her, embraced her, felt the sudden pressure of her strong hands and found himself falling, falling to oblivion on the rocks below.

"What are you thinking, Sibeal?"

I would not say it. There was no proof. Svala was mute and Rodan was dead. We would never know what had happened. That did not stop my mind from showing me Svala with her arms around Rodan, offering him her mouth. An instant's distraction, that's all it would have taken, and he would have been over the edge. I remembered the day when she had shared her fish, and the moment when I had thought she was going to drown me. "I'm thinking about Svala," I said. "I spent some time with her this morning, at the seer's cave, and she told me a very strange story."

"Told you?" said Clodagh. "You mean she finally spoke?"

"Not told in words. She showed me, in a vision." I had not intended to tell them the story but suddenly I needed to get it out. Rodan was gone; it was too late for his tale to be told. That made it all the more important to share the other, stranger story. "In the cave, with Svala, I believe I saw images that came from her mind, not mine," I told them. "I couldn't tell if it was a true vision of something that had happened to her or more of a . . . myth. It was frightening. And odd, almost like a dream. Svala became quite distraught when I didn't understand properly. One thing I am sure of: she's desperate to leave Inis Eala. She wants to go home. And home seems to be . . . somewhere impossible."

"Tell us," Brenna said, moving closer.

I related the tale as best I could: the brutal storm, the stark rocky island, the cliffs, the narrow passage. The relief on coming through to safe water, and then the monster. "A sea serpent or water dragon," I said. "It reared out of the waves and put its claw right through a man's chest. I wonder now if it was there earlier, harrying the ship forward through the gap so the men would be trapped in the bay."

My audience of three had been captured by the dramatic tale.

"You mean it was . . . *fishing*." Brenna's tone was hushed.

"Sibeal, it sounds more like an old tale than anything," said Clodagh. "I can imagine such a story as part of the adventures of Cú Chulainn or another hero. You're sure this ship was the same one that was wrecked on the reef here? The one that brought Svala and Knut to Inis Eala?"

"I think so. A substantial ship, with a hold for cargo and the capacity to go by sail or oars." I wished now that I had paid more attention to details. "But they weren't under sail. There were men rowing, a lot of men. Knut was one of them. When the storm drove them close to the rocks they panicked and lost control. Ardal's brother—the man I think was his brother—kept his head and started shouting orders. He maneuvered them through the gap. After the monster attacked he managed to get them in to shore."

"And then what?" asked Clodagh with some eagerness.

"I don't know. It finished there. A vision doesn't always show the whole story, or even the true story."

Muirrin had listened in silence. A frown of concentration creased her brow. "And Svala showed you this," she said.

"I don't know whether she has the ability to scry and to share her vision. Perhaps the feelings she had pent up inside her were so powerful that they took control over what appeared in the water. I'm certain those images came from her."

"I thought she was sad because of what she lost when the ship foundered," Brenna said. "Her child in particular."

"You mentioned Knut and Ardal," Muirrin said. "What about her? Was Svala in the vision?"

"I didn't see her. But it was a big ship. I suppose the women and children might have been down in the hold for safety." I could hardly imagine how terrifying that would be, below deck, buffeted by wind and waves, listening to the men's panicked screams as they lost control of the oars.

"If she'd been in the hold she wouldn't have seen what happened," Clodagh pointed out.

"True. But visions don't usually show a picture of something just as it was. They are not the same as memories. Perhaps that was what she thought I needed to see."

"What did you mean, Sibeal, about Svala wanting to go home?" asked Muirrin. "What has that to do with this vision?"

"She couldn't tell me, of course. But I felt what was in her heart." The power of Svala's yearning was still with me. "She wants to go back to that place. I'm sure she was trying to tell me that inhospitable island is home."

There was a lengthy silence.

"That's crazy," Brenna said eventually. "It makes no sense. Who'd live out in the middle of the ocean on a rock? With sea monsters on the doorstep?"

"It seems unlikely," said Clodagh. "The ship came from Ulfricsfjord, headed for the Orcades. That's a well-traveled sea path. Traders use it all the time. If such an island lay between Ulfrics- fjord and the north coast of Erin, we'd know about it. If a giant sea serpent lurked there, there'd be a hundred tales of it."

I was starting to think I should have talked to Johnny before I aired any of this before others, even if those others were the trusted women of my family. "What if they were not going to the Orcades when the ship hit our reef," I suggested, "but coming back?"

Everyone looked at me as they digested this.

"You mean Knut lied to Johnny?" Clodagh said, brows up.

"Svala was quite sure the island lay due north of here. It isn't between Ulfricsfjord and Inis Eala."

"Why lie about something like that?" asked Brenna. "A storm, a monster, nearly losing the ship—Knut would have spilled out everything."

I was still considering sea paths. "There's another possibility. If they were heading to the Orcades and had already traveled quite a distance to the northeast, past Dalriada, and were driven off course by the storm, they could have ended up due north of here. Perhaps the ship was damaged. Perhaps they lost so many men they gave up the original plan. They might have turned back and made for the nearest land. That would have brought them straight to Inis Eala."

There was something uncomfortable about the silence that fol- lowed. I guessed what Muirrin was going to say before she came out with it.

"Sibeal, this is conjecture. For Knut to lie about something so significant seems extraordinary. Besides, if he and Svala lived on a lonely isle all by themselves, what was he doing on the crew of a vessel heading out of an Irish port and bound for the Orcades? Given his account and this one, side by side, there's no doubt at all which people would believe." She was scrutinizing me closely. "You're close to Ardal, I know. Have you told him this story?"

I was annoyed to feel my cheeks flaming. "No. I was on my way back from the cave when Clodagh called me to join you in the kitchen. The only person I've seen since Svala showed me the vision—apart from you—is Knut, and I said nothing about it to him. Muirrin, you can't be suggesting I'd alter the facts so Ardal's story will be more credible than Knut's when it finally comes out." I was hurt and dismayed. I deeply regretted sharing the vision with them. I should have learned by now that such insights are best kept to oneself. "Besides, this is Svala's story, not Ardal's. As far as I know he still can't remember anything about all this."

"As far as you know?" Brenna asked, glancing from me to my sisters and back again a little nervously. It was unusual for us to argue.

"I think perhaps he's remembered more than he's told," I said. "But he won't talk about it. All he cares about now is getting strong again, so he can leave."

Another charged silence.

"Which is exactly what Johnny wants, isn't it?" I added, as misery crept over me despite my best efforts to withstand it.

After a while, Clodagh said gently, "He was always going to leave, Sibeal, as soon as he was well enough."

"And so are you," said Muirrin. "Best if you step back from it all, Sibeal. That's what we believe. You saved his life. That was a remarkable act of bravery. I know you care about him. But Ardal's a grown man. He will survive without your protection." When I did not respond, she added, "Sibeal, of course I don't believe you would alter the facts. But you've told me yourself how hard it is to interpret visions, and how their meaning is often something quite different from the images you see. And Svala is hardly the most reliable of guides in these matters."

I sank into silence, wishing profoundly that I had kept the tale for Ardal to hear first.

They continued to talk, moving from the voyage to other matters. After a while Biddy and Flidais came out to join us and I remembered, belatedly, why we were gathered together. I sat beside Brenna as the other women chatted about their children, their daily work, their men. Muirrin's comments were still there, nudging at my mind, unable to be forgotten. I set myself a test: while the others made guesses as to whether Clodagh and Muirrin would produce sons or daughters, I imagined myself in a situation like Brenna's. Brenna was telling a story now: how Sam had been playing with little Fergal, and had kicked a ball so hard it sent a line of washing straight into the mud. Even as she related how she'd scolded Sam and made him and Fergal pick up the clothes, her voice was warm with love, her laughter soft with tenderness.

My mind conjured up a pleasing image: there was I, firelight warming my face as I sat by the hearth. I was carving Ogham signs on birch sticks. On a table were an ink pot, quills in a jar, a sheet of parchment. A young man sat there writing. Chestnut hair over his shoulders; eyes like deep water under evening sky. A thin, strong-jawed face, a straight nose, a generous mouth. Ardal. And on the mat before the fire, an infant in a smock. The child had a crop of wispy dark hair. It sat with its legs stuck out, and between them lay a small pile of rune rods. In my imagination, the infant selected one, waved it about, then dropped it and chose another. And another. *Os, Ger, Nyd.* The child looked up at me, beaming with delight at its cleverness, and its eyes were of the palest blue-gray, so light as to be almost colorless. Like Finbar's. Like mine.

Look, Sibeal, said Ardal in the daydream. *She's chosen the same runes you were shown in that very first augury, after you saved my life.* I turned toward him, smiling, and saw that beyond the open shutters lay, not the stark open spaces of Inis Eala, but the myriad greens of a great forest. *Another druid in the making*, Ardal said.

Sudden tears sprang to my eyes, startling me. That had felt real. It had felt true. My heart ached for it; my body was full of a mindless longing. What was wrong with me? I knew it would never happen. *You thought you'd never give up your vocation*, a voice whispered inside me. *You thought you'd never even consider it. But you've met the one man who could change your mind. He is your perfect complement. He is Cathal to your Clodagh; he is Bran to your Liadan. No wonder you conjured up those images. No wonder they make you weep.*

This would not do. It could not be so. I would not allow myself the indulgence of such fantasies again. I would banish them from my mind. For my commitment was already made, if not formally until I spoke the words of my pledge, then most certainly in my inner heart. Who could deny the call of the gods? I had known my path since I was a child not much bigger than that little girl, my daughter who would never be born.

Later in the afternoon I left my sisters and returned to the infirmary, only to find that Ardal had gone out walking with Gull.

"They were heading toward the place of the boat burial," Evan said. "I don't imagine Ardal will get all the way there, even with support, but he insisted on trying." I took my cloak back off the peg where I had hung it, intending to follow them. "They're probably best on their own, Sibeal," my brother-in-law said quietly. "Ardal's had a long time of looking weak in front of you. That sort of thing is shaming for most men, especially when the woman is someone he cares about."

"But—" I was stunned by this. Ardal had not seemed to mind my seeing his weakness in those early days, and he'd been ready enough to talk and to listen. But I could not discount Evan's words. This was a man's insight, something I would not have thought of myself. The treacherous image of earlier came back to me as I retreated to my chamber: that impossible future in which I was Ardal's wife and the mother of his child. Just thinking of it, I could feel his arms around me, his fingers stroking my hair. All the sweet things he had said to me whispered through my mind, a gentle spring breeze across a harsh winter landscape. Inside me I felt something unfurl with tentative grace, reaching for the light.

I prayed. I sought wisdom in the voices of the gods. I murmured my way through passages of lore. I studied the charcoal runes I had marked on the walls that first day, before I knew Ardal existed. I watched the shadows lengthen.

Eventually they came in. I heard Gull's voice, low and encouraging, and Ardal's patchy response, a word, a pause, another word. Sitting behind the curtain that screened my chamber, I knew how tired he was.

I did not go out into the infirmary. I stayed quietly on my bed, wondering what Ciarán would think best under the circumstances. How would my wise mentor interpret Svala's vision? Perhaps he would think it best that I told Johnny before Ardal. *The answers lie within you, Sibeal.* I could almost hear him saying it. Ciarán never told me what to do. On occasion he would remind me that the skills I had learned in the nemetons would help me find my own solutions. It was the druid way. Sometimes, when the voices of the gods were silent, it felt profoundly lonely.

When it was time, I went to supper. After we had eaten, the musicians played, and I told the tale of Deirdre and Naoise, which is a sad love story. And after that, Kalev was persuaded to step up and give us a tale from his homeland, a strange, violent tale about a girl who married a snake. I congratulated him afterward and made him blush again. When I got back to the infirmary, Ardal was already asleep.

Something jolted me awake. I sat up, my heart pounding. All was silent. Had I heard the door creak a moment ago? Or was it only the wind? No: beyond my curtain, I could hear stealthy footsteps on the infirmary floor. A chill sense of wrongness filled me, leaving no room for the obvious explanations—Gull heading out to the privy, Ardal wakeful and restless. I slid out of bed and snatched up my shawl. As I drew the curtain aside, a voice screamed in my mind: *Help!*

The place was in near darkness, the fire damped down, the lamps quenched, the candles snuffed out. There was just sufficient light to show me an amorphous dark mass where the sleeping figure of Ardal should be; something was moving, struggling, and I heard a sound of stifled pain. A wash of feelings flowed through me: shock, terror, desperation, hatred. A fierce will for survival; a dark need to kill. Two men were locked in a ferocious struggle. One of them was dying. I felt the juddering, halting heartbeat in my own breast. He was fading away, leaving me forever . . .

I flung myself across the chamber, taking in the attacker's flaxen hair, his awkward stance with one knee up on the pallet, his fingers on Ardal's neck, pressing hard. I grabbed his arm, trying to haul him off. He was like a rock, immovable. "Gull!" I screamed. "Gull, help!"

The arm came back, swatting me off like an unwelcome insect, and I crashed to the floor, jarring hip and elbow. My mind edged toward blank terror. Oh gods, in a moment Ardal would be dead, and I couldn't, I couldn't . . . *You are a druid, Sibeal,* said a small, strong voice inside me. *Use what you know. Use what is already here.* A distraction. I needed him to let go just for a moment. A moment of elemental magic—use what is here—fire, glowing red beneath a blanket of ash. Now, quick! I concentrated my mind on that red, feeling its heat, feeling its strength in the beating of my heart. *Help me. Help us.* I spoke a word I had learned from Ciarán, a word of power.

The fire flared into sudden brilliance, flames shooting high. The attacker uttered an exclamation, perhaps a Norse curse, and in that instant Ardal rolled out of his grasp, toppling off the pallet and landing on the floor beside me. His breath was the scrape of metal on stone.

I struggled to my knees, then to my feet. The fire had died down now. Knut was standing very still, facing me; the flickering light played in his eyes, and set a gleam on the knife at his belt.

"You were trying to kill him," I said, hearing the cold iron in my voice. "I saw you leaning over him with your fingers on his neck. I saw you."

"No, no," Knut said, taking a step closer. "You see nothing. Mistake." His hand went to the knife's hilt. "You see nothing at all. Yes?" There was a small, metallic sound, and now the weapon was in his hand.

How Ardal managed it I do not know, but he was up in a flash, grabbing me by the shoulder and thrusting me behind him. He stretched out his arms to shield me. His hands were shaking. His voice came in a harsh whisper, and although he spoke in Norse, I could guess the meaning. *Lay a finger on her and you're dead, I swear it.*

A crash as the back door was flung open. Gull strode in. The light from his candle sent shadows leaping around the chamber. "What in the name of the gods is going on?" he bellowed.

In the moment of distraction Knut moved, slicing with his knife. Ardal cried out, staggered and fell. As he went down, his head struck the chest by the pallet with a thud.

"Hold!" roared Gull, surging toward us, and there was a flurry of movement. I crouched down, my hand on Ardal's shoulder. He was so still. So terribly still. I could hear the rumbling approach of the Ankou in his cart of stones. Then, nearer at hand, there was the sound of a blow and a thud, and Gull's voice. "Sibeal, if you can get up, take my candle, light the two lamps and bring me a length of rope. Ardal, are you injured?"

I did as I was told, knowing nothing could be done for Ardal without good light. With great presence of mind, Gull had set his candle on a shelf as he came back in. I touched the flame to the wicks of two oil lamps. A warm light spread through the chamber, revealing the prone form of Knut, facedown and evidently unconscious. Gull's foot was planted on his back.

"Ardal's hurt," I said. I did not sound like a person who had just performed an act of elemental magic. My voice was that of a frightened child.

"Sibeal, the rope. Evan has a coil out the back."

When I brought it, Gull said, "You'll need to make the knots for me. Wrists behind his back, ankles together. He'll come to soon; I only hit him hard enough to stun, and I've cause to know how strong he is."

"Ardal—"

"I'll help him as soon as this is done. Not like that, wind it through and over . . . that's it. Then I must ask you to go for help. I won't leave you with Knut, even trussed up. What in the name of the gods was he doing? Did he try to assault you?"

"He would have killed Ardal. I woke up and he was there, pressing his fingers into his neck. And then he slashed at him with a knife. Gull, please see if Ardal's all right. He's unconscious, and I think he's bleeding . . . "

"This job needs doing first. Now the ankles. I got a good blow in because he wasn't expecting it. I wouldn't like my chances a second time. Tie it firmly." He hauled the Norseman over to the wall, propping him in a sitting position.

Gods, don't let Ardal be dead, please, please . . . I'll do anything, anything you want . . .

He lay as I had left him, head on one side, face chalk white. There was a dark stain of blood on the floor by his side. *Please, please . . .*

"Bring a lamp over, Sibeal." Gull put his hand to the fallen man's neck, feeling for the rhythm of the heart. My own heart strained to beat for Ardal's; I sank my teeth into my lip, waiting.

"He's not done for yet," Gull said, and I felt tears well in my eyes and flow down my cheeks, welcome as spring rain. "Roll up his left sleeve, will you, Sibeal? I think the blood's coming from that arm. Ah, yes—a nasty flesh wound here, but it doesn't look deep. I'll wrap something around it for now. As for his head—" He moved up, supported Ardal's neck with one hand, felt the skull gently with the other, under the thick fall of hair. "He'll have a monstrous headache and a lump like an egg—it's already swelling—but my opinion is he'll survive both this and the knife wound. Ardal's a man on a mission, even if he doesn't quite know what it is. He's not going to let something like this stop him. As for Knut, he has some explaining to do, and I don't think it can wait for morning."

"Thank you," I said, scrubbing my cheeks. "Gull, thank you." *For coming in when you did. For saving us. For being so calm and wise. For telling me Ardal isn't dead.*

"Just wish I'd been quicker. You'd best go for help now. Straight to Johnny. Ask him to bring Gareth and Cathal, and maybe one of the Norse speakers, if someone can be fetched without waking the whole place. I suppose we need to hear both sides of the story, whatever it turns out to be. Likely you'll find someone on the way here already; that was quite a scream. Enough to put a man off going to the privy by himself at night for a long time."

I fetched my cloak from my little chamber, then came back through the infirmary. Gull had placed a pillow under Ardal's head and a blanket over his legs. Ardal was stirring; he muttered something in his own tongue.

"Lie still, son," Gull said quietly. "You're hurt. I'm just finding a bit of bandage for your arm, and Sibeal's off to get Johnny."

"I'll be back soon," I said, trying for a reassuring tone and managing a strangled croak.

As I moved to the door, Ardal spoke. The sound of it stopped my heart. It was as if he had opened a window and found himself gazing straight into his worst nightmare. I understood in that moment that at last he had remembered.

"We left them. Gods have mercy on us, *we left them behind.*"

CHAPTER 9

~Sibeal~

hey went to find shelter, to find a safe place—if he hadn't come back early—they wouldn't listen—when Paul tried to—"

After the long silence, now the words were pouring out of Ardal like water from a broken dam. He couldn't keep still. Despite the knife wound, which Gull had bandaged—Evan would stitch it later, by daylight—he would not sit down, but paced and gestured, his body possessed by a restless energy. He was making very little sense.

I had hammered on Johnny's door, glad that he and Gareth had their own hut, since the alternative would have meant waking everyone in the men's quarters. Gareth had gone to fetch Kalev and Cathal, while Johnny and I returned to the infirmary. By the time we got there Knut had regained consciousness, and both Evan and Muirrin had arrived, drawn by my scream.

Once the other men had come in Johnny ordered that Knut's bonds be untied. The Norseman seemed as desperate to explain himself as Ardal was, but Johnny silenced him.

"You'll get the chance to speak, Knut. Hold your tongue until I tell you it's time. And don't move unless you want to be tied up again."

"But—"

"You heard me."

Kalev and Gareth stationed themselves on either side of Knut. Cathal came over to stand behind me, near the fire.

Ardal was still talking. " . . . and we left them there. Paul tried—he tried, but—" He made a wild gesture with his good arm, missing Gull's nose by a hair's breadth. "I must go, I must go straightaway—they may still be alive—"

"Ardal," Johnny said, stepping forward to put his hands on the other man's shoulders, "we want to hear your story. But not like this, in bits and pieces. Take a deep breath and sit down."

"I cannot—I—"

"That's an order," Johnny said. "Sit there beside Gull and don't get up until I give you permission."

Ardal sat, agitation written all over his face. "My name is Felix," he said in strangled tones.

I fought the urge to go over and put my arms around him. I stayed where I was, on the other bench beside Muirrin and Evan. The best way to help him was to stay calm. I did not feel very calm at all.

Johnny nodded. "Very well, Felix. We need your story, and it's clear you no longer wish to hold it back. But first things first. I want a plain and truthful account of what just happened in here. Sibeal, let's hear your version of events."

I stood up, thinking the occasion demanded it, and found I was trembling. Clutching my hands together, I gave an account of what I had experienced—the sudden waking, knowing something was wrong; coming through the doorway to see the shadowy figures locked in struggle; the realization that Knut was trying to kill Ardal. Felix. I would have to get used to that. I told of my attempt to intervene, and Knut flinging me to the floor. I did not speak of what I had *felt*: the two men's tumult of dark emotions. "I . . . created a distraction, with the fire. Knut lost his grip on Ardal. Then I—I spoke to Knut, I accused him . . . He said no, I was mistaken. He was angry. I thought he was about to hurt one of us, perhaps both of us." My voice shook.

"Take your time, Sibeal," Johnny said.

I drew a steadying breath and went on. "Ardal moved in front of me and Knut slashed at him." I would never forget that. In the face of Knut's knife and his murderous eyes, Ardal had used his body to shield mine without a second thought. So quick. So brave. He would have died for me.

"And then Gull came in," I said. "I didn't see the next part, I was helping Ardal—Felix—but Gull hit Knut, and Knut fell. Gull told me to bring the rope and go for help, and I did."

"Thank you, Sibeal. Please sit down." Johnny turned to Gull. "Is that an accurate account, Gull?"

"Sounds about right to me," Gull said. "I was in the privy when I heard Sibeal call out. When I came in Ar—Felix was facing Knut with Sibeal behind him. Knut used his knife; Felix went down. The situation being what it was, I disabled Knut." He glanced at the Norseman. There was no judgment in his eyes. As was the pattern of things on Inis Eala, everyone would be heard before any determination of guilt or innocence was made. "Felix was hurt, maybe Sibeal as well. Someone had to go for help. So I gave Knut a tap on the jaw, just enough to put him out of action so we could tie him. Once I had reassured her that Felix would live to see the sun rise, Sibeal was prepared to go and fetch you." Gull smiled at me, then was somber again. "Felix has a bruise on his neck—show them, Felix. A man who puts pressure on that particular spot knows what he's about. His intention is to kill, quickly, efficiently, silently. If there hadn't been a seer in the next room, Felix wouldn't have lived to tell us his story. His killer could have come in, done the deed and left again before I got back from the privy. Such a man would think, perhaps, that I wouldn't notice my charge was dead until he failed to wake for his breakfast. That, of course, is not fact but theory."

"It is not important now—none of this matters—there are men in need, men suffering, I must go there—"

"Enough." There was a certain voice, a very quiet voice, that I imagined made even the most hard-bitten of Johnny's warriors take heed. Johnny used it now, and Felix fell silent, but the tension in him had me on the edge of my seat, full of unease. "Perhaps it's better if Felix goes to rest now, and gives us his story in the morning," Johnny added. "Evan? Muirrin?"

"No!" Felix shouted, springing to his feet and suppressing a sound of pain. "You must hear my tale tonight! There are lives in the balance!"

"You seem in no fit state to tell it," Johnny said.

"I've a suggestion," Gull put in quietly. "Let Sibeal ask the questions, and the rest of you back off a bit. It's quite plain that Felix needs to tell this now. But the man's been through hell. Anyone who can't see that on his face must be half blind."

It made sense. Who could be relied upon to be calm and evenhanded, if not a druid? And if Ardal—Felix, I must think of him as Felix—trusted anyone here, it was me. But to do this with all of them watching, to do it with Knut only a few paces away, Knut with his jaw clenched tight and his eyes glinting and the anger building in him with every speech that Kalev translated . . . I must view this as a test of inner strength.

"Please," Felix said. "Please hear me."

Words burst from Knut, a torrent of furious Norse.

"Knut objects to this idea," Kalev said. "He believes that because of Sibeal's attachment to this man, she cannot be impartial. She will persuade you all to believe Felix's story over his, no matter how outrageous it may be. No doubt he has already told her this tale, and she has instantly taken it as truth, as a woman does whose feelings hold her in thrall. This man is a liar, a manipulator. Knut offers his respect to you, Johnny, and asks if this can wait for morning, so it can be heard before a representative group from the island community." He cleared his throat, looking down at the floor. "I translate exactly what Knut has said."

Johnny turned quite slowly to face Knut. He addressed him in measured Norse. When he was done, he said, "I've told Knut I'll hear his story before Felix's—that will give Felix time to compose himself. I've made it quite clear that I believe we have a representative group here tonight and, in addition, that I have gathered this particular group because I have complete trust in each member of it. Knut does not understand, perhaps, what it means to be a druid." He looked at me, and I saw the ghost of a smile cross his lips, gone almost as soon as it had appeared. "Lastly, I explained again what the agitation of the moment may have caused some people to forget. On Inis Eala, I am leader and the final decision on any weighty matter is mine alone." He looked at Kalev. "Kalev, please ask Knut to give his version of what happened tonight. Tell him to stick to the facts and to keep it brief. He can start by telling us why he was in the infirmary at night, carrying a weapon."

I did not watch Knut as he gave his story, and I did not watch Kalev as he translated it. My eyes were on the man we now knew as Felix, and my heart felt the force of what was in him: grief, guilt, horror, anger. A desperate need to act, so desperate that it came close to driving him mad. It was taking every bit of strength he could summon to stay seated there beside Gull, and not to speak. I willed him to look at me, and he did. A face drained of color. Eyes full of demons. Mouth a grim line, jaw as tight as Knut's. Hands in white-knuckled fists. If ever a man needed the comfort of touch, it was this man, now. I ached to wrap my arms around him and tell him everything would be all right. I longed to feel his heart beating against me. Gods, now I was blushing; my cheeks were hot. What would he think? *Stop this, Sibeal; it is completely inappropriate.*

There was one sign I could give him, and I did. As unobtrusively as I could, I crossed the first fingers of each hand, one straight, one slantwise, to make the rune *Nyd*: inner strength, courage in the face of the impossible. I held this only for a moment, for I had no wish to provide Knut with another reason to doubt my impartiality. Felix would need help to get through his account, and I was the best one to give it. As my hands returned to my lap, Felix un-clenched his fists and made with his two hands the rune *Ken*, the torch. Light in the darkness.

Knut spoke with vehemence, illustrating his account with ges-tures. Kalev's translation was much calmer. "That man"—Felix—"has been spreading lies about me, dangerous lies. Yes, I came here to frighten him. Yes, I waited outside until Gull was out of the way. No disrespect to Gull, a fine warrior, a man of heart, but it is a standing joke among the men here that he's up to the privy three or four times every night. My intention was not to kill. I always carry the knife. Where I come from, a man would be a fool to go about by night with no weapon at the ready. I did not expect that the girl would wake and come in. I am sure I made no sound at all. My intention was to give this man a fright, a warning that he must stop spreading his evil stories. He paints me as a bad man to cover for his own failings. He wants me sent away. I have done nothing wrong, nothing. He is a meddler. He speaks nothing but lies."

"Kalev," Johnny said, "remind Knut that I said stick to the facts. You wanted to frighten Felix, you said. How did you do this?"

Knut stood with hands on hips, the bruise from Gull's blow darkening on the fair skin of his face. "I pressed my fingers against his neck, there, where he has a mark." He was making no effort to conceal the hostility in his eyes as he looked at Felix. Those eyes said plainly: *You should be dead.* "Not to kill. Why would I kill here on Inis Eala, such a good place? I wished only to scare him, to teach him a lesson. The girl ran in, got in the way, fell down. The man fell. Everything was mixed up, hard to see in the dark, shout-ing and commotion. When I tried to help, the girl thought I would attack her. She called me a murderer. Why would I do that, attack a helpless woman? In the confusion, the man was hurt. An acci-dent." When Kalev had rendered this, Knut added, "Gull hit me, and I saw no more. I am grateful that he did not hit me harder." He favored Gull with what looked like a grin of genuine admiration.

"Thank you, Kalev," Johnny said. "Ask Knut if he has anything further to say. I don't want his opinion on Felix or Sibeal or any-thing about the situation, only facts."

A brief interchange. "Knut says he has given his account, and he thanks you for your fairness. Not every leader would have allowed him to explain, given the circumstances."

"Tell Knut he can sit down."

Knut seated himself on the stool by the pallet. Kalev and Gareth remained standing, one on either side of him.

"We're ready for Felix's account, Sibeal," Johnny said. "What is the best way to do this?"

Trust your instincts, said my inner voice. I moved to sit on the rug before the fire, not far from Felix's bare feet. Breathing steadily, I blocked out my awareness of the others in the chamber, concentrating on the man beside me, and Gull seated next to him like a wise guardian. "Tell me what just happened, Felix," I said, as if the three of us were exchanging tales before bedtime. I felt the warmth of the fire; I saw its light flicker strangely in Felix's eyes, flame on dark water. "Start from the moment when you woke up, before I came in."

"But this is not—"

I reached up and put my hand over his, on his knee. "I know the other part is more important for you," I said, "but you must tell this part first. Remember that you are among friends."

"I was sleeping. I heard—I heard—at first, the creak as Gull went out. I heard this without waking. Then suddenly the hand was on my neck, the fingers pressing—I knew it was Knut. Who else could it be?"

I asked the question before anyone else could. "How did you know who it was? Could you see him?"

"I was barely awake, and the light was dim . . . I knew because he had threatened me before. Said he would kill me if I told the story of our past. I knew, as the fingers pressed down, as I felt my heart jump and my breath falter, that he had come to carry out his threat. But I have said nothing. I have spread no stories about him, good or ill. There was nothing to say. Until tonight, all I could remember about this man was that he boarded *Freyja* as a crewman."

I felt cold all over. "When did Knut threaten you?" I asked.

"Soon after we came here. Early days, when I could remember almost nothing. He thought I was dissembling, biding my time before I chose to tell. He said if I spoke of what had happened he would slit my throat." A silence, as his audience exchanged shocked glances. "And when he believed I had disregarded his warning, he threatened you, Sibeal. It was the day when you found that man's body. Knut said . . . " Felix cleared his throat. "He said he knew you and I were friends. He told me how you liked to walk on the cliff paths, alone. He . . . he suggested an accident might befall you." He looked up, and straight across toward Knut, who watched him, tight-lipped. "I did not understand what dark secret could drive a man to such baseness. Not then. So I planned to leave Inis Eala as soon as I could, knowing that if I was gone, I could tell no secrets, and you would be safe, Sibeal."

"I have a question for Knut," Gareth said.

Johnny nodded.

"Knut, if this is true, what stories were you talking about? As far as I know, Felix has hardly left the infirmary since he was washed up on Inis Eala, and barely exchanged a word with anyone save the healers and Sibeal. I've heard no tales at all about you or your past beyond what you told Johnny, and nothing at all suggesting ill-doing. I'd wager that when I say that, I speak for all the men. They think highly of you."

When Kalev had translated this, Knut fixed Felix with an icy stare. "He lies," he said. "I made no threats. His story is sheer fantasy."

"So we have one man's word against another's," said Johnny. "Sibeal, we'd best hear the rest of Felix's account."

I had a host of questions, but they would have to wait. Conducting this conversation as Johnny needed it to be done was my best way of helping Felix in the long run. Dear gods, whatever he was going to tell us, let them not call him a liar.

"Felix, we'll go back to tonight. You told us you woke to find Knut with his hands on your throat. What happened after that?"

"Everything fading, my heart about to burst, everything turning to dark. So weak, oh gods, so weak—I could do nothing against

227

the press of his hand. A sudden scream—yours, Sibeal—and my assailant struck out, but still he held me. The fire flared strangely, I saw shadows leaping above me, and the pressure was gone . . . I rolled from pallet to floor, and there you were, Sibeal, crouched, hurt. I had been scared before, with his fingers on my neck. The wheels of the Ankou's cart were creaking just outside the door. Now I really knew fear.

"You rose to your feet, like a brave warrior, and confronted Knut with the truth. He said it was all a mistake, but he lied, for as he spoke he drew his knife and moved toward you. I did not stop to think. I was there, standing between the two of you, hoping I could be strong for long enough. Then, welcome as warm sun at midwinter, came Gull. The door creaked, he called to us, Knut slashed with his knife, one, two. My head struck something as I fell. I lost consciousness. When I woke . . . " He shivered convulsively. "When I woke, it was there in my mind, the memory that has eluded me for so long. There is a tale to tell, a tale to make men weep. Before morning, that tale must be told." Felix looked across at Knut, whose face was like stone. "We have done a terrible thing," he said. "We have betrayed our comrades. Knut would have killed to keep that tale from coming out." He lowered his eyes. "A strange twist, Sibeal. Until he cut me, until I struck my head in falling, I had not remembered the story he so feared."

For a little, then, there was utter silence in the infirmary, save for the distant, restless wash of the sea.

"Thank you, Felix," Johnny said. "We'd best hear this tale of yours." He looked around the circle of watchers: Cathal with his shoulder against the wall, long form wrapped in his cloak; Muirrin and Evan seated together on one side of the hearth, Gull on the other beside Felix, I cross-legged on the mat. Grim Knut with his two tall guardians. The firelight flickered on the circle of somber faces. "Is there anyone else you believe should be present to hear it?" Johnny asked.

Felix shook his head. Johnny looked at me and gave a little nod.

"Felix," I said, still finding it quite odd to use this name, "where does this tale begin? With the departure of the ship from Ulfricsfjord, or earlier? Will you tell us what brought you and your brother to Erin?"

"I . . . of course, but I . . . " He drew a shuddering breath. "I come from Finistère, in Breizh—the region known to you as Armorica. My father is a councillor to Duke Remont, who rules there. My mother is a Norsewoman. My brother and I grew up speaking both tongues. We left our home when . . . " He faltered, eyes dark with memory.

"Take it step by step," I said quietly.

"Paul had the skills and strength to be a warrior; he was a member of the Duke's guard. I was more apt at scholarly pursuits. Full of ideas. Argumentative. Too ready to speak out. My tutors warned me, but I never learned to hold my tongue."

A sound of derision from Knut, when Kalev translated that for him. Gareth hissed something in Knut's ear, and he fell silent.

"Not all of this need be heard tonight," Felix said. "Enough to say that certain words of mine came to the Duke's ears, words challenging the authority of the Church and the influence of the bishops over Remont. My father's secure position at court, which he had held for many years, was suddenly under threat. Rather than make a groveling public apology, I left. Paul came with me.

"We crossed the water, first to the southwest of Britain, to a place where other Breizhiz had settled. Our skills found us roofs to sleep under, coins for our pockets, food to sustain us. Paul was a strong-hearted man." His voice cracked. "He could set his hand to anything. I found work as scribe and translator—I can read and write Latin, and I knew Irish already, thanks to Brother Seanan, a traveling scholar who stayed at Remont's court. So we came to Erin.

"I helped Paul. Helped him with his Irish, helped him learn. And he . . . he guarded me, he kept me safe. He was the home I carried with me." His head came up, his eyes went to Knut, and if I had seen death on the Norseman's face before, now there was a look to equal it on Felix's gaunt features. "You killed him," he said, and his tone was the punishing stroke of a flail. "If you had not bound him, he would have swum to safe shore. My brother was young. He was strong. For his courage, you fettered him, and he died."

I saw Johnny look at Gareth, and Gareth give him a little nod. What it meant, I did not know.

"Felix," said Gull, not bothering to ask Johnny for permission to speak, "how long is it since you and your brother left home?"

"Almost three years. I was seventeen when we left that shore, Paul one year my senior. For the last two years, we have been at the court of Muredach, King of Munster. I am—was—the king's translator and chief scribe. Paul was personal guard to Muredach's son Eoghan." A pause. "He became both guard and friend."

"Was it on behalf of the king of Munster that you were on the ship?" I ventured.

"We bore gifts," Felix said. His eyes were calmer now, as if he saw the bright promise of the voyage, the hope with which it was begun. "Muredach's son is to wed the daughter of Jarl Thorkel, ruler of the Orcades. Those items you showed me were chosen by Eoghan as gifts for his betrothed and for her mother. Our party was led by Muredach's senior councillor—one of the men you buried here on the island, along with Paul. Paul . . . my brother did not need to come on the voyage. There were others in our party who could have fulfilled the role of guard. Eoghan did not want Paul to come with us; the two of them had become close, and the prince said he would miss Paul too much. But my brother said that he had made a promise to watch over me, and that Eoghan would be so busy over the summer with riding and hawking and games that he would scarcely miss us. Either he stood by his little brother, Paul told the prince, or he left Eoghan's service altogether. Eoghan let him come with me. He let my brother follow me to his death."

A silence followed Kalev's translation to Knut, and then came Cathal's voice. "Have I permission to ask a question, Johnny?"

"Very well."

"How many people were aboard the ship when she left Ulfricsfjord?"

Felix sighed. "Forty oarsmen, Knut among them. Five other crew. Eight passengers."

"And how many were on the ship when she sank off the coast here?"

"Cathal—" I protested, but it seemed Felix was prepared to face this dark truth.

"When we approached this isle, seventeen were left. The last seventeen." After a moment he added, "Eighteen, with the woman."

Cathal regarded him levelly. "Only seventeen, for a ship of that size," he said. "No wonder your hands bore blisters."

Knut stirred as Kalev murmured a translation, but he did not speak.

"There were catastrophic losses, then," Cathal said, "even before you reached here. If you're telling the truth, why didn't Knut—"

"Cathal," said Johnny. "Let him tell it in his own time."

"You left from Ulfricsfjord," I said quietly. "You must have traveled some distance by land to reach the ship."

"We rode for some days, yes. Muredach had procured passage for our party of eight. A Norse vessel; there were men among the crew who intended to stay in the Orcades. I understood the plan was to pick up crewmen on the islands for the return voyage."

"You said forty oarsmen, five other crew and eight passengers— those passengers were your own party, I assume, from Muredach's court."

"That is correct, Sibeal. The councillor, Matha, who was to discuss certain sensitive matters with the Jarl; my brother and I; and five other men, all Irish."

"We know that Svala and the child were traveling with Knut," I said. "Didn't some of the other crewmen who were planning to settle in the Orcades have wives and children with them?" Knut had told Johnny this was so. The numbers did not add up.

Felix glanced at Knut. "When we sailed from Ulfricsfjord, there were no women on *Freyja*, and no children," he said. "Coming back, there was only the one woman. I cannot tell you how she came to be on board. He says she is his wife. I do not think that can be true."

Johnny held up a hand, signaling for Felix to wait until Kalev had completed the translation before he went on. Hearing it, Knut gave a derisive laugh.

"This is complete nonsense, a fabrication!" he exclaimed. "I told you this man is full of wild stories. He is jealous, like many others. What man would not wish for such a fine woman to warm his bed at night? No doubt the rest of his tale is equally foolish. There were wives on board, four or five of them. They traveled in the hold, with the cargo. All perished in the sinking of *Freyja*." After a moment, he added, "He makes a mockery of my loss."

As Kalev finished translating this, Felix got up abruptly, swaying on his feet. "How dare you lie about this?" he demanded, then gulped in a rasping breath. He was strung so tight I could feel the vibrations of his anger. I thought he might hurl himself across the chamber at Knut and perform his own act of violence. "With so many dead, with so many lost, after what we did, how can you have room in your mind for anything but the need to go back, to save those we abandoned, to make good what little part of this we can—"

"Steady, son," murmured Gull, putting his hand on Felix's arm.

I summoned a tone I had heard Ciarán use on certain occasions with argumentative novices. "Sit down, Felix," I said. "Breathe slowly, as if you were preparing for a divination. It's time for this story to come out. Tell it calmly, as a druid might."

Felix drew a deep, shuddering breath and subsided onto the bench beside Gull. The chamber became utterly silent. "We set off for the Orcades," he said. "We were following an established trade path, or so Paul told me—he knew more about such things than I. The plan was to skirt the coast of Erin, then thread a way between Dalriada and the isles before heading northeast. *Freyja* went by sail when the winds allowed. The oarsmen did the work at other times. At night we trailed a sea anchor. Each man prayed to his own god, that between dusk and dawn we would not drift too far from our true course. From the seasoned seafarer to the boy on his first adventure, each feared to wake and find himself in unknown waters. It is a potent terror to turn and turn again and see measureless ocean on every side, and not a sign of land.

"The oarsmen slept at their benches; there was nowhere else. We passengers sheltered in the hold, out of the crew's way. Most of us were sick. Matha, the king's councillor, was worst affected. The endless rocking motion of the ship, the confinement below made his belly churn. He could not keep anything down but sips of water. When the ship was under sail we were allowed on deck, but Matha could not go up.

"On the second night, what we had most feared came to pass. In the darkness we were seized by contrary currents and borne far west of our intended path, west and then north into seas uncharted. We woke to driving wind, to waves tall as mountains, on which *Freyja* was tossed about like a child's toy. There would be no going by sail—the sail would be torn to shreds as soon as it was raised. There would be no going by oars, for the strongest crew of rowers could not hold firm against such seas. We clung to whatever we could find—benches, oars, ropes, each other—and prayed for a miracle.

"The storm had come from nowhere. All that endless day, all the lonely and fearful night, and long into the next day it bore us onward. Heavy cloud blanketed the sun. What little light penetrated the thin veil revealed here two men, here three huddled close against the spray, faces like those of wan ghosts. Paul and I took turns in the hold with Matha, who could not be left on his own. I saw in my brother's eyes a reflection of my own thought: *What matters this seasickness now, when all of us teeter on the brink of death?*"

Felix had his audience spellbound. Now that he was telling the story at last, he was far calmer. I had heard a poet's voice from him before, and it was present again in this grim telling. Even Knut seemed captive to the tale. The Norseman sat very still, eyes straight ahead, and I wondered if he was living it again.

"The tempest snatched seven men from our crew," Felix went

on. "Six were washed overboard by a wave that came close to swamping us. One was knocked into the sea by a length of loose timber flung at random by the wind. He was the crewman most skilled with the steering oar. I wondered if we would all be picked off in the same way, leaving *Freyja* to sail on with a cargo of vain prayers and fearful memories.

"But I am here, as you see, and so is Knut, and so, for a brief time, was *Freyja* with the sorry remnant of her crew. At some point in our breakneck voyage we spotted land: an island like a spear, a tall, narrow rock standing alone in the wild ocean. The sight of that inhospitable isle filled me with joy. Anything, anything but this wretched boat, this storm, this empty sea . . . The men were sick, frightened, exhausted. None among them had the heart to take charge. Paul did what the crew could not: he took hold of the steering oar and began to shout orders, urging the men to help save themselves. There was no time to rig the sail. But we could row." Felix glanced at Knut. "This man, too, showed presence of mind. He kept his wits about him and helped calm the others, some of whom were near-crazed from fear. We rowed, crew and passengers alike, Paul's voice ringing in our ears, a battle cry, a call to arms. *'Pull! Pull!'*

"All the way to the lonely isle we fought wind and waves. We left the stricken Matha alone in the hold. Every able man rowed. We came closer, and it seemed the island was bordered on every side by high cliffs, and there was no landing place. Then Paul saw a narrow opening, a slit between looming headlands, through which a passage might perhaps be threaded. Beyond the gap I glimpsed a calm inlet, a strip of level shore."

Goose bumps rose all over my flesh. I had wondered if it would be the same tale. I had almost expected it. But to hear him say it, to recognize Svala's vision in Felix's account, was like watching the message of the runes become reality.

"We pulled hard toward that crack in the rocks. Paul kept up his steady guidance, easing *Freyja* one way or the other, correcting the stroke, steering a hair's breadth from the high walls of stone. We passed through, *Freyja* surging out into the waters of the bay as if borne on a freakish wave.

"Safe. Safe at last. Full of joy, forgetting for the moment that we were in a wild place and far from home, I relaxed my grip on the oar. Smiles illuminated the pallid faces of the crew. 'Pull for shore, men,' Paul said, and I heard the same gladness in his voice.

"And then . . . and then, oh gods . . . " Felix put his hands up to cover his face. I held my breath. "Then it came, out of the water right by the prow, a fearsome, long-toothed head, wild eyes, a neck like an oak trunk. It towered over us, a creature of gigantic proportions, a nightmare made manifest . . . 'Pull!' shouted my brother. Frozen in terror, none of us could obey. Besides, the thing was blocking our path. It whipped at the water with its tail, and waves splashed across *Freyja*, drenching us anew. It reared up, pawing the air above us with its long limbs. Each toe was tipped with a vicious claw the length of a man's forearm. Paul was yelling at us, bidding us summon our courage, not stand about waiting for the creature to sink the ship and us with it.

"As we scrambled for some kind of order on the benches, the monster toyed with us, making currents with its tail that carried the ship now nearer to shore, now further away. A crewman found his bow, placed an arrow with shaking hands, drew the string tight. The missile struck the creature in the neck and hung, quivering. The monster stilled, its eyes on the marksman. It shook itself and the arrow dropped into the water. I could see no wound between the glossy green scales that formed its hide. It extended its monstrous foot toward the man who had loosed the dart, and with one long claw it spiked him through the chest. Blood spurted crimson as it tossed him up into the air like a plaything. The creature opened wide its jaws. As he fell, it caught him neatly and swallowed him."

"Morrigan's britches," muttered Gareth. He and Kalev exchanged a glance. I saw in that look the recognition of a great story, and doubt that such a wild tale could possibly be true.

"We rowed for our lives," Felix said. "As we passed the sea monster it opened its jaws for one ghastly moment to reveal the remnant of that last meal, a sight I would give much not to have seen. It seemed the creature had satisfied its appetite, for it let us go. But I saw the look in its evil eye. It was sizing up each of us in turn. I imagined it thinking, *That man will be tonight's supper; that one I will save for tomorrow.* By the time we beached *Freyja* on the pebbly shore, the monster had vanished beneath the water.

"We clambered down onto the stones, our legs shaky, our minds reeling from the shock of what had just happened. Our situation was dire. The isle was high and rocky, with not a blade of vegetation to be seen. We were far off course, beaten and exhausted, our number depleted, our stores only adequate for what was to have been a few days' sailing to the Orcades. Even assuming we could get out of the bay without the monster's attentions, who knew if we could find our way back to Erin, or on to our original destination? We stood there in silence, all who had survived save for Matha, who was still in the hold.

"'Water. Food. Shelter,' Paul said, taking charge again, since it seemed nobody else was prepared to do so. 'I'll take a group to look for a cave or similar, somewhere beyond that creature's reach. Felix, you'd best get back on board and tend to Matha. There's no point bringing him ashore until we have shelter; he'll be more comfortable where he is. The rest of you, I suggest you unload a few supplies, water and food for a day or so, your warm cloaks, blankets if we have them. Get everything up higher, out of the monster's reach. When we've found shelter and fresh water we'll carry what's necessary there.' Someone said, 'Who made you the leader all of a sudden?' and others grumbled their concerns, forgetting that they had followed him without question in the time of greatest need. 'If you have a better plan, let's hear it,' Paul said, and when nothing was forthcoming, he gathered his expedition—the five men from Muredach's court and two of the Norse crew—and headed away along the shore.

"As I climbed back on board, thankful that the ship had been beached more or less upright, I heard Knut issuing instructions to the remaining men. He was quick to take control in Paul's absence, though on *Freyja* he had been a crewman, not a leader. Five men to locate and unload the supplies. The rest divided up into groups to search the terrain close at hand and see if there was any sign of fresh water, or anything edible, shellfish, seaweed, perhaps seals that could be speared. The voices faded as they went their separate ways. I clambered down into the hold, where Matha was in a bad way. It was not just the seasickness. He had injured his leg during the storm and was in great pain. I did what I could for him as men attempted to find our food stocks in the disorder around us.

"Time passed; the supplies were unloaded, and from the quiet outside I deduced the crew had taken everything to higher ground, as Paul had suggested. I gave Matha water; ripped up someone's spare shirt to make a bandage for his leg; wrapped him in a blanket that was slightly less wet than the rest. I was soaked, shivering, still unable to take in fully what had happened to us. Matha's teeth were chattering; he could not get warm. I lay down beside him, putting the blanket over the two of us and reassuring him that all would be well."

Felix glanced at me, and I saw in his eyes the memory of that first dusk, when I had brought him up from the cove, and the two of us had pressed close together for warmth. It seemed so long ago. Pebbles had touched three runes on the carven timber: *Lagu, Eh, Nyd*. The gods had told me, even then, that this would be a mystery long and painful in its revelation.

"I must have fallen asleep," Felix said. "If only I could have stayed awake . . . if I had been alert . . . I could have stopped them . . . " He clutched his hands together, and in the soft lamplight his features were a mask of anguish. "How could I have slept? How could I have been so thoughtless?"

"Felix," I said quietly, "tell us what happened next. What woke you? Did you hear something?"

"Footsteps on the deck above. Voices. I was half asleep, confused, my body stiff and aching. Someone dropped down into the hold, limp as if dead. A woman, her hair all gold, her body marble pale. Naked. Naked in the chill of that far-off place. I took off my cloak and flung it over her; she was not dead as I had thought, but deeply unconscious, a mark on her brow as if she had struck it hard in falling. Where had she come from? How could she be here? It was perhaps a wild dream, for she was the kind of woman who appears much in the fantasies of lonely seafarers, a creature formed in the mold of a goddess. Matha groaned. He had not seen her, but her fall had sent a bundle crashing into his injured leg, and he was in pain.

"Then came shouting from outside. I rose to my feet, hauled myself up to look out of the hold. Knut was on the deck, yelling, beckoning, and men were running, faces chalk white, eyes big with terror, running back toward *Freyja* as if pursued by demons. It happened so quickly. Knut bid me get down and I obeyed, not knowing what had frightened them. No sooner was I crouched beside Matha once more, the unconscious woman lying close by, than I felt movement and heard the crunch of stones under the ship's belly. They were launching *Freyja*. We were leaving the island. And my brother's group had not returned.

" 'Wait!' I shouted. 'In the name of the gods, wait!' The men heaved; the ship slid down the shore and deeper into the water. 'Heave!' Knut's voice came. 'Heave, men!' And then, from a distance, another voice shouted. 'What are you doing? Where's my brother?'

"I stuck my head up again, pulled myself up to sit on the edge of the open hold, despite Knut. My brother was sprinting along the shore toward us. He was alone. *Freyja* rocked in the shallows. Crewmen scrambled over the sides, took up oars, looked to Knut for the command to row. 'Paul!' I shouted, knowing they would not listen to me, but thinking perhaps my brother could make them see sense.

"They waited for him. Waited for him to reach us, to splash through the water, to heave himself up alongside the others. 'Why are you moving the ship?' he demanded. 'She's best left here. We've found a cave large enough to shelter everyone, and a freshwater spring. We need the supplies brought up—' The flow of words ceased. 'Don't tell me you were planning to leave without us,' he said in a different tone.

" 'No time for this,' Knut said, and his voice told me his intention was precisely as Paul had said. 'Pull, men!'

"Paul tried to stop them. There was a struggle. It was so quick I could not help him, and besides, I am no fighter. At the end of it, my brother had joined us in the hold. His hands and feet were tied, and I was ordered not to touch the ropes, or he would be thrown overboard still bound. Paul was shaking with fury, his face bruised, his eyes dangerous. The crew rowed. Every moment I waited for the roar of the serpent, the screams as it snatched one man, then another, but there was nothing but Knut's commands, the creak of the timbers, the wash of the waves. *Freyja* crossed the bay, edged through the narrow gap, headed for open sea."

Felix paused, drawing a deep breath. I felt what he must have felt then, the guilt, the horror, the powerlessness in the face of wrong.

"They did not free Paul until we were far out to sea," he said. "They let me untie his hands, but not his feet. We got an explanation for what they had done, though nothing could excuse such an act of callous cruelty. One party of crewmen had walked around into the next bay. There had been a cave there, some distance above the water and quite dry, and they had explored it, thinking it might provide good shelter. As they came out, the monster arose from the water, neck snaking, mouth slavering in anticipation. They ran; the thing pursued them, bellowing. To their horror, it came right out of the water, moving as a seal might, but far more quickly, so fast they could not outrun it. Of that group, only two survived. The rest the creature crushed with a single blow of its great tail. While it was devouring them, the two men fled. They found their fellow crewmen, told their tale and bolted for the ship. They made an unthinkable decision. They would seize the chance to leave the island while the creature was occupied in feeding. They would save themselves at the expense of Paul and his men, the eight who had gone to look for shelter. For they believed that if we stayed, all of us would inevitably die."

Johnny raised his hand, a sign that Felix should wait for Kalev to finish his translation before telling any more. When this was done, my cousin said, "Ask Knut what he thinks of this account thus far, will you?"

Knut's response was swift and fierce. "He lies! Sea monsters? I think not. The tale is complete fantasy, every word!" I noticed that he was not meeting Felix's eye, or indeed Johnny's.

"We were desperate for them to go back," Felix went on, "to save those whom we had abandoned to their fate, among them a boy scarce fifteen years of age. But there were only two of us, Matha being too old and too unwell to do much at all. They said they would kill me if Paul unfastened the rope around his ankles. We made the voyage back to Erin with a crew of only three-and-twenty oarsmen, far too few to manage a vessel of such size. We had left most of our supplies behind. It was . . . difficult. By the time the vessel foundered on your reef, we were down to seventeen, including my brother, myself and Matha. Paul and I were both rowing, he with his feet still tied." Felix lifted his head and looked straight at Knut. "If you had not fettered him, my brother would be here with us today. His death is your burden and your doom. I lay this on you, Norseman." The silence that followed this was alive with tension.

"Nonsense," Knut muttered when he heard the translation. "He is a madman to speak thus. The voyage was as I told you, no more, no less."

"What about the woman?" Gull asked. "That was Svala, I take it?"

"She came to when we were on open seas," said Felix. "She sat in the hold, saying nothing. She seemed in a daze, barely aware of what was around her. I found clothing for her. We tried to talk to her, but to no avail. Some of the men asked Knut where she had come from, and he said she was on the island, all alone, and that he had rescued her. Nobody bothered to ask for further explanation. We were too busy keeping the ship afloat and on what we hoped to be a true course back toward Erin."

"Danu have mercy," murmured Muirrin. "All alone, you say? There was no child?"

The silence drew out. The implications of this were appalling. It was unthinkable that Knut would have lied about the drowning of his son.

Suddenly I remembered the vision I had experienced in Finbar's cave, the first time I had gone there—hands seizing me, dragging me across the sand and through the water. Striking my head on something; falling. I knew without a doubt that it was Svala's experience I had felt, Svala who had come to Inis Eala bursting with grief. Grief, not over the death of a child, but over what had been done to her. She had not been rescued. She had been abducted.

Felix rose to his feet. "I must go there," he said, looking straight at Johnny. "I must go straightaway. We left our comrades behind. I must find them. This is pressing; every moment matters."

"There's no doubting your courage, or your sincerity," Johnny said slowly. "You'll understand, Felix, that after the loss of your memory and your severe illness, a man might doubt whether your recollections are completely reliable."

Felix's pale cheeks flushed crimson. "It is the truth," he said simply.

"Say we accept that," said Johnny. "This place is—how many days under sail, do you estimate?"

"It is hard to tell. We reached the serpent's isle four days after we set out from Ulfricsfjord, but we were driven off course, as I told you. The winds were extreme. Returning, we rowed much of the way."

"May I say something?" Gareth asked. At Johnny's nod he went on. "Felix, you speak as if you intend to get into a boat and head off on your own, preferably first thing in the morning. All of us would feel the same compulsion to go, under these circumstances. We understand the horror of abandoning comrades. But your idea of doing so is hardly practical. The voyage is long. It's across open seas. Your ship reached this island by accident, in a storm, with, I presume, no stars visible by which to chart a course. You'd need a sturdy oceangoing vessel of reasonable size, an expert crew, good supplies. Then there's the small problem of the sea monster, supposing your story is accurate. It's been some time since *Freyja* came to grief here. I regret the need to say this, but it seems very likely all the men you left in that place would be dead

241

by now. I assume you will ask Johnny for help. For a ship and a crew. Under the circumstances, who in his right mind would want to go?"

Cathal cleared his throat.

"You don't believe the story?" It was Gull who spoke, rising to his feet and putting one misshapen hand on Felix's shoulder. "You think the lad's memory has been turned upside down and back to front?"

"That's possible, isn't it?" Gareth glanced at Evan.

"Entirely possible," Evan said, his tone compassionate. "On the other hand, the fact that this tale is unlikely does not make it untrue. Felix has told his story in a coherent manner, and it's a complicated tale. If his story is true, I see several reasons why Knut might want to lie."

Knut responded angrily when this was translated for him, and Johnny said, "Wait, Knut. Evan, explain to us what you mean."

"Someone's lying," Evan said. "Knut's story and Felix's cannot both be true. If Felix's story is accurate, then Svala's history is quite different from what we believed. There's a great deal missing. How did she come to be on the island? Why was she brought back here? Why did Knut tell us she was his wife? And what about the child?"

"And, of course, Svala cannot give us her own version," Johnny said. "One part of this tale, I know to be true. When my folk took the drowned men from the sea, one had a length of frayed rope linking his ankles." I saw Felix flinch at this. "It was cut free when they took him into the boat, to give him some dignity. When they laid him out, his burial garments concealed his damaged skin. I asked those who had seen this to keep it to themselves, for it troubled me. I have not spoken of it until now. Of those present here tonight, only Gareth and I knew of it. Felix, it seems your brother has borne witness for you, in this particular at least. Kalev, ask Knut how he accounts for this."

After an interchange, Kalev translated, "Knut says the man was a troublemaker, violent and unpredictable. The bonds were for his own good."

Felix started to say something, and Johnny waved him quiet. "There's a further part of this tale that can be put to the test. Another message can be dispatched to Ulfricsfjord, asking certain questions as to who boarded *Freyja* and requesting more details of the intended voyage." He glanced at Knut, and there was a new coolness in his gray eyes. "We can at least establish whether Svala was on the vessel at that point. We should also send a message to Muredach's court," he added, looking at Felix, who still stood before him, fists clenched, eyes a little wild. "Sad news for your prince, Eoghan. Sad news for all."

"Thank you," Felix said on a rush of outward breath. "I will write this message in the morning. But—"

Johnny raised a hand, and Felix fell silent. "But other matters are more urgent for you. Yes, I know that. I know you believe this account to be the truth. On balance, I am inclined to concur. But we cannot be sure, and unless we can be sure, you are asking a great deal of us when you ask for help. Gareth spelled it out clearly. A rescue attempt would be perilous in the extreme. Anyone undertaking such a mission would risk his own life and those of his comrades. We might lose a ship. We might never find this place or, finding it, might be unable to return safely. That must be weighed against the slim possibility that any of your party has survived so long on that inhospitable isle."

Felix bowed his head. "I know this," he said. "But I believe it must be done. Sibeal cast the runes not long after I came here, before I had recalled any of my past. The divination showed a mission; courage in the face of death; the completion of a circle, the possibility of a goal achieved. I must do it. If you cannot help me, I will do it alone."

He stood there before us, his body rail-thin from his illness, his face all hollows, his eyes blazing, and I thought every person in the chamber, bar one, must hear the courage in his statement, and the truth.

"I have to tell you," Johnny said, "that at present we have no vessel at Inis Eala suitable for such a journey. Nor is there any such craft in the settlement across the water. Our biggest and sturdiest boat, *Liadan*, is presently in the south. She's due back soon, but I cannot say precisely when. Even if Snake's party sailed in tomorrow, there would be refurbishment required before the craft could go on such a testing voyage. As to assembling a crew, that would present its own difficulties. Felix, sit down now. I thank you for your account, which you delivered bravely. We must allow Knut his turn to speak. Kalev, ask Knut to give us his own version of *Freyja*'s voyage. Thus far he has told us very little. If he has anything to add, especially on the matter of Svala, now is the time to do so. Remind him that I don't want his opinions, only the facts."

"A simple story," Kalev translated for Knut. "It was exactly as Knut told you before—the ship set out from Ulfricsfjord for the Orcades with its passengers and its crew, and some wives, Svala included. Somewhere between the north coast of Erin and Dalriada, *Freyja* was caught by strange winds and driven west. She was wrecked on the reef here, with the loss of many lives, including that of Knut's son. Felix's story is a fabrication. Knut says he does not understand how you can give any credence to such a wild tale. He says there is no need to ask questions in Ulfricsfjord. Besides, few folk there knew Svala. She is not the sort of woman who makes friends."

"There'd be folk on the waterfront who would remember whether she got on the ship," Gull said. "Men don't easily forget a woman like that."

"There's one element in this that troubles me greatly," said Johnny. "If Felix's story is true, what was Svala doing on the serpent island all by herself? How could she have survived there? Her story could help us determine the truth, but she cannot give it to us."

"She has given it," I said into the silence that followed.

"How?" asked Gareth.

"You know I am a seer." I spoke mainly for Knut's benefit—the last thing I wanted was to be accused of making things up because of some kind of personal feelings toward Felix. "I have visions, flashes of Sight. If other people experience a powerful welling of emotion, be it sorrow or anger or frustration, sometimes that spills over and I share it. That is a phenomenon over which I have no control. It happened tonight, when I came upon Knut attacking Felix. And it has happened with Svala, more than once. I've known since the first day she came here how unhappy she was. Several times she's tried to show me what happened to her. Clodagh saw it once, too. And—"

Johnny stopped me with a gesture, waiting for the translation to catch up. As Kalev was still speaking, Knut leapt to his feet, eyes fixed on me in undisguised hostility. Every man in the chamber was suddenly on edge; I felt it.

"You cannot take her account for truth!" the Norseman shouted. "Visions, feelings—this cannot be trusted! She could be saying anything, anything at all! She and this man, they are close, too close—no doubt they have concocted this whole story together. The girl will say anything if she thinks it will make you believe him!" Perhaps seeing the look on Johnny's face, he moderated both tone and expression. "I am sorry; I should not have spoken thus. The girl has good intentions, no doubt. Perhaps she believes her own story, whatever it is. But Svala cannot tell her tale. Not only is she unable to speak, but she is . . . " He repeated the gesture I had seen once before, tapping his temple with a finger. "Whatever she has conveyed to your girl is unreliable." Kalev scrambled to keep up with the flow of words.

"Sit down," Johnny said in the tone men never failed to obey. "Sibeal, in the interests of fairness, I must ask you to respond to the accusation that you may be less than impartial where Felix's welfare is concerned. I regret the need to do so."

I felt my face flush red. As I drew breath, unsure how I might best answer, my sister's voice came, cool and precise.

"Since Knut believes Sibeal cannot give you an unbiased account," Muirrin said, "I'll do it for her. At around midday today, Sibeal came back from the seer's cave, where she had encountered Svala. She came straight from there to the dining hall, and then she joined me and Clodagh and Brenna for the afternoon. Sibeal did not return to the infirmary in between, and so she had no opportunity to speak to Felix, or indeed to Gull or Evan or Johnny.

She told us about a vision she had shared with Svala in the cave, a vision she believed was a reflection of what Svala wanted to tell her."

My sister looked straight across the chamber at Knut, her neat features calm and composed as always. "The vision, as Sibeal recounted it, was completely consistent with the story Felix has just told," Muirrin said. "*Freyja* driven toward the lonely isle, the narrow gap through which they reached the bay, the appearance of the monster, which killed a crewman and ate him. A man— Paul, Sibeal thought—rallying the crew and bidding them row for shore. That was all she saw. Afterward, Sibeal told us, she and Svala enacted the scene again, using objects at hand, so that Sibeal could be sure her own vision matched with Svala's. Sibeal told us she believes Svala is desperate to return to that place. The message she was conveying was *Home. Go there, go home.*"

Kalev's murmured translation came to an end. There was utter silence.

"Once, earlier, Svala made a sea monster on the beach, using sand and shells," I said. "A creature somewhat like the one Felix described, and very like the one in my vision, with a long tail and fearsome teeth. She tried to tell me something about it, using gestures, and grew very frustrated when I didn't understand. She kept pointing out to sea. *Home. I want to go home.* I sensed the longing in her, and the grief. Clodagh was there, too—she can confirm that part of my story." I would not tell of our encounter on the cliff path, and Svala naked in the place of Rodan's fall.

"A concocted story," Knut said. "Who is to say she and Felix did not invent this long ago?"

"I'd swear the lad only regained the last part of his memory tonight." Gull's voice was deep and sure. "I saw that in his eyes, when he came to after knocking his head. I heard it in his voice. *We left them behind*, he said. I'll never forget the sound of that." He turned toward Knut. "You'd be far better to give us the truth," he said, not unkindly. "The longer you leave it, the harder the consequences will be. I know how much you want to stay here. If you lie to Johnny, there is no way he will keep you on Inis Eala."

Nor, I thought, would he keep a man who tried to kill another to prevent him from telling the truth, a truth that would make Knut look less than admirable in this place where he had become the friend of so many men. So the Norseman wanted badly to stay on Inis Eala. Was he afraid to go back to Ulfricsfjord and account for himself?

"You speak of nightmares," said Cathal. "I must tell you that the ill dreams that have plagued me ever since the ship was wrecked on our reef were full of monstrous seas, howling gales, snapping jaws, screaming men. I have seen this island in my sleep. It is a place of towering rocks, treeless and gray amid its shawl of white water. A grim place. A place of death." He fell silent for a moment before continuing. "I know you must take time to consider this, Johnny. I know you will not make any decisions tonight. But I wish to say to you, Felix, that I believe your story. I offer you an apology. I misjudged you."

I had no idea what Cathal meant, but I saw Felix incline his head courteously, as if accepting the apology, and I saw the warmth in his eyes as he met Cathal's dark gaze. "Thank you," he said simply.

"It's late," Johnny said, rising to his feet. "We all need sleep. I will call a meeting in the morning. I will consider what's been said and come to a decision. Felix, you look like a ghost. You must rest. You, too, Sibeal." He looked at Knut, who had risen and stood flanked by the taller Kalev and Gareth. A sheen of sweat covered the Norseman's fair skin. His eyes were restless; his fingers twisted the strip of hide that held the runic talisman around his neck. "Gareth, Kalev, take Knut to the small chamber at the end of the men's quarters," Johnny said. "He'll sleep there tonight, and I want a guard on his door. Wake Niall. You two need your sleep. Knut, you'll have one of my men with you at all times during daylight hours until this is sorted out. Stay away from Felix and from Sibeal. Is that understood?"

Knut shifted his feet. He muttered something.

Kalev stifled a yawn as he translated. "He says, perhaps the story is not quite as he told it."

247

I was still on the mat by the fire, my hand in Felix's. I felt him start, as if a shock had gone through his body.

"Be quick." Johnny's face was like stone.

"In part, his story was true," Knut said. "There was another island, far north. The storm, the bay, the monster . . . it is accurate enough. I did not think you would believe it, so I said nothing of it. No man likes to be called a liar."

These words hung in the air, a judgment he had brought on himself.

"Anything further?" Johnny's tone was even and quiet. He gave no indication of what he was thinking.

"Svala," Knut said, looking down at his boots. "She is not my wife, not in the way folk mean the term, but . . . "

"But what?" Gareth asked, an edge in his voice. Everyone was weary, and whatever transpired, tomorrow would be full of fresh demands.

"She was alone on the island, naked and beautiful on the shore. All alone, abandoned there in that grim place. A woman, on her own, without shelter, without the means to make fire, without even a shred of clothing. How can anyone believe she wants to go back there? Such a place is home to nothing but crabs and shellfish. I could not leave her there, at the mercy of that monster. So I saved her, rescued her. She is mine, my wife in all aspects but the law, and that can be made good. With me she has shelter, food, companionship, all a woman needs from her man. I provide for her, I keep her safe. Most men would not trouble with a woman who was . . . " He did not make his gesture again, the one that meant *crazy, out of her wits*, but his meaning was clear.

"So you lied," said Johnny.

"You would not have believed me. It sounds like a wild invention. There was no need for anyone to know this, no need at all. He only made trouble telling it—"

"And the child?" asked Johnny.

Knut hesitated. I wondered if he was weighing up the odds: better to tell the unpalatable truth now or somehow to perpetuate the lie? "There was no child," he muttered.

"Why would you invent such a story?" asked Muirrin, clearly shocked. "Were the losses from *Freyja* not enough for you, that you had to embroider them?"

"Svala," Knut said. "Crazy. Unpredictable. I thought . . . I thought, without a good reason for such wildness, you would not let her stay here. I thought you would quickly send us away."

"I have another question for you," Johnny said, and the perilous quiet of his tone frightened even me. "Did you attempt to kill Felix tonight to stop him from telling this story?"

"No! Not to kill, only to warn him. I heard Sam talking; at supper, he was saying something about an island and a monster. How could he know this, save from Felix? I did not want the story told. I confess, it shows me in a bad light, and I . . . But I would not have killed him. Why would I do that? I came to give him a fright, to make sure he held his tongue, that was all."

"Sam," I said, seeing how it had been. "Brenna must have spoken to Sam about what I told the others earlier." I turned to Knut. "Brenna didn't learn the story from Felix," I said. "She learned it from Svala, through me. What Gull said was true. Until you attacked Felix and he hit his head, he had no memory of this."

Knut opened his mouth and shut it again. Nobody said a word. Johnny made a motion with his head, indicating that Gareth and Kalev should go, and they left with the Norseman between them. Cathal made his good nights and followed.

"Evan," said Gull, "whatever transpires from this, tell me I can give Felix something other than soup tonight, will you? It's going to be hard enough for him to sleep, after this."

"You can try him on bread and milk. Don't get up, Father. I'll fetch it." Evan looked at the exhausted, pallid Felix where he sat slumped on the bench beside Gull. I could imagine what my brother-in-law was thinking. At every turn, Felix had spoken of the rescue expedition as an enterprise in which he himself would take part. That looked nigh impossible.

"Muirrin," I said as she and Evan went out, "thank you for speaking up."

My sister smiled. "There's no need to thank me for the truth, Sibeal."

Then there were only Johnny, Gull, Felix and me left in the infirmary. I had expected Johnny to leave promptly. It was the middle of the night, and with the Connacht men on the island, he must be up early. But my cousin sat on awhile, deep in thought.

"You mean to go, whatever happens," he said eventually, his eyes on Felix, assessing. "On your own, if it comes to that. Weak, sick, not much of a sailor, not much of a fighter, you would still do it. I can't make up my mind whether you're the bravest man I've ever met, or the maddest."

Felix had begun to shake; whether it was from the relief of tension or sheer exhaustion, I did not know. To remember, to tell the story, to be half-believed—it was a great deal in one night. Not to speak of the fact that Knut had almost killed him. I knelt up beside him, holding both his hands in mine. Gull laid his cloak around Felix's shoulders. Perhaps Felix did not look like much of a hero right now, but to me he seemed a beacon of courage, a lamp of truth.

"He must go," I said to Johnny. "I know it can't happen until *Liadan* gets back, and perhaps not for a while even then. But when it's time, the runes have told us that Felix must be part of the rescue." I remembered my divinations, both of them pointing to a mission the two of us would undertake together. I recalled Felix's voice, soft and sure as he called me the flaming torch that led him forward. I saw in my mind Svala's vision of the two of us, she and I, rowing a little boat across a trackless ocean and into the north. "Svala must go as well," I said. "And so must I."

CHAPTER 10

~Felix~

I have so longed to eat a proper meal. Now I scarcely taste the wedge of bread, the cup of watered goat's milk. My mind is reeling. A trap; fate has laid a trap for me. Sibeal's words froze my heart. I saw on Johnny's face, and on Gull's, the same horror. I cannot argue with the runes. But Sibeal out in those seas, Sibeal in that godforsaken place, Sibeal in the claws of the monster . . . I see how it would be, and I shrink from it, body and mind. What if, in my desperate quest to save my companions, I draw my most precious friend, my light, my treasure, to a hideous, bloody death? I would die rather than see her hurt.

If I do not go, she need not go. But I must go. I must do my best to put right the evil thing that was done. If the least chance exists that any man still clings to life on that isle, I must find him. I must bring him home.

There was death in the runes. I did not think it might be hers.

"Eat up," says Gull, yawning. "We must at least attempt sleep before dawn, and you'll rest better with some good food inside you."

I cannot say what I am thinking. I cannot tell Sibeal I do not want her to come. The runes do not lie. To question them is to doubt her integrity as a seer. "Do you think he will do it?" I ask instead. "Will he help me?"

"Only Johnny can answer that," says Gull. "He believes you, all right; I could see that, though he won't say so plainly until he's decided how to proceed. As a leader of fighting men, Johnny's made his share of tough decisions. He won't put his men in peril for a hopeless cause, however desperately you need that to happen. Say he does decide to go ahead with a rescue attempt for these poor fellows. Nothing much can be done before *Liadan* gets back. Then there's the matter of a crew. I'd expect him to ask for volunteers, and not all men will be free to put their hands up. Johnny himself won't go, for a multitude of reasons. Cathal can't go. Not only is his wife about to give birth to their first child, but there are certain factors that bind him to Inis Eala. It's not safe for him beyond the island. Any man who's tied up in training the Connacht men must stay here while our visitors are with us. That rules out quite a few of the most capable among us. Johnny won't let such an expedition set out unless he's convinced the crew's adequate to the task. He'd be asking people to put themselves in great peril. Not that the fellows here are averse to risk, but this . . . "

He sighed and took a mouthful of his ale. "If only we could know whether anyone's survived. To be honest, Felix, I don't like the prospect of losing good men over this. Especially not if it turns out to be a fool's errand, with your comrades already fallen prey to cold or starvation or this creature. That's a little blunt, maybe, but I have to say it."

"You think we should not attempt this?" Gull's doubt unsettles me further; I feel sick.

"I didn't say that, lad. If you want my honest opinion, I think there will be enough men willing to form a crew of sorts. But if I were Johnny, I'd be wanting more certainty." He glances at Sibeal, who has moved to sit on the bench opposite the two of us, her ale cup between her palms. Her eyes are wide and watchful in the firelight.

"I could cast the runes again," she says, "but I believe they would show the same message as before. I could scry, posing a question about survivors. I might see a vision of men on the serpent isle, but I wouldn't know if I was looking at past, present or future, or whether the images meant something other than what they showed. If you want certainty, I cannot provide it. Only hope. Only my conviction that this is the right thing to do, for you, Felix, for Svala, for those men you left. Even for Knut."

"Why do you say that?" I ask.

"Because every man must at some point confront the truth about himself. I still don't understand why Knut told so many lies."

"It's a shock." Gull's tone reflects this; he is upset. He befriended Knut. He liked the man. "Maybe he started with one lie, and ended up trapped in a whole web of them."

"His explanation for bringing Svala with him sounded reasonable—she was alone on that wild, rugged island, he thought to protect her—but . . . " Sibeal hesitates. "In the light of your story, I recalled a much earlier vision, from the first time I visited the seer's cave. I think Knut may have removed Svala from that island by force. If that's true, if he abducted her, then we've done her a terrible wrong by accepting Knut's story. She's been with him in that cottage, alone, perhaps unwilling . . . "

This shocks me. I can think of nothing to say.

"I hope you're wrong, Sibeal," Gull says. "Svala has seemed content enough in Knut's company on those few occasions when she's come out in public. She's somewhat withdrawn, certainly. But who knows what happened to her before the ship reached that island? Maybe she was the only survivor of some earlier voyage. That would be enough to drive the most reasonable woman half out of her wits."

"Content," echoes Sibeal. "No, Gull, she's far from content. But she has no words to explain, and that makes her angry. Several times she has tried to show me her story, and I've failed to understand anything save how miserable and frustrated she is. She's different when Knut is not with her. Stronger. Braver. Angrier. When he comes close she shrinks into herself, like a creature hiding in a shell. I think she's scared of him."

I finish my scant meal in silence, pondering this, remembering the wan, limp creature who shared the hold with us on the difficult journey back from the serpent isle. She was neither strong nor brave. She sat huddled in a corner, and any time I went down there she shrank away from me, covering her face with her hands. At night she wept, disturbing our already patchy sleep. I recalled Knut talking to her in an undertone once or twice. Sick, exhausted and disturbed as I was, with my brother beside me in fetters and Matha moaning with pain, I did not take as much notice as I should have done.

"I don't think I'll be able to sleep at all," Sibeal says. "Felix, I'm happy that you were able to tell your story at last, and sad that it is such a terrible one. But now we can act. We can do what the gods bid us do." She smiles, her face pallid with weariness, and I manage a smile in return. The weight of what lies unspoken is heavy on me.

"You'd best go to bed and shut your eyes awhile, at least," Gull tells her. "I predict a long and tiring day tomorrow. As for you, Felix, if you really intend to be part of this, if it goes ahead, it'll be a race to get you strong enough in time. Hard work for the two of us."

I murmur a response. The magnitude of this mission is daunting. I try not to dwell on what might go wrong, what lives might be lost, what new burdens my quest might lay on the shoulders of these good people. That way lies madness.

"Sibeal," Gull says quietly. "You realize, I presume, that despite the authority you carry as a druid, your kinsmen will balk at the idea of your undertaking a venture such as this. In saying the gods intend you to go, you make Johnny's decision especially difficult."

"I must follow the will of the gods," Sibeal says, her voice clear and sure. "It was plain in the runes that the two of us would undertake this together. I mean Felix and me. I believe that if we do not both go, and Svala as well, the mission cannot succeed. I can't be more plain than that."

"You may have trouble convincing Johnny," muttered Gull. "I'm glad it's not my decision. Think what your father would say, if he knew. Or Ciarán."

"I'm a grown woman," says Sibeal calmly. "And since neither Father nor Ciarán can be consulted in time, there is no point in wondering what they might think."

Gull grins, but I see the concern in his eyes. "Ah, well, that's for the morning," he says. "Felix, do you need to go to the privy before bed?"

I shake my head. He goes; I stay. There is time to speak to Sibeal alone: brief, precious time. I can find no words. We stand facing each other. She reaches out her hands. When I take them, they seem swallowed by mine. She is made small and fine in every particular.

"You lived up to the name I gave you," she says, fixing her lovely eyes on mine. "You were brave, and you'll go on being brave, no matter what happens. We can do this, Felix. We will do it."

Now I have too many words, and none of them can be spoken. *I don't want you to go. You might die, and I couldn't bear that.* Or worse, *I love you, Sibeal. I wish from the bottom of my heart that you were not a druid.* Say that, and I will lose her friendship forever. Besides, it is only half true. Her faith is part of her; part of what makes her so remarkable.

"Sibeal," I ask, "what happened with the fire, when Knut was attacking me? What did you do?"

An odd little smile curves her lips. "I wasn't sure anyone noticed. Druid magic; elemental magic. I've never used it before outside the nemetons. Ciarán taught me. Though, of course, his skill goes far beyond mine."

"Of course." Jealousy flares up in me, deluded fool that I am. Who could compete with this beloved mentor, this much-revered teacher, this magical, brilliant kinsman of whom she speaks so frequently? I am no more than a wandering interpreter, a younger son whose inability to comply with rules led his whole family into danger and caused his brother's death. I think perhaps I hate this Ciarán.

"Felix?"

I have stood in angry silence while she watched me. I relax my grip on her hands, loosen my tight jaw, make myself breathe.

"What's wrong?" Sibeal's voice is like water fresh from the mountains, clear and sweet. Hearing it, I cannot hold on to my anger. Perhaps I should wish Ciarán was here. If *he* tried to stop her, as any reasonable man surely would, perhaps she would take heed.

"Felix?" she says again, lifting her brows.

"Sibeal, I wish—no, never mind. You should go to your bed. It's halfway to dawn already."

Sibeal is watching me closely. She knows I am avoiding something. My mouth stretches in a yawn. There is no artifice in this. I am bone weary.

"I'll bid you good night, then," she says.

"Good night, Sibeal." I hope she cannot see in my eyes how much I want to put my arms around her and feel the warmth of her lips against mine. To press her body close; to touch her. I release her hands and step back politely to let her go past me.

Halfway to her little chamber, she turns to look over her shoulder. "Felix is Latin, isn't it? Does it mean *the happy one*, or something like that?"

I feel my mouth twist, but I am not smiling. "Joyful," I say. "It means joyful. Sleep safely, Sibeal."

"You, too. Dream of home. Remember, Paul is close by, watching over you. He would be proud of what you've done tonight."

I bow my head, lest she see that my eyes have filled with tears.

~Sibeal~

Sleep was elusive. I lay with eyes closed, breathing slowly. When I judged it to be almost dawn, I got up, dressed and went outside.

From the infirmary proper there was no sound of movement, and I hoped both Gull and Felix were sleeping.

I walked to the place of the boat burial, where nine drowned men lay under their earthen mound. Grass was already starting to creep up over it. The place was serene and quiet in the morning light. I sat on the ground, thinking of the nightmare voyage those men had endured, and how cruel it was that on the very point of reaching the home shore again, the crew had fallen victim to the wild seas and the wind. I considered the long reach of Mac Dara.

"Paul," I murmured, "your brother is going back there. He's going to save the men whom you were forced to leave behind. Be proud of Felix. Now that you are gone, he has to take the lead himself, and he's not used to that. Help me watch over him, if you can. You were the best and most loyal of brothers. He loves you and misses you."

I stayed there awhile as the sun rose slowly in the sky, and the community of Inis Eala awoke and began its daily business. Men went down toward the jetty. A girl drove a small herd of goats out of one walled field and into another. Folk moved between sleeping quarters and dining hall; between dining hall and practice yard. After some time I got up and headed back, taking a roundabout way that would give me a view of the main bay and the fisherman's cottage where Knut and Svala were housed. He would not be there, of course, but she might. Some time soon, someone must try to explain to her what was planned. That task would most likely fall to me.

The fishing boat was out in the bay, trailing nets. The little cottage close to the water's edge had its door standing open, but there was no sign of Svala. Perhaps she had been worried when her husband did not come back last night. Perhaps she had been relieved.

My gaze moved to the jetty and I narrowed my eyes. Was that Fang down there, Fang who had been behaving so oddly, and who had not come in at all last night? She was hunkered down at the very end, apparently staring out across the water. There was something very strange about that frozen position. Was the little dog hurt?

I made my way down, feeling obliged to check that all was well. I stopped a few paces away from the dog, crouched down and spoke to her quietly. "Fang?" And when there was no response, "Come here, little one." I clicked my fingers, and her ears twitched. "Good girl. Come on. Breakfast."

She was shivering with cold. A whimper emerged from her throat, a sound fit to melt the hardest heart. I was trying to coax her closer to me when Biddy came down the path with a basket over her arm.

"She's been here since last night," she said. "Don't try to touch her unless you want her teeth in your hand." She unpacked a water skin and a shallow bowl, then used the one to fill the other. She placed the bowl close to the dog—Fang growled without turning her head—and set beside it a handful of meat scraps from last night's supper. "I have a theory."

"Me, too," I said. "Is this the first time Snake's been away since he brought Fang to the island?"

"First time he's left her behind. Looks as if she's waiting. Makes you wonder, doesn't it? Maybe even among dogs there are seers. Otherwise how does Fang know he's on his way home?"

"So you think *Liadan* will be here soon," I said.

Biddy looked at me sideways. "I've been told some of what happened last night, but not all," she said. "Shall we walk back up together, and you can fill in the gaps? I hear a certain note in your voice when you mention the ship, and it worries me. I hope that man of mine isn't contemplating doing anything reckless. I saw how much he enjoyed tutoring Knut in swordplay. Made him feel young again, no doubt; young and whole. Trouble is, when they start feeling like warriors, they've a tendency to rush off and get themselves killed."

Where the jetty met land, I paused and glanced over my shoulder. Fang was devouring the meat.

"Since you're such an early riser," Biddy said, smiling, "you can feed her for me tomorrow."

"Gladly. As for last night, Felix—Ardal—told an extraordinary story. It was like this . . . "

Even in a much abbreviated form, the tale took us all the way back to the dining hall, where Biddy's assistants had the fire crackling and were starting to prepare the breakfast porridge. "Johnny will call his meeting this morning, I expect," I said. "I don't imagine Gull would want to go on this voyage. But Evan might. There are reasons why a healer's presence would be useful."

"Danu be merciful," Biddy muttered. "I'm not sure I want to hear this. My son go to that godforsaken place, when Muirrin's with child at last? Next thing you'll be suggesting Cathal go too."

I said nothing to this. It was unthinkable that Cathal would sail with us, with Clodagh's baby due so soon and the powerful hand of Mac Dara poised just beyond the safe margin of Inis Eala. And yet . . . and yet . . . I wished Biddy had not said this, even in jest. I wished I had not thought of the implications. "Of course," I said, "the entire venture depends on Johnny's decision. And on the return of *Liadan*." I did not say that Felix and I were both intending to go. I suspected today would hold a long chain of shocked responses to this news, and I would not invite them before I must.

Johnny had been faced with an extraordinary series of events. He dealt with the situation like the true leader he was. There was no urgent announcement to disrupt the routine the Connacht men were used to; there was no immediate involvement of folk who had no need to know. However, by breakfast time it was apparent to me that a great deal of planning had already gone on behind closed doors. I suspected that Johnny and Gareth had been up all night, and that certain key figures among the Inis Eala men had been woken rather earlier than was usual.

Over breakfast, Rat announced that the entire contingent of Connacht men would be undertaking rope work and other associated exercises at the western end of the island. He would supervise, and three of the island warriors would assist him. They could expect to be gone all day, he told the men, so they'd best eat heartily now. This was an opportunity for the visitors to put together everything they had learned so far.

I ate without much real appetite. I was starting to feel nervous, despite my conviction that the mission would go ahead. Clodagh had her eye on me, and the expression in it told me quite plainly that she'd heard the whole story from Cathal, knew I intended to go, and thought the idea completely outrageous. But she said nothing, and neither did Cathal or Gareth, who came to join us after Rat had finished his speech to the visitors. While I had not been sworn to silence, I realized nothing would be said about the night's drama until the Connacht men, at least, were out of the way. Knut was not in the dining hall. Neither was Svala. I hoped that she was nowhere near the place where Rat would be conducting his exercise.

We ate in awkward silence. The enormity of what lay ahead made it impossible to speak of day-to-day matters. Evan went up to the infirmary, carrying provisions for Felix, and Gull came down to join us, yawning. Eventually Johnny, who had been moving about the hall talking to one group, then another, came back to our table and sat down.

"We'll meet here later in the morning," he said in a tone calculated to carry no further than our small group. "I'm calling the whole community together, but only briefly. I'll explain what has happened and put forward a proposed course of action. We'll meet again when folk have had time to think about it. Evan tells me Felix is strong enough to be brought down here for this, Gull—will you see to that?"

Gull nodded.

"It's important, or I wouldn't suggest it. I want to put an end to these ill luck rumors, and in that matter I believe he'll be his own best advocate. After last night's revelations, I've been wondering whether Knut may have been the source of those rumors. Discredit the man, and you discredit his story when it finally comes out. Gull, tell Felix he should be prepared to speak briefly. Once the community knows the situation, the visitors can be told. No doubt everyone will be conversant with it by supper time." He turned toward me. "Sibeal, I think Svala should be present. Can you persuade her to join us?"

"She wasn't in the cottage when I went down earlier," I said. "I can look for her, certainly. But even if I find her, I may not be able to explain something so complicated."

"Don't go looking on your own." There was an unusual edge in Johnny's voice. "Take Brenna or one of the other women."

I looked at him, not able to ask the question I wanted to: *If Knut is locked up in the men's quarters, what are you worried about?* It was not the first time I had wondered if he shared my suspicions about Rodan's death.

"I'll come," Clodagh said. "The walk will do me good. Don't look like that, Cathal. Yes, my back hurts, but I'm not going to make it any better by lying around like a seal in pup."

"I'll come as well," offered Muirrin, surprising me. "If all three of us together can't persuade Svala to be at this meeting, then I suppose nobody can."

We found Svala seated on the rocks in one of the small bays. It was a still morning, and the sea had the sheen of fine polished silver. Further out in open water, something moved beneath the surface, perhaps a shoal of fish, perhaps a larger creature. Svala had her clothes on this morning, but her gown was hitched up above her knees, revealing a length of shapely leg, and her bare feet were crusted with sand. She turned her head to watch us approach, large eyes wary. Her hair was soaking wet.

At a certain distance we halted, the three of us, keeping to the plan we had made on the way.

"Good morning, Svala," I said. "These are my sisters." I made a series of gestures, trying to show that the three of us had been little together, had grown up together, were linked by love.

Svala inclined her head gravely. So far, so good.

"We brought you something," Muirrin said, moving forward with our gift wrapped in seaweed. She stopped a few paces from Svala, bent down and laid it on the rocks: a gleaming, sizeable codfish, obtained from Biddy. Jouko had been out early with a hand line; this was part of his impressive catch.

Svala's lovely eyes went from the fish to Muirrin to me and Clodagh, and back to the fish again.

"You can eat it," I said. "Eat. Good." I demonstrated, hoping we would not be offered a share this time.

She moved, keeping one eye on us as if she thought we might change our minds and seize back our gift. She was quick; in the space of two breaths, she had come down, grabbed the fish and returned to her perch, holding her prize to her chest.

"Eat," I said again. "Fresh caught today."

Svala lifted the cod and sank her white teeth through scales and flesh, ripping away a mouthful and bolting it as if she had not had a good meal in days. I heard Clodagh make a little sound, quickly suppressed, and hoped she would not be sick. I *had* warned my sisters.

"Good?" I asked, then went on without waiting for an answer. "Svala, your man, Knut—not home last night. Hurt another man. Locked up." Muirrin and I performed a bizarre little mime, she taking the part of Knut—we tried to show who she was by suggesting the amulet around the neck—I of Felix. "Johnny locked him up for now." The heavily pregnant Clodagh assumed the role of Johnny, leading Muirrin to an imaginary chamber and shutting the door. "You are safe," I said. "We are all safe."

Svala regarded our performance with apparent interest, all the while tearing and chewing with vigor. No wonder her teeth were so good. But then, if she had been stranded on the serpent isle for years and had gone half wild, it was no surprise that she had acquired an appetite for raw fish and the ability to deal with it. There would have been little else on offer.

"Svala," I said, moving on, "you know we talked about the island—out there," I pointed northward. "The serpent island." I used my arm and hand to make the creature, as she had done in the seer's cave. "A boat—rowing, sailing—you go back there. You and I." It was easy enough to indicate; we had done this part before.

She ceased feeding to stare at me, her eyes suddenly alight.

"Maybe go," I said, seeing how difficult this might be if she misunderstood. "Johnny will decide. Johnny . . . " How to show this? I moved a hand around my left eye, trying to indicate a tattoo of a raven, but so many men on Inis Eala bore similar markings, I doubted she could understand. But perhaps, by now, she recognized this name at least. "You come, listen to story. You come with us? All safe now. Maybe go, little boat, row to island."

"Would you be able to show her if you were in the seer's cave?" Muirrin asked in a murmur.

"There's no time for that this morning. Besides, it was more the other way—she didn't see my vision. I saw hers." Often when Svala had been touching me I had felt the turmoil within her, but the only time she had conveyed clear images it had been with the aid of the scrying pool. "When she's had her breakfast, I'll try something else," I said.

Watching as she devoured the fish, I wondered whether Svala had been starving for most of her sojourn on Inis Eala. She never ate much in the dining hall. My sisters and I waited quietly until the flesh was all gone, and Svala laid out the bones on the rock beside her, as if in a ritual. She had consumed all but this skeleton: scales, guts, even the eyeballs.

"Svala," I said as she stood and wiped her hands on her gown, leaving greasy streaks. "Svala, come." I reached out toward her.

She stepped down from the rocks and clasped my hands. "Close your eyes," I said, closing my own. I told the story in words, for my sisters' benefit, and as I spoke I pictured each part of it: Knut's attack, the confusion in the darkness, my terror that Felix would be killed. The truth coming out at last, Knut's denials, his eventual grudging revision of his story, Johnny's calm wisdom. I conjured an image of the community gathered in the dining hall, of Knut restrained by a pair of guards, of Johnny speaking. And then I imagined a boat, *Liadan*, sailing away to the north, and on it Svala, Felix and me. My crew did not include Knut.

My mind was so intent on these images, I did not realize until I opened my eyes again how tightly Svala was gripping my hands. I felt a wave of excitement flood through her, a passionate yearning, a wild elation. Some of my message, at least, she had understood. But perhaps not the elusive *maybe*. "Today, only talk," I said, realizing how hard it was to differentiate between a biting monster and a talking mouth when one only had a hand to use for illustration. "You come, yes?"

"Fresh clothes," muttered Clodagh. "If she's to appear in front of everyone, she should change that gown."

"A little fish is the least of our concerns," Muirrin said. "Svala, will you come now?" She pointed toward the path, lifting her brows in question.

But Svala released my hands, turned away and waded into the sea, up to her knees. She stood quite still for a moment, then slowly raised her arms to the sides, palms up. A powerful, keening cry burst from her, as if she would send a message to the far ends of the world. The sound rang across the sea. We waited, but she made no move to come.

"We should leave her for now," I said.

"What if Johnny decides against the rescue mission?" Clodagh asked. "Maybe it would have been better not to tell Svala until you were sure."

"She did need to know why her husband didn't come back last night," Muirrin pointed out.

"Sibeal," said Clodagh as we headed up the path, leaving Svala oblivious behind us, "do you really mean to go on this voyage yourself? Do you realize how mad that is?"

I considered this before offering an answer. "It's about as mad as your heading into the Otherworld to rescue Cathal was," I said. There was no need to point out that I had helped her slip away from home so she could do it. Such things are never forgotten between sisters.

"Are you sure you're not half in love with Ardal? I mean Felix? I can't think of any other reason you would suddenly lose all your common sense."

I glanced sideways at Clodagh. It was wrong to be less than honest with her. But I could not give her the answer that felt most true: *If ever I were to give up my vocation for a man, it would be for this man.* "I would never give up my vocation," I told her, and that, too, was the truth. "Besides, if I cared about him, I'd want what was best for him. It's best that both of us go. The runes showed that plainly."

"Mm-hm," said Clodagh.

"And that is the story," Johnny said. "A striking one, as strange as any old tale. I can understand that you might feel some doubt as to its truth, hearing it on its own. But there are Sibeal's visions, which illuminated certain aspects of it with perfect clarity. There's the evidence of the rope around Paul's ankles, which I saw with my own eyes. And folk have been dreaming since the shipwreck, folk who had not heard this tale until last night. Their dreams bear out what Felix has told us. Perhaps the most compelling argument of all is that, after calling that tale a web of lies, Knut has now admitted most aspects of it were true. It seems this man who has become a friend to so many of us during his time here is a bare-faced liar. More than that, he has attempted to murder one who was under our protection, and has both threatened and injured my young kinswoman. For this, any other man would be banished instantly from our shore. For this man, I have other plans."

The dining hall was hushed; the assembled men and women had hung on every word of Johnny's speech. He had given a calm, considered account of last night's events, including a brief version of Felix's story. The news of what Knut had done had caused an outcry. It was plain that many found it hard to believe him capable of such duplicity. But Johnny had said it, and nobody ever doubted Johnny. Knut had stood stone-faced between Niall and Jouko as his ill deeds were made public. Johnny had not asked him to speak.

"I have faith in Felix, and I believe his story," Johnny said now. "I see his honesty in his eyes. He has made a request that, if granted, will have weighty consequences for our community. Felix, step up and explain what you're asking of us, and why it's so important."

Felix rose to his feet, waving away Gull's supporting arm. He came to stand beside Johnny. His mouth was set tight; his eyes were full of determination.

"Some here have called me an ill luck man," he said quietly. "There may be some truth in that, for my brother perished on this voyage, drowned on the reef out there. He died because he stood up for what was right. Because he would have hindered their flight from the serpent isle, the flight that saw seven men abandoned to their fate, our crew tied Paul's ankles. I could not unfasten the knots in time, and so he drowned. My brother was a good man. A good man never leaves his friends behind. Sometimes we are faced with terrible choices, heartbreaking choices that make a mockery of right and wrong. But the choice that faced Knut and his companions on the serpent isle was easy. All it required was courage.

"I am compelled to go back, by any means I can, to try to save those men. It is what my brother would do if he were here. I do not know if they are alive or dead. I have no skills in navigation, no experience in sailing a boat. You will think me quite mad. But I am saner than I ever was. The gods call me to do this. Sibeal cast the runes for me; their message was quite plain. I must go, and I will go. Last night I asked Johnny if he would help me. If he cannot, if you will not, then I will find another way to do this." He glanced at Johnny, who was watching with a little smile on his lips. "That is all I have to say."

"Thank you, Felix. Sit down, please." Johnny faced the crowd. "I will give you time to consider this. Before you do, I'll make my own position clear. This can't be done without a vessel strong enough to withstand the trip. It can't be done before *Liadan* returns. We have no reliable guide to the location of this island, since the ship on which Felix and his brother were traveling was swept off course by a freak storm. We don't know if there are any survivors. We have a sea monster to deal with, a creature that is large, fierce and not kindly disposed toward men. That is a heavy weight of risk. To balance it, we have a group of men abandoned in that place by friends they believed they could trust. A group of comrades struggling to hold on against the odds, scraping an existence in the harshest of conditions, hoping and praying that someone will have the courage to come back for them." He paused, looking around the hall. The silence was profound. "I don't believe we have any choice," he said. "I'll authorize the use of *Liadan* for this mission. If we can put a crew together, we'll go ahead."

Spider rose to his feet. "How do you intend to choose that crew?" he asked.

"I'll call for volunteers," Johnny said. "Experienced men to sail *Liadan*; others with specialized skills. You realize what kind of mission this is. I don't want anyone making a decision without thinking it through. Take some time, talk to your wives, and don't make light of the immense risk involved. You need a few days, at the very least, to make up your minds. I won't take volunteers from those involved in training the Connacht men. Our primary work is on Inis Eala, and we must maintain that."

"The boat may need refurbishment," someone said. "That could take time. Is the plan to sail off as soon as possible after she returns?"

"Every day counts for those men," said Johnny soberly. "Work on the boat will start the day she comes in. Provided we have a crew, she'll sail out as soon as she's ready. Supplies can be assembled now, while we wait for her return."

A babble of talk had broken out all around the hall now as the implications began to sink in. I felt the women's doubt and fear, the pull between pride in their men and terror that those men might be lost on a journey whose heroic intention was equaled by its appalling uncertainty. I felt the inspiration that filled the men's hearts, the knowledge that here was a mission no true warrior could refuse. There would be volunteers, all right; far more than Johnny needed. I saw the light in their eyes.

"Johnny," said Gareth, "what happens if you don't get enough volunteers to make up a crew?" It seemed to me he already knew the answer—there were no secrets between these two—but had seen a need for it to be stated publicly.

"Then the mission cannot go ahead." The implications were quite plain.

"I've got a question," said Sam, rising to his full, impressive height.

"Ask it, then."

"What did you mean about Knut? We all know a man who acts as he has is banished immediately from the island. On the other hand, he's a good fighter and to many of us he's become a friend. What are these other plans you spoke of?"

Jouko had been translating for Knut. Now Knut released a flow of impassioned words, gesturing toward Johnny. Jouko lifted his brows in question.

"Translate it, please," Johnny said.

"Knut says he wants only to stay here and earn his place in the community that has welcomed him. He believes his fighting skills could be of great use to you. He swears there will be no repetition of last night's events."

"One would certainly hope not," murmured Gull, who was seated beside me.

"Any more?" Johnny asked, looking at Knut directly.

"And he says," went on Jouko, translating, "it is his belief that all who were left on the serpent isle must have perished by now. As, indeed, he and his crewmen would have done if they had not sailed away when they did. The monster would have devoured them all. Knut says this is a fool's errand, the sort of venture only a man such as Felix here would have conceived, for he is a scholar, full of dreams and softness. He is no warrior. Such a man has not the courage to fight."

Johnny did not speak immediately; he let the poison of these words stand for a while, so that every man and woman present could take it in. Then he said, "Felix, do you wish to respond to this?"

Felix managed a crooked smile. "Few men could match my brother for courage. Now that he is gone, I must be brave enough for two."

"Well spoken," said Gull, and I heard others echo the sentiment.

"Knut," said Johnny, "you are far from understanding the way things are done in this community. Your fighting skills are exceptional, and that has earned you friends among us. We have a rule here that the past can be forgotten, provided a man or woman is ready to start afresh, with the right attitudes and the right intentions. No, don't speak—I heard what you said before, and I remain unconvinced of your sincerity. Only last night you attempted to kill this man. You put my cousin in danger. That alone should earn you banishment from Inis Eala, as Sam quite correctly pointed out. But there's the question of Svala. She is not among us this morning—"

He halted, gazing toward the open doorway. I turned my head to see a familiar figure standing there, barefoot, with her damp hair straggling over her shoulders. The look on her face was that of a deer facing a pack of wolves. I rose to my feet, walked over and took her hand, guiding her forward.

Words burst out of Knut, a furious stream of Norse, and he strode across the chamber toward us, taking his guards by surprise. He was three paces from us before Niall seized him by the arms and restrained him. Svala's hand trembled in mine. Fine, strong woman that she was, she edged behind me as if my slight form might shield her. Her breathing was shallow and quick.

"Bring him back over here," Johnny said. "Knut, stand still and face me—I'm not finished. We don't have all of Svala's story yet, but it appears you may have done her a great wrong, albeit with the best of intentions. I welcome you here, Svala," a courteous nod, "and I hope we can set matters right for you."

"Set matters right? What do you mean?" demanded Knut.

"Sibeal believes Svala was taken from the serpent isle against her will," Johnny said levelly. "If that is shown to be true, then our mission will be not only to bring back the men who were left there, but to deliver Svala safely home."

A hubbub of talk greeted this. Johnny let it go for a while, then raised his hand for silence. "Knut, you will remain under guard for the foreseeable future. You'll stay away from Svala. You won't speak to her unless she requests it. As for your future, believe me, I am sorely tempted to banish you this instant. But I have always believed in giving a man a second chance."

I held my breath. How could he even think of having Knut on Inis Eala? The man did not know the difference between right and wrong. Or knew, and cared nothing for it.

"When *Liadan* sails for the serpent isle, you will be on board," Johnny said. "I'm not offering you a choice. If Svala wants to return there, you will take her. You will help our crew navigate. You will assist in the rescue of your abandoned comrades. When you come back from that place, if I see a change in you, a change I can truly believe in, then and only then will I consider your wish to remain among us. You are a good fighter. But we have many good fighters here."

By the time Jouko reached the end of his translation, Knut was no longer meeting Johnny's gaze. He looked down at his boots, one hand nervously twisting the leather strip around his neck. *Eolh* was a rune of defense. It could not defend him against a man like Johnny, a man who saw deep inside to the fear, the weakness, the lack of self-belief. It could not keep out the wisdom and compassion that were woven through this harsh decision.

"Sibeal," Johnny said, turning toward the doorway, "does Svala wish to speak? Can she do so through you?"

Now that Knut had been moved further away, Svala was steadier, but I felt her unease. The four walls, the fire, the press of folk, the sound of voices, everything unnerved her. She had come because she knew it was important. It was taking an immense effort of will for her to stay. It had been hard enough to convey my meaning to her down on the shore with only my sisters present.

"She will be happy with what you've decided," I said. "I will explain it to her in private." After a moment I added what I sensed to be true. "She thanks you for undertaking the mission. From the bottom of her heart. She has already told me how much she yearns to go back to that place."

"Are you taking more questions?" someone asked.

"If you need the answer now, yes," Johnny said.

"It's not so much a question as a comment." The speaker stood up and was revealed to be Badger, one of the older men. "I reckon there's one thing a man would want to know before putting his hand up for this, and that's whether there's a chance anyone could still be alive in that place. I understand that we can't know that. But if we could, it would make the choice a lot easier. If they're alive, it's a heroic quest. If they're all dead, it's a fool's errand."

Cathal stirred. He had stood behind Clodagh throughout the meeting, motionless and silent, his features set grimly. I met his eye, and a kind of recognition passed across his face. Would he break his self-imposed rule and offer to scry for this information? His comrades knew his parentage was somewhat unusual. I doubted that they understood the extent of his abilities, or the risks he faced in using them. Clodagh was frowning. I looked back toward my cousin.

"It's a fair comment, Badger," Johnny said. "As you say, we can't know. We must rely on what these dreams and visions tell us, and on our sense of what is right. No man should feel any compulsion to put his name forward. I will not think badly of any man for not wanting to go."

One of the younger men stood up, a sturdily built fellow with weathered skin and a head shaven bald as an egg. "I have a question for Felix."

Felix was tired. His face was waxen pale, but he held his shoulders square. Johnny glanced at him and he nodded.

"I've been a crewman on a trading vessel between Dublin and the isles," said the young warrior. "The voyage you're talking about would mean days at sea with no scrap of land in sight; uncertain weather; no real means to chart a course. Cramped conditions, little rest, limited supplies. You tell us you're no sailor, yet you say you're coming on this trip. I'll be blunt. This is a venture suited only to the strongest and hardiest of men. You may have done the trip once already, but it wasn't as a crewman. And haven't you been confined to the infirmary since the day you got here, under constant supervision, barely able to leave your bed? Scholar, aren't you? If I were choosing a crew to undertake such a mission, you'd be one of the last men I'd pick."

"That's blunt," I heard Gull murmur.

"I understand your argument," said Felix, rising to his feet once more. "By the time *Liadan* sets out for the serpent isle, I will be ready."

A brief silence followed this statement, which was delivered in a voice both confident and strong. From where I stood with Svala near the doorway, I could see that Felix had his hands clutched together behind his back to conceal their shaking.

"Five coppers says I can get him fit in time," called out Gull, a grin spreading across his dark features. "Any takers?"

There was a roar of laughter, followed by a chorus of offers. If these men liked anything it was a wager. Thus the meeting ended in a spirit of goodwill. Whether that feeling would continue once everyone had time to think about what lay ahead remained to be seen.

Not everyone in the hall was diverted from the matter in hand by Gull's moment of humor. Cathal always looked somber, but today he seemed to be walking under a personal shadow. I wondered what had provoked his apology to Felix last night, when he had spoken of misjudging him. Gareth was not his usual cheerful self. I put that down to lack of sleep; but perhaps he sensed an impending parting. If no other likely leader for the voyage offered his services, Gareth might feel honor bound to volunteer, taking on a duty Johnny could not perform himself. Such was the complicated bond of loyalty between this pair who were lovers, best friends and fellow warriors. My sisters were very quiet. Nobody had mentioned that I, too, would be traveling on *Liadan*, cramped conditions, trackless ocean, limited supplies and all. There were still some battles to be won.

"Svala, we can go now," I murmured, motioning to the outdoors. "Come with me." I felt in her trembling grip a powerful need for flight. But I kept my hold on her until we were out in the yard, the two of us momentarily alone. "It's all right," I said, holding her with my hands and my eyes. "You will be safe now. Knut is not coming back to your cottage, or to your bed, unless you want that. And we will take you home." I willed her to understand me; I made pictures in my mind, simple pictures I hoped would make sense to her. We stood there until other people began coming out of the dining hall. Their voices broke my concentration, and the link was gone. I felt suddenly drained. My knees had no strength. "Go now, if you want," I said, releasing Svala's hands.

She was off in a flash, running down toward the bay in her bare feet with her hair streaming out behind her. Had I seen a smile before she turned away?

"Sibeal!" Clodagh was there beside me, holding my arm, keeping me upright. "What's wrong?"

"Nothing. I'm a little dizzy. I need to sit down."

"Come back inside, let me get you some mead—"

"I'm fine, Clodagh . . . "

"Rubbish, you're about to faint. Now do as you're told."

Spots danced before my eyes; I felt sick. Quite clearly, my legs were not going to carry me anywhere. I allowed my sister to steer me to a bench outside the hall, where I sat with my head bent over my knees, waiting for the weakness to pass. In the light of that man's comment about Felix not being fit enough to travel, this was unfortunate. It became even more unfortunate when Johnny came out of the hall and moved to crouch down beside me. "Are you ill, Sibeal?"

I shook my head. A bad idea; my stomach roiled. "No, I'm . . . it's just . . . with Svala, it can be exhausting . . . "

"Clodagh will take you over to the infirmary to rest," Johnny said. "After last night, this is not surprising. Sibeal, you and I need to talk later. I'll come and see you when you've had some sleep."

"I need to go," I said with my eyes shut. "The gods . . . "

"Shh," Johnny said. "We're going to do this calmly, carefully, with the best preparation we can. Time enough to talk when you've rested. Could you walk now?"

People were streaming out of the hall and back to their work. The eyes of every potential crew member of *Liadan* might be on me. "Of course," I said, rising to my feet and feeling the earth tilt beneath me. "I'll just—" I took one step, then fell into darkness.

I woke in my little chamber, feeling perfectly well though still somewhat weary. I lay there awhile, looking at my charcoal runes and wishing very much that I had not demonstrated such weakness in public. I could remember little after I fainted, but I did have a dim recollection of someone carrying me, and Clodagh tilting a cup of water so I could drink. The light around the door suggested it might be midafternoon. I must get up, dress, prepare myself. Some time today I would have to present my case to Johnny; I had no doubt that was what he wanted to discuss with me. My collapse was not going to make things any easier. Perhaps I should be asking Gull to train me as well as Felix.

It was very quiet in there. Maybe everyone was catching up on sleep. I got out of bed, picked up my shoes and pulled the curtain aside.

The only person in the infirmary was Felix, and he was not asleep but standing by the hearth looking straight at me, as if he had been waiting for me to emerge. I wished I had brushed my hair before I came out. I wished . . . And then, without thinking much about it at all, I walked straight across to him, and he opened his arms, and I went into them. He had held me once before, briefly, but this was different. It felt like coming home from a long journey, and at the same time it felt like the first day of spring, when all the beauty and possibility of the season lies ahead. We stood there without speaking a word, his arms around my shoulders, mine around his waist, my cheek against his heart, his fingers moving against my hair. *I will not think beyond this moment*, I told myself. *I will store this up to remember always.*

It was Felix who stepped back first, taking my hands in his and lifting them to his lips for a moment. "You look pale," he said in a voice that was markedly unsteady.

I had thought my cheeks might be as bright as rosebuds. My blood was surging; inexperienced as I was, I recognized the signs of desire in my body. "I'm quite well," I said, but in truth I was confused, troubled and perilously happy all at the same time. "I was tired, not sick. I must have been sleeping for ages—where is everyone? Did you rest?" I heard myself babbling, filling the silence with empty words. I made myself stop. I sat down on the bench by the hearth, and Felix sat beside me, holding my hand.

His touch warmed me all through. I could not make myself with-
draw my fingers from his clasp, though it seemed to me I should,
for what had just occurred between us must not be encouraged.

"I worked with Gull for a while, then he sent me back here to
rest. But I have not slept; my mind is too full for that. Gull has
gone down to the married quarters to sleep. He was struggling
to stay awake. Evan and Muirrin are talking to Johnny. And I am
here, as you see. Waiting for you to wake up, Sibeal."

After what had just happened, I felt oddly shy with him. "You
seem different," I said.

"I am the same man I was yesterday."

"Stronger. More sure of yourself. Yesterday, I would have
thought you could never be ready in time to make such a voyage.
Today, I don't doubt that you will be."

"Johnny believes me," Felix said. "That makes all the difference. If I seem stronger to you, that is good. I must convince every
man who goes on the mission that I can play my part." He hesitated. "Sibeal . . . there is something I must say to you. I think it
will not please you."

I had no idea what he meant. I hoped he was not about to say
anything that would spoil the memory of his arms around me, his
tender touch, the touch not of a friend, but of a lover. I could still
feel it, a gift, a promise, a rare thing to be cherished, wrong as it
was.

"Sibeal," he went on, "I believe in you, I believe in your capacity to guide this. Who else can interpret for Svala? Who else can
hear the voices of the gods? I understand why it is important for
you to come on the voyage. The runes do not lie. If you were a
stranger to me, I suppose I would think what most of the island
folk will think: that you cannot possibly have the strength to endure such a mission. The people of Inis Eala know you are strong
in spirit, wise beyond your years. They also saw you faint away
this morning. They see how slight you are, how delicately made.
How could they imagine you on a ship sailing through mountainous seas toward an isle of myths and monsters?"

"I know that, Felix," I said. "But I don't need to convince the entire population of Inis Eala that I'm more than a helpless young girl. I only need to convince one person: Johnny."

Felix did not reply, simply sat there looking at me.

"Go on, then. Say it, whatever it is."

He cleared his throat. "Sibeal, I do not want you to come on the voyage."

It hit me like the punch of a hard fist. Any trace of druidic calm left me; I felt winded. "*What?*" I said, springing to my feet.

"Sibeal, I speak not as the man who shared that runic divination, but as the man who held you in his arms only a heartbeat ago. The mission is too perilous. You should not go." He reached to take my hands again, but I folded my arms. My heart had become a cold stone.

"How can you say that?" It was not the voice of a serene druid, but the shaky tone of the vulnerable girl who fainted when overwhelmed; the quivering voice of the young woman who had melted in his arms a few moments ago. I was losing myself. This could not be allowed to happen.

"Sibeal, let me explain, please. All I am trying to do is be honest with you, but . . . "

"But what, Felix?"

"You're angry. I have upset you."

"I thought you believed in me. I thought you were the one person who trusted me completely. I thought you saw my strength and not my weakness." Oh gods, now I was crying. "I thought you understood."

"Oh, Sibeal." He reached up to brush the tears from my cheek, and I shut my eyes, unable to bear the naked feeling on his face. There was such tenderness in his touch, I could not armor my heart against it. I knew I should step away, but my feet refused to move. "Sibeal, please listen. I believe in you. I know why you must come on the voyage. If you wish, I will support you when you speak to Johnny. But . . . now that it seems this journey might be real, that we might actually go there and find them, I cannot stop thinking of what might happen to you. If you were killed, if I lost you, I think my heart would break. I weigh it up—your death against the rescue of the men we left—and I begin to doubt the wisdom of the mission. I cannot doubt. I must do this for Paul."

My eyes were open now. "Oh, Felix," I said, and I put my hand against his cheek. "Don't think that. Don't doubt." His hand came over mine. "Besides," I made myself say, "I'm destined for a future in the nemetons. We'll be saying goodbye at the end of summer, whatever happens."

Felix closed his eyes. His voice was so quiet, he might have been speaking for himself alone. "That makes no difference," he said. "It cannot alter what I feel."

And despite myself, I knew this for the deepest kind of truth; for the same conviction had awoken in my own heart. "I know," I murmured. "And I'm sorry." *Sorry for you. Sorry for myself; oh, so sorry.*

"Sorry that you met me?" Felix was trying for a smile, without much success. "Or sorry that we must risk our lives together, for a mission with such small likelihood of success?"

"I will never be sorry that I met you, Felix. It was . . . a privilege. A gift. As for the mission, I trust the gods. They've shown us we can achieve this if we are brave enough. And we can be very brave, the two of us. The day you were washed up on the shore here, we proved that."

"You are brave, Sibeal. I, not quite so courageous. Twice you have saved my life, once on the shore and once last night, with your . . . diversion. I hope I can be brave enough to take you into danger and still act with balance and wisdom. I hope my terror for you does not paralyze me."

"When I was a little girl," I told him, swallowing tears, "sometimes my sisters would tell me I did too much thinking, when I should have been running about and climbing trees. Right now, we're probably both doing too much thinking. If we trust each other, we'll get through this. Other considerations don't matter."

Someone was coming; I heard footsteps outside and the rattle of the back door.

"Sibeal?" Felix murmured.

"Mm?" My fingers brushed his cheek, moved away.

"You have shown me both your strength and your weakness," he said. "That, too, was a privilege. It was a gift of great worth. More than I deserve."

Then, as Muirrin came in carrying a basket, with Evan close behind, Felix stood up and moved away, and I turned my back, finding myself quite unable to enter into an ordinary conversation. Feeling the opposite of brave, I mumbled something about the bathhouse, headed out the front door and fled.

I allowed myself the luxury of a long soak. Clodagh washed my hair for me and lent me fresh clothing, a skirt and tunic of her own weave in two shades of green. She did not ask if I had been crying. Indeed, she seemed unusually distracted, and not in the mood for talk. When I was clean and tidy I went out walking. I would talk to Johnny when I came back. Fang was still down on the jetty. Not far from her, two lads were fishing with hand lines. As I watched, one of the boys threw a small fish, and the dog caught it with the ease of long practice. Fang would not starve before her beloved Snake came home.

On the cliff path, halfway to the north point, I found Cathal sitting on the rocks looking out to sea. With his dark cloak wrapped around him and his black hair lifted off his long face by the afternoon breeze, he looked like a sorrowful prince from an ancient tale. As I came up he shifted over to make room so I could sit beside him. We watched the play of wind and water for a little, and then he said, "They're alive, Sibeal. At least three of them."

Perhaps I should not have been shocked, but I was. "You went to the seer's cave?"

Cathal sighed. "There seemed no choice. I can't let men put their lives at risk over this if it might be a pointless mission. Not when I possess the ability to summon a true vision. Yes, I made use of the scrying pool. I saw the three survivors in a cave, high up among the crags. That isle is a desolate place. They had a few supplies: some kind of large covering that they were using for warmth, one or two other things—I don't suppose Knut and his friends paused to reload what had been taken from the ship before they put back out to sea. The three I saw were . . . not in good condition. I hope *Liadan* gets here soon." A shiver ran through him. "Sibeal, that place is just as it was in my dreams. It makes me wonder who, or what, had the power to bring those dreams to Inis Eala. That's a remarkable gift, if gift it can be called. Someone has drawn us into the shadow of his own nightmares. Or hers."

I considered this awhile. "Do you still think Mac Dara could be involved?" I asked eventually. "It would be a convoluted way of exposing you to danger."

"He cannot exert his influence within the borders of Inis Eala," Cathal said, staring out across the ocean. "He must draw me out. My father is completely unscrupulous. He cares nothing at all for lives lost by the wayside. And he's easily bored. A sea monster is precisely the sort of detail that would amuse him."

"There's no certainty, is there?" I mused. "You can't know whether your father is involved unless you leave Inis Eala, and even then you might not be able to tell. He might be manipulating this from far away."

"Correct, Sibeal. All of this, everything that has happened, might be entirely unrelated to his struggle with me. I will not summon *him* to the scrying bowl. To do so would imperil all I hold dear." He drew a deep breath. "Your friend will be relieved to hear that some, at least, of his comrades still live. He interests me. So weakened by his experiences, clearly no warrior, yet full of courage where this mission is concerned. I misjudged him badly. I believed him an agent of my father. But even my father is not subtle enough to use an agent such as this. Unless he does so without Felix's knowledge."

"Cathal," I said, not sure if he would listen or snap at me for interfering, "you're doing what Felix was doing; you're thinking too much. The mission will go ahead, whether what happened is Mac Dara's doing or not. Every person on the ship will be there of his own free will. Except for Knut, I suppose, but he brought this on himself. As for your father, he doesn't want Felix or Svala or me, he wants you. Or your son. You know you can protect Clodagh and the baby. All you need do is stay on Inis Eala."

And then there drew out a terrible silence, a silence in which I was the one who was thinking too much, and cringing from what Cathal was not saying.

"You wouldn't go," I said in a horrified whisper. "With Clodagh's child coming so soon, you wouldn't even think of being part of this." But I saw it clearly: the waves, the tide, the monster and Cathal's particular skill in water magic. His presence on this particular mission might be the difference between success and bitter failure. Between life and death.

"Go back to the settlement, Sibeal." Cathal used his most forbidding tone, the one that said with perfect clarity, *Leave me alone.* "Johnny wants to talk to you."

And, since only Clodagh was prepared to stand up to him when he was in this particular mood, I obeyed. I walked back oblivious to my surroundings. How could he consider being part of this? How could he leave, when it almost certainly meant he would not be here for the birth of his first child? I knew some men placed little importance on such things, but Cathal was no ordinary man. He loved my sister with heart and soul. And the child . . . this was the child Mac Dara wanted, the child Cathal's father would do anything to take for his own. If Cathal left the island he put himself straight into Mac Dara's path. If he was killed Clodagh and her baby would be all alone. For Cathal to go away was . . .

Stop it, Sibeal. Do not judge him. If I were choosing the crew for the voyage, whom would I select, a young woman with no sailing skills at all, or a proven warrior, a leader, a superb fighter? A fainting, weeping girl who was starting to lose sight of the druid she purported to be, or a practitioner of powerful water magic? I must not let my emotions get the better of my common sense. Above all, I must banish the feeling of guilt that was rising in me as I imagined first one, then another of my family hurt or killed because I had believed this voyage was the gods' will. I could not allow myself to be crippled by doubt, for if I lost my faith in this mission, I could not help Felix hold on to his.

*   *   *

I had been rehearsing what I would say to Johnny, thinking how best to convince him that the will of the gods must overrule his feelings of responsibility toward a young female cousin in his care. I found him in the garden outside the back door of the infirmary, sitting on the bench waiting for me. The sun was dipping down to the west; it touched Johnny's tired features with a soft gold light. Not that there was much softness about this man. He could be both kind and compassionate. But he was a warrior and a leader, and when it came to difficult choices, he would not waste time. He would make his decision and stand by it.

Perhaps that was why he did not wait to hear the arguments I had carefully assembled, but spoke before I could even begin.

"A question for you, Sibeal. Would you agree that if I allow you to go on this voyage, and you are hurt or killed, a wedge will be driven between me and your father that will remain for the rest of our lives?"

No trivial question, this. Not only were there strong bonds of kinship between us, but Johnny was my father's heir. If they fell out, the succession at Sevenwaters might once more become fuel for territorial conflict. The next in line, my brother, Finbar, was only four years old.

"The situation contains sufficient cause for guilt," I said, "to cripple every one of us. Did you know Cathal was going to the seer's cave today?"

"He went of his own choice, not at my bidding. Have you seen him?"

"He says there are three men still alive on the serpent island. And . . . " No, I would not say more. Let Cathal tell Johnny what he intended, if my suspicions were proven correct. Let no whisper of it reach Clodagh before Cathal could tell her. "As for your first question," I said, "before we leave I will write a letter to my mother and father, a letter which I will place in your keeping. I will explain that this is my choice, and that I know it is right." I imagined my father reading such a letter after being told that

I had perished far from home, perhaps devoured by a sea monster, perhaps fallen victim to cold and hunger. "I should think it would cause some bitterness, yes," I felt obliged to say. "Perhaps not lifelong. My father is a wise and balanced man. In many ways he resembles you. But you have no children, and I think children change a man's attitudes."

Johnny smiled. "It is difficult for any man to send a loved one on such a mission, Sibeal. In this community everyone has learned that lesson over and over. It becomes no easier with time. Despite that, you'll be interested to hear that I have sufficient volunteers to go ahead with the mission."

"Already!" On the same day. In a heartbeat, men had thrown their lives into the balance.

"They did not need the time I offered them. It's not unexpected. They were captured by Felix's tale. They see themselves or their friends in the shoes of those men, clutching onto the last scrap of courage in the face of the impossible. It is the stuff of legend. So . . . " He gave me a very straight look. "It would seem this is going ahead, provided *Liadan* is back in time."

"She will be."

"How can you speak with such certainty?"

"I feel it, Johnny. I know it. The gods want Felix to accomplish this. They will not let him fail for the lack of a ship."

"Your faith impresses me, Sibeal. While I have not quite the same degree of certainty, I feel in my bones that this will happen."

"Do you have a leader among your volunteers?"

"Yes. Gareth."

There seemed nothing to say. *I'm sorry* was not appropriate. Gareth was a seasoned warrior. He was the kind of man who could lead an expedition with calm confidence. Whether or not Johnny wanted him to go, and whether or not Gareth had offered himself because he knew Johnny could not go, was none of my business. "He'll do a fine job," I said eventually.

"Yes."

"Johnny, I—"

"I have a favor to ask of you, Sibeal."

I had expected him to tell me, next, that I should leave this crew of professionals to do the job and stay here where I would be safe. "What favor?"

"I want you to cast the runes again, in my presence. You can have anyone you want there, or just the two of us if you prefer." When I did not reply, he added, "I don't doubt that first divination, Sibeal. I know you will always give us the truth. I don't doubt Cathal's dreams or his scrying vision or what Svala has communicated to you. I'm asking this because I'm hoping it may shed more light on the situation."

"Very well," I said. "Is there a particular question you would have me pose?"

"You might ask which weighs heavier in the balance of this venture, salvation or sacrifice."

A solemn question indeed. "And if the answer was sacrifice, would you refuse to let me go?" I asked. "You know my first divination suggested the mission could not succeed unless both Felix and I were there."

"At the very least," said Johnny, "the divination will provide some clarity. We're in sore need of that."

Instinct told me Svala should be present when I cast the runes, since these matters affected her so closely. When it was time, I went down to the fisherman's hut to fetch her. She was sitting not far from her open doorway, on the shore in the fading light, humming to herself and setting out shells in a long, snaking line on the ground. When I gestured that I wanted her to come, she got up and followed me quite willingly.

All of those I had asked for were there when we reached the garden: Johnny and Gareth, Cathal and Clodagh, Muirrin and Evan, Gull and Biddy. And Felix, whose eyes were on me the moment Svala and I came into the garden. I tried not to look at him. His presence made my heart race. My well-governed thoughts threatened to become a jumble of raw emotion. I must not allow this. A runic divination required calm, control, detachment.

Johnny had stationed Kalev and Niall further down toward the dining hall, out of earshot but close enough to intercept anyone who might think to interrupt us. I had prepared the ritual area earlier. It was simple: a circle of swept ground, a folded blanket to kneel on, an oil lamp. Gull and Biddy sat on one bench, Clodagh and Muirrin on the other. Evan and Felix were on the back steps; the other men were standing. When she saw how many were gathered, Svala stopped in her tracks.

"Come," I said, beckoning. "You are among friends."

She came a certain distance but no further. Just beyond the circle of light cast by the lamp, she halted and squatted down, waiting.

"Good," I said, giving her a reassuring smile. I hoped she would stay. Perhaps she was already familiar with the runes. Before she found herself on that lonely island she had most likely lived in a Norse community. That race was generally fair of coloring and robust of build, as she was, though Svala's beauty was something exceptional.

I had warned everyone that I must take time for preparation. They sat in silence as I knelt down on my blanket and spread out the ritual cloth on the ground. I closed my eyes and moved step by step toward the state in which my mind would be receptive to the gods' wisdom. There was no rushing this. I slowed my breathing. With a great deal of effort I banished wayward thoughts, making my mind calm. Time passed. In the darkness behind closed lids, I could not disregard what was creeping in from my silent audience. Someone's mind was working hard, planning, thinking ahead. Someone was edgy, uneasy, wanting a particular answer from the runes. Someone was wracked with indecision. Someone was walking with me down the path, every step of the way; I knew who that was. And someone was suffering an anxiety so strong I could almost touch it. Who was that? Who sat on the edge of the seat, every part tensed in fearful anticipation of the runes' message? I did not open my eyes. I breathed more slowly still, letting it all pass, and when I was ready I picked up the bag and loosened the tie. For the benefit of the others I posed Johnny's question aloud.

"Which weighs heavier in the voyage we plan, salvation or sacrifice?"

With my eyes still shut, I turned the bag upside down, spilling the rune rods out onto the ritual cloth. Svala sucked in her breath.

I opened my eyes. It was wrong to try to guess in advance what a divination would show, but part of me had expected the three significant runes to be exactly the same as in my first divination, when I sought to help Felix: *Os, Ger*, and *Nyd*. But here, atop the others, lay *Rad, Ken, Eolh*. All different. All unexpected.

I sat there awhile, letting the symbols work within me, blending and changing. I observed which signs lay directly below those three. There were several possibilities here. I owed it to Johnny to select what I believed most apt as a response to the question. It would be all too easy to choose an interpretation that would win me a place on the boat. But that was not the druid way. A selfish choice would anger the gods, even if it was the will of those selfsame gods that I travel to the serpent isle. The runes did not lie. But a seer could come close to making them lie, if she allowed her own will to influence her.

To avoid a throbbing head and a state of confusion, I came out of the trance gradually, with several changes of breathing. As I did so I became once more aware of my surroundings; of the small circle of onlookers, their faces illuminated by the warm light of the lamp; of the moon rising in the night sky; of Felix's eyes fixed on me, the knowledge on his face telling me that he, too, had read a message in the signs. Of Clodagh sitting on the very edge of the bench, biting her nails. Svala's utter stillness drew the eye. She sat cross-legged now, back straight, head high, eyes tranquil as she watched me.

"Water, Sibeal?" Muirrin came over, offering a cup.

"Thank you." I drank, as thirsty as if I had not had a drop all day. "I will tell you what I see in this. There are two signs predominant: *Rad*, the journey, and *Ken*, the torch. Taken simply, this could mean that there will be light on the quest, or that the travelers will find enlightenment. There will be learning in it. I think we would have known that without a divination. *Rad* and *Ken* are a pair; there's a rightness in their coming up together. The third, less prominent sign is *Eolh*: a rune of defense." I picked up the rod with its three-pronged hand or claw, and Svala made a little sound. She recognized it, perhaps, as Knut's choice for self-protection. "*Eolh* is a shield. It guards against all kinds of attack, not only the physical. If I could give those men on the island one rune to keep them safe, it would be this one. When I pray for their survival, I will thank the gods for sending this sign."

I paused. That much was simple. "Johnny," I said, "it would be easy for me to give you the interpretation that suits me best. You know I believe the mission cannot succeed unless I am present. That conviction was based on another reading entirely. In these three runes, the need for both myself and Felix to travel to the island is less clear. *Rad* tells me the gods believe in our venture. *Ken* tells me those who undertake it may go down a dark path indeed, one in which the light of knowledge may be all that can show them the way. A shadowy path; a path that may bring the travelers close to death. The presence of *Eolh* could be taken to show that they will nonetheless come through safely, shielded by the love of the gods and by their own courage. I see both sacrifice and salvation in these runes. But I do not see myself." I made myself say it. I had been trained in ways of truth.

"But Sibeal," said Felix, his voice warm and sure, "of course you are there. *Ken*, the torch." He looked over at Johnny, who stood with arms folded, his tattooed face somber. "I, too, understand the need for honesty where this interpretation is concerned. I will tell you that I learned the runes from my mother's brother, a wise man skilled in certain arts. I do not pretend to Sibeal's expertise, but I see what she cannot: the meaning that pertains to herself. *Rad*, the journey: it is the gods' will that we go to the serpent isle. *Eolh*, the shield against harm. Perhaps the gods will protect us. Perhaps the shield is the skill and courage of those who are prepared to undertake the mission. And *Ken*: light in the darkness; clarity amidst confusion. The torch that illuminates our way. That is Sibeal."

For a man who not so long ago had told me he did not want me to go, he had done an eloquent job of supporting my case.

For a while, everyone was silent. Then Johnny said, "In times of old a chieftain would take his druid with him everywhere, even onto the field of war. But one does tend to imagine those druids as bearded ancients."

"Conor was present at the battle with Northwoods," put in Gull. "I doubt very much that he'd think of himself as a bearded ancient, though he does have the look of a venerable sage. And Fainne was also on that field of war."

"True," said Johnny. The memory had shadowed his eyes. "At the time our cousin was no older than Sibeal is now. It was Fainne's presence that tipped the balance in our favor, though she achieved it at great cost." He sighed. "Sibeal, I am impressed by your honesty. And by yours, Felix, since I suspect your personal inclination is for Sibeal to stay behind."

Felix inclined his head in agreement. "The runes do not lie," he said.

"Sibeal," said Johnny, "you must understand that your presence on the venture would probably have a twofold effect. On the one hand, there is your expertise in the druidic arts, backed up by your conviction that the gods intend you to be there. On such a mission, spiritual guidance may play an important part. My crew will understand that. Against that understanding we must weigh your vulnerability, and the impact that might have on the men's capacity to carry out what must be done. Every man on that ship will see it as his duty to protect you. Without that distraction a man might be better able to sail, to make decisions, to fight if need be. Cathal, what is your opinion?"

A hand fastened on my shoulder, making my heart jump. Svala had come up in silence. She made a little sound of inquiry.

"Johnny," I said, "I must try to explain to her what we've been discussing. Can you wait while I try to reach her?"

I rose to my feet and took Svala's hands in mine. I pictured the boat setting out from Inis Eala, its crew including Gareth and Felix and a number of other men whose faces I did not imagine in detail. I added Svala herself, standing in the bow with her hair blowing in the wind as the men raised the sail and set a course due northward. I showed a party of folk on the jetty waving goodbye: Johnny, Gull, Biddy, Clodagh and myself.

A sound burst out of Svala, a high, chittering noise of protest. Further down the garden, Niall and Kalev turned their heads in surprise. Closer at hand, eyes widened. Even Johnny looked taken aback.

Svala let me go and took a step toward Johnny, her fear set aside for now. She pointed to me, to herself, to Felix, then performed the same gesture as she had in the cave: quite clearly, rowing a boat. Her arm swung around to indicate due north.

Nobody said a word. As far as I knew, this was the first time Svala had revealed the extent of her understanding in the company of anyone but me and my sisters. When she was done, she stepped back and put her arm around my shoulders, pointing again. *Her. Me. The two of us. Two women.*

"There is one thing you men didn't think of," said Biddy. "If Sibeal doesn't go, Svala will be the only woman on board. That doesn't seem quite proper."

"But then," put in Muirrin, "if Svala really is going to stay on that island, Sibeal would be the only woman on the way back."

"We are perhaps getting ahead of ourselves," Johnny said. "It's clear Svala believes Sibeal should go, though she cannot tell us why. As for this question about propriety, Gareth and I would not select any man for the crew unless he was completely trustworthy." In the pause that followed, I thought of Knut, who would be on the boat, and who was one of the least trustworthy men I had ever met. "Believe me, I have given the whole matter considerable thought. Sibeal's personal safety has loomed large in my mind, along with what her father would deem appropriate. The perils of the voyage itself were foremost in my mind; I didn't imagine there could be any threat from our own men, and I still don't."

"I wonder if you *have* thought it right through," Biddy said quietly. "There's consequences here to freeze the marrow in your bones. It takes a lot of courage to go out and battle monsters. But it takes even more to wait. To see the ones you love put themselves in the path of the storm."

Gull glanced at her and cleared his throat. "Seems as good a time as any to speak up. You'll be needing a healer on this trip. Those fellows who were left out there are going to need attention. Not to speak of someone to deal with possible mishaps on the way." He glanced at Muirrin, then at Evan. Biddy was white. Her lips were pressed tightly together. "Seems that healer should be me, bearded ancient as I am. And while I can't claim to be a woman, I have been acting as Sibeal's chaperone, more or less, since she came to Inis Eala. In place of a father, you might say. My presence on the voyage should answer those concerns about what's proper." After a few moments of stunned silence, he added, "Sibeal can be my hands. Between us, we'll do a good job."

I was shocked and elated both at once. I wanted to protest; Biddy's words and the look on her face told me this would alter our friendship forever. Johnny was expert at masking his feelings, but right now shock was written all over his face. Gull was his father's oldest friend, revered and loved by all on Inis Eala. He was like a father to everyone on the island. It would be simple enough for Johnny to point out that Gull, with his maimed hands, could not combine the duties of healer with those of crewman as Evan might. But I knew Johnny would not say this.

"Father—" began Evan now, getting up from his position on the steps.

"Hush," Gull said. "You're my son. Your wife's expecting a child. Nothing more need be said on the matter."

"A pox on this!" The voice was Cathal's, wretched, furious. "With every step the ripples widen to take in another! It's not Felix who's the ill luck man here, it's me."

Clodagh got to her feet, her anger almost palpable, and walked off down the garden without a word, hugging her shawl tightly around her. Cathal muttered something under his breath and strode off after her. Muirrin got up as if to follow, then sat down again.

"Biddy," Johnny said, "I do understand what this means, both for those who go and for those they leave behind. Every time I send men into battle it is the same. You've cause to understand better than most, I know. But we've all had losses."

I looked around the circle of faces, each one of them beset by doubt. Meeting Johnny's eye, I dug deep for my most confident tone and the look to match it. "We must think of this as the heroic rescue mission that captured your men's imagination," I said, "and not as a wild and perilous venture in which lives may be lost. You have an expert captain," I nodded toward Gareth, "and a fine crew. In Gull, you have a steady beating heart for your mission. In Svala you have one who knows the way. Her fierce desire to return home will carry *Liadan* across those stormy waters. In Felix you have the fair wind that fills the sails, a fresh breeze of courage and determination. As for me," I thought fast, not being prepared to call myself a torch to light the way, "my presence acknowledges the will of the gods. I am attuned to their voices, and while I travel with *Liadan*, she goes under their protection. We cannot afford to dwell on possible disasters, on personal grief, on guilt and uncertainty. Now that the decision is made to do this, we must set our course forward."

A smile spread slowly across Johnny's features. I saw its echo on Gareth's face, and on Gull's.

"Well spoken, Sibeal," my cousin said. "You speak with the voice of hope. And that, I believe, is essential on a voyage into the unknown."

I struggled to maintain the tone and demeanor of a druid. "You're saying I can go," I managed.

"I am. As leader here I take full responsibility for the venture and the safety of those who are part of it. May the gods look kindly on all of us. I cannot imagine a better team with whom to share this burden, and I only regret that I may not travel with you and stand beside you in that far place." He glanced at Gareth. "Tomorrow we'll let the community know who's going. From that point on, Gareth's in charge. And, Sibeal, you might ask the gods to set a favorable wind in *Liadan*'s sails. The sooner she gets back here, the sooner she can set sail again."

Now that he had said it, I was seized by terror. This was real:

the ship, the perilous voyage, the island at the end of the world, the monster . . . I'd had a choice, and instead of a quiet summer's stay with my sisters and a safe ride back to Sevenwaters, I had chosen this. "I must tell Svala," I said and, turning toward her, I took her hands again. This time the picture in my mind showed the two of us on *Liadan*'s prow. Svala stood as before, a living figurehead, proud and lovely. Beside her, I was somewhat green in the face but doing my best to match her bold look. Among the others on the boat, I included Gareth, Felix, Knut and the dark-skinned, smiling figure of Gull. On the jetty, watching us, I pictured Johnny, Biddy, Muirrin, Evan and Clodagh. Cathal, I did not put anywhere. The ship in the image sailed off to the north under the sky of a rosy dawn, her sail filled by a fair wind.

Svala dropped my hands and threw her arms around me. When she let go, I saw that her mouth was stretched in a wide smile, and that her eyes were streaming with tears. *At last, at last!* She moved to kneel before Johnny and, taking his hand, touched her brow to his fingers in a gesture of acknowledgment. Before he could say anything she was on her feet again and bolting away through the garden.

"Gods have mercy on me if I've made the wrong decision," Johnny said. "Now to rest, all of you. Remember Sibeal's words of hope, and make sure your doubts, if you have them, are not aired in public. We've a strong team, and we'll perform this mission as we always do, with courage and professionalism. I'll bid you good night now. Gull, I wish my father had been here to see you volunteer."

"I wonder if he'd have said yes or no."

"No, if he had any sense," Biddy commented, though she had her arm linked with her husband's. If she was angry, I thought it was not with Gull himself, but with the complex set of family loyalties that had obliged him to offer his services. "But more likely he'd be getting on the boat with you. Every old warrior believes he's got one more adventure in him."

CHAPTER 11

~Felix~

Liadan returns to the island within ten days of Johnny's decision. I am at the place of the boat burial, high on the hill, when I spot her approaching the bay with a steady westerly filling her square sail. My heart lurches. *We can go*, I tell my brother. *The ship is here.*

I wonder if Paul, so brave and strong, ever felt as I do now: torn between utter terror at the magnitude of the task and a powerful will to achieve it. Perhaps my brother never knew doubt. *I will be brave*, I say to him. *I will be as brave as you were.*

I walk back toward the settlement. Others have seen the ship now, and folk are streaming down to the bay to greet the travelers. People are laughing, smiling, gesturing, chattering. Men come from the practice area to join the throng of women and children. From the cliff path above the bay I see Deiz poised on the very edge of the jetty, a quivering ball of anticipation. Her small form vibrates with the desire to leap, to swim, to fly, to close the gap in whatever way she can.

It would not be right for me to go down there, so I find a place at the top of the path, on the stones. Not long after, while *Liadan* is still some way from shore, I feel a presence behind me. "Sibeal," I say, smiling.

"How did you know it was me?" She comes to sit beside me.

"I knew."

We sit watching as the boat comes closer. *Liadan* is smaller than *Freyja*. I shiver, closing my hands over the blisters long healed. The rocks, the splintering timbers, the wave . . . *I will be brave*, says a voice inside me. "She looks a sturdy craft," I comment, and this much is true. *Liadan* seems made for trading, not war. They're lowering the sail, and using oars to bring her in: two pairs forward, two aft, the rowers standing. Amidships is the deep open hold. It looks big enough to accommodate a considerable cargo, though it is near-empty; this was no merchant voyage. Men crowd the walkways to either side, their eyes fixed on home.

Sibeal has heard the reservation in my voice. "If Johnny and Gareth believe the job can be done with this vessel," she says, "then it can be done. After all, she's just been all the way down to the south and back."

Neither of us adds that such a voyage can be completed without any need to sail beyond sight of land; at any point her crew might have headed for a safe bay to ride out storm or trouble.

"Sometimes I wish I were the kind of man who does not think too much, but simply believes," I say. "A man of blind faith. It would make life much easier. Yet it was seeing that kind of faith in action that lost me my own belief, back in Breizh."

"Perhaps you have more faith than you realize," says Sibeal, lifting a graceful hand to tuck her dark hair behind her ears. The breeze is rising. "You presented a strong case for me, and for yourself, based at least partly on my runic divinations. I'm sure you mentioned the gods more than once."

When I do not reply, she looks at me and smiles. The honesty in her eyes is a shining light. How can a man see that and not believe? It is hard to put this into words for her.

"I think your faith is so strong," I say, stumbling a little, "that some of it may have rubbed off on me. In your company I can no longer say outright that I do not believe in gods of any kind."

Sibeal brushes her hand against mine, sending a wave of desire through my body. To be so close to her, these days, is to suffer both delight and torment. I think she is quite unaware of what she does to me. "Say rather that you are still searching," she tells me. "You're on a journey, an interesting one full of possibilities. Full of opportunities for debate, for learning, for the development of the mind."

The boat is almost home. On the jetty a woman is jumping up and down with excitement, waving frantically, screaming *Daigh! Daigh!* A man leaps overboard, amid laughter, and swims for shore. The little dog is making a high-pitched yelping sound.

"But first, another journey," I tell Sibeal. "Also interesting, but in a somewhat different way."

"Are you scared?" she asks me.

"To the marrow," I say. "You?"

"It will be better once the waiting is over."

"You didn't answer the question. Perhaps a druid does not feel fear. Faith might outweigh any misgivings."

Sibeal gazes out toward the horizon, while down at the jetty, the swimmer is hauled up and enfolds his woman in a dripping embrace, to the accompaniment of cheers. A rope is thrown; *Liadan* is secured, and an extraordinary-looking warrior takes one long step from vessel to shore. Deiz leaps into his arms, to be cradled as if she were a baby.

"I don't think I was truly scared until I saw *Liadan* coming in," Sibeal says. "Now it's real, Felix. We're actually going to do this, you and I."

I clasp her hand, discreetly. Once we are on the boat, all of us in uncomfortably close quarters, such a gesture will not be possible. And perhaps that is just as well. "Uncanny," I murmur.

"What is?"

"How often we think the same thoughts."

"That is not uncanny, it's . . . " Her voice falters. Whatever she was going to say, she's thought better of it.

I could complete her sentence. *It's because we are the same. It's because each of us is half of the other. It's because we are a perfect fit. A pair. Made to be together.* "So that's the famous Snake," I say, watching the tall man on the jetty with the wriggling, licking white bundle in his arms. Snake's hair is cropped stubble-short. He has an intricate pattern graven all across his brow, and marks like broad twisted bracelets on the skin of his wrists. Over his tunic he wears a garment that appears to be fashioned from a serpent's skin. I am reminded that our journey involves a sea monster, and wish I had not thought of it.

There are others disembarking now, bundles being unloaded, folk hugging, men hoisting children onto their shoulders. Snake puts the dog down to throw his arms around Gull's shoulders, then Johnny's, and to exchange friendly punches with several other men. Deiz scampers about at ankle level, yapping.

"That's Snake," Sibeal says. "One of a kind. He's an old friend of Gull's, from the earliest times. The very big man with the dark beard is Wolf, another of the original Painted Men. He's a Norseman. The one in the blue shirt is Sigurd. And that young man there is my cousin Cormack, Johnny's brother."

Cormack has seen us and is bounding up the path, his face wreathed in smiles. He is like Johnny, yes; but not quite like. He's taller, thinner, livelier, without the reserve and composure that make Johnny seem older than his years. This man is close to my own age. From his keen eyes to his well-muscled arms to the long legs that take the hill in their stride, Cormack is every inch a warrior. He reminds me of my many deficiencies as a man.

"Sibeal!" He's beaming. He seizes Sibeal around the waist, lifts her off the ground and whirls her around a couple of times, then sets her back down with a smacking kiss on the cheek. "Morrigan save us, you have grown up since I last saw you! You'd be the image of Mother if it weren't for those eyes of yours. And I suppose this scowling fellow is your jealous sweetheart." He turns toward me, and I cannot think of anything to say to him.

Sibeal is laughing. She's flushed scarlet. "This is Felix," she says. "A scholar. From Armorica. Felix, this is my cousin Cormack." Suddenly serious, she adds, "There's a lot to tell you, Cormack. Too much for now. Welcome home. I'm happy that you're safe."

Perhaps I am jealous. Not in the way he meant it, but jealous of Sibeal's family, her sisters, her cousins, even those like Gull and Biddy who are family at one remove. There is a strength in their love for one another, something deep and sure. She has five sisters and a brother; Johnny, three brothers. I only had Paul. *I can be brave.*

"Walk back with me," Cormack says, and I'm sure he doesn't mean me.

"I'll stay here awhile," I tell Sibeal. Her eyes see right to the heart of me. She nods understanding. Cormack drapes his arm around her slender shoulders and they walk off toward the settlement. *Jealous sweetheart.* I am not even that. I am the man who loves her more than life itself. And I am the acquaintance of a single summer.

~Sibeal~

With the efficiency that was part of everything on Inis Eala, the boat was ready within a few days of her return. Men swarmed over her, busy from sunrise to sunset, while in the net-mending shed a group of industrious women patched an area of the sail that had sustained some damage. The supplies that had been prepared while we waited for the boat included materials to deal with all manner of possible damage at sea. I hoped we would not need them.

Even I had doubted that Felix could be strong enough for the voyage so quickly, though I had not told him so. But he had worked with the determination of a man preparing for battle. From dawn till dusk each day he prepared himself for the task ahead, only resting when Gull ordered him to do so. Under Evan's supervision he gradually increased his diet to include meat, fish, bread, the things that had been forbidden. It was not only the healers who helped him now, but many others as well. I would see him out walking with Kalev; I would come across Felix and Cathal seated in a quiet corner, deep in intense conversation. I saw Gareth, Felix and a small group of other men on the path from the jetty one morning, going up and down the steep slope with packs on their backs. They gradually increased the pace until the upward slope was taken at a jog. And there was Felix, maintaining the same speed as the others, though I noticed Gareth was keeping a close eye on him. At the top of the path there was no fuss, simply a nod of acknowledgment from Gareth, an equal recognition of each man's effort.

While Felix was so intent on his recovery, there was little time for me to see him alone, and perhaps that was just as well. His presence affected me oddly these days. When he was close I found it hard to concentrate on anything. My mind had a troubling tendency to revisit that afternoon when he had held me in his arms while I soaked his shirt with my tears. I wanted that closeness again. In his embrace I had felt like a wandering creature returned to its home field. At the same time I had felt full to the brim with life, as if I were on the brink of a great adventure. Not the adventure we faced now, with its cold seas and long-toothed monster. An adventure that was between man and woman; a secret and remarkable journey that was forever denied to me.

With all the druidic skills I had acquired over the years, the fact that I could not quickly banish these feelings made me doubt myself. It made me ashamed. I might have spoken to Clodagh, who was a good listener, but after the divination something had changed between the two of us. She was perfectly courteous in public. In private she was avoiding me. Any time I referred to the voyage in her presence, she went silent. As for Cathal, he had not sought me out again, and I had decided I'd been wrong to think he would consider coming with us. After all, neither Gareth nor Johnny had spoken of the possibility, and it was far too late now to volunteer. So why were both Cathal and Clodagh looking as folk might look in the face of a looming disaster? Had Cathal seen a vision of *Liadan* sinking with all hands?

The day before our departure, Clodagh came to see me late in the afternoon. I was in my little chamber, going through my meager store of belongings for the twentieth time, trying to match the small size of bundle allowed on the boat with what I might need for the range of possibilities that lay ahead. Rune rods or a second warm shawl? Ceremonial herbs or a roll of linen in case I had my monthly courses before we got home? And what about Svala, who might also need the linen but would likely not think of it? She knew we were leaving in the morning; I had made that clear to her earlier, showing her the sun passing across the sky, the time of sleep, the dawn rising, the boat setting out. In the fisherman's hut, the items of clothing she had been given by Biddy and others had lain carelessly heaped in a corner, along with a kettle, a ladle and a jug. I had seen no sign of packing.

Clodagh did not come through the infirmary, but tapped on my door. "Sibeal, I need to talk to you."

I let her in, and with her I let in a wave of anxiety. "What's wrong?" I asked, setting aside the awkwardness that had lain between us. I motioned for her to sit beside me.

Clodagh lowered herself slowly onto the bed. She glanced toward the curtain and lifted her brows.

"Evan's gone over to the practice yard to bind up a wound," I said. "Gull's out somewhere with Felix. And Muirrin's feeling sick. She's gone to rest."

Clodagh was as solemn as I had ever seen her. "I need a favor, Sibeal," she said.

I kept working, attempting to fold a garment with the same degree of precision as she herself might use. "Go on," I said.

"I want you to find Cathal and talk to him in private. I think he's at the seer's cave again. This is tearing him apart, Sibeal. He needs help, and this time I don't seem to be able to give it."

Whatever I had expected, it was not this. "If I ask questions about the voyage now, will you answer them?"

She simply looked at me. I could see she had been crying.

"I've been thinking perhaps he feels he should come with us, out of the same kind of family obligation that made Gull volunteer," I said. "I did wonder if you were upset that night because Gull put his hand up, and you thought that meant Cathal would be next. I understand all the reasons why he shouldn't come, Clodagh. I'd never suggest he leave the island, even though he has some abilities that could make all the difference out there. Nobody expects him to risk his whole future on another man's mission."

Clodagh grimaced. "Isn't that what everyone in the crew will be doing?"

"You could put it that way, yes. But nobody else has Mac Dara to contend with."

"You think we've been fighting because he wants to go and I'm trying to stop him," she said.

"The two of you have been looking somewhat tense for the last few days. That seemed to me the most likely explanation. You should have talked to me sooner, Clodagh. It's my job to help when things are difficult."

"I'm not consulting you as a spiritual adviser, Sibeal." She gave a crooked smile. "I'm talking to you as my sister. You're wrong about this. Certainly, Cathal understands that his presence could be immensely helpful on the voyage. Indeed, if he'd volunteered at the start it could have saved Gareth from needing to go, since Cathal could have led the expedition. But he says he won't go. He's not afraid for himself. He can't bear the thought of me and the child left on our own, at Mac Dara's mercy, should anything happen to him."

My hands went on folding and packing away, while my mind reeled in shock. "You're saying that Cathal doesn't want to go, and that *you* want him to do it?"

"I want you to be as safe as you can be," my sister said quietly. "Believe me, I'm horrified at the thought of his going. Ask any of the women how she feels about her man risking his life on this venture, and she'll tell you she wishes your wretched Felix had never come to the island to spark the men's imagination with his crazy rescue mission. Ask her what she thinks of her man's choice to be part of it, and she'll tell you she's so proud of him her heart might burst with it. That's all part of loving a man, Sibeal, something you'll never really understand. Of course I don't want Cathal to go. I want him here, safe. I want him to be able to hold his baby on the day it's born. But I believe he needs to go. I know the crew are experienced, brave, strong, able to deal with all manner of crises. But they can't do what Cathal can. None of them has any ability in magic. If Mac Dara *is* involved, the rest of you will have no protection at all. I don't want you to go, Sibeal. You're my little sister. I don't want Gull to go, though I hate the idea of Evan going even more—that would be too cruel for Muirrin. But it's decided, and you're going. If Cathal is with you, at least I'll know I've done everything I can to keep you safe."

My eyes were suddenly full of tears. It was the most selfless decision I could imagine, and typical of Clodagh.

"Don't cry, Sibeal," my sister said. "Go and find him. Tell him I really mean it. Tell him you believe I will be safe until he gets home. Women have babies all the time. And Mac Dara can't reach me here."

No, but he will be able to reach Cathal the moment we sail out of the bay. "Are you sure?"

"I'm quite sure. We're fettered by our fear of Mac Dara. His influence governs our every thought. We've talked about it, and we both feel the same. It's wrong. It's letting Mac Dara win. We've gone over and over it, and now Cathal's in such a state of guilt and confusion that he won't listen to me anymore. I think he'll listen to you."

Gods, this was fraught with peril. If I managed to persuade him, and then he was killed . . . If he came with us and failed to protect me from harm . . . If we both sailed away, and came home to find that Clodagh had died in childbirth . . .

"Go now, please, Sibeal," Clodagh said. "I'll finish your packing. I can fit twice as much in that bag. It's all in the folding."

It was late in the day, and the seer's cave was full of soft light: violet, lavender, gray. Shades of sadness. Cathal had spread out his cloak and was sitting on it, not scrying, simply gazing straight ahead of him. On his troubled features I saw the shadow of a far older man.

I sat down at a little distance.

"Clodagh sent you," he said after a while.

"She asked me to talk to you, yes. I wish she'd done so somewhat earlier. My chances of changing your mind are not great, one day before we leave."

"True. I can't imagine why she thought you could do what she cannot."

Cathal's tone was scathing. I was tempted to get up and walk out, but I swallowed my annoyance. *You'll never really understand*, Clodagh had said. I must use what limited understanding I had to reach him. I owed it to her.

"You know, I suppose, how much courage it has taken for Clodagh to decide that you should go," I said.

"I don't need to hear this."

I drew a deep breath. "You will hear it, Cathal. That choice is based on love; nothing more, nothing less. She's putting her own wishes aside to do what's right for everyone she cares about. Me, you, Gull, Johnny, your child yet unborn. Love will govern Clodagh's choices, always. That's the woman you married. If you do as she asks, you honor the woman she is."

He did not so much as blink an eyelid. I might as well not have been there.

"Besides," I said, "deep down you're like all the other warriors. Their hearts were captured by this mission: loyalty beyond terror, survival beyond endurance. Don't tell me part of you isn't longing to rush to those men's rescue."

I thought he might turn on me in a fury after that; his face was full of darkness. I sat quietly, watching the still water. I waited. The silence drew on and on.

"Sibeal," said Cathal, and his voice was not angry at all, but sounded more as if he were choking back tears, "how can this be the right choice for our child?"

"You ask the most difficult of all the questions. Clodagh believes that to stay here, to remain forever within the safe margin, is

301

allowing Mac Dara to govern your existence. Keeping out of your father's reach is living in a kind of prison. That's what she implied. A druid might debate that issue at considerable length and not reach a conclusion one way or another. But that is the pattern of Clodagh's thinking, and who is to say she's wrong?"

"We've talked about this already. Endlessly. We've gone through all the arguments."

"She says that at a certain point you stopped listening to her."

Cathal picked up a handful of small stones and threw them into the pool with some violence. The calm surface shivered under the impact. "What she wants feels wrong," he said. "How can I leave them? But it also feels right. There is indeed a part of me that wants to go. I cannot make a choice. I came here to scry one last time before *Liadan* sails, and I can't do it, Sibeal. I came prepared with several appropriate questions relating to the likelihood of Otherworld interference on the journey. But Clodagh and the child fill all my thoughts. Sibeal, how can I go away? The baby might be born any day now."

"If your mind is made up, why are you here?"

He glanced at me. "You're a druid today," he said, making it sound like something bad.

"I only ask the questions that must be asked. Does Gareth know there's a possibility you may go? Does Johnny?"

"I suppose my state of mind has been easy to read, these last days. I was relieved of responsibility for training the Connacht men soon after the crew was named, even though my name was not on the list." He thought for a moment, then added, "Sibeal, I understand that much of druidic lore and teaching is secret. It would help me if you could explain the extent of your own abilities. I know Ciarán has a certain facility with magic, born as much of his lineage as of his druidic training. I know he is your mentor. And Felix said you did something with the fire, that night when Knut attacked him."

"I have learned the rudiments of natural magic. I'm a beginner, Cathal. I might be able to make a fire flare up, or conjure a momentary breeze. No more than that. I would not be much help to

you, though of course I would try. I do have the ear of the gods."
Of recent times there had been some cause to doubt that. "And the
ability to find answers to problems. We're trained to do so."

"You have much more," Cathal said, "for it seems you can hear
Svala's voice, a voice silent to the rest of us. For that alone, your
presence on the voyage must be of great value."

"I believe each of us will have a part to play: Felix, Gull, Gareth,
every other person on board. That includes me, though what my
part will be, I don't know. I suppose I'll find out on the way."

"I understand that I, too, may have a part to play. I know that if
I stay behind, the loss of that part may doom the mission."

"You must weigh that up in making your choice."

"I hear the voice of a wise old woman coming from the lips of
a lovely young girl," Cathal said, "and it makes me feel sad. I'm
not sure why. Oh, for some certainty, Sibeal. Oh, for a promise that
we would return safely, all of us, and that those we leave behind
would be safe as well."

"We cannot know the future. All we can do is face it bravely.
We should take heed of those we love and respect. But in the end,
we make every decision alone."

When he did not reply, I rose to my feet. Cathal was not looking at me. He had his head bowed, his hands linked on his knees.

"Tell Clodagh I'll be back before sunset," he said. "I should
thank you, I suppose. I find I cannot bring myself to do so, not yet.
I acknowledge your honesty, Sibeal."

"I need no further thanks than that," I said.

The scene I had created in my mind for Svala became reality. We
stood on the jetty in the morning, those who were leaving, those
who were saying farewell. The real goodbyes had been made in
private, behind closed doors, and perhaps there had been tears,
or anger, or some bitterness. Here, on the jetty, every face was as
brave as the banner that flew from *Liadan's* masthead. The supplies
had been loaded the day before, foodstuffs, fresh water, materials
to mend the boat, the wherewithal to make a rudimentary camp

should it be necessary to linger on the serpent isle or elsewhere. Weaponry. The means to make fire. Space had been left for our personal items: one small bag apiece. There would be no washing, no changing clothing, no privacy at all for the performance of bodily functions. I imagined I might hold up a shawl, down in the rocking hold, while Svala used the bucket, and she might return the favor. It was the best we could hope for.

Since the night when Felix told his story, Knut had been forbidden to approach Svala. It was easy enough to ensure they stayed apart on the island, but within the cramped confines of the boat it would be impossible to maintain a distance. Svala would stay in the hold for most of the time, with me, Gull and Felix. It was understood that the crew would sail the boat, and the passengers would keep out of the way. But everyone needed to rest, which meant all the men, Knut included, would be in the hold sleeping at one time or another. Gareth had asked me to keep an eye on Svala; to make sure she did not grow too agitated.

She stood on the jetty now, still and silent amid the noisy crowd, gazing out to sea. She had no luggage with her.

"Ready, Sibeal?" Gull was beside me, his bundle under one arm. A larger bag containing his healer's items was already stowed in the hold. Behind him stood Biddy, a well-controlled smile on her face.

"As ready as I'll ever be," I said. "But I'll wait until everyone's on board. Johnny wants me to say a prayer for a safe journey."

"Here, I'll take your bag."

"I will." There was Felix, back straight, head high, pale as a winter morning. He sounded as if he was speaking through clenched teeth. I felt his terror deep in my bones. *The wave coming . . . Paul's eyes widening . . . a great rumbling sound like cart wheels . . .* It was the first time he had set foot on a boat since the shipwreck. In all of Gull's rigorous training, they had not prepared for this.

"Thank you," I said, passing him the bag. "One step at a time. And remember, Paul is right beside you."

I watched them board, all of them. When Knut walked past her, his face stony, his fingers nervously twisting his amulet on its cord, Svala cringed. The light left her eyes. A familiar shuttered look came over her features. Then Gareth, who was already on board, reached out a hand to help her down onto the deck. She ignored him, stepping over lightly on her own.

I watched the faces of those left behind, wives and lovers, children, parents, comrades. The loss would indeed be great if our expedition came to grief. How hard it must be for a woman to live in a place like this, where every season might bring another farewell. How hard to be a warrior, torn between the heart-stirring mission and the love of home and family.

"Sibeal?" Clodagh was beside me, holding out another bag. "I've packed this for Svala. It has practical items, the things she probably wouldn't think of for herself." Her freckles were stark against the white skin; her eyes were pink-rimmed. Like Biddy, she wore a smile.

"Thank you." I was looking around for Cathal when something crashed into my legs, almost toppling me. Fang bolted along the jetty, coming to a sudden halt at the spot where Felix had just stepped over onto the boat. The dog's voice arose, silencing all others with its shrill howl of woe. Clodagh's smile faded, and so did Biddy's.

"Morrigan's britches, what's got into you?" Snake strode forward; the crowd parted for him. He reached to pick up the little dog, but the anguished crying went on. Fang was in a frenzy, trying to do everything at once: bite Snake's hand, leap off the jetty onto the boat, scream her confusion to the world.

"It's Felix," I said, coming closer and wondering why, all of a sudden, I was on the verge of weeping. "She wants to be in two places at once: with you, here, and on the boat with him. Let her say goodbye, Snake, and perhaps she'll quieten down."

Snake stepped onto the boat, holding the dog, and Felix took her in his arms. The howling stopped. Felix murmured something, resting his cheek against her head for a moment. She wriggled around to lick his face. Then Felix passed her back to Snake, who returned to the jetty. Fang began a forlorn whimpering. Snake held her firm.

"Sibeal, I think we're ready," Johnny said. "Will you say your prayer now?"

I glanced at Clodagh again. She stood perfectly composed, pale and still. I saw that there was still a bag in her hand.

"If we're ready, yes," I said, and turned to face the boat, the bay, the great ocean beyond. I lifted my arms. "May the gods of wind and waves look on this voyage with understanding. Manannán, let not your creatures harm us, nor storm and tempest wreck us. We go in peace, to make good what was done in error. We go to find men cruelly abandoned in a far place. May fair winds fill our sails, may we travel safe and swiftly, may we return all together with our mission achieved. May those we leave on shore be guarded and shielded from all harm. We ask your solemn blessing on *Liadan* and on all who sail in her."

It was time. And here, as if summoned by my words, was Cathal, taking the bag casually from Clodagh's hand, giving her a chaste kiss on the brow, walking with me across the jetty as if there had never been any doubt about his being part of this. He held my hand as I made the awkward jump required for a short-legged person to reach the boat, then boarded himself in one elegant stride. Gareth called a series of orders and the crew obeyed, one man moving to the steering oar, eight to the rowing oars, which were situated at either end of the boat. I went to stand beside Svala on the deck at the bow. We would have to go down in the hold soon enough, but it felt wrong to start a brave mission amidst the cargo.

The folk on the jetty grew smaller. The gap grew wider. Felix came to stand on my other side. The ghost of that other voyage lingered in his eyes. "It will be all right," I said. "We can do this."

Far sooner than I expected, we were leaving the bay and heading into open water. The crew shipped oars. They raised the sail. *Liadan* began to move up and down, up and down, and I wondered if I might be sick, and if so how long it would last. I wondered how far from Inis Eala we would need to go before Mac Dara could once again sense his son's presence. Looking for Cathal, I saw him working with the rest of the crew, all orderly purpose.

Beside me, Svala was perfectly balanced against the increasing movement of the boat. She wasn't even holding on. Her golden hair flew about in the wind, so bright it seemed the morning sun was trapped there.

Felix murmured something in his native tongue.

"What was that?" I asked.

"The great eagle lend you the shelter of his wings," he said. "The wolves of the forest guard you from shadows. The creatures of the deep swim by your side. And may your courage bring you safely home again."

"Is that an old blessing from Breizh?"

"A new one."

Gareth shouted something I failed to catch.

"Time to move to the hold," Felix said. "They'll be wanting to make good use of the favorable wind. Let me help you down, Sibeal. If it's any comfort, the sickness doesn't last."

~Felix~

Liadan has some advantages: there is space in the hold for several men to rest among the baggage, while the women still maintain a corner of their own. And she has some disadvantages. The hold may be large, but it is open to the weather. Everything is damp, ourselves and our clothing included. The only shelter is under the boards of the fore and aft decks, and even there the wind bites. Sibeal is miserable: she sleeps a snatch at a time, waking to retch into a bucket, her face drawn and white. Gull tends to her as best he can. Svala is no nursemaid. She crouches among the bundles as she did on *Freyja*, watching as each man comes down to rest, and as each goes up on deck again. Her hands are restless, plucking at her gown, twisting her long hair.

I think of voyages past. Setting out from Breizh with Paul, a few silver pieces buying us passage to Britain with a trader, Paul's brawn ensuring we were not relieved of the remaining contents of our purse along the way. That vessel was like this, a merchant boat, sturdily made, designed to go mainly by sail. Whatever happens, I suppose I will not need to row.

The trip from Britain to Erin, we made on a fishing boat. Paul helped with the nets. I studied the clouds, the intricate patterns of the waves, the harsh, musical sound of the language as the crew laughed and joked, balanced against the swell. That was a good journey; our hearts were high.

The last voyage: *Freyja*. I am trying not to think of that. I am trying not to remember the wave that took my brother away.

It is night. We sail on by the stars, heading for the place where the storm took *Freyja*, or as close to that place as Gareth can calculate. The men rest in shifts, a few hours' sleep, a watch on deck. When Knut comes down, Svala backs further into her corner. She bows her head; her hair veils her face.

Sigurd comes to sit by me. He is the only man from Snake's expedition to be sailing out on this voyage. He was chosen, I imagine, for his fluent Norse. Besides, he has neither wife nor children. He is about Johnny's age, fair-skinned, blunt-featured, with the short-cropped hair favored by many of the Inis Eala warriors. The markings that decorate his brow and cheek put me in mind of a seal. "You're from Armorica, yes?" he asks. "Which part?"

This is the warrior who had a countryman of mine as a friend. I remember the name: Corentin. "The region of Finistère," I tell him. "In the far west."

"Mm. Strange tales in those parts. Corentin was full of them. Monsters and transformations. You going back, after this?"

I shake my head. "I doubt it."

"Got family there?"

"My parents."

"Corentin and I used to talk about it." Sigurd lies down with his hands behind his head, but he seems in the mood for conversation, not sleep. "We made plans, not that either of us thought we'd leave Johnny's band, but there's no harm in plans. I'd take him to see the north, snow and ice, bears and wolves. He'd take me to that realm of strange stones left by the ancients and islands that appear and disappear. Have you heard of that? There's a bay he used to talk about, where there are over three hundred islands. He said that when folk try to count them, they always come up with a different number. We thought we'd get a little boat and keep exploring until we found every last one." Sigurd grins. "Imagine what you might discover in a place like that. But Corentin had to go home in a hurry, and I couldn't walk out on Johnny. I wish I knew how he got on; whether he managed to save his family holdings. He could be a big landowner now. He could have a wife and children. He could be dead." The smile is gone.

I thought I did not want to talk about home. After all, this man is almost a stranger. But his manner disarms me. "Do you know where his family lives? What region?"

"Near that bay I mentioned, if that's any help."

I nod. It is close to home. "I know the place," I tell him. "I hope your friend was able to secure his land. The region is beset by territorial disputes. In that, it is not unlike Erin. It is possible Corentin's holdings lie within the overlordship of a certain nobleman, a person with much influence and little conscience. I hope he managed to stand up for what was rightly his."

"Oh, he'd stand up for it all right," says Sigurd grimly. "It's whether he was cut down afterward that troubles me. There are moments when I wish for the gift of Sight." He glances over at Sibeal, who is bent double, gasping, while Gull presses a cloth to her forehead. "But when I think about it, I wouldn't want that. Could be more curse than blessing. A man wants to be free to make his own choices. That's what I think, anyway."

In the semidark I find myself smiling. There is no lamp down here; the risk from fire is too great. But the nights are never quite dark in summer, and we are heading northward. A lantern up on deck casts a slanting beam down into the hold, picking out Knut's inimical eyes, Sibeal's ghost-white face. "Sibeal would say she still has choices, even though she has a window on a possible future," I tell him. "The Sight helps a person choose right. It doesn't tell what will happen, only what could happen."

"Mm." Sigurd closes his eyes. "Fond of her, are you?"

I say what I must say. "She's a druid. Destined for the life of the spirit."

"That's no answer."

"It's the best one I have," I say.

Sigurd does not reply. *Liadan*'s progress has slowed; the wind has died down. Manannán, the sea god, cradles this frail vessel and its human cargo: the sure and the brave, the uncertain and the doubtful, the resentful and the furious. It is time to sleep. *You would like that plan*, I tell my brother. *A quest to find every last island. A little boat, the two of us rowing, a fantastic, crazy mission . . . Sweet dreams, Paul.* Sigurd's breathing slows; he is already asleep. In the shadows Knut lies still, watching me through narrowed eyes.

The second night. Our progress has been slow, the conditions calm all day. Now it is overcast. The stars are in hiding, and we cannot go on. The sail comes down. We trail a sea anchor. Gareth orders most of the crew to rest. It is cold, wet and cramped in the hold, and my joints ache.

Sibeal has stopped being sick and is taking sips of water. Her eyes are sunken; her jaw is set with fierce determination. I make myself get up and stretch as Gull has taught me. A crewman named Garbh is in charge of rations: hard bread, cheese, strips of wind-dried mutton. I make myself useful fetching supplies for Gull, for Svala, for myself. At Gull's suggestion, I soak my bread in water before eating. No nourishing soups on this voyage. Gull can provide herbal potions, but cannot brew any freshly until we make landfall and can light a fire. If I get sick, he may not be able to save me this time.

Svala will not eat. I have not seen her swallow so much as a mouthful.

"I don't think she eats this kind of food, Felix," Sibeal says. "If we could fish . . . "

"No way to cook it," says Gull. "More's the pity."

"She eats it raw."

"Now, why don't I find that surprising? Catches it with her bare hands, does she?"

Sibeal stares at Gull, taken aback. "Possibly," she says.

"I expect someone has a hand line. We might try in the morning. Depends on the conditions. And on what Gareth decides to do."

Neither Knut nor I can be a reliable guide to finding the serpent isle. I spent much of that voyage in the hold, and I know nothing about navigation. As for Knut, his wish to be elsewhere can be read in every part of his body. When Gareth asks for his advice, he answers briefly, giving as little as he can. I understand his fear.

Gareth has several means of path-finding: landmarks such as skerries and islands, the stars by night, and by day a sun stone such as the Norsemen use. Far from land, under cloudy skies, instinct is the only guide. He believes tomorrow will see us close to the spot where the tempest fell on *Freyja*. The uncertainty of it hangs over all of us. What if we sail northwest from that point for two days, three, and do not find the isle? Do we abandon the plan and turn for home? Sail on to the end of the world?

"Felix." Sibeal has got up and come over to me, looking so frail the next roll of the boat might fell her. She seems transparent as fine glass. "Are you all right?"

"I'm fine. You look—" I stop myself from telling the truth: that I want to wrap her up and transport her safely home, right now. "You look as if you're getting your sea legs," I say.

"I hope so. I'm not much use to anyone with my head in a bucket. Maybe tomorrow Gareth will let us go on deck for a while." She glances across at Svala, who is crouched in her corner, an awkward bundle of unease. "I'm sure she'd be happier up in the open air," she adds in an undertone. "She hates being confined, and she hates being close to people."

And she is afraid, I think, but do not say it. For the three of us, *Freyja*'s only survivors, this is that ill-fated voyage all over again. The creaking of the timbers, the endless rolling motion, the tang of sea air, the sound of rushing water, everything takes us back to our dark place. If Svala is frightened, it is with good cause.

Paul, I will be brave. I will be as brave as you were, my brother.

*   *   *

The third day. Tempers fray; we are all on edge. It is overcast. The sun stone is useless. The wind is a mere breath.

Sigurd catches a fish. Svala receives it with wary hands. She takes her prize to a dark corner of the hold, where she squats down and guards it. Eating, she turns her back to us. Her feast is soon gone.

Late in the day, Gareth calls me up on deck. Cloud blankets the sky from north to south, from east to west; if it does not lift, there will be another night at anchor. On every side the sea stretches to the horizon, an endless expanse of heaving gray water. No island; no reef; not the smallest skerry. The sky is empty of birds. We are alone.

I lean beside Gareth at the rail.

"We're near the place, aren't we?" I ask him. "The spot where *Freyja* was taken?"

"As close as we'll get with little more than guesswork to go by." Gareth sounds somewhat dour. "What do your instincts tell you, Felix? Does it seem right? Can you remember any signs, anything at all we might use to help us find a way?"

I wish I could help him. "My instincts would be a poor guide. As I said, I was down in the hold for the best part of *Freyja*'s voyage. What will you do?"

"This breeze feels like a southeasterly to me, and it's gradually rising. But I won't go on until I can be more sure of the direction. Pray for clear skies."

By night, in the hold, I overhear Knut telling Sigurd that I am the ill luck man, and that this wild and crazy voyage has been born entirely of my madness. My goal is to get everyone killed, he says. My ambition is to exact vengeance for my brother's death and my own inadequacies. Sigurd listens without comment, then changes the subject to fishing.

When Gareth comes down, he and Cathal argue in lowered voices. Cathal believes that if the wind strengthens we should head in the direction we believe is northwest, even if the clouds make our tools of navigation useless. Gareth disagrees. Cathal sounds edgy, his tone full of the need to go, to move, to get this job done. Gareth's is the voice of reason: our captain's voice. Cathal goes up to take his watch with nothing settled. Glancing across the hold, I see that Sibeal is awake, sitting up with her eyes closed and her hands in her lap, a blanket loosely around her shoulders. I wait until she is finished: a long time. A poem forms in my mind as I watch her, a poem I will never speak aloud.

She returns, blinking, stretching, the veil of that other world slow to lift from her features. I am ready with a water skin.

"Here. Drink."

She smiles. "Thank you, Felix."

We speak in whispers; around us many are sleeping. I have found it hard to sleep on board the boat. While I no longer suffer from seasickness, I cannot lie here without feeling the immense power that lies beneath our fragile cradle. I cannot close my eyes without seeing the wave come over. With every breath I take, I feel the water's chill embrace, carrying me away.

I do not ask Sibeal what she has seen. I wait for her to tell me.

"We'll find the place," she says. "I'm certain of it." Nothing of what came to her in meditation; nothing of whether the gods still smile on our endeavor. She wears her contained expression, the look suited to the enactment of a ritual. I wonder if she has seen disaster and wants to spare me. "Best sleep now," she says. "Rest well, Felix." She looks over at Svala, whose eyes are on the two of us, watching, watching. Sibeal mimes sleep, resting her head on folded hands. "Good night, Svala."

But as Sibeal and I lie down, a discreet distance apart, Svala makes no move, save to turn her gaze up through the opening toward the starless sky. I close my eyes and wait for the wave to come.

There is no need for further dispute between Gareth and Cathal. The choice is made for them. In the darkness a strange fierce wind rises, and suddenly we are all wide-awake. No need for the guidance of stars or sun. It is the same wind, blowing to the northwest; I know it in my bones. Something severs the rope that holds our sea anchor. With commendable calm, Gareth orders the crew to hoist the sail. We must ride before the storm or become a scrap of flotsam, helpless under the buffeting of the waves. *Liadan's* joints creak and groan. Above us, on deck, crewmen exchange shouts as they fight to get her under some measure of control. The seas are rising. Spray dances high above the rail, splashing into the hold and drenching us.

Gareth calls Knut up on deck; in such conditions, every able crewman on board must be put to work. Knut obeys. I am forced to recognize how brave he is. Once he is out of sight, something changes in Svala. Or has the storm done this? Her eyes are bright, her back straight, her head held proudly. She stands up and moves toward the opening as if she, too, would haul herself up there into the wild wind and the ocean spray.

"No, Svala!" Gull has to raise his voice to be heard over the gathering storm. "Sibeal, tell her it's not safe."

Sibeal staggers over to Svala, takes her arm, says something I do not hear. Svala seems to understand either words or touch, for she comes back and sits down, but there is a restless energy in every part of her. She could be a different woman. As for me, I am glad we have this crew, this captain. If the men of Inis Eala cannot stand fast against the storm, I think nobody can.

I am not sure I believe in the sea god, but I pray to him: *Keep Sibeal safe, at least.* I go to sit by her and hold her hand. Who cares about propriety? On her other side is Gull, calm and quiet. As the sky lightens to a tentative dawn we hurtle through monstrous seas, our sail bellying, on a path straight for the serpent isle.

CHAPTER 12

~Sibeal~

e sailed on before the storm. The pace was unrelenting. Keeping *Liadan* on a steady course and in one piece became the only thing that mattered. Days and nights passed in a blur. A man would climb down, white-faced and shaking with exhaustion, to snatch brief rest; another would struggle up to take his place on deck. They lay down and were instantly asleep, inert as felled trees. Gull told stories to the rest of us to help the time pass, but even he could not go on forever. The memory of death shadowed Felix's eyes.

As a druid I was trained to endure. I made body and mind quiet; I slowed my breath. My thinking shrank to the kernel of a nut, the petal of a flower, a single blade of grass. Night followed day. A small part of me was aware of the purposeful, grim-faced men, the violently rocking ship, the waves washing over, the white face of Felix beside me.

On the third night I dreamed of violent struggle, of screams and clawing fingers. I woke abruptly to a hand on my shoulder, and swam up to full consciousness to see Cathal crouched beside me. It was morning. Through the opening above the hold, the sky was a clear light blue.

"What is it, Cathal?"

"We need to talk."

I sat up. Gull and Felix were both awake, seated not far from me. Felix had dark circles under his eyes. And Svala—what was wrong? She was standing awkwardly, her hands up in front of her, and . . .

"She's tied up!" I exclaimed in horror. Was this real, or was I still dreaming? Svala's wrists were bound together with a rope, and a length of it tethered her to the timbers of the hold's interior. No wonder Felix looked as if he'd seen a ghost. "What happened?" I demanded, struggling to rise. My legs were cramped from my uneasy sleep. "Who has done this?" I must release Svala right now.

"Leave her, Sibeal." Gull reached out a hand to hold me back. "Captain's orders. You slept through it all, but last night she got up on deck while the ship was under full sail. I was down below, but Gareth said she caused chaos up there so he ordered the men to bring her back to the hold and restrain her. She fought off four crewmen. Did a lot of damage. I've been kept busy attending to scratches and bruises. Believe me, Sibeal, Gareth had no choice."

This was wrong, utterly wrong. It made a mockery of the mission; it was akin to caging a beautiful sea bird. And I couldn't bear that look on Felix's face, the look that told me he was remembering Paul; I couldn't bear it a moment longer. "How can you be so calm about it, Gull?" I burst out. "I don't care what she did! She's frightened—just look at her!" Svala was pulling against the ropes with some violence. A raw bracelet of damaged flesh encircled each wrist. A whimpering came from her, the hoarse, defeated sound of someone who has raged and wept all night long. "I'll set her free myself if none of you is prepared to do it!"

I was moving toward her when Felix's arm came around my shoulders, holding me, halting me. "Sibeal," he murmured in my ear. "I know how you feel. Wait."

His touch slowed my hammering heart. His steady voice told

me I had been on the brink of behaving in a manner not befitting a druid. Perhaps there was another way to do this, a better way. "I can keep her calm," I said, looking at Cathal. "Please ask Gareth if I can untie her bonds. She has a link with me. She'll listen to me."

"No, Sibeal, I won't ask him. You didn't see her. No seafaring man wants to risk a madwoman on his vessel. And that was what she was, laughing, singing, screaming, climbing in the rigging, leaning over the side with waves like mountains crashing all around. What if there had been a reef? The crew were so distracted that we'd have sunk with all hands. I won't ask Gareth, and I won't untie her. And you won't either. In a matter like this, you don't go against the captain's orders."

A slap in the face. My authority as a druid counted for nothing. I stood silent beside Felix. To restrain Svala was to mock the gods. My chest ached with the wrongness of it. Standing beside Felix, with his body touching mine, I felt his pain. How could he be so stoic about this?

"What was it you came down to say?" Gull asked Cathal.

"We can't sustain this pace much longer," Cathal said flatly. "The toll on men and boat is too great. I'm starting to have doubts about the course. Could we have sailed right past the place?" He looked at Felix.

"I can't tell you," Felix said. "The conditions feel the same, the wind, the seas, the light. This part of the journey was shorter for *Freyja*. But you must allow for a different vessel, almost certainly a different starting point, the speed of the wind, and . . . " His voice faded away.

"That is the question. Is this an ordinary storm, a phenomenon that is perhaps quite common to this particular place? Or is it something more? What great hand stirs the seas? Whose fell breath drives *Liadan* onward?"

"I take it you're not referring to Manannán," I said. I was furious with him, with Gareth, with Gull for allowing this to happen to Svala. That did not take away all my common sense. We were in danger. The situation was perilous. If Cathal needed my advice, I would give it.

"No, Sibeal, I do not refer to any godly power. It is in my father's nature to toy with folk, to play tricks, to exercise his particular form of cruelty. We might sail on and on, and . . . "

"And never reach land?" put in Gull. "The wind doesn't blow in the same direction forever. Sooner or later it will change. If it's later rather than sooner, Gareth will have no choice but to turn and head for home, our supplies being limited."

"It's not blowing in the same direction, Gull," says Cathal soberly. "Some time in the night we veered off closer to due north. Just now, the clouds lifted long enough for Gareth to check it with the sun stone, and his reading bears that out."

Felix was silent, his jaw clenched tight.

"That need not mean we're off course," I said. "We started from Inis Eala, not Ulfricsfjord. The wind may have picked us up at a point further west than it did *Freyja*. If we accept that the storm is an uncanny thing, whether sent by the gods or by some other power, then perhaps it blows in whichever direction will bear us to the serpent isle."

"So if you were Gareth you wouldn't even attempt to steer a course?" Cathal's brows went up.

"I'm offering a theory only. And no, I wouldn't suggest any such thing to Gareth. Didn't you imply that the captain's word is law?" Anger rose in me again, and I might have spoken rashly, but there was a different kind of sound from Svala, and I saw her looking toward a particular corner. "Gull," I said, "how can Svala use the privy if she's tied up?"

Without a word, Gull went over to unhook the long rope that anchored Svala to the timbers. He made no move to untie her wrists, or her ankles, which I realized were linked by a rope perhaps two handspans long.

Beyond words, I made my way to the corner where the privy bucket was wedged between various other objects. In the storm it had not always been possible to keep the contents where they belonged. Fortunately, it seemed Gull had been up to empty it over the side this morning.

I was sure none of the men had considered quite how difficult performing this function might be for a woman with her wrists and ankles tied, however loosely. I helped her as best I could. As I smoothed down her skirt, she held up her bound hands, moving them to and fro. Her eyes pleaded with me. I had never felt so strong an urge to disobey a direct order. I would not let Gull fasten her to the timbers again. I could not let it happen. I opened my mouth to say so, and Felix spoke instead.

"Cathal, you said the wind changed during the night. When? What was happening at the time?"

Standing beside Svala, with my hand on her arm to reassure her, I felt a sudden calm possess me. I understood what Felix was thinking of, and it made perfect sense to me.

"I believe it was about the time Gareth gave the order for Svala to be taken below. I can't be certain, Felix. All of us were somewhat preoccupied."

"So she was manhandled down here and tied up, and then the wind changed?" I said.

"I noticed it when we came back up on deck," said Cathal, and I saw on his face that he was starting to follow our thinking. "I didn't make much of it at the time—I wasn't sure. Then Gareth asked me if I'd noticed a difference; he'd felt it, too."

We sat silent for a while, listening to the scream of the gale and the pounding of the waves against the hull. Eventually I said, "She knows the way. Svala knows the way. Gareth must untie her and let her go back up on the prow. It doesn't matter, for now, who's stirring the seas and making the wind blow. Without Svala, we won't find the serpent isle."

"The wind changed *because* she was not there to guide us?" Gull sounded somewhat sceptical. "What is she, a goddess?"

"I don't understand it either, Gull, but my instincts tell me this is what we must do. Tell Gareth, Cathal, and get her back up there quickly, before we go too far off course." I realized I was giving orders. "Please tell him I'm sure that's what he must do."

"Felix?" Cathal lifted his brows. "You concur with this?"

"I do," Felix said. "The sooner Svala is set free, the sooner we will reach that place. Perhaps today. Perhaps today we will find them."

Cathal went on deck. Very soon after, he came down again. "He's prepared to try it. Felix, will you untie Svala's bonds?"

I had not thought it possible for Felix to go any paler, but he did so now. "I will," he said. "Sibeal, I may need your help."

I stood by Svala, using gestures to explain as best I could what was happening. My link with her was weak here in the hold; there were, perhaps, too many others close by to allow that joining of thoughts we had sometimes shared. But I could keep her calm while Felix undid the knots and freed her hands. I could murmur to her while he knelt to unfasten the ropes around her ankles. It was a slow job; his hands were shaking. I understood why Cathal had laid this particular duty on him.

"It's done," Felix said eventually, and rose to his feet. Tears were running down his cheeks. "You're free."

I had expected Svala to dart away as soon as the last knot was untied. But she laid her hands on Felix's shoulders—she was slightly taller than he—and nodded gravely in recognition. Then she took my arm and pointed up to the deck, giving voice to a sequence of liquid sounds that were somewhere between speech and song. A series of clear gestures followed: *you, me, up there.* Then a sweeping, almost imperious movement of the arm, indicating Felix. *And him.* She motioned to Gull. *That one, too.*

"We should do as she wants," I said, trying to ignore the quavering terror in my belly. Up there in the storm, in the open, amid those heaving seas . . .

"Are you sure, Sibeal?" Gull was getting to his feet. He winced as he straightened. The close confinement of the hold and the lack of opportunity to stretch our legs had taken their toll.

"Yes, I'm sure," I said. There was a reason for everything Svala did; I was more and more convinced of that. Even the things that seemed wild and uncontrolled had their purpose. "Cathal, is it possible for us to be somewhere on deck but out of people's way?"

"If you can keep Svala from wreaking havoc, I expect Gareth might agree to it."

"I'll do my best."

"Let me go up first, then. I'll find you a spot."

Up there, in the teeth of the wind, I could think of little but staying on my feet. I wedged myself against the rail, and Felix stood between me and the gale. As for Gull, the moment he came up on deck he changed from healer to sailor. There were tasks even his crippled hands could manage: stowing equipment quickly and neatly, lending his strength to jobs requiring the force of several men, keeping an eye on which crewman needed to rest, calling the next to take his place. I realized that if it had not been for my presence on *Liadan*, his voyage would have been quite different. I saw a purpose and pride in him that touched me even as I clung to the rail with one hand and to Felix with the other, praying wordlessly to Manannán to let us live.

Svala was restored to herself. She stood tall on the prow, heedless of the salt spray, the fearsome swell and the scourge of the wind. She was at one with the sea. Her golden hair flew wildly above her, tossed in all directions. Her bare feet were planted firmly. While I could not have taken a step on my own without falling, for the deck was tilting one way, then the other, she had no need to hold on. I watched her in awe. There was a freedom about her, and a power, that awoke a yearning in me, a longing for something I could not name. Now and again she turned to me, eyes alight, as if to share her excitement. *Here we are! Isn't it wonderful?* I managed a grimace in return. Truth to tell, I was not able to face this with the fortitude I would have wished for. I was terrified.

Felix bent to say something—the only way he could make himself heard over the wind and the waves was to put his mouth close to my ear. "I'll hold on to you, Sibeal. I won't let you go, I promise."

He put his arm around me, and although the sea was immense and the gale was mighty, I was reassured. I slipped one arm around his waist; my other hand would not release its death grip

321

on the rail. For a moment my head was against his chest, and it seemed to me that under the filthy, wet wool of his tunic I could feel his heart beating, steady and sure. "I know," I said. "I won't let you go, either."

For a while I repeated passages of the lore in my head. When I no longer had the strength for that, I simply stood where I was, knowing that without the warmth of Felix's body close to mine and the knowledge of his hope beating into me, I would be scuttling back to the hold to huddle in a pathetic ball among the baggage, wishing I had never set out on such an ill-conceived journey.

At some point I heard a series of sharp commands. The sail crackled. *Liadan* shuddered, then settled into a barreling, forward course.

"The wind's changed, Sibeal," Felix murmured in my ear. "You were right."

"Mm," I managed. It was indeed remarkable. The gods had smiled on us and should be thanked. But I was beyond summoning even the simplest of prayers.

For what felt like hours we stood there on the shifting deck, holding onto each other, watching as Svala balanced strong and confident in the prow and the crew toiled to exert a measure of control over the racing *Liadan*. There had been some uneasy looks after the wind changed, for sailors have a well-founded dread of the uncanny. But nobody made comment; they were too busy. Eventually, through the howl of the wind and the crash of the water, I heard a man shout: "Land! Land ahead!"

Svala stretched out her arms as if reaching for something that lay before us. She threw back her head and released an ear-splitting scream. And from the north a sound came, a bellowing that sent a chill up my spine. Felix started as if someone had hit him. It was an uncanny cry, deep and sad, a sound so profoundly strange that no words could fully capture it. Svala had called. Someone— *something*—had answered.

I saw the island. It loomed ahead, alone in the wild seas, a bastion of darkness fringed by white water, a towering fortress of sharp pinnacle and sheer cliff with no visible landing place. I could see no entry to a secret bay, no break in those improbably high bulwarks, no smaller isles nearby that might furnish a mooring.

Felix muttered words in his native tongue, most likely an oath. Gareth gave a series of orders and the crew scrambled to obey. Sigurd was on the steering oar; a second man went to help him. The rowing oars were readied. If the approach to the serpent isle was as Felix had described it, the men would need to maneuver *Liadan* through a narrow channel to reach sheltered water. Crewmen stood ready to lower the sail. All was steady purpose.

"I can't believe it," Felix said. "But here we are."

The eldritch bellowing sound came again, rattling my very bones. And closer at hand, someone was scrambling along the narrow way beside the open hold, a frantic figure shouting out a tirade of furious Norse. I did not understand Knut's words, but my mind reeled from the power of his feelings—rage, terror, the utter panic that attends a recognition of impending doom. *No! Not in there! I won't go back, I can't, I can't—*

Every crewman on deck was occupied in sailing the ship. Gareth shouted, "Stop! What are you doing, man?" but Knut continued his wild progress along the vessel, scrambling ever closer to the forward deck where Felix and I were standing not far from the oblivious Svala. I could almost smell his fear. As he passed a crewman whose hands were busy adjusting a rigging block, Knut snatched a knife from the man's belt.

Felix grabbed me and shoved me behind him with my back to the rail. Knut was on the tilting foredeck now, fighting to keep his balance, his features like a grim war mask. "Ill luck man!" he shouted in Irish, taking a labored step toward us. "You bring fear! You bring death! A curse on you!" Another step. Felix tensed. Knut had the knife up before him, ready to strike. He moved to take the step that would bring him close enough, but Felix was quicker. He let go of me, sprang forward and kicked out in the space of an instant. Caught unbalanced, Knut toppled and crashed to the deck. Felix backed, arms out, shielding me once more. Knut snarled like a wounded animal, struggling to get up. His eyes were on Felix, and the word they spoke was death.

"Svala!" I squeaked in a voice too faint to be heard above a gentle breeze, let alone this wild gale.

But she whirled around. In two long strides she was beside us and hooking her fingers through the cord encircling Knut's neck. She yanked hard; he wheezed in pain as the narrow strip of hide dug in, cutting off his breath. Svala hauled him up bodily. His face turned purple; his eyes bulged. He was going to die right in front of us. *No*, I whispered, *that wasn't what I meant you to do.* Or perhaps I only thought it. Peering around Felix, I knew I could do nothing to stop whatever was about to unfold.

She held him a moment, the strength of her arm formidable, and her face was indeed that of a goddess, stern in her judgment. Something had changed; his presence no longer cowed and frightened her. The cord snapped, and Knut collapsed to the deck. Set free, the talisman graven with *Eolh* flew through the air, tumbling on its way, and fell into the sea. Svala touched the frayed cord to her lips in an oddly tender gesture, then tucked it into her bodice. To my astonishment, I saw a tear spill from her eye and roll down her perfect cheek.

Now here was Cathal on the deck beside us, lifting the wheezing Knut, dragging him away. Sigurd came up to help; together they conveyed the Norseman below. Svala had turned back toward the north. No screaming now, no singing, no calling. She stood calm and quiet.

"All right?" Felix asked, somewhat breathlessly.

"Mm. You?"

"In one piece. Sibeal, you'd be better down in the hold for this last part. It's—a little dangerous."

Laughter welled up in me. It owed more to sheer terror than amusement. "I thought you once said you'd always tell me the truth," I managed.

"This, now, is frightening," Felix said, and there was no trace of laughter in his voice. "But the passage between the rocks is . . . different. And there's . . . "

There's what lies beyond, I thought. *The monster.* "I know," I said. "But I'm not going down in the hold with Knut, even if they've tied him up." It was the first time I had seen a man crazed by fear. With difficulty I summoned a confident tone. "This is the very best crew we could have. They'll get us through."

"We're almost there, Sibeal," Felix murmured, wrapping his arms around me. His warmth flooded into me once more; my heart lifted. "We could find them before sunset. We could be on our way home tomorrow. I'll owe you a debt for the rest of my life."

"Don't say that." Oh, this felt good. Here on the deck, with *Liadan* plowing ahead through heaving seas and the air full of salt spray, with the unforgiving rocks of the serpent isle drawing closer and closer, for a moment or two I felt as safe as I had ever felt in my life. "Your courage made this possible. Your hope kept the mission alive. Without you, nobody would have come to the rescue."

"My courage is your courage, Sibeal. My hope is your hope. You led me out of my own Yeun Ellez, the place of mist and shadow."

I closed my eyes, holding on, wishing the moment would last forever. *Fix this in your memory, Sibeal. Lock it up well, for it is rare beyond price.*

As we approached the island, both Gareth and Cathal came up to stand on the foredeck beside us.

"Ask Svala where the entry is, Sibeal," Gareth said. "I'd hoped Knut would be able to show us, but he's not making any sense."

There was no need to ask. As the sail came down and *Liadan* advanced cautiously under oars, Svala pointed with complete confidence to what appeared to me a sheer, unbroken wall of stone. *That way.*

"Manannán have mercy," Cathal said. "Can you see anything?"

"Not a break anywhere. Sibeal, can you—"

Gareth broke off. Svala had turned. Her lovely eyes widened as she looked past us, along the boat. She hissed, a sound of outrage. I followed her gaze to see crewmen passing up spears, bows and throwing knives from the hold.

The hiss became a flood of sounds, not the warbling songlike speech of better times, but a furious, shrieking challenge. Her anger filled me; I staggered with the force of it, and Felix had to grab my arm to stop me from falling.

"No weapons," I gasped. "Tell the men to put them back. If you want her to show you the way in, do as I say."

"Dagda's britches, Sibeal," protested Gareth, "there's a man-eating monster through there!"

Everything began to turn around me; my vision filled with spots. "No weapons," I murmured, swaying. I clutched onto Felix, willing myself not to faint.

"Put the weapons away!" Gareth shouted. "Gods help us, you'd better be right about this. Any sign of an opening yet?"

Surely we were too close to land. I could see shawls of weed on the rocks, and ledges higher up where gannets might nest. Gull was shouting commands to the oarsmen. Their faces were red with effort, their bodies straining hard. *We will not founder*, I said to myself, as if repeating the words might make them true. *We will not be wrecked. We will find the way.*

"There!" Felix was pointing ahead. And there it was: a narrow opening, visible only as a subtle variation in the gray of the rocks.

"Pull!" yelled Gull, moving to a position beside Sigurd and his helper. "Pull!"

I thought of a childhood game my sisters had often played at Sevenwaters. We would find a stream in spring spate, with cliffs and waterfalls and rapids all in miniature. We'd float ships of bark and leaf down this watercourse to see whose vessel would come first to the pool at the bottom. I saw myself sitting under an oak, watching as the others shrieked and ran and got their gowns soaking wet. Now we were in one of those fragile craft, and this was our own rapid, a turbulent mass of water churned by currents that were surely too violent and wayward to be conquered by the strength of a mere eight men rowing. *We will not founder. We will not be wrecked.*

Liadan skirted the rocks, approaching the place where a narrow inlet opened in the cliff face. A heaving body of white water filled the channel, swirling and eddying one way, then another. Gull shouted commands; *Liadan* shuddered as the oarsmen fought to guide her through the center. Above Gull's steady voice came Svala's, ululating high and strong, ringing off the rocks above us, as if a hundred wild women sang the song of our passage. From the other end of the channel came an answering roar. Between the rock walls we coursed, their weathered surfaces rushing past not two arm's lengths from us.

"Hold fast, men!" called Gareth.

"Ship oars!" shouted Gull, and the crew obeyed. *Liadan* surged forward like flotsam before a spring tide and shot out into the waters of the bay. When I could breathe again, I murmured a prayer. "Manannán be blessed. We give thanks." I realized I was clinging to Felix like a barnacle to its rock, and stepped back, releasing him. Here within the protective barrier of stone the water looked perfectly calm. *Liadan* moved forward, the crew rowing with precision, though their faces were white. Those who were not rowing stood in their places, eerily silent. Only Gull moved, coming to join us on the foredeck.

Svala's cry had ceased. Her gaze moved around the bay as if to drink in every corner of the bleak landscape. And it was indeed bleak: the picture I had formed in my mind, hearing Felix's story, was nothing to what I saw now. It was a nightmare vista in which everything seemed exaggerated. The high slopes were impossibly sheer, the lower reaches a tumble of misshapen stones like crouching monsters, all sharp edges and sudden holes. The bay or inlet was bigger than I had pictured it, a long, curving expanse of sheltered water with one patch of pebbly beach. I could not see a single bush or tree or clinging piece of foliage anywhere. Not a strip of weed; not a blade of grass; not a stunted, desperate plant. "It's like a place abandoned by the gods," I whispered.

"Perhaps there are different gods," said Felix.

And all the time we were waiting, waiting. Everyone had heard Felix's tale now. Everyone knew what came next.

"Row for shore!" Gareth called, and his voice was an intrusion in this empty place. It did not belong here. None of us did. The oarsmen obeyed the captain, and *Liadan* glided across the still water toward the narrow strip of pebbles.

Svala made a little chirruping sound. Looking out, I saw a widening patch of turbulence on the water's surface, a shoal of small fish, or maybe larger fish, or maybe very big fish indeed—

It rose in a shimmering burst of green-blue scales, rearing so high it blocked the sun, towering over us. The oarsmen froze; their blades went everywhere, clattering. The creature was huge, longer than *Liadan*, its girth massive. Its eyes shone like dark gems; its long jaws were studded with serrated, purposeful teeth. We stood stunned, silent. The weapons would have been no use at all; a pinprick to a wild boar.

Gull recovered first. "Pull!" he shouted, striding back along the walkway toward the stern, where Sigurd stood immobile, hands on the steering oar, shocked eyes on the monster. "Put your backs into it! What do you think this is, a leisurely fishing trip?"

Svala chirruped again, and the creature came down, its forequarters plunging into the water on our port side, its body snaking, its tail rising to smack the surface once, twice, three times. *Celebrating,* I thought crazily as I ducked to avoid a soaking. *It's celebrating her return with drumming and dancing. Liadan* rocked wildly, her deck tilting one way, the other way. The creature was making a storm all by itself, cavorting around the boat, diving and leaping. On the prow, Svala laughed and clapped her hands.

The thing swam away; I breathed and stood upright once more. Thank the gods, it was going to let us reach the shore. In my mind I saw Svala on the beach at Inis Eala, making her great sand creature, touching him with loving hands, displaying him to me in all his splendor. Singing him songs. Sitting by his side as the tide came to claim him. Hard as it was to believe, it seemed the man-eating monster was her friend. It—*he*—was glad we had delivered her home.

The creature dived beneath the surface and was gone. The water settled, calm as before. There was no ripple, no disturbance, nothing to show it had been there. Only the blanched faces and shocked eyes of *Liadan*'s crew, and the thunderous beating of my heart.

"What are you, men or mice?" roared Gull. "Pull, you useless sons of vermin!"

They gripped their oars. They pulled. The shore drew closer.

I felt it a moment before it happened, as if fate tapped my shoulder with a cold finger. The water swirled, and like a missile from some giant's catapult the creature leaped up, high into the air, right over *Liadan*, so close I saw the cunning pattern of interlocking scales on its belly, so close I thought the mast would snap, so close I was sure it would crush us. In a heartbeat it was down again, plunging head first back into the water on the other side of the boat. A surge of water crashed over *Liadan*, flooding into the hold. And where Gull had been standing on the walkway, now there was nobody at all.

A moment's stunned silence. Then men moved, tearing off their boots and scrambling for the rail. A scream welled up in me.

"Wait!" yelled Gareth. "Nobody jump—that thing's still in there! Man your oars!"

I was cold to the bone. What was he saying, that Gull should be left to drown? "We have to save him!" I shouted. "Gareth, someone has to go in after him!"

But Gareth was silent, jaw set, eyes on the shore. I didn't understand. Had this mission made him into a different man, one who could let an old friend die without a second thought?

Be calm, Sibeal. Think of a solution. Cathal. He was right here. He could calm the water, he could—I saw that he was already at the rail, arms outstretched, looking out over the place where Gull had vanished and speaking words in a tongue unknown to me. Thank the gods. Thank all the gods Cathal had come with us.

Gareth gave another order; the oars stilled. Time passed, time measured in the frantic drumbeats of my heart. In the water below us, nothing stirred. Cathal called again, his voice powerful and ringing. The only answer was silence.

He lowered his arms and turned toward us. His face was a mask in pale stone. "I can't do it," he said. "There's a force here, a contrary force . . . something is blocking me." His voice cracked. "I can't save him."

"But—" I began, then realized I had forgotten something. Svala was the monster's friend. She had called and he had answered. "Svala, help us!" I grabbed hold of her arm, hoping she would feel my desperation as I had once felt hers. She turned her lovely gray eyes on me, but made no move. "Please, Svala! The sea beast is your friend, surely you can do something—" Oh, gods, this couldn't be happening.

A flurry of movement behind me. "No!" shouted Gareth and Cathal together. I couldn't move; I couldn't breathe. For, of course, there was one man on board who was not a member of the crew, one man who might, at an extreme, disobey the captain's orders. Felix was astride the rail. He steadied himself, brought his other leg over, then dived, straight as an arrow, into the bay. The waters closed over him, and he, too, was gone. Gone in a heartbeat. Gone between one breath and the next. Gone as if he had never been.

I rushed for the rail, scrabbling to climb up. If I jumped now I could save him, I had to, it wasn't too late, he couldn't die—

A pair of hands closed around my arms, restraining me firmly but gently. "No, Sibeal," said Cathal. As I twisted and kicked and fought, shouting my rage, he held me firm all the way to shore.

I was on the beach. *Liadan* lay at anchor some little distance out in the water. Crewmen had conveyed me to shore in a small rowing boat. The pebbles were hard underneath me; the air was chill against my wet cheeks. I heard Gareth giving sharp orders, his tone forbidding comment. And someone was making a whimpering sound like the cry of a whipped dog. Maybe it was me. There was no druid here, no brave woman with the ear of the gods and a spirit honed to strength and wisdom by years of discipline. The last spark of that person had dwindled and died out there on the water. There was only a hollow where my heart had been ripped out. Cast away. Sunk deep as death.

"Sibeal?"

Cathal was crouching beside me, his tone unusually kindly. He put his hand on my shoulder.

"Don't touch me!" I shrank into myself, hugging my anguish close.

"Sibeal, we need your help. Take a deep breath and look at me. Sibeal, look at me."

"Go away."

A crunch as he settled on the stones beside me. A silence. Then he said, "Being leader of a mission means certain responsibilities. That includes making decisions on the instant. Sometimes those decisions seem wrong. If you're not a fighting man they may seem very wrong indeed. Sibeal, Gareth can't afford to lose any more men. If our numbers drop below a certain level we won't be able to get home. That could have been a trap, designed to draw one after another of us into the water in a vain rescue attempt. He had to do what he did." After a moment he added, "Both of them vanished the moment they went under the water. We could go out in the small boat. We could search until nightfall, putting ourselves in the perfect position to be snapped up by that creature. Chances are we'd still find no trace of them."

I tried to close my ears. *Gull. Felix. Gone.*

"Gareth's sending a search party along the shore, in case they've come in further up."

"And then he'll ask me to conduct a burial rite, I suppose." My voice was someone else's, someone bitter and furious.

"Sibeal, we haven't a lot of time. I want you to answer a question for me." When I made no reply, Cathal went ahead and asked it. "Why did we undertake this mission?"

Felix. My whole body ached with sorrow.

"Answer, Sibeal. Or do you lack the courage?"

I turned on him. "Courage? Don't talk to me about courage! There was only one man among all of you who had the courage to jump in after Gull, and that was a man who had more cause than anyone to be afraid of the water! Every night, when he closed his eyes, all he could see was the wave coming over and taking his brother! How dare you? How dare you talk to me about—"

331

The flow of words stopped. Now that I had lifted my head and opened my eyes, I saw orderly activity all around us: men bringing gear ashore in the little boat, others passing items hand to hand up the rocks to higher ground, Gareth and Sigurd scanning the hillsides and talking in low voices, a small group putting on packs and collecting spears from a stack of weaponry. And Svala, not prancing and singing and celebrating her return, but crouched up on the rocks as if waiting for something. She was looking directly at me. The waters of the bay were like fine glass under a clearing sky. The storm had passed. "All right," I said. "We're here because Felix believed in his cause." I could hardly bring myself to speak his name. "Because he is—was—a good man, a brave man who knew he must do the right thing."

"Mm-hm."

"I can't believe he's gone, Cathal. And Gull . . . So quickly, like flames blown out in a draft. So quickly, as if they didn't even matter."

"I know." He bowed his head. I realized that he, too, was grieving, mourning the loss of a beloved old friend and a fine new one. Through the fog of my own sadness I recognized what he was trying to tell me. "We must find those men," I said. "Find them and bring them home. We owe it to Felix, and to Gull, to complete the mission."

Cathal nodded. "If we don't do it," he said, "then Felix's sacrifice was all for nothing." He rose to his feet and offered me his hand. I stood. My legs were shaking. We were soaked; our clothing hung around us, dripping. "We'll move up this slope to the shelter of those overhanging rocks, if shelter it can be called," he said. "Gareth's insisting on time for food and rest; the men are on their last legs. The only exception is the search party he's sending along the shore. When they get back, a group of us will head out to look for these survivors. Some must stay here to watch over the boat, and . . . " He glanced up toward the rocks where Svala was perched. "And her, I suppose. She's shown no sign of wanting to bolt off to wherever she was living before. Knut's still disturbed;

he can't be sent out foraging. If he's to be left here with you and Svala, we need several men on guard."

Knut was sitting on the beach, a short distance away. He had a rope around one ankle, tethering him to a slab of rock. He was hunched over, a picture of misery, his arms around his knees, someone's cloak draped over his bent back. Two men stood at a little distance. One leaned casually on a spear; the other had knives at his belt.

"I'm not staying here," I said, trying to dry my eyes on my wet sleeve. "I'm coming with you to find those men. Since Felix can't do it, I must take his place." I recalled those first divinations, cast after the waves brought Felix to my doorstep. Had I put too much trust in *Nyd*—fortitude beyond endurance? Had I placed undue emphasis on the beneficent power of *Os*? In Felix's own choice of runes, he had included *Is*. In tying that to his loss of memory, had I failed to consider that *Is* could also signify a disaster that came from nowhere? And if I had seen it coming, could I have changed the pattern of this? Could I have saved him?

"Sibeal," said Cathal.

I started, blinking. He'd been saying something and I had missed it completely. "What?"

"This could be difficult. Even Felix didn't know where those men were. Nor did Knut. All we have to go on is my vision, and the only thing that showed was a cave. It may be a lengthy search." He did not mention the monster, which, according to Felix's account, could go on both land and water.

"I'm coming with you."

Perhaps it was something in my stance, or in my eyes. Perhaps my brother-in-law thought anything was better than the whimpering wretch I had been not so long ago. I could not be that woman, not now. There was work to be done.

"So be it, then," Cathal said. "See if you can find yourself some dry clothing—Garbh and Rian are sorting out the things from the hold, over there on the rocks." He hesitated. "I think Svala wants to tell you something. Maybe she can help us. If she really does belong in this place, she should know the likeliest spot for folk to shelter in."

Rian and Garbh found me a shirt and a tunic that had missed the worst of the water, and I went behind a protrusion in the rocks to change. No spare skirt. I took mine off, wrung it out and put it back on again, shivering. When night came it would bring a cold to freeze the marrow. My stockings were soaking and filthy. I thrust my bare feet into my shoes. I rolled my wet things up. Coming back out, I almost crashed into Svala, who was standing with legs apart and arms folded, waiting for me. The stance was not encouraging, and nor was the tight set of her mouth. I put down the bundle and reached to take her hands, and I felt a trembling running through her. I closed my eyes, hoping that here, with open space around us, her thoughts might come to me more clearly than on the boat. Was she scared? Angry? Cold? How could such wild elation be gone so quickly?

Don't reproach her, I told myself. *They were not lost because of her. They weren't even lost because of the monster.* For though I wanted someone to blame, I had seen that the creature's wild antics were no attempt to kill, only sheer exuberance. What had happened was mischance, no more. I breathed slowly; I made my mind open to Svala's thoughts.

A wild jumble of conflicting images poured in. She was bursting with what she felt, what she wanted, what she needed from me. Something about getting dressed, getting undressed . . . The creature, its tail splashing on the water's surface, the wave coming over . . . Now I was the one who was shaking. Her feelings welled into me, making me dizzy and nauseated. She was angry, scared, confused. She wanted . . . oh, she wanted, she needed . . . *Where is it? Where has he hidden it?* For a moment there was Knut in the image, and her hands ripping his talisman from his neck. *Give it! Give it back!* She pulled one hand from my grasp and thrust it down the neck of her gown, bringing out the twisted, fraying piece of cord she had taken from him. Her eyes were wild as she shook it in my face. *This! This! Mine!* The images in my mind were changing so fast that I could not understand any of them.

I couldn't do this. I was too weak to withstand it, too small to hold her powerful feelings as well as my own grief. I had no idea at all what she meant.

"I don't think I can help you any more, Svala," I whispered, releasing her hand. In the back of my mind were thoughts that shamed me: *Why should I? You wouldn't help me. You stood there and let them drown. And now Felix is gone, and if you think you love this place, monster and all, it is nothing to how I feel!*

As I moved away she made her chittering sound, and I turned my head to see her miming the same idea her thoughts had suggested: putting on clothing, perhaps a hooded cloak or similar all-enveloping garment. She smoothed the imaginary cloak down, swirled it around her, nodded. *Now everything is all right.* When the odd performance was done, she stretched out her hands toward me and made the noise again. Now it sounded as much threat as plea. She pointed to the water. *Do as I ask, or I will make him come again with his sharp claws and his long teeth. Do it.* Beyond her, out in the calm waters of the bay, I thought I saw something rise just above the surface, the sleek suggestion of a great body, the ripple of a long tail. I blinked and it was gone.

I turned away again and walked back toward the men. *Oh, Ciarán,* I thought, *I need your wisdom now. But I am glad you are not here to see me come to this.* And it seemed to me his voice murmured in my ear, wise and calm as always: *In all experience, there is something to be learned. In deepest sorrow, wisdom is found. In the well of despair, hope rises.*

Men slept, rolled in anything they could find that was tolerably dry. The rock shelf made a hard bed, but these warriors were used to taking their rest where and when it was offered, and they were bone weary. Those who were to form the rescue party were ordered to rest first, Cathal and me included. He lay down and closed his eyes, his dark cloak spread over him. Perhaps sleeping; more likely not. I knew I would not sleep.

Four men stood guard around us, three of them facing the bay with spears in hand. Gareth paced. I found I could not look at him. I saw the logic in what Cathal had told me, but I could not accept it. This was Gareth, Johnny's beloved, a man who always put others' needs before his own. A joker; an arbiter; a peacemaker. The captain who had ordered his crew not to save a comrade's life was worlds away from the man I knew. A familiar friend had, in an instant, become a stranger.

"Sibeal," Gareth said now, speaking in an undertone so as not to disturb the sleepers, "if you're going with Cathal, you must lie down and rest."

I ignored him, moving to sit a short distance away from the others. Further down on the rocks, Svala still crouched. She was humming a mournful little tune, over and over. I settled cross-legged, my hands palm upwards on my knees. I closed my eyes. Gareth said nothing more.

I needed all my strength to achieve a meditative trance. My body was tight with grief; sorrow was in every part of me. It beat in my heart and ran in my veins. In my mind, over and over, Felix dived off the boat, graceful as a swallow, and vanished under the water. I called upon my training. I called upon the discipline that had been so hard-won. I breathed. I banished my tears. I thought of Ciarán's wise eyes, his measured voice, his reassuring presence. And of Finbar, long gone but still present in spirit, a power for good. After a long time, when at last I was ready, I prayed. *Help me be strong enough. Help me survive this.* And then the hard part. *Lead them kindly on their journey, guardian of the great gateway. They were fine men, the two of them. Gull, warrior and healer, beloved of his family, a friend of utmost loyalty, a lamp of goodness to all who knew him. And Felix . . .* Breathe, breathe . . . *And Felix, so strong in heart, so gentle yet so brave . . . Morrigan, I pass him over to you. But oh, if his hand were still in mine I would fight to keep him, I would fight like a she-wolf to win him another chance. Manannán, you took him too soon. Surely it was not his time.* Despite my best efforts, a tear spilled.

It had been so long since the gods had granted me answers that I was shocked when a voice spoke in my mind, a voice as powerful as a thundering waterfall and as quiet as a sleeping child. *Would you challenge the gods, Sibeal?*

Why would it be the gods' will that Felix should die before he completed his quest? If it were possible for the mind's speech to be brittle with fury, mine surely was. *The runes said he could do it! They spoke of a mission fulfilled! If I had known, I'd never have encouraged him to undertake the voyage, never!*

The mission can still be fulfilled.

I was supposed to go on and rescue the survivors without Felix. Well, I was doing that. As soon as the rest period was over, we'd be setting off.

He was never for you, said the voice. *You are promised to the service of the gods, Sibeal. Your destiny is a higher one than his could ever be. You know this.*

I let the words sink inside me, reminding me of what I had long known to be true. This knowledge had guided my steps since I was a small child. Was this the gods' answer to the question, *why?* Why was he taken from me? Because he did not fit into the picture. Because he was a complication.

"Oh, no," I breathed. "No! That's wrong! It's more wrong than I can say! To sacrifice him so you can secure my loyalty . . . I will not stand for that!" Ciarán would have been appalled; to address the gods thus was akin to putting one's neck on a chopping block. I did not care. "If this is what being a druid requires, then I renounce that life! I am not yet sworn to it." I was shivering, shocked, held halfway between the calm of the trance and furious recognition of a betrayal that set my deepest convictions on their heads.

Did not you once promise you would do anything, anything at all, if he could survive?

"But he didn't survive," I muttered aloud. "He wasn't even allowed to live for long enough to find his friends and make good his promise to his brother. Don't toy with me—this is cruel."

Wait, Sibeal. The voice was calm and grave. Beyond being offended by my disrespect; beyond caring about something as trivial as human love. *Only wait.*

"Sibeal? Are you all right?"

My eyes sprang open at the sound of a real voice. Cathal had come over to sit a short distance away. His dark eyes were full of concern.

Still caught in the trance, I could not answer. I shook my head, then closed my eyes and fought to recapture the pattern of my breathing. I must quiet the storm of feelings that had no place in a meditative mind. I must let it go. I must let him go. I must . . .

"I can't," I said, opening my eyes again. "I can't accept this. Cathal, we should go now. Now, right away." I tried to get to my feet, but my head reeled and I sank back down again. "Danu preserve me," I muttered. "I'm as weak as a newborn lamb."

"Did you eat?"

"I wasn't hungry." While the men had downed their hard bread and dried meat I had sat apart. It had occurred to me that I might never want to eat again.

Cathal went off then, while I continued to stare out over the water. I had never challenged the gods before. I had never refused their counsel. I felt as if I were standing on the edge of a cliff, looking down into a vast empty space that was my future.

"Here." Cathal was back, bearing a cup of water, a smallish lump of the rock-hard bread, a piece of cheese. "It may be a long climb. It will surely be taxing and dangerous. Even the most spiritual of folk can't undertake such a challenge on an empty stomach. Come on, Sibeal. I'll break it into mouthfuls for you."

His kindness disarmed me, and I found myself accepting each small piece as he passed it over, and managing to chew and swallow.

"You must be missing Clodagh," I said quietly.

A curt nod. After a moment he said, "More than I can possibly tell you."

"You don't say, 'more than you could understand,' as Clodagh might. She was quick to challenge me when I told her the life of the spirit was higher and better than the life of the flesh, marriage and children, family and home hearth."

Cathal dipped a piece of bread into the water and passed it to me. "Today, I know you can understand," he said. "I'm sorry,

Sibeal. We're all sorry, even if we don't speak of it. On a mission there's no time to grieve. We lay our fallen to rest with what respect we can manage, then we put our feelings away inside and get on with what must be done. When we return home, our wives and mothers do their best to pick up the pieces."

"They can't be laid to rest," I said, my throat choked with tears. "They're out there somewhere, floating with the weeds and the fish, eyes open on nothing, just like most of *Freyja*'s crew."

"And I wonder," Cathal said, "whose hand is behind it?"

I swallowed the last mouthful of bread, then took a sip of water. I did feel slightly better. "The gods told me to wait," I said. "For what, I don't know. But I can't wait. It's like that day when I was drawn to the little cove to find Felix. And the day when I was too late to save Rodan from falling to his death. I feel a pull, a need to go. How long before the men are sufficiently rested?"

"You were sitting there a considerable while. We can leave soon, I think." His gaze had moved to the shore, where the party that had gone along the water's edge could be seen returning, spears in hand. If they had found drowned men, they were not bringing them back. "He'll rest those fellows next. We must leave soon or we risk being caught up among the crags after nightfall." He glanced skyward. "We're far north. At this time of year we won't have true dark, but the place is full of pitfalls. We'd be fools to climb in the half-light. And if we find these fellows, we may have to carry them back."

"Cathal," I said.

"Mm?"

"Thank you."

"Any time. I'll have a word with Gareth, see if we can move things along." He hesitated. "Felix was a fine man, Sibeal. Some time, you'll want your moment to scream and shout and cry your rage to the sky. It's hard to hold it all in. Even if you're a druid, I suppose."

"I thought I could. I thought I could deal with anything."

"Nobody's as strong as that," he said.

*   *   *

And then we were walking, climbing, edging our way across precipitous slopes, traversing cracks that opened on subterranean shadow, scrambling up small mountains of broken boulders. Following instinct; my instinct. Nobody knew where to go. Felix had stayed on *Freyja* for his whole visit to the serpent isle, tending to a sick man. Knut had been on the shore, close to the point where they'd beached the vessel; he had seen only the general direction in which Paul's party had first headed, and that was the path we took now.

I'd intended to try once more with Svala, in the hope that she might tell us where to search. But the look on her face had warned me not to come close. She was angry, frustrated, poised on the verge of some violent action, I was sure of it. I need not touch her to feel it. Her urgency was twin to mine, but without a better understanding I could not help her.

We were a party of eight. If there were indeed three survivors, as Cathal's vision had indicated, and if none was fit enough to return on foot, we would leave some men there and come back for help. Gareth had not been prepared to send more than eight, and I understood his reasons. The group that stayed behind must keep watch not only over *Liadan* but also over the unpredictable Svala and the white-faced, shivering, tethered Knut.

Besides, the monster was still out there in the waters of the bay. From time to time it rose just enough to reveal a glint of brilliant scales, the curve of its back, the claws of one great forelimb before it sank again beneath the water. Waiting. Svala and the creature were both waiting. Now that I had challenged the gods, now that I had, more or less, told them I was disappointed in them, perhaps I would never again have the ability to read Svala's thoughts. Perhaps I would never find out what she had lost and so desperately wanted back. What might she do if she believed I had failed her? Beneath my sorrow, my shock, my need to get the mission done, fear lay like a cold hard stone.

The pace was fast, even when adjusted to accommodate my shorter legs. Cathal led the party. Sigurd was the only other among our number whom I knew at all well. Nobody wasted time on talk. The men advanced, grim-faced, getting on with the job that had to be done. All were armed. I had seen Svala looking at the axes and cudgels and knives. Her eyes had narrowed as the other party came back along the shore with spears in hand, spears that would have been used against the serpent had it struck. It seemed to me fighting a creature of such size would be entirely futile. Still, I understood why they would try. In that moment at *Liadan*'s rail, I would have leapt in to save Felix, even though I knew I was not strong enough to rescue him, or even to survive the attempt. Sometimes the only choice was to fight.

Time passed. *Liadan* and her crew had long ago dropped out of our sight, and we were moving along a ridge high above the bay. At a certain point Cathal called a halt and ordered us to rest our legs. A water skin was passed around, and I drank gratefully of its brackish contents. Sigurd and Cathal were talking together, scanning the island all around, looking for possible paths through terrain that seemed devoid of any softness, for it was all rock and scree, with not a scrap of green.

"Sibeal?" Cathal lifted his brows. "There's no sign of a path. Whatever we decide, the going will be at snail's pace, and the day is passing. What do your instincts tell you?"

I stood up to get a good look around. My instincts were pulling me in the least likely direction, toward a set of tower-like pinnacles surmounting a vertiginous rock stack to the west. On this unlikely castle roosted many birds. The air above it was alive with wheeling shapes. From where we stood we could not see the stack's base, only its jagged crown.

"There," I said.

"You're joking." Sigurd looked at the place, looked at me again. "You're serious."

"It's a fair distance," Cathal observed. "Are you sure, Sibeal? I'd judge we've barely time to get there and back before it's too dark. Wouldn't it make more sense to continue in this direction, following the natural curve of the bay?"

"I think we should go that way." The feeling inside me was powerful, drawing me westward. *Nearly there, Felix. We'll find them for you.*

341

"Very well," said Cathal. "Men!"

A few of them glanced at me when he explained where we were going; it did indeed seem the least promising direction to take. But they were professionals, and within a short time we were making a cautious way toward the place. My feet hurt, and I wished I had kept my stockings on. I could feel blisters forming. The closer we came to the cliffs, the more uneven was the ground. It was all too easy to imagine cracks opening under our feet, or slabs of solid rock shearing off to crumble into the sea far below. As we came down from our vantage point the rock stack was less visible, its oddly pointed peak often the only part showing above the cliff edge. Gulls screamed in the air above us, perhaps warning us away from their nests.

And yet, in its starkness, its myriad shades of gray on gray, the place was beautiful. Here, sky met sea as if the two were one. Here, where all was harsh and clean and barren, there was a curious peace. It was a hermit's place, a place of prayer, a place of deep and eternal power. Beneath my feet I sensed the heartbeat of an ancient god. I glanced at Cathal, who was walking beside me, and when he looked back I saw the same awareness in his eyes. I remembered that he was descended from the Sea People.

A long walk, and difficult. Nearer the cliffs, the ground was broken by jagged holes that opened to a subterranean realm of cavern and tunnel, a nightmare honeycomb. Here, for the first time on the island, we saw lichens and mosses growing on the rocks, tiny, creeping things that clung and cowered under the force of the elements. The wind had turned to a vigorous westerly that whipped color into our faces and robbed us of breath. We came down a pockmarked slope and saw another first: some yards to the north of us, a deep ravine split the rocks. Down the inmost face of this chasm splashed a delicate waterfall. We could not see its source, likely a spring higher up the hillside, but along its channel small plants grew, making a startling ribbon of green in the relentless gray. Birds chirped and hopped and danced above this watercourse, not the gulls and gannets and great sea birds we had seen elsewhere, but smaller ones, some no larger than a wren.

I wondered at their survival in this far-off place. They must be under the protection of a benign spirit.

"Your instincts are sound, Sibeal," Cathal said. "This may be the only source of fresh water on the island. And we've seen already that there are caves, unwelcoming as they appear. If those men are still alive, this does seem a likely area."

"It's far from the landing place," observed Sigurd. "If they came all the way over here, they cannot have been in much hope of prompt rescue."

We fell silent. Perhaps, I thought, they had been in no hope at all. But how could a man survive without hope?

"Perhaps we should call," one of the crewmen, Oschu, suggested. "That's if you really believe they might be here somewhere."

"It can't hurt," Cathal said. "Sibeal, do you still want to go toward the rock stack? That would take us perilously close to the edge of the cliffs. Why don't we head for the stream? Maybe there's a way down through that ravine, and we can at least refill our water skins."

I nodded. The compulsion that had drawn me westward was gone. Either I'd been wrong, or we had come far enough already.

We reached the lip of the chasm and gathered on a patch of level ground. It was possible to see, just, how a man might make his way down to a lower point, if not right to the foot. The ravine was so narrow and uneven that I could not see the point where it opened to the sea. But there could be no benign anchorage down below, only a storm-battered cliff face and a ledge or two where seals might snatch brief rest.

Higher up the abyss, where the blanket of green foliage softened the stones, there were hollows in the rock face. They were too small to be called caves; I saw none big enough to provide good shelter even for one man. All the same, in storm and cold I would far rather be here than in the bay or out on the hillside. There was an odd charm about this place. It was as if a goddess with a warm heart had laid her hand on this one corner of the stark isle. After that, no doubt she had departed for gentler climes.

"Anyone there?" shouted Sigurd, startling me so badly that I nearly fell. "Hallooo!" Then he called something in Norse.

His ringing voice started up a chorus of echoes. A small army of birds flew upward, then settled again, only to be shaken anew by Cathal's cry: "Men from the *Freyja*! Where are you? Call out to us, comrades!"

The echoes died away. There was only the washing of the waves, the sighing of the west wind, the peeping cries of the birds. And . . .

"Did you hear that?" I whispered, not believing it. "Shh! There it is again."

A cry. Undoubtedly, an answering call from somewhere below us in the ravine.

"Here! We're here!"

I stood frozen. His voice. Felix's voice. I must be dreaming.

"Down here!"

The rescue party muttered various oaths, then moved into orderly activity, retrieving ropes from bundles, slinging bags on their backs, gathering what I now saw were the parts of a stretcher on which an injured man might be carried. I couldn't move. I could hardly trust myself to think. It couldn't be. Grief and loss had finally sent me out of my wits. And yet . . . and yet . . .

"Sibeal," said Cathal, "was there a man among the *Freyja*'s crew with an Armorican accent?"

Fighting the mad hope in my heart, for it was impossible, I opened my mouth to say no, only two brothers, and they were both dead. Before I could speak, another voice came. "Sigurd, is that you? Get a move on, will you? We've got three injured men here and it'll be dark soon!"

The face of every hardened warrior was instantly illuminated with a smile.

"By all that's holy," someone said, then shouted, "Gull! How in the name of the gods did you get down there? We thought you were done for!"

"Stop wasting time and get on with it, Berchan! Bring everything with you. There's an easier way out, but the two of us can't get these fellows through on our own."

My heart had stopped; or that was how it felt. "Gull!" I called, and my voice was an old woman's, cracked and tremulous. Let it be true. Let me not have heard wrong. "Is Felix there with you?"

I waited for the longest moment of my life.

"Sibeal! Sibeal, are you up there?"

The greatest gift. A gasping sob racked through me. *Did not you once promise you would do anything, anything at all, if he could survive?* Now, possessed by joy, I would not consider how devious the gods could be. "Felix!" I screamed, entirely heedless of my audience.

They sent the lightly built Berchan down first. A series of narrow ledges did provide a path of sorts into the chasm, though it was hardly safe even with the rope Cathal fixed at the top. When Berchan reached the others, he secured the bottom end of the rope to provide a handhold of sorts. I suspected this was mainly for my benefit. At another time I would have needed all my reserves of courage to tackle such a climb. Now, joy crowded out fear. Never mind how; never mind why. He was alive. Felix was alive. After all, the gods had smiled on us.

I climbed down with the confidence of a spider traversing a strand of filament. Sigurd was just below me, ready to arrest a fall, but I did not need him. We reached a ledge, and from the ledge an opening led into a cavern, and just inside the opening stood Felix, wet, bedraggled and beaming with delight. Behind him the shadowy space was full of activity, but I had no eyes for that. I threw my arms around him, and his came around me, and the world vanished for the space of a few breaths. *I'm home again*, I thought. *Home.* And even as I savored the joy of the moment I thought, *This is what Svala wanted. This is what she was expecting when we reached the island. She lost the one she loved, and she thought she was coming back to him. I know how she felt on Inis Eala, as if she were so broken she could never be mended. And I know how she thought she would feel when she came to the serpent isle. She expected to feel the way I feel now: healed, whole, brimming with happiness.*

We could not stay here forever, holding each other and getting in everyone's way. Time was running short and there were things to be done. We moved back, making way for the last men to enter the cave with the pieces for the stretcher. What had seemed a sizeable space became quickly crowded.

"I am so happy to see you," Felix whispered in my ear. "My heart sings with it, Sibeal. But I must help here—as you see, we have men to bring out of this place."

"You're alive," I choked. "You're not drowned. How can that be?"

Gull was kneeling by a man who lay against the wall, covered by what looked like a big, rough blanket. The man was emaciated, his features hollowed by privation, but his eyes were bright with hope. So wasted was he that I could not guess his age—he could have been twenty or fifty. Of the other two survivors, one was very young, the other a man in his twenties. They were rake-thin, with sores on their faces and their hands and feet all cuts and grazes, but both were standing and making an attempt to greet the rescuers.

"We were carried swiftly along the bay, mostly underwater," Gull said in answer to my question. "This place is full of strange currents. When we first surfaced, Felix managed to grab hold of me, but there was no getting to shore. We were pulled around that curve of the bay, far beyond sight of the rest of you. The current was fierce. The strongest swimmer couldn't make headway against it. I did wonder if that thing, that creature, was somehow making it—that's a sheltered inlet, after all, not some wild river. Eventually we were washed, not onto the shore as we'd hoped, but into a kind of tunnel, an underground passage. We thought we were dead all over again—it was dark and the place was half full of water. There was a ledge to one side, but we couldn't get up on it. After a while the ground rose, the water grew shallower, and we stepped out onto rocks. Since there was no going back, we went on. There was an opening or two overhead—you'll have seen what a maze of passages this place is—so we could find our way, more or less. When we came out, here we were. These fellows thought they were seeing ghosts."

"Dagda's britches," said Cathal. "That's the least plausible story I've heard in years, Gull."

Felix was coughing. It hurt me to hear him. It took me back to those nights in the infirmary, when I lay awake listening to him struggle and begged the gods to let him live for one more day.

"Cathal," said Gull, "we must get these fellows out of here as soon as we can. I don't want them spending another night without proper attention, and I can't give them that without my healer's supplies. We can't get Thorgrim here up the ravine, but we can go out through the tunnel."

Cathal gave him a direct sort of look. "Didn't you say part of it was underwater?"

"The fellows tell me there's a big tidal flow here. Judging by what they've said, if we go soon we'll be out before it starts to rise again. I reckon it'll be knee deep at most when we get to the other end, and we should be able to make our way back to *Liadan* around the edge of the bay." When Cathal did not immediately reply, Gull added, "Unless you want to go back the way you came, and leave us here until tomorrow."

Felix's coughing fit had passed. In the quiet of the cave, the wheeze of his breath was like wheat stalks rustling in the wind. Everyone could see the look on Thorgrim's face, a naked longing to be safe again, warm and dry and tended to by kindly hands.

"The creature." It was the young boy who spoke now, a lad of perhaps fifteen. "The monster. Is it still there?"

"It is, Colm," Felix said. "But these men won't run away. They'll stand and defend you if it comes again. And there's a boat waiting, a sturdy boat with a crew well able to take you home."

The boy was trying his best not to weep. His jaw trembled. "It took Artan," he said. "Before we found this place. It took Demman. It took one of the Norsemen. It ate them up right before our eyes."

"We know, son." Gull's voice was very quiet. "You told us. And we're here to get you away before any more are lost. Cathal, if we're doing it we need to move."

I was reminded, again, of what people said about Johnny's men: that they were the best of the best. They worked with no fuss, assembling the stretcher, moving the sick man onto it with strong but careful hands, deciding who would carry it and who would help the two men who could walk. Few words were exchanged; every man knew exactly what he was doing. I waited quietly, watching them. This small cave had been home to hunger, cold, loneliness and fear. It had seen men near death; men desperate for survival in a world turned hostile. There was no fire here. There was nothing to burn. How in the name of the gods had they survived the harsh northern nights? Where had they found hope?

I glanced around me as the men began moving through the back of the cave and into the tunnel. There was very little in the chamber. A stone with a natural depression in it might perhaps have been used to collect water. Spray from the waterfall, maybe, or rain. In a corner lay a heap of empty shells; they had foraged for food, then, on the rocks nearby. Perhaps they had stolen an egg or two from the gulls' nests. If they had stayed in the cave, they would have starved. I wondered what had happened to the other man, the one who was not taken by the creature. Perhaps he had died of despair. The place stank; the men had performed all their bodily functions here, and it smelled not only of that, but of sickness and defeat. I must say a prayer as I left, or the sad shadow of its human tenants would linger on.

The stretcher-bearers had not taken the unwieldy covering that the sick Norseman, Thorgrim, had used as a blanket. It lay on the cave floor, humped in awkward folds. "Shouldn't we take that with us?" I asked Cathal. "It could keep Thorgrim warm on the way back."

"It's too big and heavy. It would take two men to carry it. We can't afford anything that will slow us down. Thorgrim will do well enough with a cloak over him." He glanced at the covering.

"Where did it come from, Donn?" Felix asked. He had his arm

around young Colm's shoulders; the lad was ashen, his memories close to the surface. Getting him through the subterranean passage would not be easy.

"Fiac found it down by the shore," said the third survivor. "He made us bring it up so we could keep warm. We slept under it every night. Would have died, if not for that, all of us one by one. Fiac died anyway. His dreams sent him mad. Fell down the drop." His expression was impassive, his tone flat. Perhaps he had seen so much that he was beyond feeling anything.

"Time to go, lads." Berchan nodded at Donn and the two of them headed out together. Felix followed, shepherding Colm. The last of the others went after them, leaving only Cathal and me.

"Danu, look kindly on this place," I murmured. "Accept our thanks for the shelter it provided when men were in trouble. May the breath of the gods purify it; may the soft voice of the waterfall bring peace once more. May it be cleansed of all sorrows. May this be holy ground."

The first part of the tunnel was not so bad. Light came down through chinks and holes high above, showing us where to put our feet on the uneven, often slippery rock floor. The way was narrow in places and we were slowed by the stretcher, which was hard to get around corners. I could hear Felix coughing. I prayed that he might not fall sick again. For I could see a possible future that would be the stuff of a grand and tragic tale, and the thought of it chilled me to the bone.

Donn seemed in the best health of the three we had rescued. He made a resolute effort to walk without support, and managed well, though his pace was slow. Berchan stayed beside him. Felix was still with Colm. Donn was grimly silent, all his energy concentrated on moving forward. Colm was talking: a stream of words flowed from him, as if, now that the rescue party was here at last, he must release all he had held bottled within him during those long, lonely days and nights. He spoke about the monster, about seeing men die, about coming back down to the shore to find *Freyja* gone, about how Fiac's body had been wedged in a crevice further down the chasm and how they could not reach it, and how the gulls had come, and—

"Shut up, Colm," grunted Donn, and, much to my relief, the boy fell silent.

The passage began to slope gradually downward, and it grew darker. In these lower reaches there were fewer apertures up above. Perhaps, outside, the sun was already setting.

We reached the water. It stretched ahead into darkness. On the left side of the tunnel was a ledge perhaps two steps wide, at the height of a tall man's head.

"Which is it?" Cathal asked, looking at Gull. "If you're right about it being shallow all the way, wading will be easier and probably safer. But we don't want to be caught down here if the tide comes in."

"If we're going up on that ledge, we'll be leaving the stretcher behind," said one of the bearers. They had laid the sick man down at the water's edge, and were flexing their arms and rubbing their shoulders. "Thorgrim here will have to go on someone's back."

"How long have we got?" Sigurd asked. "Are you sure about the tide, Gull?"

"I'm sure. Provided we go straight through, we'll be well out the far end and up on the rocks before it reaches knee deep, even on Sibeal." Gull gave me a searching look, as if remembering belatedly that I was not one of Johnny's warriors. "All right?"

"I'm fine." If there was an edge in my voice, it was due less to the anticipation of a wet, dark wade to a tenuous kind of safety, as to some other unease whose cause I could not quite identify. It made sense, all of it—the rescued men were weak and tired, the tunnel was the quickest way back, Gull knew the tides . . . So why did this feel so horribly wrong? "I just . . . no, it's all right, it's nothing." I could not expect these men to wait while I spent precious time going over my vague doubts and half-formed anxieties. "What is it to be, the ledge or the water?"

"The water," Cathal said. "Move steadily ahead, and don't rush it. I don't want anyone injured. We can get through." He glanced at the others. "Sigurd and Oschu, you go first." Both were tall men. "Stretcher-bearers next, and remember that you'll be carrying Thorgrim all the way through before you can put him down. Keep him out of the water; a cold bath is the last thing he needs. Felix, you look after Sibeal. Sibeal, stay close to him. Gull, you go behind them. The rest of you with Donn and Colm, and I'll come last. Ready?"

We moved on. The passage grew darker, the water gradually deeper. I hitched up my skirt, not so much to keep it dry—it had hung in clammy folds for the best part of our journey—as to make wading easier. The ground was treacherous, and often it was only Felix's steady hand that stopped me from falling headlong. My mind began to fill with craven thoughts, thoughts unworthy of a druid, even one who had not yet made her final promise. *I wish we had a lamp. What is that rustling sound? I want to go home.*

"Take heart, beloved," said Felix. He spoke softly, for my ears only, but in the stillness of the underground passage, it carried clearly.

My cheeks were hot. I had not spoken a word, but he had heard me. He had heard what I would not say: *I'm scared.*

I squeezed his hand. In my mind I said, *I love you.*

As if in response to my fear, the tunnel turned a corner and the darkness was relieved. A chink high above admitted a ray of dim light, as welcome as rain after drought.

"Back up!" Sigurd's shout turned my blood to ice. We backed a few paces.

"What is it?" Cathal came past me, heading for the front of the line. I clutched Felix's hand and peered forward into the shadows. "Sigurd, what—"

A pair of great eyes gleamed ahead, familiar eyes, bright in the gloom. Behind the eyes, the monster's body filled the tunnel. There would be no going past. The eyes drew me. I saw the wild beauty of them, the myriad colors in their depths, the unshed tears of sorrow. I thought . . . I almost thought . . .

The creature opened its jaws wide. Its long white teeth caught the filtered light as it drew breath. It roared. The sound rang from every surface, powerful as thunder. I clapped my hands over my ears. Colm was crouched down in the water, his arms curled over his head, his whole body shaking. The men with the stretcher staggered in shock, almost dropping Thorgrim. The roaring went on and on. It set a vibration through every part of me. My heart raced; my head throbbed. I closed my eyes.

Nothing was right, he'd thought it was right, she came back, it should have been the way it was before, but something was gone, something was missing, and now he would weep, he would rave, he would blast his sadness into the depths of the earth until the whole island burst with it. He would destroy these outsiders, these puny creatures that dared steal her away, and brought her back incomplete . . .

There was only one thing to do. I let go of Felix's hand and moved forward. Past the stretcher-bearers and the pallid Thorgrim. Up beside Sigurd, Oschu and Cathal. I took another step.

"No, Sibeal!" hissed Cathal, grabbing my arm and holding me back. "What are you doing?"

The creature had quieted, though the roaring still rang from the rocky surfaces. Its strange eyes were fixed on me now. Deep, distant eyes. Eyes that held the stone and the sky, the wind and the waves, the lonely beauty of a far place, a fortress and refuge. Wildness. Wisdom. Eyes like Svala's.

CHAPTER 13

~Sibeal~

Let go, Cathal," I said, as my mind put together the pieces. "If you want us to get through unharmed, let me do this."

"No, Sibeal! This is crazy!"

"Let her go, Cathal." Felix and Gull spoke with one voice.

Cathal released me, muttering an oath. I moved forward again. I looked up. I concentrated all my will on the serpent. In my mind, I formed a clear, simple message. *I can help you.* For in those eyes I had seen the solution. I had realized, at last, what Svala had been so desperate to tell me.

Quick as a heartbeat the creature moved, scooping me up in its forepaw and lifting me toward its face. My stomach lurched. So close! I could smell its breath. I could see the tears in its great eyes. Its skin was made up of glimmering eight-sided scales. Its claws closed around me, making a neat cage. There was a sliding sound as several knives were drawn out of their sheaths.

"Tell them no, Cathal," I called. "No weapons." My voice was weak and shaky; it would not do. I had never negotiated with a sea beast before. I hoped it would be the only time. It was not a job for a fainting, weeping girl. It was a task for a druid.

I lay down on its palm; it was cold and smooth. I slowed my breathing. In my mind, I made an image of Svala standing tall and proud on the shore at Inis Eala, her perfect form clad only in the gold cloak of her hair. I showed *Liadan* at anchor in the bay here, and our party searching across the barren landscape. I pictured Knut crouched on the sand with a rope around his ankle. A vibration passed through the serpent's body, and there was a creak as its claws closed tighter.

But it's going to be all right. I made my inner voice calm and strong. *I know what you need and I will fetch it now. I will help you. I am her friend.* I made an image of Svala putting on an item of clothing, somewhere between a cloak and a gown; my imagination could take me no further.

It felt like a long time, but perhaps was not very long at all, before the creature lowered its paw with care, and opened its claws to release me into the shallow water beside Cathal. The others had retreated a short distance up the tunnel.

"Cathal," I said, "it's a skin. That thing, that blanket the men were using to keep warm, it's her skin."

"You mean—" He fell silent.

"Didn't they say one of the men found it on the shore after *Freyja* had sailed away? It's Svala's—it's what she wants. I can't believe it's taken me so long to work this out. I know dozens of selkie tales. Cathal, we must fetch it here and show him."

"Him?"

"The creature. I'm sure this is right, Cathal. If I run all the way there and back, maybe we can still get through before the water is too high. This can't wait for tomorrow."

Cathal's eyes passed over the three survivors: Colm now huddled against Gull, sobbing with fear; Donn sheet-white in the gloom; Thorgrim lying limp as if dead on the stretcher, still held above the water by the two stalwart bearers. "You're saying the rest of us should wait here with that creature breathing in our faces while you run all the way to the cave and back again?"

"That's what I'm saying." I had not felt the will of the gods so strongly since the day when I first met Deirdre of the Forest. The runes had not lied. There was a part for me in this mission, and the time for it was now.

"Someone else should go," Cathal said. "You'll never carry that thing back on your own. Didn't you see how big it was?" We stared at each other as the implications of its size sank in.

"I'll go," Felix said, moving up beside us. "This is my mission; it is my responsibility. Sibeal and I should go together."

"No, lad." Gull spoke, the voice of experience. "If you don't want to die of an ague on the way home, you're not going any-where. Besides, I need you here." He glanced at the weeping Colm. "Cathal, you go with Sibeal. I'll keep an eye on things at this end. We'll lift Thorgrim onto the ledge and cover him up until you get back." He eyed the creature, which was shifting restlessly, its gaze moving from one man to another as if making a selection. Higher up the tunnel, nearer the cave, I thought the way would be too narrow for the creature to pass. Here, it would be able to move forward and snatch a man in its jaws.

"Sibeal," Gull said, "if you've got some way of talking to our friend here, could you ask it not to eat any of us before you get back? And be quick about it, will you? If anything's calculated to give me nightmares for the rest of my life, this is surely it."

I looked into the monster's eyes and spoke the message in my mind. *I am going now to fetch what you need. Do no harm while I am gone. Wait. Only wait. I am a friend.* I showed him Svala embracing me, her tall form close to engulfing my far slighter one. I showed the serpent's dance of joy in the bay when we first sailed in and he saw that she had come home. I made a picture of the men waiting in the tunnel, and the serpent sleeping where he was, and Cathal and me coming back, holding the blanket—the skin—between us. Then I stepped away. The creature was quiet. He hunkered down in the shallow water, closing his eyes to slits, but behind them he was watchful.

We ran. I fixed my thoughts on the cave; I concentrated on staying on my feet. Here and there we slowed, and Cathal took my hand to help me. Once or twice we stopped to get our breath back, though Cathal did not seem in the least breathless, only rather paler than usual. We did not waste our energy in talk, for reaching the cave was only half the journey. Eventually we came under the arch and into the space where the lost men had sheltered. Beyond the cave mouth the ravine was dim; it was close to dusk.

I bent to pick up the covering that had kept three men from death all through the lonely days from *Freyja*'s departure to *Liadan*'s arrival.

"By the Dagda's manhood," breathed Cathal, "I think you're right. If this isn't a skin, I don't know what it is. Great gods, Sibeal, that poor creature. I wonder if Knut knew what he'd done to her."

I was examining the skin more closely. It was all in dull duns and grays, and curiously patterned in even, eight-sided shapes. And here, at the very edge, was a damaged patch, as if a clumsy hand had wielded a knife without due care. "He had an idea, at least," I said. "He cut off a strip of it and put it around his neck— see here, it's torn at this edge. He hung his lucky charm from it. Not quite the same as taking the whole skin, but enough to keep her under his control, at least while she was far away from here and could not reach the missing part of herself. No wonder she ripped the cord from his neck with such violence. Perhaps it was being close to *him*—the creature, I mean—that made her bold enough at last."

We regarded each other across the dimming cavern, awestruck by the strangeness of it. Then Cathal said, "You amaze me, Sibeal. You are truly remarkable. Now, how are we going to carry this?"

Inevitably, the way back was slower. We rolled the skin into a long bundle and each carried one end. I went first, setting the quickest pace I could, and Cathal came behind me. It grew darker. It grew so dark that we could not go on with any degree of safety. We came to a halt.

"Sibeal."

"Mm?"

"Can you make a light? My craft is useless here; I cannot conjure so much as a candle flame to show us the way. So much for my decision to leave Clodagh and join the rescue mission. It seems anyone could have taken my place."

"I don't believe that, Cathal. Time will show why your magic is blocked here. There will be some wisdom in it, I'm sure."

"Not if my father is responsible. Can you do it, Sibeal?"

Elemental magic. I knew the rudiments. I had made the fire flare up on the night Knut attacked Felix. At this moment, I was so weary that only the compulsion of the task was keeping me going.

"I'll try. Can we put this down for a bit?"

We had not yet reached the water: water that would be deeper now, perhaps much deeper. What would happen when the creature moved? I would not think of that. I would summon my deepest reserves of strength. I would make myself calm and open. I would use what I already had—the last dim trace of day, the little creatures that slithered and scuttered on the tunnel walls, the creepers and crawlers that hid in nooks and crannies. I would use the memory of the men who had perished in that cave and in the ravine, men who had held on as long as they could. I would use the moment when Felix had dived in after Gull, like a flame of pure courage made flesh. I would make light.

I closed my eyes and spoke the words of an ancient charm. I breathed. I sent the warmth of my breath out through the darkness, touching each small penumbral life. *Help us. Help us bring her back.*

I heard Cathal's indrawn breath before I opened my eyes to look. The tunnel was transformed. Myriad points of brightness pierced the gloom. It was as if the stars themselves had come down to guide us on our way. Each was tiny; each was a glow as small as the heartbeat of a fly. Together they revealed the stone floor, the ledge, the high walls and vaulted roof of the passage. Together they illuminated the way forward.

Wordless, we moved on, bearing the great skin carefully between us. *Cathal*, I thought, *you will have an amazing tale to tell your baby son or daughter one day.* Unbidden, a vision came to me. It was the same little house I had seen once before, the same window opening onto trees, the same mellow lamplight over the peaceful interior. I was there, before the hearth. Felix was seated opposite me, restored to perfect health, his color high, his glossy hair tamed by a ribbon at the nape. The child on his knee was older than she had been last time; instead of an infant's smock she wore a little gown embroidered with owls. Her big eyes were fixed on her father in fascination as he told her a story. *And then your mother walked up to the serpent, right up to it, and it lifted her in its hand.* Our daughter protested, *But Papa, serpents don't have hands. They are the same as snakes only bigger. Aren't they?* He smiled. *This one had hands. Hands with long sharp claws. Perhaps it was not so much a serpent as a sea dragon. Your mama is the bravest woman in all Erin.* Our daughter turned her beautiful eyes on me for a moment and said, *I know that, Papa. Tell me what happened next.*

The vision began to fade. I stumbled, desperate to keep it, desperate to say, *I love you, I wish with all my heart that you were real, don't go!* Foolish Sibeal.

"Wait." Cathal stopped to adjust his grip. "Are you all right?"

"Fine," I said grimly. "Prey to unhelpful thoughts, that's all."

"I know how that feels."

We reached the water sooner than I expected. Or maybe the water came higher up the tunnel now. We splashed in, our awkward bundle between us. Here, there were fewer of the little lights. My facility for natural magic was limited; beside Ciarán's it was nothing.

"I told myself I wouldn't think about Clodagh." My companion's voice came to me softly through the half-dark. "But I've thought of nothing else, all the way."

"Hope," I said. "Leading you forward. The knowledge that home is waiting for you when the mission is over." Even as I spoke, it came to me that my idea of what *home* meant had changed entirely over this summer. What was waiting for me?

Silence for a while, as we moved on through the water. Now it was almost up to my knees. "I don't suppose it matters," I said, "if we get the skin wet." I imagined the sea creature leaping and diving in the bay, at one with the waves.

"I suppose not."

The remaining lights were winking out one by one. *I will not be afraid*, I told myself. *It's much worse for the men waiting than it is for us. All we need do is walk straight ahead and we'll get there. Even if it's dark. Even if it's late. Even if . . .*

"Sibeal," said Cathal.

"Mm?"

"Do you know that song about the lady and the toad?"

"Mm-hm."

"What, even the rude parts? I'm shocked."

I smiled, though he could not see it in the darkness. "You'd be surprised what we pick up in the nemetons, Cathal. How shall we do it, one verse each and the chorus together?"

"Sounds fair to me. You start."

Step by step. Line by line. Verse by increasingly scurrilous verse. When we got to the end of that song we sang another, about the love of a hapless clurichaun for a young lady ten times his size. I'd had no idea Cathal was a singer, or that he possessed sufficient humor to enjoy tunes of this kind, the sort the rowdier inhabitants of Inis Eala liked to sing after a good supper and a few jugs of ale. Gull, now, or Snake, I could imagine participating with some enthusiasm. When the clurichaun had been sent, sobbing his woe, back to his ancestral hill, we started a ballad about a faithless lover. After two verses Cathal stopped singing, leaving me all on my own with the chorus. My voice faltered.

"We're almost there," he said. "See, it's lighter up ahead, where the roof opens to the sky."

It was barely lighter. There would be a full moon tonight, but it was not yet late enough, surely, for it to be high in the sky and casting its beams down into this hidden space. But I could see a little more. The water was up to my thighs. I would not think of the current that had borne Gull and Felix into the tunnel, the current Gull had said even the strongest swimmer could not combat.

"Good," I squeaked.

We rounded a corner and there they were. All were up on the ledge, high above the water level. Thorgrim lay with his head in

Gull's lap. Felix had his arm around Colm; his smile of welcome lightened my heart. The others sat stoically waiting. And there was the creature, his eyes suddenly wide-open as we approached.

"Show him, Cathal," I said. "Hold it up and spread it out."

Sigurd and Oschu came down to help us. The four of us unfurled the skin, holding a corner each. The width of the tunnel was not sufficient to accommodate it held flat. I met the serpent's eye. *This is what you need. See, we have brought it. Now I ask you to help us take it safely to her.* I showed him all of us wading out of the tunnel, stepping up onto the rocks, forming a procession along the shore to the place where *Liadan* was moored. I showed Svala waiting for us, smiling. I prayed that the creature would not seize the skin in his jaws and back out of the passage, letting the tide enter in his place. I closed my eyes.

A feeling like a great warm smile spread through me. *Good. Friend.*

The men were getting up, standing along the ledge. Two had spears in their hands; others had drawn their knives.

"Wait," Cathal said quietly. "Trust Sibeal—she knows what she's doing."

The creature moved, rising to its clawed feet. A rush of water came around it, catching me at waist level. I staggered before its force. Sigurd grabbed me and held me safe against the current, and the water subsided. Still I held my corner of the skin, and Cathal and Oschu did likewise. "Roll it up," I gasped. "We must move on." *Let us move on. Let us take it to her now.*

"Move on?" echoed Gull from the ledge. "It may not be far from here, but—"

The creature had half turned, maneuvering his long tail with some difficulty in the confined space. He edged toward the side of the tunnel until a long-legged man could have stepped across with ease from the ledge onto his broad, scaly back. He became still. He seemed to be waiting.

Up on the ledge nobody was saying a word, though I could hear Colm weeping. Down in the water Sigurd, Oschu and Cathal rolled up the skin. I regarded the creature. His head was turned back toward me; his fey eyes looked into mine. What I sensed in his mind was, *Come. Come then. Make haste.* But he did not move forward. Nobody could pass his bulk.

"Sibeal." The soft voice was that of Felix. "Could the creature be offering to bear us on its back?"

"Dagda's bollocks," commented someone.

Come now. Make haste. The water rises.

It would be possible even for me to step over from the ledge to the serpent's back, given a helping hand. That back was broad enough to accommodate all of us if we sat close together. Perhaps it was high enough to keep us safe even at peak tide. A creature that could leap right over an oceangoing boat might well be strong enough to withstand the current Gull had described.

"That's what we must do," I said. "Sigurd, will you lift me up to the ledge, please?"

He obliged, hoisting me as if I weighed no more than a child. They passed up the skin; then Cathal, Sigurd and Oschu hauled themselves up beside the rest of us.

"Are you sure?" Cathal asked me, though I saw that he knew this was our best chance. He was asking for the men's sake. *Liadan*'s crew would face even this nightmare test with professionalism. If they were afraid, they hid it expertly. Felix and I were drawn by the mission; our convictions were stronger than our fear. But for Thorgrim, Donn and Colm, to be so close to the monster that had devoured their companions would be a test almost beyond endurance.

"I'm sure," I said.

Oschu stepped over first, then gave me his hand for support as I half stepped, half jumped across. I settled myself close to what might be considered the nape of the creature's neck. The others followed. Sigurd carried Thorgrim in his arms. Donn's face was ghastly white in the semidark, but he stepped over with Berchan by his side, and the two sat down without a word.

Colm screamed, fighting those who sought to aid him, and Gull and Felix, one on either side, manhandled him across to the serpent's back. The creature was perfectly still. He did not twitch so much as the tip of his tail; he did not utter so much as a sigh of exasperation at how slow we were. I tried not to remember that he had pierced a man's chest with his claw, or that he had almost sunk *Liadan* through sheer exuberance. When the last man— Cathal—had moved over from the ledge, I lay facedown against the creature's skin and made again an image of all of us emerging safe and sound onto flat rocks at the bay's edge. *We trust you. We honor you, and we honor her. This is your place. When we have done what must be done, we will sail away from this isle. You will be at peace again. All will be to rights.*

No answering thoughts now, but the sea beast moved, completing his turn and lurching forward so suddenly he came close to dislodging us. Colm opened his mouth to cry out again, and Gull gave him a flat-handed smack on the cheek. "It's time to be a man, lad," he said.

The creature waded forward into the dark. Now there was not a song left in me to keep away the shadows. I could not hold Felix's hand. It was taking the combined efforts of him and Gull to keep Colm from leaping off the serpent's back to be smashed on the rocks or stamped to death. Or drowned. Water gurgled and gushed around the creature's legs, a rising surge.

"The hand of Danu lie over us," I prayed. "The courage of the ancients fill our veins. The wonder of wild things be not terror to us, but inspiration. The memory of good companions, of hearth fires shared, of brave deeds achieved, beat in our hearts and give us strength."

There was quiet for a while, and then a voice rose in song. Not my voice or Cathal's, but that of Felix, singing in Irish.

> *Farewell, my mother and my home*
> *Farewell my sisters three*
> *For I am bound for oceans far*
> *And isles of mystery.*
>
> *A talking bird I'll bring for you*
> *Gold brooches and fine rings*

A chain of pearls, a silver clasp
And other costly things.

A refrain came next, full of *oh-ree-oh*s and somewhat melancholy in its style. Felix's voice was as strong and sweet as fine mead, and commendably steady. If his chest was still tight, there was no trace of that in the lovely flow of the ballad. Gull was quick to join in the refrain, followed by Sigurd and, after a moment, several others. The sea beast moved steadily forward in the darkness.

The brave young sailor crossed the sea
To places near and far
Until he found a treasure rare
As bright as any star.

She sat upon a rocky shore
Combing her golden hair
A princess from an ancient tale
Lovely beyond compare.

"*Oh-ree-oh,*" we sang, a ragged chorus indeed, but full of new heart.

Come here, come here, you creature fine
Oh come away with me
And I will give you hearth and home
And children one, two, three.

We started the refrain once more; even Donn had joined in now. As we sang on I became aware of another sound. Beneath the tune a low, humming accompaniment had begun, a sound surely conjured from sea and shadow or arising from the very depths of stone. I felt it vibrating up through me, filling my whole body. One by one we faltered and fell silent. Gull cleared his throat.

"*She laughed to hear those words so bold,*" sang Felix. I could no longer see him, for the darkness was almost complete, but I imagined him sitting bolt upright on the creature's back, arm around Colm, eyes fixed ahead. Where others saw only shadow, he saw the shining light of a mission achieved. *If ever your hope falters*, I thought, *I will remind you of this moment.*

> She laughed to hear those words so bold
> And shook her tresses free
> She gazed upon the surging waves
> And never a word spoke she.

Felix went on to relate how the sailor boy found a sealskin on the rocks nearby and, while the beautiful creature was distracted, hid it away under the decking of his boat. Then he took the woman home with him, not back to his mother and three sisters, who would likely have been less than impressed, but to a little hut by the sea. And there they lived for some while. He was happy enough, wed to the loveliest woman anyone in those parts had seen in a lifetime. But she pined. She wandered the shore; she tossed and turned by night; she was always searching for what had been stolen from her.

As the story unfolded verse by verse, there was a gradual lightening of the gloom around us. The water in the tunnel was higher. The creature made a sloshing sound as it waded on. My mind was on Gull's description of the monstrous current that had caught him and Felix, sweeping them far up the underground passage. I put my cheek down against the sea beast's hide, closing my eyes. *You are strong. You are brave. I know you will keep us safe.* The deep humming continued; I took it as a good sign.

Felix's ballad drew toward its close. A wise woman from the local village helped the selkie to search for her skin, and they found it hidden under a pile of fishing nets. As the passage lightened around us, and the sound of lapping water could be heard ahead, Felix sang the final verse:

> She slipped into the silvery skin
> A seal once more was she

She dived into the briny depths
Joyous and strong and free.

Before we could draw breath for one last refrain, the creature threw back its head and roared. This was no sound of challenge, no trumpeting of war. It was a shout of triumph. Before us opened the mouth of the tunnel, and beyond it was the water of the bay, and the night sky overhead, and the moon sailing high, full and cool and lustrous.

"Hold on tight!" ordered Cathal.

Water was surging in on either side of us now as the tunnel broadened. The tide was rising fast. An image came to me, of the creature leaping forward and diving into the depths, as the selkie in the ballad had done, and of the human passengers being thrown hither and thither to be tumbled in the wild flow or pulverized on the rocks. But no. He would not do that. We were carrying Svala's skin.

Before, the creature had edged sideways so we could step onto his back. Now he made a bridge of his neck and head, laying his chin on a rock shelf to one side of the passage entry. If we were bold and kept our balance, we could walk across to safety. From here, the moonlight would allow us to make a way around the bay to the place where Gareth and the others waited.

The sea beast's neck was broad enough to walk on, though doing so would require a degree of confidence—his scaly skin was wet and slippery. I judged the length to be about eight strides. The hardest part would be walking on his head; to reach the rocks we must pass between his great eyes and within easy snapping range of his formidable jaws. Cathal took charge.

"Sigurd, you're first. When you get to the brow, you'll wait and help the others over the last part. Gull, you're next—go right over, stand on the rocks and make sure everyone moves up and out of the way quickly. Oschu, you'll take Thorgrim on your back. Berchan and Felix, you're with Colm. Donn, you all right to go with the warriors?" Donn gave a stiff nod. I saw how much this would help him. Cathal had just recognized him publicly as fit, capable, ready to move on. "Sibeal," Cathal said, "you and I will carry the skin over. We're going last. All right?"

"All right," I said. Oh, he was wise. The precious skin had won us safe passage from underground. The creature might be well disposed toward us at present because we had retrieved it. All the same, the sea beast was a wild thing, and the workings of its mind were largely beyond our understanding. Cathal knew, as I did, that while we carried Svala's salvation her beloved would not harm us.

Johnny would have been proud of this team. We crossed to safe ground in orderly procession. Even sturdy Oschu, with the sick man balanced across his shoulders, was as steady as if walking on an ordinary bridge of wood or stone. When everyone else was over, Cathal and I picked up the skin. He made me go first this time. I had thought I might cross as easily as the warriors had, but balancing was hard while carrying the heavy bundle. At one point I slipped, and in regaining my footing I made the mistake of glancing down. A rushing tide under moonlight is a stunning sight: natural magic at its most powerful. I thought I would be quite content if I never saw one again.

"Three more steps, Sibeal," said Felix, and I looked up. He was waiting right by the creature's mouth, holding out a hand. I walked on, and Cathal came after me, and as I stepped onto solid rock, Felix took my end of the skin so I could clamber up higher, to a flat area where the others were standing in a silent group. Cathal was on the sea beast's muzzle; he was stepping over its mouth; he was on dry land. He gave his end of the skin to Berchan, who stood ready, and turned to face the creature. "We thank you," he said gravely. "We honor you. We go now to take this to her, and to make good the injustice that was done." And perhaps, after he had spoken the words in Irish, words the sea beast surely could not understand, he also sent the creature another kind of message. For Cathal's ancestry was, in part, that of the Sea People, folk not unlike Svala in their power and their wildness. In the moment when he stood facing the creature, still and silent, perhaps like spoke to like. Then Cathal turned to us. "Let's get these fellows to shelter," he said. "Everyone all right to walk?"

Save for Thorgrim, everyone was, and Oschu announced himself fit to carry the sick man all the way to the camp. I hoped there was a camp. I wondered if the others had found anything to burn on a fire, and whether they had managed to catch some fish. Suddenly, it seemed a very long time since I had eaten. As we set off over the rocks, I turned my head to see the creature swim powerfully out into deeper water and disappear below the surface.

No songs now. Even the strongest men must have been exhausted, and the way was difficult despite the moonlight. The distance was not so long, but the pace was slow. The patch of pebbly beach where we had first come ashore seemed the only such place on this side of the bay. We clambered over heaps of stones that lay holus-bolus like the remnant of a giant's juggling game. We picked a route through narrow chinks in what at first seemed impenetrable buttresses of rock. I walked beside Felix. From time to time we brushed against each other, not quite by accident. Once or twice I looked up and found his eyes on me, and what was in them filled me with joy and sorrow both at once. Sometimes I watched him without his being aware of it. I found myself memorizing his features, the strong jaw, the straight nose, the chestnut hair, pleasing even in its current salt-crusted, unkempt state, the deep lake-blue eyes, like those of a sage in an old tale . . . And when he looked up and saw me watching, he smiled.

"We're nearly there, Sibeal," he said.

I nodded, but said nothing. Nearly there. Nearly at the end of the quest. Nearly at the point where, one way or the other, my heart would surely break.

~Felix~

Gareth and his companions have made a fire. We see it as we approach along the shore, a welcome sign of warmth and life. I do not realize until this moment how cold and wet I am, shivering and weary. Something beyond my own frail body has carried me to this point. Soon the mission will be done, and whatever it was—inspiration, compulsion—will be gone. For a brief time, I have been more than an ordinary man. Soon I will be myself again. But not my old self. This has changed me. I think it has changed us all.

When they see that Gull and I are with the others, the men who have stayed behind shout greetings and run to meet us, helping to bring the three survivors in to the fireside. They have found driftwood to burn. A good supply stands neatly stacked, ready for use. I smell fish cooking.

I am watching Gareth. He has not spoken; he did not run forward when he saw us, but stayed by the fire. Back on Inis Eala, he seemed a man of even temperament, more given to smiles than anger, a man whose pleasure was to make others happy. He seemed the kind of man anyone would want as a brother. On the journey he has been all leader, making a leader's hard, swift decisions. I see now that those decisions have cost him dear; they do not come naturally to such a man as this. When he sees us, his face shows naked relief. It is as if an unbearable burden has been lifted from his shoulders. As we reach the level place where they have made their fire, he moves forward to throw his arms around first Gull, then me. He greets the survivors; he acknowledges all the men who undertook this mission. He sends someone to find Gull's bag, the one with his healing supplies. The men who stayed behind start organizing dry clothing, places near the fire, food and drink for both survivors and rescuers.

Only then does Gareth come over to Sibeal, where she stands quiet and composed, watching it all. I saw how she was on the ship, when he ordered Svala bound; I saw her expression when Gareth ordered the men not to dive in after Gull. I wonder if Sibeal will refuse so much as to glance at him. But she takes his hands, looks up at him with her face all peace and speaks quiet words. I am too far away to hear what she says. Gareth nods and lifts a hand to his face. It is possible he is wiping away tears. Sibeal has been true to herself. If she has perhaps not offered forgiveness, she has at least given understanding. Can a man be warrior and peacemaker both at once? Not without great cost. Only in a person like Sibeal, whose weapons are courage and conviction, compassion and inspiration, can the two be truly combined.

At her mooring, *Liadan* rocks gently in moon-spangled water. Close to this little beach, there is no hint of the monstrous tidal rush that washed Gull and me up the rocky passage earlier today. Today. This same day. So brief a time to contain so much.

I think that if I sit down I may never get up again. As soon as I stopped walking, pain flowered in every part of me. My joints ache. My chest aches. There is weariness in the very core of my body, and I long for sleep. But not yet. The mission is not complete.

They are both here, Knut and Svala. A rope still tethers his ankle, lest he run mad and injure himself or others, but they have moved him to a place nearer the fire's warmth. He has a blanket to sit on and a cloak around his shoulders. The moonlight touches his skin, white as pearl. His eyes are wide. He is staring at the skin, as Cathal and Gareth unroll it on the rocks at a safe distance from the fire. They handle it as carefully as they might a weaving in fine silk.

Svala has been perched on a vantage point high above the camp. Now, as the skin is revealed, she creeps down crabwise, wariness in her every move. It is as if she cannot quite believe what she sees. I believe it. I grew up on tales of sailors and mermaids, selkies and the misguided men who loved them. This tale, Svala's tale, is full of pain, sorrow and beauty. When it is finished I will make a new song.

"Felix!" Sibeal calls softly. "It's time."

I move to stand beside her. The skin lies before us, an oddly shaped mat of earth shades, slate and shingle, sand and pebble, stone and shadow. The firelight touches it gently.

Svala reaches the flat ground and walks toward us, slowly, so slowly. I think even now she doubts the evidence of her own eyes. She comes to the far edge of the skin. A trembling courses through her body, but she stands as tall and proud as a queen. Her eyes are on the two of us, Sibeal and me.

"Felix," Sibeal murmurs, "you say what must be said. I think she will understand."

In my heart I hear the tolling of a great, solemn bell. I remember the sound of the creature singing, joining me in celebration of wrong put right. I think of Paul. "What was cruelly stolen from you, we now return to you," I tell Svala, making sure I meet her eyes and trying to form the right images in my mind, as I know Sibeal does. "It is yours; take it. We are sorry. We are more sorry than we can say. We will never trouble your shore again." I do not ask her to let us go safely out of the bay. Now is the time for this one thing only.

"Take it, Svala," says Sibeal in a voice lovely as the nightingale's song. "Be yourself again, in all your strength and dignity. Take it."

Then, without a word or a glance at each other, we step back from the skin. Around us the men of the crew are still and silent, caught in the moment. They have forgotten, for now, how many lives were lost here.

Svala nods. It is an acknowledgment of what we have done. She bends to take the edge of the great skin in her hands. I stare, not knowing what I will see, not understanding how this can possibly work, but aware that we are about to witness something truly remarkable.

Svala lifts the skin one-handed, flipping it up and through the air as if it weighs no more than a lady's silk kerchief. As it rises above her, Knut screams. "No! No! In Thor's name, no!" He is on his feet, wrenching at the rope that binds him, desperate to get away. Nobody helps him. All eyes are on her.

The skin comes down, settling around her form. All happens in a few moments: under the moonlight she changes, growing taller, taller still, as tall as an ancient oak. Wider, longer, her form stretching, her limbs thickening, the features of a lovely woman becoming those of a serpent, a monster, a sea beast like the one in the bay. Her jaw lengthens; the skin that clothes her seems to swell as her form expands to inhabit it fully. Only the eyes are the same, liquid, lambent, full of the moon and the wild sea, but larger, so much larger. They are just like those of the creature that vaulted *Liadan* in one great leap; the monster that brought us safely out from underground. She is done. She is complete.

"Morrigan's curse," someone mutters, and another man makes the sign of the cross.

Svala rears high, pawing the air with her long-clawed forelegs as if to test that everything is working as it should be. She switches her huge tail from side to side; men shrink back against the rocks. The moonlight shines on her scaly skin, and now it is not a patchwork of duns and grays and browns, but a triumphant garment of sparkling silver and glittering gold. Svala was beautiful as a woman. As a creature, she is magnificent.

Knut is wailing. "Save me! Oh gods, save us all!"

One or two of the men bid him be brave. His collapse is unnerving; it compares ill with the bravery of our three survivors. Even Colm is standing quiet now, his arm in Gull's.

The creature tips back her head and roars. The sound rings out like the braying of a great trumpet, echoing all around the bay. It fades away. There is a heartbeat of silence. Then comes the answer. From the moonlit water rises a great head, a sinewy neck, a broad, scaled back in gleaming blues and greens. The toothed jaws open wide, and Svala's mate bellows his response. There are no words in it, but I understand his call. *Here! I'm here, beloved! Come to me!*

But she is not quite ready for that. There is one job to do first, one act to make this tale complete. She turns. I grab hold of Sibeal's hand and we retreat to safety, for the creature could crush us without even noticing. "Get back!" Cathal shouts, and the men scramble for the other side of the fire. There are no spears in hand, no knives or clubs. The men recognize Sibeal's authority as a druid, and though every instinct must tell them it is folly to stand before such a monster unarmed, all have obeyed her.

"No! No!" shrieks Knut. "Help me!"

Too late, far too late to take any action, the men realize what is about to happen. Several shout and one or two move forward, but there is no time. The creature bends her neck, her head comes down. She seizes the Norseman in her teeth, lifts him, shakes him as a dog shakes a rat. There is a high squealing sound. Sibeal blanches in horror. Svala tosses her prey high. Blood sprays as he falls. The creature catches him in her mouth, closes her jaws and swallows. He is gone.

The silence is absolute. The men who rushed to help Knut are frozen where they stand. I am still as stone with Sibeal's hand in mine. I hear her forcing her breathing into a pattern, steady and slow. I make an effort to do the same. Too late to help. Too late for anything.

The sea beast in the bay trumpets again. Svala moves. Her progress down the rocks to the water is fluid and graceful, remarkable for a creature with such bulk. She slithers, glides, dances her way to the sea. She reaches the water's edge, and for a moment she pauses. She turns her massive head, looking back at us. Sibeal sucks in her breath sharply, as if she has been hurt.

"Are you all right?" I whisper.

"Mm."

Sibeal bows to Svala. It is acknowledgment and farewell. I do the same. The moon shines down on the creature's glimmering skin like a mother lighting her lost child home. Svala wades, swims, dives, is gone.

Nothing to say. Nothing at all. After a while the men behind us start to move about, talking in low voices. Sibeal and I stand there, hand in hand, watching. She is trembling now. I wonder what she felt in that moment when Svala's eyes met hers. Eventually, far out in the bay, the creatures surface. They swim and tumble and dive, moving in perfect unison, as if they were two parts of one whole. It is a dance of ecstatic greeting, a graceful, powerful celebration of love. My heart trembles to witness it, for it seems deeply private. Yet they have chosen to celebrate in the moonlight. They know they have a spellbound audience, and honor us by sharing their joy. They circle and play, roll and leap around each other, churning the quiet water to great splashing waves. Glancing sideways, I see that Sibeal is crying. On her other side Cathal has come up silently. He looks out over the bay, his black cloak around him, his grave face transformed with wonder. Oh, there is such a song in this!

"I saw it, Felix," murmurs Sibeal. "I saw everything in a moment, as if, in creature form, Svala could show what she thought and felt with perfect clarity. As a woman, she struggled to make me understand. But in that sliver of time when she looked back at me, it was all there—the abduction from this island when she came down to the shore, curious about the ship; the rough confinement in *Freyja*'s hold; the terror of Inis Eala, an alien world for her, a world in which only I had the slightest understanding of her misery. And . . . and Knut. Knut holding sway over her because of that tiny strip of skin he wore. Knut taking her unwilling to his bed. Knut filling her with disgust, loathing, terror. *We* did that. We were responsible, because we believed his story and lodged them together, away from the community." A shudder goes through her body. "I even saw her with Rodan."

"Rodan?" I do not remember this name.

"The Connacht man who fell from the cliff. He . . . he made advances to her and she pushed him over. She was always stronger, bolder, more sure of herself when Knut was not close by. Oh, gods." Sibeal lifts a hand to wipe the tears from her face. "That was harsh justice. And Knut . . . I wish I had not seen that. But it brings the story to a fitting close. At the end, she was bursting with happiness. She was herself again, like the selkie woman in your song, Felix. *Joyous and strong and free.*"

We are all bone weary. Gareth sets watches for the night. Two stand guard while the others rest. Sibeal believes we are in no danger, provided we do not linger on this isle too long. The camp grows quiet. The fire dies to a glowing mound.

I thought I would fall instantly into the deep sleep my body craves. But I cannot sleep. My mind is wakeful. I have lived a lifetime since I arrived on Inis Eala with my past wrapped in shadows. In time I will write of this adventure. Perhaps not a song. To capture such monumental events in the form of a ballad would be to render them smaller; to force them within the limits of what our minds can readily accept. This tale calls for something longer, larger, a recounting that evokes all the horror and the grandeur, the peril and the profound mystery. Some day I will set it down. Not yet. I do not know what the future holds. I cannot guess. I only know that soon she will be gone. After that, a chasm yawns.

I lie awake long, under the moonlight. At some point, as the night wears on, I look across to where Sibeal has been lying not far from me, and I see that she is no longer there. Since I know I will not sleep, I rise and go to look for her. I do not know if this is the time to speak of what comes next. For some while I have closed my mind to that, thinking only of the mission. But soon we will be back on Inis Eala. We cannot part with so much unsaid between us. I do not know what Sibeal thinks about this; I do not know how she feels, only that she is unhappy. To me our parting is the hewing asunder of a lovely growing thing; the smashing of an instrument whose music holds the power to change the world; the sundering of a single self. It is wrong. Even in the light of her vocation, her remarkable druidic skills, her dedication to the gods, it is wrong. In the great pattern of flower and tree, bird and beast, stone and star, what is between Sibeal and me fits perfectly. How can it not be right? Surely even the labyrinthine mind of a druid such as this Ciarán of hers must know it is right.

I find her not so far away, at the other end of the strip of pebbly shore. She is seated on the rocks, so still she might herself be a stone, formed by the forces of nature into the semblance of a delicate young woman. And Cathal is here, down on the strand near the water. The moonlight throws his long shadow behind him on the shore.

He is surrounded by seals. I walk up to Sibeal; she puts a finger to her lips, and I sit down beside her without a word. Her hand creeps into mine.

I look again. They are not seals, but small beings in hooded cloaks of gray. Or perhaps those are their pelts. Within the darkness of each hood the moonlight finds a pair of bright eyes that belong to a creature surely not listed even in the most comprehensive of bestiaries. Whatever they are, they are Other. If I did not trust the evidence of my eyes, I would know this in my bones.

They are conducting a conversation with Cathal. I cannot be

sure if they speak in Irish or in some Otherworld tongue that, by its very nature, can be understood by folk such as Sibeal and me. I had thought the day could hold no more wonders, but I was wrong. The strangeness of this stops my breath.

"He is close," one of the beings says, and its voice is like the stone of the island, hard and strong and forbidding. "Only *she* keeps him out; her power is great. While she was gone, we fought a hard battle to hold our isle against him. She came home just in time."

"You say my father is close." Cathal is exerting hard-won control over his voice. "Then why could I not feel his presence on the voyage here? I thought he would challenge me. He has waited four years for me to leave Inis Eala and come back within his reach. Why did he not confront me as soon as I came out from my safe place?"

Another being speaks; the sound reminds me of a gurgling stream. "She is home. Mac Dara will not come here while her protection lies over the island. No sorcerer has the power to challenge her. No mage may pass within her boundaries, save when she chooses to allow it. As with you, Mac Dara's son."

"And beyond the isle, on the journey?"

A third being speaks. I hear in its voice the shrill crying of gulls and the endless song of the ocean. "You are of the Sea People," it says. "You are kin. On the way to this place, you bore our Queen on your ship. Her protection lay over you and the two who walk with you." The hooded head swivels; the pinpricks of light that form its eyes are on Sibeal and me. "Druid and bard; teller of tales and singer of songs." After a moment, the being adds, "Lamp of hope and questing spirit."

"Left hand and right," puts in another of the small creatures.

"Moon and sun."

"Shadow and light." They are all joining in now, as if it were some kind of game.

"Still pool and waterfall."

"Conscience and courage."

A silence after this, as all of them turn their eyes on the one who has just spoken, as if its contribution was somehow inappropriate. For myself, I like greatly what was said, for it recognizes the depth of the bond between Sibeal and me.

"My father troubled you, then, before we brought your Queen home," says Cathal. "How?"

"Storms."

"Great waves."

"Days of darkness."

"Cloud. Tempest. Icy chill."

"Monsters from the deep. A plague that killed the fish and left us hungry."

"Sea-Father fought for us," a creature said. "He was weakened by that, and by the loss of her whom he loved. If she had not come home when she did we might have lost him, and our isle with him. Mac Dara is strong."

Cathal stares out across the water. "I cannot fight him," he says in a low voice. "My craft is gone. There is not a shred of magic in me. I could not so much as raise a spark to make light when it was needed. Even before, I struggled to match my father's power. Now, he would simply laugh at me. I cannot wage war against a prince of the Otherworld. I cannot even defend my family."

The silence draws out. The little gray ones start to fade away, merging into rocks and sand and water as if they were the stuff of dream.

Sibeal rises to her feet. "Wait!" she calls softly.

Eyes turn in her direction.

"Cathal is no coward," she says. "What he needs is an explanation. Do not judge him before he has heard it."

They seem to be waiting for more.

"Is it not true," Sibeal says, "that within the margins of this isle your Queen holds total sway? If her power is sufficient to keep Mac Dara at bay, might it not block the spells and charms of any mage who entered her domain?"

The faces of these beings are obscured by the shadow of their hoods; the bright eyes give little away. But I sense a warming, a softening. "It is true, wise one," one of them says. "Mac Dara's son will leave the confines of the isle without the Golden Queen. Beyond the barrier of our cliffs, he will be free of the restraints her presence has placed on him."

"But—" Cathal says, and his voice is less guarded now, "Sibeal used a druid charm to make light, in the underground passage. Why was *her* magic not blocked?"

"Aaah." They make the sound as one. It is a sigh, and a song, and a deep and fervent prayer of thanks. "She is the goddess-friend. She is the one who sees true. They are blessed, the wise woman and the one who walks beside her. But for them, Mac Dara's son, you would not be here. You would not be here to receive our gift."

"A gift." Cathal sounds as if, even for him, this is all too much to take in. "What gift is that?"

The small beings move, breaking the circle around him, and converge in a huddle. They resemble a collection of weed-covered rocks. In this place of stone and water, they blend seamlessly. At length one of them glides forward, stopping before Cathal. It stretches out what might be a hand. I cannot see what it offers.

"Take this." It is the one with the sharp, emphatic voice. "Guard it well. Use it well. The time is coming when Mac Dara must be challenged. He must not continue to stir the seas with his capricious hand, or spoil a realm that once was peaceful and just. No, don't speak"—when Cathal was ready to argue—"only listen, and take heed. You are too ready to say this is not your task, you cannot do it, you will not do it. One way or another, it must be done. Without you, it cannot be done. But a quandary vexes you; we understand that. This talisman is our Queen's token. It will protect what you hold most dear until your task is complete. Wear it around your neck on the voyage home, and the Sea People will guard your vessel from the storm."

Cathal has taken the tiny item in his long-fingered hand, and is examining it in the moonlight. "Thank you," he says. Nothing more.

"Come forward, Bright Heart," says the being.

I look at Sibeal; they must mean her.

She shakes her head. "It's you they want, Felix. Go on." She releases my hand.

I walk down the pebbly shore, the crunch of my footsteps an intrusion in the quiet of the night. Now I am beside them, and scarce able to breathe for the strangeness of it. The being stretches out its hand again. The hand has three fingers, and is as soft and gray as the creature's cloak. On its palm lies something that might be a shell, or a stone, or an artifact. Such is its gleam, I think the moon has lent it some of her light.

"For you," the being says, and, inverting its hand, drops the talisman on my palm. "Not for yourself. Not for the wise one, for she has no need of it. She carries her protection within her. This is for your daughter. Use it wisely. Guard her well."

I am unable to ask the question that fills my heart. I cannot speak a word. I close my fingers around the talisman. I bow to each of them in turn. A silent prayer fills me, a prayer made up of hope and fear and hard choices.

By the time I am sitting beside Sibeal once more, the beings are gone. They have not vanished in a puff of smoke, simply faded back into their surroundings. Cathal has taken his talisman and gone to the other end of the shore, where he sits alone on the rocks with his hands around his knees. We will not disturb him; not tonight.

"Felix?" Sibeal asks in a low voice.

"Mm?"

She does not answer. I think perhaps she is crying. "I didn't tell you, but I saw her. Our daughter. I saw her in visions, twice. That was the cruelest thing." The tears flow in earnest. My wise druid is, at this moment, adrift and helpless.

My throat is tight; my eyes brim. I open my hand to examine what lies there.

The talisman is like a little moon. Pearlescent, glimmering, radiant with light, it is wafer thin and hard as shell. There is a tiny hole close to the rim. A vision. Our daughter. I would thread this on a silk ribbon for her to wear around her neck. For a moment I allow myself to imagine it, as I lift her dark curls out of the way and tie the bow, and she says, *Thank you, Papa.*

"Sibeal."

She says nothing.

"Sibeal, I must tell you how I feel. I have held back; I have tried to match your self-restraint, but I cannot do that any longer. It is time to tell the truth, to speak out. Sibeal, I love you." She bows her head as if these words set an intolerable burden on her slender shoulders, but I have begun now and I must go on. "I respect your vocation; I honor your link with the gods, your druidic wisdom. But I love you as a woman; I love you as the one woman I want to spend my life with. I love you as a tree loves rain; I love you as a flower loves the sun. Sibeal, I know your feet walk a path toward the nemetons and a celibate life."

Gods, my heart is going like a drum; my skin is all cold sweat. Still she sits there, eyes down, hands in her lap. "I know you are convinced this is the one future the gods have determined for you. But . . . " I draw a shaky breath. "I cannot believe there is no alternative, no way by which we could be together, you and I. I would honor, love and cherish you all my life, Sibeal. I would protect you. I would walk with you step for step, wherever you chose to go. I know in my inner heart that the two of us are meant to be together. I believe that if your gods rule otherwise, they deny an essential truth." I pause; Sibeal lifts her head and looks at me. She is deathly pale. The moonlight shows me her bright eyes, full of tears.

"There, I have said it. I have told the truth. I want you to do the same, Sibeal, even if it breaks my heart. It hurts me to see you there, closed up within yourself, holding your feelings tight lest they disturb that druidic calm. If you think me presumptuous, if you think me misguided, tell me so. If you find my words offensive, shout at me, rail at me, strike me if you will. And if you can for a moment entertain that your future might follow a different path, one on which I might walk beside you, speak of that now. I challenge you, Sibeal. Or would you spend your whole life shut in and locked away, like the kernel of a nut that never ripens? You give much of yourself; you are full of compassion and wisdom. But if you never let that other self flourish, the one who weeps and rages and doubts, the one who once melted into my arms as if seared by the same flame as I, then you will not lead a full life, not even if you are the wisest and most devout druid in all of Erin. That is the opinion of this poet, scholar and fool who never learned how to keep his mouth shut. Please, Sibeal. Please let me hear what is in your heart."

She gives a great, choking sob and folds her arms around me, and I gather her close.

"I'm sorry," she says with her face against my breast. "Felix, I'm so sorry. I don't see any way it can be. You speak as if this were easy for me, and it's not. When I thought you were drowned, I . . . it was . . . I've never considered abandoning my vocation before. At that moment I was only a breath away from it."

My heart is leaden. I hear in these words that she will not be diverted from her path. Yet her body tells me what her mind will not allow her to say, that mind so trained to control. I feel in her embrace that she wants me as I want her; that we are a perfect complement, two halves of one whole. Oh, Sibeal, let go. Let go for just a moment.

"The gods still need me," she says. "There was Svala and the skin . . . I could not have spoken to her as I did without the gift the gods have granted me. How can I set their will aside for my own selfish ends?"

Selfish. It does not feel selfish to me, but absolutely right. Sibeal lifts her face to mine and I kiss her. Our first kiss, and likely our last. I taste salt tears and the aching delight of what might have been. And still, even now, I cannot keep silent. "Ask yourself this," I say. "When your every breath is taken in reverence, why do your gods choose to punish you so?"

We are two nights on the serpent isle. *Liadan* is scoured clean; clothing and supplies are brought ashore and laid out to dry in the sun. Water casks are replenished from the spring. Stocks of hard bread and dried meat are checked for the voyage home. A new sea anchor is fashioned from rocks and cunningly knotted rope.

Gull tends to the three survivors. He makes me drink a potion brewed with seaweed and a brown powder that he carries in his healer's bag. I do as I'm told. Since this vile mixture can stave off the illness that nearly killed me before, or so Gull tells me, I drink it as readily as I might the finest mead. I was given a second chance at life when Sibeal found me half drowned on Inis Eala. I fought a fight then, for Paul, for the men abandoned here. Now the mission is fulfilled, and it seems a new challenge lies before me. Perhaps I must summon the courage to live my life without her, and to live it well. But I will not accept that, not yet. Bright Heart, they called me. I am still fighting.

On the third morning we assemble on the shore, all of us, waiting to be rowed out to *Liadan*. The weather is calm, the sky cloudless. The men have worked hard, and all is shipshape. It is time.

We board. For a moment all are gathered on the deck, and Gareth steps up before us. His features are grave, and I wonder what he will say. A rallying speech, maybe, or a reminder that while we are at sea, his word is law. But all he says is, "Friends, we're going home."

Under oars, we head out to the perilous channel. We catch no glimpse of Sea-Father and the Golden Queen, but as we pass through the narrow, high-walled passage, I sense their large eyes on us. We emerge to open sea. A kindly wind fills *Liadan*'s sails, and she makes a course to the south, and Inis Eala.

CHAPTER 14

~Sibeal~

We had made the voyage from Inis Eala to the serpent isle in five days. The homeward trip took much longer. We were not harried by storms or driven off course by howling gales; quite the opposite. After one day's brisk sailing, nature decided to remind us that it was summer. The clouds departed. The air warmed. The winds took a rest. We floated, trailing our new sea anchor, for six days before a northerly came up. The crew raised *Liadan*'s sail, the square of woolen cloth bellied out, and to the accompaniment of cheers, we headed for home.

I had been seasick only for the first day or two. After that I kept myself busy helping Gull tend to Thorgrim. Indeed, I kept myself very busy. I managed to present an outer shell of calm, lending a hand wherever I might, sitting in silent prayer, keeping myself to myself. Under that still exterior I was a stew of raw feelings, and every day they bubbled closer to the surface. There was, in truth, no silent prayer. When I sat cross-legged with my eyes closed, I could neither pray nor meditate. All I could think about was Felix. The passages of lore that had once come so easily, the patterns of breathing I had been able to summon in the most difficult situations had slipped away; they were beyond me. When Felix was up on deck, fishing with Sigurd or talking to Cathal, I longed for him to come back so I could look at him. When he was close by, the merest glance brought back the thrilling sensation of his lips on mine, and the desolation of stepping out of his embrace. I could hardly bring myself to speak to him, lest I break down completely. Ciarán would have been horrified.

I was not too preoccupied to feel pleasure at our survivors' progress. Thorgrim was managing to keep his food down, and looked better by the day. Though weakened by his ordeal, Donn had from the first been eager to work. Gareth had asked him to join the crew, allocating him tasks that were within his reduced capacity. As for Colm, little ailed him physically that rest and good food would not quickly mend. His mind was a different matter. Felix listened patiently to the boy's endless recounting of what had happened, what he had seen, what he had felt, and reassured him that his old life waited for him back in Munster, and that in time the nightmare would fade.

As Thorgrim's condition improved, we learned that he had known Knut in Dublin. "Knut had a wife and children there," Sigurd translated, to our astonishment. "But he was in trouble twice over. He owed money, a lot of money. Although he was a fit, able sort of man, there never seemed to be any funds to mend the house or clothe the little ones. Too keen on a wager, Knut was, and on women other than the one he was wed to. Things came to a head with his wife, and he took to her with his fists. Seems he forgot that she had five brothers. He left Dublin in a hurry, with no intention of going back, and headed for Ulfricsfjord in the hope of getting a place on a ship. He was almost lucky. He would have stepped off *Freyja* in the Orcades and made a new start, if the boat hadn't been swept off course."

"Danu save us," murmured Gull. "So when he saw Svala on the shore he thought he'd found himself the perfect replacement for his wife. Not only was she beauteous beyond compare, but once he'd helped himself to a piece of her skin, she was biddable and silent, too. No wonder he was so keen to win a place on Inis Eala, where folk valued his skills and nobody knew about his past. It must have seemed perfect. And no wonder he was so desperate to keep Felix quiet."

"That sea monster," mused Sigurd, "the other one, I mean—if Svala could shed her skin and become human, does that mean it could, too? That thing would make quite a figure of a man."

Felix kept busy, as I did. He talked to Gareth, to Cathal, to Sigurd, to Gull. He plied a fishing line and even on occasion helped with sailing the boat. He turned his hand to any task he was given. The crew treated him as a friend. And I watched him, seeing the fit, healthy man of my vision emerge from the shaken invalid by whose side I had kept so many anxious vigils. I had new vision now; I saw the strong shoulders, the proud carriage, the long legs and grace of movement. I saw him laughing, somber, reflective, purposeful. When I thought of the time ahead, I wondered how long it would be until I forgot these fine things; how long before he faded to a beloved memory, and then to nothing. Or would I keep his image in my mind forever, a piercing reminder of what I had sacrificed to follow my destined path? *An alternative*, he had said. How could he understand? There was no alternative.

Cathal made it his habit to take me up on deck at least once a day. Too much time in the hold was bad for anyone, he said. No doubt this was true, but he had another reason: he wanted to talk.

"Every day I expect it to happen," he said to me the first time, as we stood together looking out across the vast ocean. A small flock of gulls had joined us as temporary passengers. They perched in the rigging, feathers ruffled by the breeze. "I expect my father to act. A storm; a mighty wave; a thunderbolt; an eldritch vessel crewed by uncanny warriors. If those little creatures on the serpent isle spoke true, the talisman should protect my loved ones and also keep *Liadan* safe on the voyage home. But it is a great deal to entrust in a tiny scrap of shell, however magical it may be. I cannot believe my father would not seize this chance to sink us. To drown me and have Clodagh and the child at his mercy. Why would he hold back when he has the power to stir the seas and conjure tempests? Why wouldn't he meddle, when he has no scruples at all? He's a man who kills for no better reason than to amuse himself. He's a man who turns folk's lives upside down without a second thought."

I struggled to find the wise answer that would once have come so readily. "You are his only son. True, perhaps he is more interested in your child now. But he will not harm you if he need not, surely."

"You don't know him."

"There is another possibility," I said. Felix had just come up through the open hatch; he was heading to the bow to talk to Sigurd. He lifted a hand in casual greeting. The wind caught his hair and lifted it around his head like seaweed on the tide. What beautiful eyes he had, eyes of drowning blue.

"What possibility?"

I struggled to remember what I had been about to say. "Those little folk implied that someone must stand up to Mac Dara, and that the one to do it might be you. I know you have no intention of going back to Sevenwaters, Cathal. But you should consider the possibility that your father is holding back because he fears you. Because he fears your magic has the power to overcome his."

"What about *Freyja*, the wreck, the losses?"

"There is no way to know if that was his doing. It was odd, yes. But there are many oddities in this tale, and not all of them are of Mac Dara's making."

"Mm." Cathal fell silent for a while. Then he asked, "Sibeal, are you all right? You seem . . . not yourself."

"I'm fine." The sharp note of my voice made him narrow his eyes at me. "A little tired, perhaps," I added. "This has taken a toll on all of us."

More than half a turning of the moon after we had set out, we sailed past the reef on which *Freyja* had foundered and into the sheltered bay at Inis Eala. A crowd stood on the shore to welcome us home. Above the shouts of greeting came one penetrating sound: the shrill yapping of a little dog.

"It sounds as if she missed you," I said to Felix, who stood beside me at the rail.

I do not think he heard me, for he was staring intently toward the shore. I followed his gaze and saw that among the familiar faces on the jetty was one that had not been there to watch our departure. He stood a little apart, a tall, still figure, his hair deepest auburn, his features gravely handsome. He was clad in an austere gray robe. Ciarán. He was already here. Time after time, in this testing summer, I had longed for his wise advice. Now I felt something akin to despair.

"That's Ciarán, I take it?" Felix sounded less than delighted.

I nodded.

"Felix," said Gareth, coming up on Felix's other side. "That was a mission to test the most adventurous of men. Scholar you may be, but in courage and tenacity you surpass the most peerless of warriors. And without you, Sibeal, this could not have been achieved."

I was hardly listening. The gap between *Liadan* and the jetty narrowed as they edged her in under oars. There was Snake, catching one rope, and Niall ready for the other. And Ciarán's mulberry eyes in his pale, solemn face, watching me. I managed an awkward, jerky nod of greeting, and he favored me with one of his rare smiles. Fang was on the very edge of the jetty, making more noise than everyone else put together.

"I don't see Clodagh." Cathal was beside me now, scanning the faces.

He was right. Evan was there, and Muirrin. Biddy stood beside them, beaming and waving both arms to Gull. Among the women were Flidais and Suanach, Alba and Brenna. Johnny was helping Niall secure the second rope so we could step across from deck to jetty. He looked up at Gareth and smiled, and I saw not only relief and love in it, but also an apology. Leading the mission had tested Gareth hard, and the marks of it showed on his face.

Cathal was first off the boat, and heading over to Evan and Muirrin before I so much as moved. There was a brief interchange, then Cathal was off up the track at a run, with Muirrin following at a more sedate pace.

Felix offered me his hand as I jumped over to the jetty. Ciarán was there to catch me. We looked at each other. My mentor put his hands on my shoulders and bent to bestow a fatherly kiss on my brow.

"You're safe," he said.

Felix was beside me now.

"Ciarán," I said, "this is Felix. He is a scholar from Armorica. Felix, this is my kinsman and teacher Ciarán, of whom I've told you." Even the semblance of calm deserted me; my voice shook.

All along the shore, women were embracing their men, men were hoisting their children onto their shoulders, mothers were greeting sons, and warriors who had stayed at home were slapping the adventurers on the back and talking about jugs of ale and the exchange of stories. The Connacht men were mingling with the rest. The place was awash with relief and delight, save for here, where the three of us stood in our own little world. Ciarán and Felix exchanged a look. What was yet unspoken filled the air with tension.

"Sibeal, you have a new niece." Evan came up, smiling broadly. "And a new nephew."

My jaw dropped. "Twins?"

"They were born on the sixth night after you sailed. Clodagh's well. I'm not sure I can say the same for Cathal; he looked deeply shocked. You'll want to come and see them straightaway. I'll take you."

Twins. No wonder my sister had grown so large. "Are they healthy?"

"They're healthy indeed. And it won't surprise you to learn that Clodagh's the most capable of mothers. There was a certain point in the process when she cursed Cathal for his absence, but all's well now. And their hut is finished. She wanted to be in her own place. Shall I carry that bag for you?"

"I'll take it." Felix relieved me of the bag, then melted away into the crowd.

"Who is he?" Ciarán was walking beside me as we followed Evan up the steep path to the settlement.

This was not the obvious question it seemed.

"You'll have heard the story," I said. "Unless you only just arrived."

"I have been here a few days. It's earlier than we arranged. I hope that does not inconvenience you, Sibeal. If you wish, I will be happy to remain on Inis Eala until the end of summer. I need to talk to Cathal, and to Johnny."

"Once you've done that we may as well go," I said, failing utterly to match his equable tone. Why delay the pain of parting? Whether it happened tomorrow or the next day or at summer's bitter end, it would hurt no less.

He gave me a sideways look. "Is something troubling you, Sibeal?"

"No."

"We'll talk soon," Ciarán said quietly. "First you must see your sister." He glanced at me and added, "Clodagh will want to look on smiling faces."

"Here we are," Evan said as we came up to the hut Spider had built for Clodagh and Cathal. It was finished, and Clodagh had already started planting a garden in the walled area behind the house. I could see freshly dug earth and a row of green seedlings. Nearby, linen cloths flapped on a line. Ciarán had left us, disappearing with as much alacrity as Felix.

I took a few deep, measured breaths. I summoned a smile. Evan knocked, then opened the door at Clodagh's call, "Come in!"

My sister was seated on the edge of a shelf bed, feeding one of the babes. It was suckling busily and pounding its mother's creamy flesh with a small clenched fist. Cathal stood before the hearth with the other babe in his arms. Father and child regarded each other with dark and shining eyes, taking long, slow measure. And although I had thought myself drained of tears, fresh ones welled in my eyes. The infants were as perfect as rosebuds.

"Clodagh!" I bent to wrap my arms around my sister and the babe she held. "They're beautiful!" I had expected to love them instantly. I had not anticipated this aching longing for my own child. "Are you well?"

"Very well, Sibeal, though I do feel somewhat like a milch cow. I've never had so many people bringing me food, and offering to do my washing and my mending, and making me rest during the day. Biddy says I should accept any help I'm offered. I do welcome the food. I always seem to be starving."

"What are the babies' names?" I asked.

"Our daughter will be Firinne, for Cathal's mother," Clodagh said. "We haven't chosen our son's name yet. We're hoping you'll conduct a naming ritual for us while you're here."

I was looking around the little house, seeing how brimful it was with Clodagh's loving presence. No wonder Cathal looked so different, his features transformed with happiness, the anxiety that had tightened his features in those last days of the voyage quite gone. It was not only the miracle of the son he held in his arms and the daughter at her mother's breast; it was Clodagh's presence that changed him. The bond between them was strong enough to survive anything. Modest hut this might be, but it was as much a home as the keep of Sevenwaters had been to generations of children. My mind was full of the vision I'd had, Felix and I in our own little house, with its warm lamplight and its windows opening on trees. That was the right home for the child in the owl-embroidered gown, the little girl whose eyes were just like mine. *Let it be real*, something within me whispered, something treacherous that, like Felix, could not keep silent. *Oh, please let it be real*. I sat in silence, watching Clodagh and her daughter. I fought the tide that was rising within me.

"You seem different, Sibeal," Clodagh observed as she moved the babe expertly to her shoulder and began patting its back. "This voyage—Cathal has given me the bare bones of it, and it seems you've been exceptionally brave and done some amazing things. Ciarán's already here—did you know?"

"Sibeal?" It was the first time Cathal had spoken since I came in. I saw something on his face that I had never seen there before: a beaming, spontaneous smile. "Would you like to hold him?"

I was used to infants, having helped with my brother since the day he was born. I took the baby boy and cradled him in my arms. Under his blanket he was clad in a little gown of Clodagh's making, embroidered with berries and leaves. Around his neck was a cord fashioned of fine-spun wool, and threaded on it was a talisman in the shape of a half-moon, made from the same glimmering shell-like substance as the one Felix had been given on the serpent isle.

"What they gave me was a single talisman, pierced with two holes," Cathal said. "When I brought it out to show Clodagh, it had split neatly down the center. If the gray ones are to be believed, our children now walk under the protection of the gods."

I did not reply. As I felt the warm weight of the child against me, as his solemn gaze met mine, something snapped inside me. A sob burst out; tears poured from my eyes. I sank down onto a bench, hugging the baby against my breast and rocking back and forth. "I can't do it anymore!" I wept. "It's too hard, everything's wrong, I can't even pray properly, and Felix is going away, and I'll never have it, I'll never have what you have, there never will be that cottage in the woods and Felix writing by lamplight and that little girl with her wise eyes, because if I choose that I'll spend my whole life knowing I gave up my vocation and turned my back on the gods and disappointed Ciarán and did something utterly selfish! But I love Felix! What he said was right, it was completely right, he and I should be together, we're like wind and rain, like leaf and flower, like—how can I let him go away and never see him again? I know I should be calm about it, I'm a druid, if I haven't learned acceptance by now I haven't learned anything in the nemetons, but I can't be calm, nothing works anymore, everything's wrong . . ."

I was dimly aware of an interchange between Clodagh and

Cathal, after which he went out, closing the door of the hut behind him. My sister rose and put the baby girl into a basket. A few moments later, Clodagh sat down beside me. Her arms came around me and her son, and she held on, not saying a thing. She waited until the words and the sobs and the tears came to a hiccuping end, then took the infant from me—he had remained remarkably calm throughout—and moved back to the bed to feed him.

"There's a clean kerchief on the shelf there, Sibeal. Wipe your eyes and blow your nose. Then put the kettle on the fire, please, and brew us a drink. Feeding the twins makes me thirsty. Then we'll talk some more."

Kettle. Fire. Water. Cups. A dried leaf mixture in a corked jar. Someone came to knock at the door, and Clodagh called out, "We're busy! Come back later."

While the water heated I went to look at the girl child in her basket. She was sleeping, long-lashed eyes closed, tiny face wreathed in mysterious dreams. She had more hair than her brother did, a downy crop with a distinctly reddish tinge to it. My own daughter had been dark . . . More tears welled. I couldn't hold them back. What was wrong with me? I couldn't even face the thought of walking out the door. I couldn't face anything. "I hope I didn't upset him," I mumbled. "The baby, I mean."

"Children are more robust than they look. And it clearly hasn't affected his appetite." After a moment Clodagh added, "You should give yourself a little time. I know it feels bad right now, but you've only just got off the boat and you're tired . . . "

"There, there, Sibeal, everything will be all right in the morning?" It's not all right, Clodagh. It never can be. Whatever I do, whichever choice I make, I'll spend the rest of my life regretting what I gave up. I wish Felix had never come here! I wish I'd never met him!"

She looked at me, her green eyes full of compassion and understanding. I looked back at her. "I don't mean that," I said, sniffing. "I love him. I could never be sorry to have met him. I could never be sorry I was part of his great mission. But this is breaking my heart."

"You said, *whichever choice I make*. Does that mean you would seriously consider giving up your vocation for Felix?"

"How can I? How can I turn my back on the gods? How can I deny the call I've heard since I was a small child?"

"Folk occasionally do, I believe. What about Ciarán himself? He was a novice druid at the time he met Aunt Niamh. And he left, even though they were forbidden to wed."

"This is not the same. Besides, he came back to the nemetons."

"Only years later, after Niamh had died, and after Fainne had grown up and gone away to serve the gods on the Needle."

"It doesn't matter how long it was. He managed to put it behind him. Ciarán is strong in faith. I thought I was strong; I never had any doubt until this summer. But I know that if I give Felix up I'll regret it every single day of my life, Clodagh. No matter how wise I become as a druid; no matter how well I study and pray and meditate. This has shaken my belief. Denying what is between us feels wrong; it feels like denying the turning of the seasons or the growth of a tree or the pattern of waves on the shore. And the love of those things is what makes a good druid. I just don't understand."

"Congratulations," Clodagh said.

"What do you mean?"

"You've grown up, Sibeal."

"Grown up? I've just burst into tears and babbled complete nonsense! I've completely lost sight of that calm, self-contained person I thought I was! I haven't grown up—I've become a child again!"

"You're in love. It's a condition well-known for making folk leap from happy to sad to mixed-up and perplexed at the least excuse. As for growing up, we all love calm, wise, reserved Sibeal; she's the person I know and value as a dear sister. You've just found out, to your surprise, that she's only half of you. The other half is a woman: a woman who laughs and cries and loves, a woman who makes mistakes and has to work hard to fix them. A woman who doubts herself; a woman who sometimes can't find answers without help."

I busied myself pouring hot water over the dried leaves, stirring, straining the brew into the cups, placing one where she could reach it easily.

"I have a challenge for you, Sibeal."

I gazed at her, unable to imagine any challenge at which I would not fail miserably at this moment.

"From now until you finish drinking that tea," Clodagh said, "set aside the druid part of yourself, the part that wrestles with philosophical arguments and worries about loyalty to the gods. Be the woman, the one who's just found out that love can fill you with joy one moment and sink you in sorrow the next. I'm your sister, and we're given sisters so we have someone we can talk to at such times. Tell me about Felix. Forget about what might happen, or what you think should happen. Tell me why you love him."

So I did, and I was still telling her long after our tea was finished. I brewed us each a second cup, and Clodagh found some honey cake that had been set away, and I discovered I was ravenously hungry. Some time later, the knock on the door came again, and I opened it to see Biddy standing there with an apologetic smile on her face.

"Sorry to disturb you. I thought you'd be ready for a bath by now, Sibeal. The men are all out of the bathhouse, and I have fresh hot water waiting, and Flidais says she'll wash your hair for you." She could hardly fail to see that I had been crying; it felt as if my whole face was red and puffy. But she made no comment.

"And after that," Clodagh said firmly, "Sibeal must eat and sleep. A piece of honey cake doesn't go far. Biddy, will you tell Cathal he can come back now? I assume he's had his bath."

Biddy grinned. "Scrubbed clean as a whistle, and sitting in the hall telling anyone who'll listen that his children are the most perfect ever born. Sibeal, what a tale Gull had to tell me! Svala some kind of sea monster! And Knut . . . " She shook her head. "I'm still trying to take it all in."

I said nothing, but gave Clodagh a kiss and followed Biddy out. As I turned to shut the door, my sister said, "Ciarán is the other part of this, Sibeal. Tomorrow you must talk to him."

~Felix~

Stepping off *Liadan* onto dry land, I felt strong. The mission was done, and I could report to my brother that I had kept my word. I had been brave.

After we made landfall, Sibeal went away to Clodagh's hut, and I did not see her again. Sigurd took me to the bathhouse, and the two of us emerged freshly clad and smelling fit for company. In the dining hall, we ate seethed fish and baked vegetables. It was a feast fit for the gods. Gull helped me move my things out of the infirmary to make room for Thorgrim, and Sigurd found me a bed in the men's quarters. I lay down when the sun was setting, and if I dreamed, on waking I remember nothing of it. There is only one thing in my mind. Today holds a new challenge. I must speak to Ciarán.

I find him out of doors, seated on rocks, gazing toward the reef where *Freyja* foundered; the place where the Ankou rose from the sea and took my brother away. Sibeal's mentor is a person of striking appearance, his skin pale, his hair a deep red, his eyes the shade of ripe berries. His features are handsome, but there is a reserve in him that makes him seem aloof. Like Cathal, this man bears a touch of the uncanny. Looking at him, I think of a well deeper than sorrow, of moon shadow, of realms beyond the ken of humankind. I am almost afraid to disturb him, but I walk up, greeting him courteously.

"Master Ciarán. I would speak with you."

He rises. His movements are fluid. Sibeal said he was her father's uncle, but he cannot be so old, surely. He looks forty at most. "Felix." The tone is neither warm nor cool. "Shall we walk?"

I have it all planned out, how I will put my proposal to him, how I will keep calm, for such a man will be unimpressed if I let my feelings get the better of me. He is a person of erudition and subtlety. I am a scholar. In this fight, that may be my best weapon. "I wish to speak with you about the future," I begin as we head along the path. It would be easier to do this seated opposite one another, so I could see his face. But he wants to walk, so we walk.

"Ah."

It seems he is not going to help me.

"Sibeal and I have become very close over the summer." A calm voice; a relaxed demeanor. All it takes is slow breathing and concentration. I try to remember that. "I have been deeply impressed by what she has done, and what she has taught me of the druidic path. I was raised in the Christian faith, but my belief was shattered by the wrongs I saw enacted in the name of the Church. I left home because of that; because I could not remain silent."

"Mm-hm." He walks on steadily.

"This summer, during our strange adventure, I have begun to see a glimmer of light in the spiritual darkness I felt after leaving my home shore. Sibeal's unswerving faith in her gods has opened my mind to something real and true. I have observed the deep magic of earth, sky and sea, and I have seen the remarkable abilities of a druid to reach others, to make peace, to find solutions to impossible problems. Master Ciarán, I have been a scholar since I was a boy of twelve. I love ideas. I love reading and writing. I love debate and discovery. There is a hunger in me for more. I cannot return home; my outspokenness earned the wrath of the nobleman in whose household my father is employed, and if I went back I might put my family in danger. I will not remain at the court of Munster, where my brother and I were employed, for that would be full of cruel memories. I was hoping . . . "

I pause as we reach a stile. Ciarán waits for me to cross first. He says nothing at all as I clamber up and over. I stand there as he follows me, all graceful economy of movement.

"I was hoping there might be a place for me among your novices at Sevenwaters." There, I've said it. Now I dare not look at his face. I take heart from the fact that he has not broken into derisive laughter. "I am prepared to work hard. To learn. You will have heard the story of our mission by now. I hope that shows you I am a man of principle. I have not been raised in your faith, but I believe there is a lifetime of learning in it, and I love and respect learning. I have some skills that could be useful: languages, scribing ability."

"And singing, I hear," Ciarán says. He could be thinking anything at all, so little does his tone give away.

"I can sing, yes. I can make poems." I wonder who has told him this.

"Let us sit down here awhile." Ciarán seats himself on a convenient rock; I find another. I look into his eyes and am none the wiser.

"Felix," he says, "Sibeal is the most outstanding novice to enter the Sevenwaters nemetons in living memory. She has certain very special gifts, gifts we believe may be unique to her. You'll have seen some of them at work during your mission. Her gifts make her precious to our kind, not just in the nemetons at Sevenwaters, but everywhere in Erin. But they also make her vulnerable."

The silence draws out as I try to guess what it is he wants from me. "I understand," I say eventually.

"Do you? I think not. After less than a full summer's acquaintance you believe you know Sibeal. Yes, you have seen a little of her ability; you have caught a glimpse of her fine qualities. But your understanding is a drop in the ocean; a blade of grass in a meadow. Sibeal is my kinswoman, my protégé, my student. She is closer to me than a daughter. I have taught and guided her since she was twelve years old. She will make a druid of exceptional power and goodness. Within the nemetons she can develop her talents to their full capacity. And she can be protected."

"Protected? From what?" I am unable to keep my voice calm now; my outrage trembles in it. I draw breath deeply, once, twice, three times, as she might.

"From herself, perhaps."

In my head, I count to ten. "Sibeal is like nobody I have ever met before," I say. "Rare, precious and wonderful. The brightest star in the sky; the fairest flower in the field; the subtlest and most beguiling of tales. The loveliest note of the harp. I do know her. Her vocation may be as strong as iron, but she's deeply unhappy. If you are so close to her, why can't you see that?"

"Answer me one question, Felix."

I wait.

"You request a place in the nemetons at Sevenwaters. Are you telling me you have a spiritual vocation?"

Breathe, Felix. Be calm. "That depends on how you define a vocation, Master Ciarán. I have not been visited by Otherworld presences, as Sibeal was in her childhood. I have not heard the voices of gods or spirits whispering in my ear. It is as I described it before—the sense that a light reached me in a place I thought would be forever dark. The merest candle in a catacomb of doubt, but a light nonetheless. I saw it in Sibeal's gift with the runes, in her ability to reach Svala, the sea woman, in the wisdom of her tales and the kindness of her advice. I saw it in Gull's friendship, a friendship that came with no conditions. I saw it in my brother's raw courage. Now I see it every day in the power of the waves, the flight of the sea birds, the wild dance of clouds across the sky. I hear it in the cry of a newborn babe. I see it in the tranquil face of an old man, waiting for death." My grandfather's parchment skin; his soft, beguiling voice, telling me tales. His eyes closing for the last time, with as little fuss as if he were taking an afternoon nap. When the Ankou came for him, he came gently.

Ciarán regards me for a while. He seems to be giving my words serious consideration. I allow a fragile hope into my heart.

"You'll have business to attend to, I imagine," he says. "I've heard a good deal of your story from Johnny and Gareth. The king of Munster will need your report, at the very least. You will not quit such employment without some negotiation."

I wait for the next part: *But after that, if you haven't changed your mind, you can come to Sevenwaters for a trial.*

"Come back to me in ten years' time," Ciarán says. "In those ten years, go off and live your life. Your parents have lost one son. You will only punish them if you allow your principles to keep you from home. Would you leave it to a stranger to tell your mother that her firstborn is dead? Make peace with your family. Ply your trade as scribe, translator, poet, lover of ideas. If your mind is unchanged in ten years, come to Sevenwaters and speak with me again."

He might as well have hit me. I am breathless with fury, and a bitter sorrow fills my heart. I quell the urge to shout at him. "Ten years," I say, and despite my best effort, my voice is shaking. "That is a long time."

"You are young. Sibeal is even younger. The two of you, together, in the austere, celibate setting of the Sevenwaters nemetons . . . I think not."

"I—"

"Felix. You are transparent. Your feelings for her are written on every part of you. I saw it the moment the two of you stepped off the boat. Your plan is nothing but a rod for your back, and perhaps for hers as well. Go home to Armorica. Before ten years have passed you will have found a wife, fathered a child or two and made your parents happy."

I spring to my feet, too angry now to guard my words. I meet the druid's impassive gaze full on. I square my shoulders. "You diminish what I feel, and what she feels, when you speak thus," I tell him. "What is between us is as deep as the earth, as wide as the sky, as boundless as the great ocean. To deny it is to deny the turning of the seasons, the ebb and flow of the tide, the journeys of sun and moon. I have always respected Sibeal's vocation. I have not tried to divert her from it against her will; all I have done is confront her with the need to be honest in her choices. I know how unhappy she is. She grieves for the parting to come. What I suggested to you is not what my heart most desires. I make no secret of that. I want her to choose me as her husband and the father of her child. I know the little girl she has seen in visions is our daughter, hers and mine."

A subtle change crosses Ciarán's face at this, masked almost as soon as it appears.

"But Sibeal believes there is no third choice, no compromise by which she can honor both her feelings for me and her love of the gods," I say. "I cannot leave her forever, Master Ciarán. I cannot bear to be parted from her. If we cannot be husband and wife, then let me be close to her, let us live as colleagues." I bow my head. "I will never wed another. She is the other half of me."

"Are you sure Sibeal's feelings are as powerful as your own?"

I would like to strangle him, right now. "Perhaps you dismiss her sorrow as fleeting and insignificant," I say. "Maybe you do not know her as well as you think."

He opens his mouth, and I expect that he will say something like, *All things pass*, or *You are young*. But what he says is, "I respect your sorrow, Felix. Tell me, how old are you?"

"I am in my twentieth year, Master Ciarán. You will tell me, no doubt, that I am too young to know my mind on such matters; too much of a boy, still, to understand true love with its wild joy and its piercing heartache."

He looks at me then, and his eyes are full of a terrible sadness. "At nineteen," he says, "one understands it only too well. We will talk again, Felix." He rises, gives me a nod and leaves.

We will talk again. I could laugh at that if I were not so full of bitterness and rage. This is like one of those cruel tales of lovers parted. The hero can win his lady if he undertakes a mission, and the mission is of such long duration that by the time he returns for her, they are old and gray and beyond the pleasures of the flesh. Or worse, she is dead or wed to another man. After ten years in the nemetons, Sibeal will have become like him, so deep in the study of lore and the love of the gods that she will have forgotten how it feels to weep and shout and laugh and be alive. If she remembers me, it will be with regret and kindness, not with love and longing.

I run. I cannot stop running. I run until my chest heaves, my breath whistles, my head reels. When I can go no further I stand on the cliff top and hurl stones over the edge. Each missile bears my anger out into the world. I have no words for what is in me; I only know my heart might burst with it. I run out of stones. All around me, gulls are rising in startled, squawking protest. I stand still, breathing. Slowly, piece by piece, Inis Eala comes into focus around me. The waves far below, crashing against the cliff's base. The sea stretching out before me, transformed by the summer sun to a carpet of deep blue-green and glittering gold. The birds. The vast, open space. Smaller things: a fern-like plant between the rocks at my feet; a juniper some distance away, like a tenacious old woman, clinging on against the westerly wind. There must be something to learn from what has passed today. A druid finds learning in everything, success and catastrophe, triumph and bitter defeat. In the destruction of the lovely flowering thing that grew between Sibeal and me, I can find no wisdom at all.

It is some time before I return to the settlement; the sun is high. When I seek out Sibeal, I find she has disregarded Muirrin's advice to rest, and has gone to the seer's cave. She is not expected back until supper time. As I head back toward the men's quarters, Sigurd comes to fetch me—Johnny wants to talk to me.

Sigurd leads me into the practice area, through the iron gate. Pairs of men are locked in intense, expert-looking battles all over the open area. Swords seem to be the weapon of the day. Rat is up on one of the benches, arms folded, eyes narrowed as he watches. Snake stands at the other side in a similar pose.

"The Connacht men are near the end of their training," Sigurd comments. "Final display of battle-craft soon, before they leave the island. Johnny's sending some of the new swords back with them. Not compensation, exactly; Rodan's was an accidental death. But such a gift silences talk of possible negligence. That's what I've heard. This way, Felix."

We enter a small chamber set within the massive double wall that rings the enclosure. Johnny, Gareth and Gull are standing around a table on which documents and writing materials are spread. I see a map showing the southern coasts of Erin, Britain and part of Gaul. Sigurd closes the door, remaining inside.

"Welcome, Felix," Johnny says. "Be seated, please." He has already congratulated me on the safe return of the three abandoned men; he spoke to each of us in turn last night, before we slept. He gave me his personal thanks for diving in after Gull, though our survival that strange day owed little to me. As a leader, Johnny misses nothing.

"I'll get to the point quickly," he says now. "Gull tells me both Donn and Colm will be fit to return home in about ten days' time, provided an adequate escort can be arranged. I don't know what your plans are for the long term, with your brother gone, but you'll be wanting to report back to the king of Munster about the voyage and the losses, at the very least. The items salvaged from *Freyja* should be returned to him. Gull says it would be ideal for Colm if you were to accompany him on the journey. I understand he is plagued by nightmares."

"He will need me, yes," I say. "He will recover more quickly at home. His father is one of Muredach's grooms; his mother works at court as a seamstress. He has brothers and sisters." Lucky Colm. But unlucky Colm, to witness such horrors before he is a man. Once safely home, he may never want to leave again.

"I regret the need to act on this so soon after your return, Felix," Johnny says quietly. "But I know you have duties to fulfill elsewhere. What are your plans after you speak to King Muredach? Will you stay on at his court awhile? From the story you told us that night, I understand it could be difficult for you to return to Armorica." He is taking care not to ask me who will bear the news of Paul's death to my mother and father.

"I will not linger at Muredach's court," I say. "I regret greatly that I cannot take the ill news to my parents. Duke Remont is not a just ruler. He is greatly influenced by the local bishops, whom I angered by speaking too freely. My presence would, at the very least, lose my father the position he has held for twenty years. It could cost him even more dearly. I cannot take that risk. I suppose I must dispatch a letter." Such a letter is long overdue for writing. I have not been able to bring myself to do it.

Sigurd clears his throat.

"We have a proposal to put to you, Felix," Johnny says.

I find I do not care very much what his proposal is. After my interview with Ciarán I feel shattered and weary, caring little for the future. "Yes?" I say.

"Sigurd will explain it to you."

"You remember we spoke of my Armorican comrade, Corentin," Sigurd says. "A close member of the Inis Eala team; a valiant, fine man and a great friend to me. Since we had that talk, I've been thinking how good it would be to know how he's getting on and whether he managed to win back his family holdings. I've explained to Johnny what you told me, that the region where your folk live is close enough to the place where Corentin was headed when he went back there. Johnny's given me leave to come with you, Felix. It'll lighten the job of getting Donn and Colm safely back to Munster if there are two of us. I was thinking, if you're not set on staying at the court there, that we might find a ship for Armorica."

I am about to interrupt with my reasons why this cannot happen, but Sigurd holds up a hand to silence me.

"I know why you're reluctant to go, and I respect that, Felix. But the thing is, Corentin's most likely a wealthy landholder now, an influential man in the region. Even if you can't get back to your home, if we find him he'll be well-placed to get a personal messenger to your parents, someone who can break the news kindly. If your father can travel, we can probably arrange a safe meeting. We're Inis Eala men, Corentin and I. We're expert at organizing this kind of thing." After a moment he adds, "I'd like to see him again."

His big, blunt features are softened by a look that disarms me completely. And, after all, I have nowhere else to go. Not now. Ten years of nothing loom ahead.

One thing troubles me. "My brother came with me to Erin," I say, "and on to the north, to watch over me. For his care of me, Paul paid with his life. I would not have the same fate befall another good man."

Sigurd gives me a searching look. "Taking risks is part of being a man," he says. "It's part of living, Felix. You can't wrap up every friend you have and put him away in safe storage, lest he trip and hurt himself. Nobody would thank you for that. If you're still thinking of those ill luck rumors that once dogged you, forget them. I'm offering to go with you because I want to, and because I think we can help each other. That should be enough for you."

I nod. I cannot argue with this.

"Our man on the mainland will arrange horses and supplies for your trip south to Munster," Johnny says. "There will be resources at your disposal. It'll be up to the two of you how you use them. What do you say, Felix?"

"It is good to have a purpose," I say. "I will do this. I thank you, all of you. I thank you for your faith in me."

Now they are all looking at me, and I see that perhaps my tone has not matched my words. Right now, it is not possible to sound anything but sad.

"Good," Johnny says. "I'll leave you and Sigurd to work out the details in your own time. You may need to make haste if you're to secure a passage from the south before the worst of the autumn storms. I've given Sigurd up to a year's leave of absence."

A year. Once, that would have seemed long. Now, it only tells me that there will then be nine more years to wait. Nine years in which I grow older, and Sibeal grows older, and our paths grow steadily further apart.

"Felix." Gareth speaks now, quietly. He is the affable, friendly man he was before the voyage, and yet not quite the same. His eyes are more guarded; his mouth holds something in reserve. "I realize your plans for the long-term future may be somewhat hazy at present. I must tell you that several of us, independently, have suggested to Johnny that he offer you a place on Inis Eala, a permanent place, once you have completed this other business, and that he has agreed. You might return here when Sigurd does. The men hold your courage in high regard. We would welcome you as one of us."

I am astounded. I know what an honor this is, how rarely a place on the island is offered. "I am no warrior," I say, "nor ever will be one."

"You are a young man of exemplary bravery." Gull speaks. His voice is soft and deep. It makes me think of oak wood and shadows. "That is a weapon stronger than the most finely crafted sword, Felix. You are a man of great heart. Besides," he adds with a grin, "we like your songs."

"Thank you," I say to all of them. "I am more honored than I can say. Much in my future is unknown. Much is still to be decided. Whether my path brings me back here or takes me far away, I will never forget that you recognized me thus."

Nobody says anything. Johnny nods. Gareth smiles. Gull gives me a look that reflects his knowledge of the truth: that my courteous speech and calm demeanor conceal a bitter, wretched, sorrowful man.

"We might row over to the mainland and talk to Biddy's son Clem, Felix," says Sigurd, putting a hand on my shoulder. "He's the one who'll be arranging the first part of the journey for us. If we go now, we can take advantage of the incoming tide. Clem will give us a bed for the night, and we can come back in the morning."

"Why not?" I say.

It is the beginning of the end.

CHAPTER 15

~Sibeal~

iarán is the other part of this, Clodagh had said. The spiritual part; the wise, measured part. I woke from a night of tangled dreams and knew I was not ready to face him. What could I tell him? That I was torn two ways and could not think straight anymore? That I had soaked my pillow with still more tears, and that, when at last I had fallen into an uneasy sleep, my dreams had all been of Felix? How could I explain to my wise kinsman that my body was full of longing for the touch of Felix's hands and the warmth of his lips on mine? How could I say I regretted now that the two of us had not slipped away together on that moonlit night, the night the gray ones spoke to Cathal on the serpent isle? How could I admit that I wished we had found a secluded corner and taken our joy of each other? At least, then, I would have had that memory to carry with me into a future of austerity and seclusion. How could I tell my mentor that the voices of the gods had fallen deeply, profoundly silent?

I could not face anyone. I needed to be alone. I dressed, then drew aside the curtain to see that Evan was already up and tending to Thorgrim.

"Evan? If anyone asks where I am, please tell them I've gone to the cave for the day. I will be back by supper time."

I withdrew and headed out my door before he could give words to the doubt I saw on his face. No sign of Fang this morning. Perhaps it was too early even for her. But not for everyone. As I walked toward the cliff path I saw two figures down by the water, near the fisherman's cottage, deep in conversation. One wore a druid's robe, the other was clad all in black. One had hair of deepest red, the other was dark as night. Ciarán and Cathal. I shivered. Enmeshed in my own woes, I had lost sight of what was to come for them, and perhaps for us all. Out beyond the safe margin of Inis Eala, Mac Dara still waited. I thought of the tiny tokens around the fragile necks of those two babes. What if a talisman was lost or broken? What if the cord snapped? What if the child was out playing and . . . No, I would not think of that. As soon as I imagined Firinne and her brother at three or four, I saw my own daughter running and climbing and being swung up high by her father, with her own talisman around her neck, and that was simply too hard to bear.

I passed the cove where Svala had crouched over her pile of fish bones. I passed the place where she had pushed Rodan to his death. I could almost understand that now. She was in thrall to Knut, bound to do his will, bound to share his bed although she shrank from him; that little sliver of skin was enough to let him control her while they were close, at least until we came to the serpent isle and the call of her beloved put new strength in her veins. But Rodan had no such talisman, and when he approached her, she did to him what she had long wished she could do to the man who had called her his wife. The man who had stolen her away, and lied about her, and used her as if she were a possession, not a living, breathing woman. A living, breathing creature. Gods, it was like an ancient epic of heroes and monsters.

Musing on this, I reached the narrow passage in the rocky headland and slipped through into Finbar's cave.

So early in the morning, the cavern was dim. Blue shadows haunted the corners, and the water of the pool lay dark amid the stones. I lay down on the flat rocks, suddenly as tired as if I had climbed a mountain. There seemed no point at all in attempting to pray, or to scry, or to meditate. My mind was all Felix—Felix diving off the boat and vanishing beneath the water, Felix challenging me to be honest with myself, Felix using the rune *Is* to explain that he had lost his memory. Felix looking in wonder at the talisman he had been given to protect our daughter—how had those gray ones known of her, if she was never to be? Felix with his arms around me and his lips on mine. Felix singing as we made our way through the dark, riding on the monster's back. My brave, beautiful man.

I lay there a long time; perhaps I slept. When I opened my eyes the cave was much brighter, and I sat up to see the pool before me filled with a faint gold light. I had not expected visions. I had not expected anything save that perhaps, in the quiet of the cave, I might attempt to get my thoughts in order. But there in the water was the figure of a man. A tall, brown-haired man, a well-built young man with a good-humored mouth and smiling blue eyes. Not Finbar. Paul. Paul who lay beneath the earthen mound in the place of the boat burial.

There was no sound in the cavern, but in my mind I heard his voice. *I want him to know that I am content*, he said. *He should feel no regret for what happened. We always knew, my father, my mother and I, that he was the one who would make his mark, break new ground, find paths hitherto unexplored. It was in him from the first, when he was only a scrap of a boy. It's not his fault that I'm gone. I made my choice, and this is where it led me. He should go forward, speak out, be the brave heart he always was. I don't think he ever knew how proud Father was of him; I don't think my brother ever understood how rare such courage is.* Paul looked out of the water and straight into my eyes, and he smiled. *With you by his side, he will be happy*, he said, making tears well in my eyes. *Look after him for me, will you?* And with a ripple and a passing shadow, he was gone.

"I can't," I whispered into the silence. "I can't do it. I can't honor your wishes. I can't obey the gods. I can't do anything at all."

It seemed I still had not yet wept all my tears, for they flowed now as they had the day before, helpless tears, the tears of a child lost in a maze and running out of choices. I sobbed until my nose ran and my chest hurt. There wasn't a scrap of druidic strength to be found in me, and I wasn't sure I wanted it anyway. I buried my head in my hands and let sorrow claim me.

Much later, when the worst of it was over, I lifted my head, wiped my face on my sleeve and became aware that I was no longer alone in the cavern. Ciarán was sitting a short distance away, in his usual cross-legged, straight-backed pose, not looking at me, simply waiting, his eyes calm and clear as he gazed across the water. In a moment he would ask me what was the matter. I had no idea what to say to him.

"Perhaps it will help if I tell you I'm aware that you are struggling with your vocation, Sibeal, and that I know your young Armorican, Felix, is part of the problem. Don't look so surprised; I had only to see him take your hand on the jetty to be aware of the bond between you."

"I'm—I can't—you won't understand. Even I don't understand." If this was what it meant to grow up, I thought I might prefer to stay a child forever. And yet . . .

He gave a little smile. "Try me, Sibeal."

"You won't like it."

"You know better than to anticipate my response. I see how unhappy you are. Tell me why."

I drew a deep, unsteady breath. "Ciarán, I love Felix. I love him with my whole heart. He has transformed my life. Up until this summer, I never had the slightest doubt about my vocation. You know how hard I've studied, how much I've applied myself to learning, how I've tried at every turn to be the best druid I could be. Now I'm full of doubt. The voices of the gods do not come to me readily anymore; they are often silent." I shivered, finding I could not meet his eyes. He would be so disappointed in me. He would be shocked by my weakness. "I love life in the nemetons with its tranquility and purpose. On the voyage to the serpent isle I discovered new ways of using my gifts, ways I had not known were possible. I love the gods, and I believe they still call me to their service. But I love this man too; I want to be his wife and bear his children. I want the sort of life Clodagh has, full of tenderness and passion and surprises. I can't have both. Felix has spoken of other paths, of compromise, but in truth there are no other paths. There is only this choice. This impossible choice."

"Tell me why it is impossible."

"Because—because whatever I choose, I'll live a life of regret. If I marry Felix and walk away from the druid path, I will always think of the vocation I was called to as a child, the peace of the nemetons, the myriad byways of the mind, the companionship of other scholars, the wondrous opportunity to serve the gods with all that is in me. And if I have to let Felix go, I won't be the druid I should be. Part of me will always be thinking of him, wondering where he is, wondering if he's dreaming of me, weeping for the life we might have had together."

"Felix must be a remarkable young man," Ciarán said quietly, "to have awoken such feelings in you so quickly."

"You will probably dismiss it as young love, a passion that burns brightly and is soon over, a candle flame that gutters and dies at the first cold draft," I said. "But it's not like that. Please believe me. Felix and I belong together. I love him as my counterpart, my perfect completion. I love him body and spirit. He is a fine man, an exceptional man, a scholar and thinker, sensitive and wise. And brave; outstandingly brave. There is no other like him."

He put his palms together and brought the tips of his fingers to his mouth. He seemed to be giving my arguments consideration.

"I know what you will say," I went on. "That the love of the gods must always outweigh the love between man and woman. You'll tell me that in time I will forget; that the pain will go away. But it won't, Ciarán. This love is deep and long-lasting. It's as vibrant as the notes of a harp, and as enduring as the heart of stone. It's as big as the sky and as broad as the ocean. It's as grand as a high mountain; it's as lovely and delicate as a single drop of dew."

Ciarán smiled. "You seem unusually ready to put words in my mouth," he said.

"I'm sorry," I said. "But it seems obvious what advice you would give me. You've devoted years of your life to the gods. If it weren't for the fact that Conor is your brother and that you'd never challenge his authority, you would have been chief druid long ago. You are respected throughout Erin for your scholarship and your wisdom. You're not going to counsel me to drop it all and run off to get married."

"True, Sibeal, I would not do that. I rarely tell anyone what to do, least of all a fellow druid."

I waited for him to say *The answer lies within you*, or *There is learning even in loss*.

"Sibeal," he said, and I saw a look on his face that I had never seen before, a look of the most profound sadness, "I'm going to tell you something I've never told anyone else. Not one day goes by, not one, when I do not mourn Niamh's death. Not one hour passes when I do not wish my life had been different, and that I had not lost her a scant three years after I found her again. Every moment of the day she is in my thoughts, tossing her hair, glancing at me over her shoulder, dancing on the sward, cradling our child in her arms. If I could have her back I would quit the brotherhood without a second thought. She was the light of my life. She was the other part of me. We were young when we first saw each other, as you and Felix are, and from the first meeting of our eyes I was changed by her. We loved each other in the way you spoke of, with body and spirit, forever and always. Oh, Sibeal, I know exactly what the two of you are feeling. And I also know what it is to experience a lifetime of regret for a path not taken. Death robbed me of that path. I had no choice. But you are blessed, Sibeal. You do have a choice."

I was so shaken by the passion of his words that I could hardly respond. "I'm sorry." My voice was uneven. "And you lost Fainne, too. I saw my own daughter, Ciarán. I saw the three of us together, in a little house in the forest. Felix and me and a lovely child with eyes like mine. It hurt me to see her, and to know that it is my choice that she never be born. That feels so wrong. It goes against everything I know as a druid. It goes against the knowledge that all living things are sacred."

"I believe I have taught you all too well," Ciarán said. He sounded calm now, but his hands were tightly clasped together, the knuckles white. "Yes, I lost Fainne, but that was different. I know that my daughter is alive, and has a companion of the heart, and that she is doing a great work on behalf of the gods. I see her in visions; she sees me. That is not so cruel. And I have you, Sibeal. You have a wise and loving father of your own, but I have long looked upon you as my second daughter. It hurts me to see you so unhappy. There, now I have said something inappropriate to a druid, so we are even. Let me ask you a question."

"What question?"

"You said Felix had spoken of compromise. It seems to me that there is a possible solution to your problem. It depends on how far you are prepared to compromise. This is not all or nothing, Sibeal. There is at least one other choice available to you."

I could hardly breathe, let alone speak. I did not dare to hope.

"There's a community in the south, in Kerry. They call themselves the Brethren of Brighid. They are stalwart in the old faith, but they are not druids, at least, not in the sense you and I understand the term. They live communally, and there are married couples and children among them. There is far less emphasis on lore and prayer than we are accustomed to in the nemetons. Less rigor, less discipline. More freedom of thought, demonstrated in robust nightly debates; they're as fond of those as they are of their music. But principally they show their love of the gods in daily work, either on the land they farm or out in the wider world, where they teach and heal, perform hand fastings and burials, comfort the dying, and conduct the seasonal rites for farm folk and fisher folk. A very different life, Sibeal, and far away from Sevenwaters. I know several of the people who live there, and I have only good to say of them. I am convinced they would welcome you and Felix to their hearths and their hearts. In turn, you would have much to offer them, and so, I believe, would he."

I stared at him, unable to think past the conflicting feelings that rushed through me—joy, horror, hope, shock, disbelief. "You—*you*—are advising me to give up my vocation?"

He smiled again, but his eyes were sad. "You know, I don't believe I am. Yes, this choice would mean you did not make your final vows at Sevenwaters. It would mean we lost you to our own nemetons, and that would be a great loss indeed, to Conor and myself especially. But, Sibeal, my dear, you are so full of spirit, you are so rich in faith, it matters not at all what path you choose. Whether as wife and mother, or as druid, or as teacher in Kerry, or even at court in Armorica if your path should lead you there, you will live your life fully in the love of the gods. They laid their hands over you when you were a small child. You have never wavered, Sibeal; and their love for you has never weakened, even when their voices could not reach you. You should go forward in joy and confidence, knowing whatever you choose will be right."

His words sounded in me like a song. They were a precious gift, as precious as Felix's love. They held a wisdom that could keep me strong until the day I died. "But I thought—didn't you send me here because I couldn't cope?"

"Sometimes your ability comes close to overwhelming you, yes, and that concerned me. I weighed that in the balance before telling you of the community in Kerry. Certainly, your gifts would be better guarded if you chose to stay in the safety of the nemetons. But with Felix by your side, I know you would be strong enough to live your life in that more open world. Sibeal, my reasons for sending you to Inis Eala were many. Among them was my wish that you spend time with your sisters. I wanted you to reach a fuller understanding of what you would be giving up to become a druid. I did not send you here to have your heart broken, Sibeal. We can't have that, my dear." He stepped forward and put his arms around me as a father would, and I held on, feeling his deep strength pass into me, and thinking, not for the first time, how remarkable he was, how selfless and how wise. As was Clodagh. How lucky I was in my family and in my friends.

"Take time to consider this," Ciarán murmured. "But not too long. I've been talking to Johnny. Felix has a great deal of unfinished business to attend to, starting with a trip to accompany the survivors to Munster. Then he should go to Armorica to take the news of his brother's death home. He'll most likely be gone a year, Sibeal, and he and Sigurd are leaving in ten days' time."

"Ten days?" I lifted my head from his chest and looked up into his mulberry eyes. "So soon?"

"It is perhaps not such a bad thing, if you decide you will go to Kerry. A year provides time for you to speak to your father, and for me to speak to Conor, and then for you and me to travel south so I can introduce you to the Brethren of Brighid. By the time Felix returns, you will be fully informed about what this decision means. Of course, I am assuming he will be amenable to the idea. Have you at any stage suggested to him that he might consider a spiritual life?"

"No, I . . . " Oh gods, let me not be dreaming. Let me not wake to find myself alone by the scrying pool with my heart still weighed down by sorrow.

"You might put it to him. It seems your Felix never shrinks from a challenge. He may have no religious vocation—that rather depends on how you define vocation—but from Gull's accounts and Johnny's, he is a man of good heart and open mind. That, along with his bond with you, would be sufficient to earn him acceptance into the Brethren of Brighid. Sibeal, there's plenty of time for you and Felix to consider this. The final decision could wait until he comes back from Armorica."

"I don't need time," I said as something bloomed within me, a great, warm, beautiful thing made up of sunshine and moonlight and waves splashing and leaves unfurling and birds winging through a cloudless sky. What Clodagh had said was true. I had grown up. I had learned that being a woman was knowing when to stand firm and when to compromise. I had learned to laugh and weep; I had learned that I was weak as well as strong. I had learned to love. I was no longer a rigid, upright tree that would not flex and bow, even though the gale threatened to snap it in two; I was the willow that bends and shivers and sways, and yet remains strong. "If Felix agrees, I will go to Kerry. It is a long way from Sevenwaters; I'll miss the family. And I'll miss you and Conor and the others more than I can tell you. I know I'll feel lost, at first, without the lore and the ritual and everything that makes the nemetons a sanctuary and a haven. But I'm sure this is right." I stood on tiptoe and kissed Ciarán on the cheek, something I had never done before. "You've just given me a wonderful gift," I told him.

"Then why are you crying, Sibeal?" His smile was a little crooked; were those tears I saw in his eyes? "Go then, take this news to Felix. I will be surprised if he does not agree to the proposal. I believe you'll find him close to the place where his brother is buried. At least, he was there when I walked out to find you. We shall speak more of this later."

"I don't know how to thank you," I said as we left the cave. "It's too much to put into words."

"Be happy, Sibeal. That is all the thanks I need."

I saw Felix before he saw me. He was up at the place of the boat burial, sitting on a flat rock with his head bowed onto his drawn-up knees. He looked as I had never seen him before: defeated. And that could not be, not for Felix, who was brave enough for anything. I glanced at Ciarán, who had halted beside me.

"Go on, Sibeal. You don't need me." Ciarán headed off along the path toward the settlement, and I began to climb the rise. Walking. Then, as Felix lifted his head and turned swollen, reddened eyes on me, running. He stood up just in time as I reached him and threw myself into his arms, making him stagger.

"Sibeal! What is it, what's wrong?"

"I—I—" This was no good; he would think disaster had struck. "Felix, I—" I made myself step back, holding his hands in mine. *Quickly, Sibeal, say something that will take that forlorn look off his face, say something that will make this right straightaway.* "Felix," I said, "I love you. Will you marry me, and go to live in Kerry in a religious community? You might like it, it isn't like the nemetons, there is music and debate and farming and all kinds of other things, please say yes, it means we can be together after all, and everything's going to be all right, I can't believe it, I can't believe there was this other choice all the time, I can't believe Ciarán's prepared to let me go, he even seems to think it's a good idea—"

The flood of words ceased. I looked up into Felix's face and saw there the expression I had hoped for, a dawning delight, a wondering smile, blue eyes filling with a hope still tinged with disbelief but growing stronger by the moment. As I gazed, taking my fill of him, knowing there would be more to learn of him every day and every night for all the remaining years of my life, his cautious smile turned to a broad grin, complemented by dimples.

"I say yes, Sibeal, to the only part of that speech I made much sense of. Yes, I will marry you. I can't believe you asked me. I can't believe any of it, but I do, because only the most remarkable news could have you laughing, crying and running up a steep hill all at the same time."

"Now you're laughing and crying too," I said, moving close again and putting my arms around his neck, under the fall of his chestnut hair. "You looked so sad. I couldn't bear it."

"Oh gods, Sibeal, tell me I'm not dreaming. Is this real? Can it be?"

"It's real. It's something Ciarán knew about, but of course he never mentioned it to me, because before I met you there was no need. And before I met you, maybe I would have scorned the Brethren of Brighid—that's what they're called—as not being real druids, because they honor the gods with the work of their hands more than with prayer and contemplation. You've changed me, Felix. This summer has changed me. And yet, I seem to have kept the old Sibeal as well as finding the new one."

"I'm glad of that, dearest," Felix said, and touched his lips softly to my brow, and my temple, and my cheek, and lastly to my mouth. A shiver of delight ran through my body. "The old Sibeal was the one I fell in love with the first day I saw her, though at the time I thought she was a figment of my imagination. I love my little wise druid, with her air of self-containment and her keen analysis of ideas. And I love the woman in my arms, Sibeal. With mind, body and spirit, until the end of time and beyond."

"You might make a song about that."

"I expect to make many. Did you say these Brethren of Brighid enjoy music?"

"I'm told they love it. I think we will do very well, dearest." Speaking thus brought a blush to my cheeks, which was foolish indeed. All the same, it was a good feeling. "Later, we'll ask Ciarán to tell us more."

"Come, sit down here with me." We sat, leaning close, his arm around my shoulders, mine around his waist. Before us lay the settlement of Inis Eala, smoke rising from the kitchen chimney, men moving in and out of the practice yard, someone calling a flock of hens back into a walled enclosure, and the tall figure of Ciarán making his way toward the infirmary. "Did he tell you he had spoken to me?"

"Ciarán? No. What did he say to you? Obviously not what he told me, or you would not have looked as if your world were turning to ashes."

"I think he was testing me; assessing whether I was a man of good intent or a good-for-nothing fellow who sought to divert his precious Sibeal from her true path. It seems he was satisfied. And it seems he is not the man I took him to be. At the time I was . . . displeased. Unhappy. I did not leave him as courteously as I might have done."

"He's heard good reports of you, Felix. Especially from me. He thinks highly of you. Whatever you said, it made the right impression."

"Sibeal."

"Mm?" The sensation of his fingers stroking my arm was making it hard to concentrate.

"I have to go away. Perhaps for a whole year. I wish it were not so, but it is necessary."

"I know. He told me. The time will pass; it must. For now, we have ten days before you must go, ten precious days. We must savor them; store them up for the long time ahead."

"Sibeal, you may think me foolish, but . . . Paul. I want to give him our good news."

"He knows," I said. "Feel how these rocks hold the sun's kiss.

416

That warmth is Paul's blessing. His love for you is in the salt air and the smell of smoke from the cooking fire; it's in every tiny flower and every blade of grass that grows here on this mound." I would not speak of my vision; he had more than enough to come to terms with. In time, I would tell him. "But speak to him if you will; I believe he hears every word."

So he spoke; and it was from brother to brother, from heart to heart, private and tender, and not for writing here. When he was done, Felix asked me, "What would you like to do now, my heart?"

"Sit here with you awhile longer," I said. "And then run down there and tell absolutely everyone."

~Felix~

The boat is ready to take us across to the mainland. Today we start our long journey south to Muredach's court. The box that holds the sad remnant of Eoghan's courting gift is stowed, and six oarsmen wait to row us over. On the jetty and along the shore, many folk wait to wave us farewell. It has been a strange season at Inis Eala. The summer of the shipwreck. The summer of the sea woman. For me, it was the summer I lost my brother and found my true love. Now summer is nearly over, and it is time to say goodbye.

We stand near the top of the path, with the wind in our hair and the vast sweep of ocean below us, stretching all the way to the stark pinnacles of the serpent isle. Sibeal's hands are in mine, warm and sure. Her eyes hold something of the sea and the sky in them. Today they are wide, clear, full of hope and love.

"It may not seem so long," she says. "Every day, every moment I'll hold you in my heart, Felix. With every breath I'll think of you. I promise."

I lift her hands to my lips, thinking how composed she is, and how different she was when she came to me laughing and crying, and threw herself into my arms, and asked me to marry her, all at once. As long as I live, I will treasure that moment.

"I, too, dear one," I say. "When I make a song of this, it will not be a lament, but a celebration. We may travel far from each other, but each turning of the season will bring us closer together." A year. At this moment it seems an eternity, but I will not say so. I study her sweet, grave face, her skin pale as moonlight, her lips both enticing and severe, her beautiful eyes. I have already committed these things to memory; I will need them in the time to come.

"I love you, Felix," Sibeal says softly, and puts her arms around me. "More than the stars in the sky. More than the trees in the forest. More than the waves in the sea."

I gather her close and kiss her on the lips. Someone down on the jetty gives a piercing whistle; we are in full view. "I love you," I say, and suddenly there are no words left in me, but those three are enough. We hold on fiercely. The last precious moments slip away.

"Felix!" someone yells from down there. "Get a move on!"

"I'm not saying goodbye." Sibeal's voice is barely audible; a tear trembles in her eye. "Wherever our paths take us, you will be with me, and I will be with you. Come, we'd best go down."

Hand in hand we descend the steep path to the bay, where Sigurd, Colm and Donn are already aboard the small boat. I embrace Gull; I bid farewell to Johnny, to Gareth, to Cathal, to all the fine friends of this summer. I step aboard, and the rowers take up their blades.

She stands on the jetty, a slight, upright figure in her blue gown. The wind lifts her dark curls around her face. I will see her in my dreams, every night. A year of dreams. I lift my hand: half wave, half salute. She raises hers: half wave, half blessing. The oars move; the boat turns. We head for the mainland, and the long journey home.